'A gripping, haunting novel about loss and reconciliation, driven by a simple but clever plot.'
Sunday Times

'The strength of the writing and the author's brilliant evocation of how a child's mind works combine to terrifying effect. A novel one cannot forget.'
Shots Magazine

'Skilfully evokes the era and the slow-moving quality of childhood summers, suggesting the menace lurking just beyond... A study of memory and guilt with several twists.'
Guardian

'This emotionally charged thriller grips from the first paragraph, and a nail-biting level of suspense is maintained throughout. A great novel.'
She Magazine

By Lesley Thomson

Seven Miles from Sydney

A Kind of Vanishing

The Detective's Daughter Series

The Detective's Daughter

Ghost Girl

The Detective's Secret

The House With No Rooms

The Dog Walker

The Death Chamber

The Runaway (A Detective's Daughter Short Story)

Lesley
THOMSON

ghost girl

HEAD
of
ZEUS

First published in the UK in 2014 by Head of Zeus Ltd
This paperback edition first published in the UK in 2018
by Head of Zeus Ltd

9 7 5 3 1 2 4 6 8

A catalogue record for this book is available from
the British Library.

Paperback ISBN 9781788542999
Ebook ISBN 9781781857663

Printed and bound by CPI Group (UK) Ltd, Croydon, CR0 4YY

Head of Zeus Ltd
First Floor East
5–8 Hardwick Street
London EC1R 4RG

WWW.HEADOFZEUS.COM

To Mel

And for Sarah Baylis, an inspiring writer
(1956–87)

The power to concentrate exists in everyone; but few can concentrate sufficiently to drive a motor car with complete mastery in all circumstances.

Roadcraft: The Police Drivers' Manual, 1960

Jack is alive and likely to live,
If he dies in your hand you've a forfeit to give.

The Oxford Dictionary of Nursery Rhymes,
edited by Iona and Peter Opie

Prologue

In the pale light the girl might be a ghost risen from one of the graves. Zipped up in a chequered anorak, insubstantial, she trips along the asphalt path, her hood drawn up, her face a pallid oval in the twilight. Apart from the anorak she is dressed as if for a party in black patent-leather pumps, white socks gartered to her knees and a swaying skirt. A duffel bag is strapped across her back. She slips with apparent confidence through the maze-like cemetery.

She stops before an angel; the statue dwarfs her. The angel is sculpted to hold the gaze of a mourner and her considerable height means that from below only darkening sky frames her covered head. Fast-moving clouds make her appear to incline towards the child in solemn greeting. The girl returns the stare. Alone in a London cemetery, she does not seem afraid.

She rummages in her bag and brings out a hammer. Managing the oversized tool with both hands, she clambers on to the low marble surround. Her pumps crunching on the decorative surface are the only sound in the votive quiet.

She wields the hammer and with a precise arc smashes at the angel's wrist, severing her hand. A clean break. The hand lands with a thump away on the grass. The girl positions herself on the other side of the angel and aims again. This time she swings too wildly. On the downward return the hammer head clips her knee, breaking the skin, but she appears not to feel it. She executes the perfect swing of her first attempt and shears off the other hand. She slips the hammer through the neck in her bag. She collects up the two marble hands and pokes them inside.

She rushes away pell-mell, pretty pumps kicking out, flitting over graves and around mausoleums to the central avenue. She leaves the way she came.

One

Fog skimmed the bonnet and wreathed around wing mirrors which reflected only darkness. Lamp-posts and telegraph poles swooped out of the swirling mass when the headlights washed over them; phantoms bowing in obeisance, they melted into the night.

Hunched over the wheel, Charlie Hampson, middle-aged, ruggedly tousled and used to commanding all he encountered, judged the intervals of light had become fewer, despite his even speed. Hardly bloody speed; more like a funeral cortège. Good call since the place was crawling with dead people. He nudged closer to the car in front – the only vehicle apart from his own that seemed to be out on this filthy night – and again unsuccessfully coaxed it to accelerate.

Hampson, in his sparkly new BMW 318i, found scant comfort in the blue shadow Alcantara upholstery for which he had paid extra and from which a gentle heat now emanated. He was inclined to be impervious to mood or atmosphere but the bated stillness within the car was getting to him.

'Get a move on, shithead!'

Despite the closed windows and vents, tendrils of fog had found their way inside the car and he fretted that the damp reek of corpses and exhaust fumes would taint the pristine interior. The fog had seeped into his jacket and trousers and chilled him. This was what decades ago his ma would have called a pea-souper. Nowadays such weather in London was rare; tonight it had come out of nowhere. It was a fucking inconvenience and he took it personally.

His digital display warned of black ice and the clock read 10.56 p.m. He had four minutes.

'Child on Board'. He read the sticker in the car's rear window. 'Fuckwit on board, go!' He got a flash image of the kid; the doctor said that was normal, and like that day, he touched the accelerator. The car responded instantly. Lovely. He blotted out the boy.

The fog thinned briefly and revealed a tree. His four-cylinder engine with high-precision direct injection was soundless. It might be he who was stationary and the wall that was moving. This impression brought back the kid. He had not had the vision for ages; the fog was playing tricks. He turned on the radio and was instantly soothed. Andy Williams returned him to a bright and jaunty youth. Charlie lustily boomed out the chorus of 'Music to Watch Girls By'.

The effect was mesmeric and he nearly pranged the other car. He stamped his foot on the brake. He leant forward to see into the toy-like Renault but the silhouette of the headrests blocked a view of the driver or of any frigging child on board. The sticker was typical of that kind of holier-than-thou shitbag. What made kids more important than him? What did they add to the economy? He rode the clutch and revved the engine, relishing the rising purr. He would put the fear of God into the risk-averse parent in the Twingo. He twiddled his headlights to manual and flashed a Morse Code-like order in time to his words: 'Shift. Your. Arse!'

The music deteriorated to white sound. He pressed the station scanner but the crackling got louder and more intense. The car was deliberately going at walking pace to fuck with him. In a forty-mile-per-hour zone it was topping no more than ten. Had to be a joke. Hampson pulled out to overtake and was deafened by a blaring horn and dazzled by lights. He pulled on the wheel as the gigantic hubs of an articulated truck filled his side window,

4

the forty-four-tonner making a wafer-thin corridor. It was gone. This wasn't a route for artics; stupid bugger must have tried to find a short cut off the Great Chertsey Road. The geriatric box on wheels was doing eight miles per hour. Got to be a woman. Mother and child shouldn't be out at this time of night. Hampson heard the pounding of his heart. He tried turning the radio on and off to locate Andy Williams. The impenetrable noise from his surround-sound speakers matched the thickening fog. He could not bear to switch it off and kill all hope of hearing the music. In the unnatural silence it was a lifeline.

The clock said he had two and half minutes. He might do it if 'Mummy' put her sodding foot down. The kerb-hugger was stopping at the speed humps. He could ram her – she would never trace him – but he didn't want to damage his car. Although now he could afford the repair. Hell, he could get another one.

A thirty-mile-limit sign glided out of the gloom. The bitch wanted him to shunt her so she could cash in on the insurance. He pulled back.

This made him remember why he was in this godforsaken place. Forgetting the fog and the late hour, Charlie cheered up; soon he would be a free man.

'Move it!' This set him coughing, which made his eyes water. 'Whiplash, baby, yeah!' he yelled above the white crackling to the imagined tune of 'Love Shack'. He depressed the accelerator and surged forward.

One minute. Certain there was nothing coming, Hampson swung out again. He preferred night driving: even in foggy conditions there was less room for error than on a sunny day in Hammersmith when the schools were out. He gnawed his bottom lip and powered the BMW through thirty-five to forty, readying himself to gesture at the careful lady-driver.

Charlie Hampson saw a version of himself: a grey-haired, overweight bloke who no doubt liked a scotch, his Formula One and Andy Williams on the radio.

He sliced in on the Renault, accelerated then braked, and

looked in his rear mirror to see the car swerve. It had gone. The bastard had got away. Now he was officially late.

He could just make out the perimeter fence of the cemetery. 'Keep your doors locked and don't stop for any reason. A driver was ambushed there last month.' Great meeting place. Still, no houses or speed cameras. No Big Brother. Those were the days.

Too late Hampson saw that the form by the kerb was not another trick of the eye. He wrenched at the wheel, but, unused to the car's sensitive response, over-compensated. The high-performance saloon mounted the pavement at fifty-eight miles an hour. In the fog, as in the hot sunshine on Brackenbury Road W6 months before, Charles Hampson had the impression of weightless stasis. Impassive he noted a tree zooming in on him as if it were a digital simulation. At the same moment Andy Williams returned full volume.

Oliver Twist, with blue eyes curious and trusting, locked him in a staring contest as, like an angel, he flew past Charlie, up to the sky. Hampson shut his eyes.

On impact the BMW bounced off the hundred-year-old oak tree and smashed a car-shaped hole in a Victorian wall feet away. The London Stone bricks needed repointing, which marginally lessened the secondary impact. In the convivial telling later Charlie Hampson would have rendered this as comic, what with the Andy Williams soundtrack. He would have boasted how he might be fifty-four with a heart murmur but his avoidance reflexes were spot on: he had avoided the speed bump.

Except for Charlie Hampson there was no later.

Two

Stella pressed the doorbell, initiating a 'Big Ben' chime. The freshly painted window sashes told her all she needed to know about David Barlow. Bereaved men came in two kinds: those in denial who fled to an irresponsible past and those who spruced up and replaced the dead wife. The first group stopped shaving, drank and fed off takeaways until a tide of bottles and cartons spilling out of the kitchen prompted a relative to call in Clean Slate. The relative paid the invoices until a new partner came along and cancelled the contract.

Barlow was in the second camp. His having contacted the office told her he disliked the break in routine; for him Clean Slate was a dating agency and he would resent stumping up for cleaners who proved unsuitable marriage material. He would pay late or not at all. Stella had learned to avoid his sort. Compassion had limits.

Her assistant Jackie Makepeace had let Barlow in under the wire. He had read the article in the *Chronicle*. Supposing the piece to be about Terry Darnell's funeral, Stella had agreed to the interview and then was dismayed to see it headed 'The Detective's Daughter'. It described how single-handedly (single generally, it was implied, as if she were open season) she had succeeded where her cop-dad had failed and solved the famous Rokesmith murder, a cold case from the eighties. Set into a shot of Terry's flag-draped coffin on the blustery damp day at Mortlake Crematorium, watched by a solemn crowd of mourners from across the Met, was a photo of Stella at her desk. The caption beneath, 'Sleuth at

7

Work', was a blatant misrepresentation of Clean Slate's brochure picture of Stella drawing up a cleaning schedule that Jackie had sent through to the paper. Jackie had stopped her complaining. 'All publicity is …' The thrust of the piece – written by a woman with two first names like the characters in *The Waltons* – was how Stella had built up a cleaning empire in West London yet found time to clean up crime. Stella, so the article decided, had laid her dad's ghost. He could rest in peace. What bloody ghost? Stella fumed to herself again on Barlow's doorstep, noting with some approval the daisies ranked each side of the tiled path. She hadn't worked on the case alone – but Jack did not want to be mentioned. Wise move. Although published a year ago, the piece still attracted a trickle of business. Barlow was the latest. Pleased by this PR success, Jackie made Stella promise to pop by on her way home and seal the deal. Stella promised herself that the meeting – crowning a hectic day – would be short with no deal.

Her resolution wavered when David Barlow opened the door. Neat hair, aquiline nose, he was trim in a slick suit with a silk tie. But for it being a modest terraced house near Hammersmith Broadway and therefore unlikely, David Barlow might be David Bowie. The resemblance was striking.

'Come in.' He ushered her inside with a sweeping hand. He was her height – six foot – but Stella banished this as irrelevant.

Aware of Barlow behind her, she made for a doorway on the left of the hall. She rehearsed her exit: the sitting room was too large, too small, impossible to clean – whichever was applicable.

Barlow had put tea things out on a glass-topped table. With doilies. Stella set her shoulders. If he expected to win her over he would not.

'Do sit down.'

She sat down in a spacious armchair by the fireplace and found herself agreeing to a cup of tea. Barlow sat on a sofa, his back to the window.

'She was in that recliner, sitting where you are. Towards the end she couldn't concentrate and she'd doze off with the telly. I

kissed her and whispered it was bedtime. She wasn't breathing.'
He handed her a cup.

Stella quelled an inclination to rush out to her van. She took a
sip. It was exactly how she liked it, a dollop of milk and one sugar.
She sank into the cushions.

So it was that Stella Darnell – aged forty-five and indeed single
– director of Clean Slate Cleaning Services (For a Fresh Start),
came to be sitting in a dead woman's riser-recliner, taking tea on
a Monday evening in Hammersmith when she had planned to be
clearing out her dead father's house and compiling a quote for a
car dealership in Chiswick.

David Barlow chatted peaceably from the corner of an austere
sofa with little padding, his legs crossed, one foot twitching in
emphasis of certain words. '… it was a Friday, too late to ring the
doctor or undertaker.'

'Medics work through the night.' Stella drained her cup and
placed it on the little table. A furtive finger test confirmed the job
would be unrewarding: no dust. Apart from random black lines
on the walls, the room – spanning the length of the house, including a conservatory extension – was clean.

'My wife had passed away, no one could help her and on a
weekend they are run off their feet.' Mr Barlow cleared his throat:
'And to be honest, after so many years, I wanted her a little longer,
you understand.' He smoothed his tie. Jack said the gesture was a
sign of dishonesty. What did he know? He never wore a tie. 'You
are too young to have known death.' Barlow smiled, looking over
the top of his rimless spectacles. Perhaps referring to the article
he added, 'Although that isn't true.'

Stella was trying to conjure her escape so did not correct him
about her age or elaborate on her experience of death. Jack had
worn a tie to her dad's funeral, she remembered.

David Barlow's thick brown hair had no grey and his symmetrical good looks showed only a few lines. He was younger than
Bowie, anywhere between forty-five and fifty-five. In over twenty
years of running Clean Slate, Stella's stringent appraisal of her

9

clients had begun to include their dress sense. This, coupled with her assessment of their attitude to the cleaning, had contributed to a shrewd business acumen that brought Clean Slate considerable commercial success. Barlow had trodden silently over his spotless carpet in understated soft brown leather loafers. He had not smartened up for their appointment; he took this trouble for himself.

Aside from David Bowie, he put her in mind of her dad. It was not his appearance, she decided; Terry was an off-the-peg man, in a hurry, his clothes lacking Barlow's attention to detail. But Terry was a charmer; he always broke the ice and could elicit information and confessions from suspects or indeed anyone. Barlow's mild manner had to be an act because, like Terry, no wool would surely ever be pulled over those gimlet eyes. He had already got her to have tea. Time to go.

'Clean Slate would not suit you, you need—'

'Of course.' He laid his cup and saucer on the tray. 'Your firm is too successful.' He got up, apparently accepting Stella's refusal before it was clear in her mind. 'We were burgled a while back and Jennifer felt the place was violated. I should have had the house cleaned while she was alive.'

He shot her a brief smile. His eyes were a greenish blue. Absurdly, because there were more important things that she forgot, she recalled that Bowie had different coloured eyes. Stella struggled to her feet, snatched up her rucksack and glanced behind, half expecting Mrs Barlow to be there.

'I chose Clean Slate because you list "deep cleaning" among your services.'

Stella stopped, her hand on the door jamb. 'It's for industrial environments, hospitals, hospices…' she managed.

'Deep cleaning is what I want.' Barlow addressed the recliner. 'Your website lists the eradication of kitchen grease, offensive odour control, duct cleaning. This would be a sanitizing…' He folded his arms. 'I want cleaning that is as deep as can be. I want everything cleansed, all traces eradicated. To make this a home again.'

He looked around the room as if surveying the devastation that the burglary must have caused. Stella brightened. David Barlow appreciated order and cleanliness. Her heart began to race and she strode back into the room.

'I want the walls washed, all furniture pulled out and cleaned, vent panels, everything removed, taken apart. Retribution.' He turned to her.

Stella now saw that the marks on the wall were not random as she had assumed but were shapes outlined with dirt where objects had once hung. There were the outlines of three crucifixes between the oblongs and squares of pictures. Not a believer in God, Stella did not rule his existence out. She supposed that the theft of a crucifix – three – might incite retribution. Yet she wasn't convinced that deep cleaning would do it. How would the thieves know?

It was not her policy to dwell on her clients' motives. However, inspired by David Barlow's determination to get his house back, she found herself hoping it would help.

'I'll do it.' She swung her rucksack down and ferreted in it for her estimates pad. 'When were you thinking?'

'Clean Slate must be too busy to bother with me.'

He crossed to the recliner and depressed a foot pedal. The chair tilted slowly forward like a person getting to their feet. Stella found the sight unsettling. Was he not serious after all? She knew that type.

'I used to run a sales team for an internet company. I wasn't meant to fuss with customers only making small purchases like dial-ups or modems. Time is money.' He let the chair down. 'You have to be pragmatic.'

Barlow would have been a soft touch: too nice. Her dad would have made a crack salesperson; he got what he needed from any situation. Now that Barlow was prevaricating, Stella was determined to close the sale. She flipped to a fresh page in her pad and, clicking on her Clean Slate branded pen, jotted down what she could see. Thankfully the wife had not been one for ornaments – unless the burglars had taken them. 'I'll send you a quotation.'

She was particularly formal to hide a rising excitement; it was a year since she had deep cleaned.

'Invoice me after each visit. I will pay by return.'

He didn't ask for a cash deal; exacting a discount was another trait of one species of widower. The less they paid for their new wife the better. Barlow was what he seemed: a decent bloke wanting a job done.

'It will be expensive,' she warned, rat-a-tatting the page with her ballpoint. Were Jackie here she would suggest Stella talk up the benefits of Clean Slate so when she priced the work the client was primed to think it worth every penny. She had killed the job.

Barlow nodded. 'I want it sorted.' He repeated, more to himself, 'I will pay.'

Reprieve. Stella flipped open her Filofax. They decided on two sessions a week. She scratched out a recruitment meeting with Jackie that clashed with one day.

Standing in a shaft of sunlight from the conservatory, Barlow enquired: 'Who will be coming?'

Stella looked out at a green lawn so neat it looked synthetic. 'Me.'

Halfway up Aldensley Road, braking to avoid boys kicking a football across the kerbs, Stella reappraised David Barlow. He wasn't sizing her up as a bride. He wanted his house cleansed of bad memories so he could move on. Maybe this was why she hadn't sold Terry's house, she would tell Jack next time he asked. David Barlow was her kind of person. He valued order, free of dust or grime. Just as she did, and she had been quoted on it in the article. The piece had appeared in the paper before his wife died; Barlow had not rung earlier because she was too ill. Stella exhaled with relief as she turned on to King Street and headed for Young's Corner. Deep cleaning. Perfect start to her week. The last domestic client to commission cleaning at a forensic level had died; she missed the work.

David Barlow was exactly whom she needed.

Three

The noise made her ears hurt. She clapped her hands over them but it got louder. Around her sandals dots of light sparkled, white and blue and pink.

'I told you not to touch them!' her mum cried. 'That's all our crockery!'

Mary Thornton stayed perfectly still in the hallway while her mother scrabbled about on the parquet floor, shuffling broken china and bits of glass on to newspaper which she wrapped up into a parcel.

'Don't stand there. Get the dustpan and brush!'

'Where from?'

'Where it usually is, under the sink.' She shook her head at Mary.

'Will it be there already?' They had only moved to the house that day.

'No it won't.' Her mother sighed. 'Look in the box labelled "Under Sink". Don't try to carry the whole thing this time. Lord knows what we'll drink out of.'

Mary pushed open the door to the new kitchen and found her brother Michael sitting at the table. He was eating yoghurt out of a glass jar. She walked over to him and saw that somehow amongst all the boxes, wooden cases and newspapers he had got his special spoon. He eyed her, the spoon suspended; then, evidently considering it safe to do so, he resumed eating.

'Who said you could have that?'

'Mummy did. Are you in trouble again?'

'No,' she asserted, although Michael, three years her junior and never in trouble, must have heard her drop the box and listened to everything that happened afterwards.

'Give me some,' she demanded, even though she wasn't hungry.

'You hate yoghurt.' The small boy snatched away the jar and cupped it on his lap when his sister lunged for it. He opened his mouth to shout and she halted her hand in the air.

'If you say anything I'll get you later,' she hissed. 'Give. It. Here.'

Mary pulled Michael's wrist. Her brother wriggled free and, kneeling up on his chair, crouched over the table shielding the jar. Both children were engaged in the struggle for its own sake. After tugging and shoving, Mary detached herself and wandered over to a box by the back door. She had written the words 'Under Sink' on its side herself. She knelt on the lino and, lifting the flaps, rummaged inside.

'You're bad,' Michael uttered, apparently arbitrarily, now that he had a clear route to the door.

'I'm not.' She was bad. This had not occurred properly to her before. Dimly she pondered that ever since the buried children had been dug up on the Moor she had been bad. That was why she had a new name.

Despite her labelling, the box was full of pans, the rolling pin, her nan's cheese grater and the metal measuring jug for making Michael's favourite cakes. Mary could not see the dustpan and brush. She wrapped her arms around the cardboard and, disobeying her mum, hauled it up and staggered to the sink. She dumped it on to the draining board with a terrible clang and whipped around. Michael was smearing out the last of the yoghurt from the jar with his finger. Her mum did not appear.

'Will our milkman come here?' he asked conversationally.

'How do I know?' Mary barked at him. 'No, of course not, we've moved miles and miles away. Go and wash your hands.' With private triumph she fished out the dustpan and brush from another box also called 'Under Sink'. She examined the galvanized dustpan, mildly perplexed that it looked the same in the new house where otherwise so much was different.

'Where shall I wash them?'

'Don't be an idiot. In the bathroom.'

'Where's that?'

'Stop asking me things. Go and see.' Mary brandished the brush at her brother; he scampered out of the room. 'Stop!' Michael's head bobbed back.

'Wash them in the sink here.' Mary did not want to be alone in the new kitchen.

Michael pattered to the tap and by going on tiptoe he could just reach it. Mary vaguely registered that in their proper house he stood on a chair. He must have grown. Wistfully she pictured that kitchen with the sunbeam that on some school mornings warmed her cheeks while she ate her Cornflakes and made her feel special. She did not feel special any more and the idea of the new school made her tummy ache.

Mary Thornton clasped the dustpan and brush and trotted back to the hall. Her mum had gone. She crouched down and played at housework. She took today's paper from her father's coat pocket and spread it out on the floor.

The little girl was momentarily unnerved by the photograph of a woman looking right at her. She read the headline above the image: 'MOORS MURDER TRIAL OPENS'. She dabbed a thumb over the lady's name, blotting it out.

She snatched up the brush, scooted the remaining tiny fragments into the dustpan and tipped them out on to the paper until the face of the glary lady had nearly disappeared and the floor was clean. She bundled the paper up the way her mother had and carried it like baby Jesus into the kitchen.

Michael had gone. The empty jar was on the table. Mary rinsed it in the sink and plonked it upside down on the draining board. There were round circles from cups on the silver top, which was strange because they had not had a drink in the new house. Michael had whispered there were ghosts. Stupid. She rubbed at one of the rings until it was gone. Daddy had been cross that her mum had packed the tea leaves in the wrong box and so there had been no tea. She looked in both 'Under Sink' boxes for a dishcloth but it must also be in the wrong box. It was not her fault, she said to herself. None of it was.

When Mrs Thornton breezed in twenty minutes later, straining with the weight of a bulging string bag, her daughter had filled the cupboard under the sink so that it looked the same as in their last house.

'That's nice, love.' She pushed aside two empty boxes and laid down her shopping. 'Fish fingers, lamb chops, baked beans, tea, bread and cornflakes. And some veg. Please start the tea for you and little Mikey. Daddy's driving back for the last load and I'm doing the beds.'

'Can I go in the van with Daddy?'

'What did I just say?'

'Is Michael going?'

'No, My— Mary! For goodness' sake, do I have to ask a thing twice?' Mrs Thornton clapped her hands to shoo Mary along and whisked out of the room. From the hall, she called: 'Use the fish fingers and beans, they're your baby brother's favourite and he must have a treat to get used to the house.'

'I'm off.' Her dad was in the doorway.

Mary grasped the chance. 'Can I come?' she pleaded.

'You heard your mother. Don't play games. No means no. Look after your brother.'

Mary stood alone in the room. She heard a bang and then silence. In their old home she knew all the noises, but this house was foreign to her; its corners were sharp and the floors cold and hard. She was not bad and would show them by doing what she was told or she might be buried on the moor too. Mary wished Michael would come back. He would come soon enough if she made his tea.

She counted out four fish fingers from the box. The cardboard was damp from where the food had thawed and she accidentally tore the flap; another fish finger fell out. She deserved an extra one. She lined up the tin of Heinz beans, the loaf of bread and a box of Brooke Bond tea beside three brown paper bags with twists for ears. She peered in each bag: carrots, potatoes and onions. Mary played being the greengrocer and announced each item out loud while tapping out the prices on the table with stubby fingers as if working the giant till. They would not see the nice greengrocer with the funny eyes who gave her penny snakes any more.

As Mary had anticipated, attracted by the cooking smells Michael slunk in while his sister was at the stove and slid on to a chair. He lolled over the table between his rabbit knife and fork, which she had found for him, and enquired chirpily: 'Are you meant to use the frying pan?'

'How else can I make fish fingers?' she retorted, forking them out on to two plates. She scraped splodges of congealing beans out of the saucepan and ladled them next to the fish fingers, spilling some on the tabletop. Michael snapped them up.

'You're not allowed,' she added with some triumph.

'We've got a bedroom each.' Michael tucked his hands between his knees happily. His hair stuck up at the back and his wrists poked out like white sticks from the jumper knitted for him by their nan, who liked boys best.

'Take your elbows off the table.' Mary was now their mother. She banged down a plastic beaker of milk. 'Sit up.'

'Yours is bigger, but I can see my new swing from mine.'

'What new swing?'

'The one Daddy's going to make in the garden by the willow tree.' As he chattered he lined up the fish fingers with his fork making a train with two carriages. 'It'll be very, very high so I can kick the sky.' He chanted the phrase, obviously pleased with it. 'It'll be very, very—'

'Be quiet, Michael!'

'You don't have a willow tree in your tree album.' He kicked his legs against the chair as he chomped his food.

'I do,' Mary said without thinking, although she did not

remember a page with a willow and certainly didn't have the card.

'It's not a "Trees of Britain" tree.' Michael smiled good-naturedly at his sister.

'It is.' Too late Mary sniffed a trap of her own making.

'The weeping willow comes from China. It's in my en-cyc-lop-paedia. You won't get it from this tea.' Michael lined up the last three beans on his fork and nudged the packet of Brooke Bond with his other hand.

'Who says?' Mary pulled at his hand. 'Don't play with your food.'

Michael shrugged and squirmed on his chair while he chewed. 'I've never had my own bedroom. You're always there.' He looked suddenly less pleased.

'Nor have I,' Mary conceded. She sat down and gathering up a dainty forkful of beans popped it between her lips.

'Yes you have.' He slurped his milk. 'Mare-ree.'

'No, I have not and do not call me that. Close your mouth when you're eating, I can see mashed-up food.' She swallowed a bean without chewing and coughed.

'You have, you had a bedroom by yourself before I was even born. For three years you had a bedroom.'

'That doesn't count.'

'It does. It's a very lo-ong time. In three years I'll be ten like you. Except then you won't be ten, you'll—'

'Shut up!'

Her brother reddened and pronging a bean on his fork nibbled it off ruminatively. 'I want to go home,' he muttered after a bit, so quietly Mary only just caught it.

'This is home.' Impatient with trying to eat politely in the strange kitchen, she heaped beans and fish fingers on to the convex side of her fork and shovelled them into her mouth. When she had finished she rinsed their plates without washing-up liquid because it was not in the 'Under Sink' boxes.

Neither child voiced what each had decided must be true, that although they had been told their father had a new job, the move to Hammersmith from Holloway, away from everything they knew, was in some way Mary's fault.

'I don't like it here.' Michael spoke to the lino with brimming eyes.

'Nor do I,' his sister replied without turning round.

Four

Terry had painted an outline of each tool in white on the wall in the understairs cupboard. It had put Stella in mind of the police marker for a corpse at a crime scene. She positioned the vacuum cleaner on a shelf and hooked up the hose according to its outline. She cleared the house, only the white shapes would remain. She thought of the black outlines at David Barlow's. In this house she was the intruder.

Each evening Stella Darnell came to her father's end of terrace in what had once been a modest cul-de-sac off the Great West Road but was now quietly chic. She cleaned already clean rooms, consumed a microwaved shepherd's pie from the freezer before catching up with emails on his computer in what had been her bedroom forty years earlier. She never stayed the night nor, although Terry Darnell had been dead a year, had she begun getting rid of his belongings.

Fresh from meeting David Barlow, and still in her dark blue business suit and the sturdy black boots she used for cleaning, Stella decanted tonight's ready meal – the potato topping pleased her, furrowed with straight fork lines – on to a white china plate and placed it off centre in the microwave, which Terry said captured the hot spots. When Stella had let slip to Jackie what she ate for supper, Jackie had suggested Stella liven it with veg from the mini-mart below the office. Or better still have supper with her and her family, a suggestion Jackie made about once a month. Stella had ignored her advice but sometimes accepted the invitation. She did not say she preferred to eat alone. Although in Terry's house, she was not alone. The fancy-named journalist had been wrong. Terry, a retired detective chief superintendent, was dead, but Stella was conscious of his ghostly presence – like a chalky outline – in every room.

She keyed in the timing and at the same moment heard a distant clunk. The liquid-crystal screen went black and displayed only her frown. The fridge had stopped humming. A power cut.

At eight o'clock it would be light for another hour, but Stella could do no more without electricity. She had tidied and vacuumed; there was no point in staying. She wrapped the plate of food in clingfilm and fitted it in the fridge beside a tub of margarine. The half-litre of milk should last; she had bought it yesterday. She would leave the other shepherd's pies in the freezer; the outage must be temporary.

On the path outside she clutched her keys to stop them jangling. So far she had avoided meeting Terry's neighbours. The lamp-post on the other side of the street had been flickering on and off for months. Stella intended to tell the council. It should not be on now: it was not lighting-up time.

In a power cut it should not be on at all.

She glanced in through the window of next door and saw the green of a football pitch on a television screen. She jogged back to Terry's and tried the hall light. Nothing. The sound when the power failed must have been the lever tripping on the fuse box.

During her cleaning Stella had not seen a fuse box beneath the stairs or the sink and from the few times she had ventured into the attic after her dad's death she knew it wasn't there.

She contemplated the panelled door to the basement set beside the tool cupboard with stirring dread. She had avoided Terry's particular lair. The fuse box would be in the basement.

Terry Darnell had moved into the Victorian house in the London Borough of Hammersmith when he married Stella's mother in 1966, six months before Stella was born. Suzanne Darnell left him seven years later and took their daughter to live in an austere mansion apartment in Barons Court. Terry lived on in the house until his death in January last year. At first the Darnells had rented the property, but Terry's journey up the police ranks had been smooth, swift and steep, so by 1981 he was already a detective inspector and could afford a mortgage on the property. Suzie complained that he was ambitious, too busy for a wife and daughter. Eventually Stella had grown to consider her father a stranger about whom she knew little.

She did know that Terry always carried a camera; it had frustrated her that he would interrupt a conversation to snap a photograph: of a suspect, a bicycle chained illegally to railings or a passing car. He developed the negatives in the darkroom in his basement.

As Terry Darnell's only child, Stella had inherited his house – the mortgage long paid off. She had resolved to sell it, but instead was preserving Terry's routine and keeping it clean.

If her dad's presence could linger in rooms scrubbed with carpet cleaner, vacuumed with maximum suction and mopped and polished to a flawless shine, it would be manifest in the darkroom where he had spent most of his spare time.

In light through panes in the door, she tried the handle. The latch slid through the strike plate but the door did not budge. It was locked and Stella did not have the key.

Soon it would be dark. She could not leave, although it was cold for the start of spring: the contents of the freezer would not survive. The clocks on the DVD, the microwave and the boiler and the myriad timers triggering and extinguishing lights, her father's ploy to fool burglars, would slip out of sync. His intricate system would break down.

Terry's stuff, his clothes, the few books and his computer were as he had left them the morning he drove to a seaside town in Sussex where he had died. Stella did admit privately that she saw herself as only the custodian of her father's home against the day he would return.

She retrieved Terry's keys from her rucksack. Two for the

front door, one for the back and the spare for his Toyota, which she had forgotten to give the new owner. No basement key.

Terry Darnell said that burglars rely on ease of egress not entrance, so make it hard for them to get the goods out. In a house where everyone is sleeping, oblivious, a draught from an open front door might be the first sign anything is wrong. She wondered how David Barlow's burglars had left. Her own fifth-floor flat was fortressed above a foyer protected by a code and a camera, her front door strengthened by a London bar, a mortice lock and a chain.

Again she was struck by the conviction that had Terry wanted her in his house he would have left instructions about watering plants, the trick with the boiler or the optimum programme for the dishwasher. He had never shown her where he kept the key to the basement. Jack would say that the power cut was a sign that she should leave.

Stella tried the kitchen drawers, the cupboards and unlikely places like the door lintels and the grille fronting the sitting-room heater.

Outside it had grown dark and the landing was in shadow. A new stillness increased her unease. Mustering calm, she tried to second-guess Terry. Jack would suggest she 'became' him; he imagined they were alike. Stella tried to remember Terry and realized that she could not.

One stair at a time. At the top it occurred to her that some burglars defecated in people's homes, shitting on beds, pissing in wardrobes. A reason to deep clean. The bathroom, with less to steal, was where they were least likely to go. The key would be there.

To her mum's horror – although Suzie had left by then – Terry replaced the 1920s bathroom fittings with a sale-priced cream fibreglass suite. Now the shower curtain rail sagged and a fine crack ran across the lavatory lid. Stella opened the mirrored cabinet door above the sink. Terry's toothbrush and toothpaste were in a beaker beside packets of aspirin, a bottle of Warfarin, deodorant and a canister of shaving foam. She had had no difficulty chucking out Terry's condoms. Burglars would check the cabinet. He would not hide the key here.

The cast-iron cistern, the only original feature, rested on brackets she found a fiddle to clean. A chain with a grip of perishing grey rubber defied cleaning but Stella did not think it hers to replace. She had missed a cluster of cobwebs between the tank and the wall. If a prospective recruit had cleaned the room, she would not have hired them. She shrugged off shame that for Terry her standards had slipped. The condoms had thrown her; she would deep clean the bathroom.

The cistern. Stella climbed on to the toilet lid, steadied herself with one of the iron supports and peered over. No key. About to jump down, she paused. She would hide a key here. She looked closer. The cover was not flush to the tank. She nudged it and it shifted. Careful to avoid it sliding off, she inched it aside. Grit scattered down; she blinked and brushed it away with her sleeve, noting crossly that the cuff was flecked with dust.

She strained on tiptoe and dabbled her hand into the tank. The water was tepid and, even though there had been a cover on, she was nervous about dead birds. She paddled her fingers out as far as she could reach and felt something soft. A sparrow. She snatched away her hand, but then, swallowing hard, nerved herself. She yanked up her sleeve, plunged her hand in and grasped the bird.

Snap! She teetered on the toilet bowl. Her dad's toilet lid had broken in two. Stella felt a flash of guilt; she'd have to replace it. She pulled her hand out; water streamed down her wrists, soaking the dirt into the linen.

The 'bird' was a folded plastic pocket, the sort with holes for filing, and inside was a mortice key. Stella knew without trying that it would open the basement door.

After a year Stella expected the lock to be stiff, but the key turned easily and the door swung silently on oiled hinges. She had been so fixed on the search she had not considered actually going into the basement. A memory of the first time she had come here after Terry's death flooded back, as vivid as if it were yesterday. She had walked around the house, dark then too, convinced she was not alone. It was one of the few times she had been truly frightened. This time it was a simple power cut and she knew how to mend a fuse. She shone the torch down the steps and descended.

The sharp tang of photographic solution swept her further back in time to when she used to help her dad develop pictures. Stella grasped the banister rail. It was new – perhaps Terry had felt less sure-footed in his last years. She stopped the thought.

Matt-black brick walls absorbed the light. At this time of night the Great West Road, yards away, was busy, yet the quiet was absolute. The beam revealed the folds of a blackout curtain, the sink, the table and chair where Terry sorted his pictures. The room was uncannily familiar yet unfamiliar.

Terry's enlarger was floor to ceiling; he could blow up images to poster size making large the smallest details. Nowadays Stella did this with a mouse click. Terry had never got to grips with computers.

She had stood on a box in her crackling plastic apron and swished the paper about the tray with tongs encouraging the picture to emerge. The enamel dishes were still by the sink. There was no paper there now. Terry had not processed prints for years. No purist, he had not clung to old-fangled methods for an authentic look; he snapped photographs for record, not for art's sake.

Two lever-arch files were on a shelf above the sink. One, in Terry's laborious capitals, read: 'Commodore Fire 1981'. That was the year of Terry's major case: the Rokesmith murder, which the newspaper article had said Stella solved on her own. At the time she had felt proud, she had done something for him, but after the article she suspected she had betrayed him. Inside the file was a sleeve of negatives. She slipped out a strip and held it in the beam of light: the silvery figures of firefighters, some caught in movement as they dragged on hose reels and wielded ladders. They looked like phantoms. An arc of water sprayed into a hole in the Commodore wall, from which smoke billowed like steam; everything dark was light. The end frame showed the departing fire engine, a ghostly outline. She flipped the page and found the corresponding contact sheets. Terry had captured the entire incident.

Stella knew the Commodore. It had been on Young's Corner in King Street. School tennis champion in her teens, on visits to Terry she would perfect slamming returns against its vast wall. She had forgotten this. Opened as a concert hall by Hollywood actress Tallulah Bankhead in the 1920s, it became a cinema. In the late seventies, when people stopped going to films, it became a bingo hall, the crimson velvet and mahogany furnishings tawdry and tired. During its demolition a dropped cigarette butt ignited the detritus of half a century. Terry couldn't have taken the pictures for the police; it was not his job. Stella would never know why.

The other file was scribbled with the catch-all 'Misc' and had pictures of the Broadway, including Butterwick bus station where she caught the 27 bus to Terry's, gone now to make way for extra lanes on the Broadway. Terry had snapped the Hammersmith of his youth; some of it had been hers too before it vanished. Stella shoved the file back and, kneeling down, scanned beneath the counter. No fuse box.

She found a row of yellow Kodak cartons for photographic paper. Terry had written on the nearest one. Stella took a breath. 'Hammersmith Murders'. Another unsolved case. She grabbed the box and pulled off the lid. There were no case documents, just two eight-by-ten-inch prints. One was of a barge on the river with a building on the far bank, its dark shape reflected in the water. On its wall was a sign: 'Watneys Brewery'. That dated it. The other picture was of a willow tree with the river visible through the fronds that made shadows on the grass around the tree. So Terry did take arty pictures. Nothing about a murder; Stella was disappointed.

When engaged in a task do not to be distracted by the client and move to other tasks. Page ten in her staff handbook. Stella clambered to her feet. Terry was distracting her.

The fuse box was tucked behind the enlarger. It needed fuse wire. About to despair she spotted a card reel of wire and a pair of pliers on top of the box. Terry was always prepared. She snipped off the precise amount, threaded it into the Bakelite housing and levered down the handle. It made a dull clunk. With no light she couldn't tell if the electricity was on. Stella flashed her torch about for a light switch and found Terry's black angle-poise lamp.

Faces, some smiling, some gazing through her, others staring as if trying to recognize her. Stella staggered against Terry's chair and sat down heavily. The panelled partition to the steps was lined with photographs, a crazy wallpaper. Some life-size, some eight by tens, others holiday-print dimensions. Most were black and white, but a few were printed in Technicolor, giving them a lurid quality.

All the photographs were of Stella and, she calculated, documented her life from a baby in a Santa hat to the Christmas a couple of weeks before her dad died, when she had dropped off his present: a bottle of Gillette aftershave popped into a gift bag, since he knew what it was. She had no idea he had taken a photograph that day, but there she was, glancing up unsmiling from her phone, as unwilling to stay then as she had been tonight at David Barlow's. She had drunk a cup of tea and left. She had never seen him again. At least not alive. The partition was entirely covered. There was no room for more pictures. Just as well. Stella wheeled the chair closer.

Suzanne Darnell still grumbled that her husband had never taken 'snaps' of her or of his daughter. In the Wimpy on Hammersmith Broadway, aged eight, Stella worked her way through a banana split while her dad let his coffee cool. She did not remember his camera, yet there on the top row was Stella spooning ice cream from a tall sundae glass and grinning sheepishly at the lens.

As he had monitored the phases of the Commodore fire, so Terry had recorded his daughter's forty-five years. Stella had dreaded finding something unmentionable in the basement, something worse than condoms. Instead she had found herself.

She swivelled around to the table and, leaning on her elbows, rested her chin on her fists. Terry sat here to crop and trim the prints with his metal rule and the scalpel Stella must not touch under any circumstances. They were not there now. Instead there was a blue plastic ring binder that made Stella vaguely think of a visitors' book for comments. She was a visitor. She eyed the folder.

Snapping into action, she angled the lamp and gingerly, wary of finding more pictures of herself, opened the folder. She need not have worried. Inside were more eight by tens slotted back to back in reinforced wallets like the one in the cistern. All were framed in landscape mode so Stella turned the folder around. Street after street, the sort of boring shots she had seen Terry take countless times on the access weekends. Tarmac receding from the foreground, lines of uninterrupted kerbstones, some parked cars, lamp-posts and railings. No people. Her mother often said Terry couldn't relate to people; she would say these pictures proved it. Stella found one that she had missed because she had turned two pages at once. Two legs stuck out from under a VW beetle parked on a wide pavement. More cars were on a ramp leading out of a low white building running down to the kerb. Beyond the depth of field, and so out of focus, were a bus and cars waiting at lights.

She supposed it was a grisly accident until she recognized the garage. It was on the corner of St Peter's Square, five minutes' walk from where she was now. The legs belonged to a mechanic mending a car. There was the Commodore, which put the shot before 1981. She skimmed through the folder: more streets.

All the prints were black and white, some on eighty-gram photocopying paper using an inkjet printer of poor quality. Lines were blurred and lighter areas were faint. Apart from the garage, she didn't recognize the locations. Terry had taken the pictures at different times of day and on different days. In some, the pavements glistened with rain and puddles had formed in gutters; in another, a horse trough made a stark shadow in bright sunshine.

Terry had numbered each print; Stella counted fifteen. The garage was number '1' while some digits like the picture numbered '7' also had a '7a' and a '7b'.

After Terry died, Stella had found all his private papers and files categorized alphabetically, chronologically or numbered. This folder was an exception: nothing on the front or the spine. He had left no clue to what it was. Thinking of Terry's efficiency reminded Stella that she hadn't answered her emails. She glanced at her watch: twenty-five to ten. Unbelievably she had been in the basement for over an hour.

Stella shut the folder, turned off the light and ran up the stairs. The house was dark, but for the street lamp which was now on and sending a wash of light through the glazed door panels. She locked the basement and pocketed the key.

She did not heat up the shepherd's pie; she had lost her appetite. Outside on the step, to the 'meep-meep' of the house alarm, she locked up. When it stopped she heard her phone ringing from deep in her anorak pocket.

Mum.

Stella hesitated and then pressed the green button. 'Hi.' She kept her voice low to avoid the neighbours hearing.

The voice was indistinct, the words intermittent. Stella cocked her head for a better signal, although reception was not the problem. Suzie never spoke into the mouthpiece.

'It's Mu… I… can't open… Come and… Stella!'

Stella fired her key at a green and white van by bushes on the opposite kerb. The phone clamped to her ear, she tossed her rucksack on to the passenger seat and climbed in.

'I can't hear you, Mum.' She was playing for time; she knew what her mother wanted. What she always wanted: for Stella to come immediately. Suzie called at all hours of the day and night with urgent requests that could always wait. One day there would be a true emergency; in the meantime she had to play along.

'I'll be there in ten minutes. Stay where you are, OK?' she added unnecessarily, hoping that day was not now.

Five

'Sing a song of sixpence,
A pocket full of rye;
Four and twenty blackbirds,
Baked in a pie.'

Jack twittered the song under his breath and ducked down an alleyway between the gardens. The raggedy pathway was a topographical leftover from cramming in dwellings in the sixties and was probably the bane of residents' lives since it offered intruders a convenient route to their houses. He hummed softly. The muddy ground was sticky after the rain and mulched with rubbish: packaging, plastic bottles, cans. He hopped aside to avoid shit: a fox or dog. Possibly human.

The alley was lined with a hotchpotch of walls, fences and hedges. Privets and sturdy panelled fencing offered him nothing and threatened to dampen his spirits. Then he came upon a ramshackle barricade of patchworked corrugated iron and warped slabs of MDF with a gap through which he spied a lawn and a weed-strewn stretch of concrete. Plastic furniture was heaped higgledy-piggledy down the side of the extension next to a rusting barbeque. The house had a terrible air of neglect. He mulled over the options. Not uncaring tenants: the lease would require minimal standards of care. More likely the house owner had been left behind in the dilapidated dwelling, and was waiting to die. Jack tugged at the corner of an MDF panel and a rotten chunk broke off into his hand. This would be too easy and offered him nothing.

The windows were dark. He did a quick reorientation: he had passed this house many times and seen a 'For Sale' sign nailed to the gatepost. He recalled that an old man lived here. He did not fit Jack's profile; he didn't offer him a home or look like a murderer. And now perhaps he had died or gone into a home. Jack was losing his touch.

He continued down the passage.

'When the pie was opened,
The birds began to sing;
Was not that a dainty dish,
To set before the king?'

Someone with a window open might catch his lilting tones on the night breeze.

A break in a pyracantha hedge was the challenge he craved. The hedge was planted to curb the likes of him. Through spiky branches he saw an outbuilding.

White light drenched the scene. A security lamp. He kept still and dropped his singing to a low whistle. After a while the light went out. When the yellow blob faded from his retina Jack made out the lamp fixed to guttering above French doors. He noted every detail: the outbuilding, the garden laid to lawn. The doors were ajar. It was a cold night and they were open? A sign; certainly an invitation. No gravel to give away his approach. Perfect.

He pulled his coat over his head and, keeping low, pushed through the branches and stepped on to the lawn. The light came on. He crouched in a ball but, as he expected, no one came out. People got blasé and assumed an animal had triggered the light. He dressed in black to merge with the night.

Again the light went out and, coat flying, head down, Jack skimmed along the edge of the lawn and flattened himself against the house wall. The security lamp did not cover the patio. How often had he observed expensive alarm systems not activated, top-of-the-range locks on the latch while their owners popped out to water plants or fetch shopping from the car? This one was asking for him.

Tonight there was no moonlight; Jack had consulted the application on his phone in readiness. Yet in London it was never truly dark. Glistening leaves of the cherry laurel hedge were etched by a silver sheen from the street-lit sky. He edged up to the doors and peered in. A sitting room was brightly lit, the décor muted and bland. It reminded him of Stella Darnell's flat. There the similarity ended. Stella was regimentally tidy, while here papers and files were spread out on a coffee table, on a sofa facing the garden and over a dining table with document boxes stacked on chairs. The only place free of stuff was a wide-screen television, the centrepiece of a glossy black console that also housed a DVD and a hi-fi system.

Jack felt a burst of euphoria and stopped himself singing. In films and books, villains disguised by balaclavas spied through windows or plied doors with long blades and sneaked inside. No one believed it would happen to them. Until it did. This had been handed to him on a plate.

He gave a start. A woman was sitting feet from him. She was looking straight at him. Jack ducked back against the stuccoed wall. He counted to ten and then inched around. The woman was still staring, but not at him. Light from the room would blot out the garden; she could not see him. She must have become aware of her own reflection because she put her hand to her face and brushed back a strand of hair, patting it into place. She was at a desk and now began leafing through papers strewn there, occasionally jotting something down in a notebook.

Keeping below the sightline of the security lamp, he flitted to the other side of the doors, truly excited now. An ample marble mantelpiece below which flickered the flames of a fire. He sighed; he could sit cross-legged on the rug in front of the hearth and make himself at home. His attention was drawn to a picture above the mantelpiece: a middle-aged man with unruly grey hair in a matching grey suit. The modern image, a scan of a photograph, was incongruous in the sumptuous gilt frame. This man was staring at him. Jack shrank back. It was a picture, but he could not shake the impression that the man could see him.

He had seen no signs of evil in the set of the woman's features, but staring back into the grey eyes in the framed picture, Jack knew he was looking at a killer. It was to stop murderers like him that Jack went on his night-time prowls. He occupied their homes without them knowing and meticulously undermined their plans to take lives. At least he had done this until Stella got wind of it and said he must stop, it was illegal. Tonight when he left his house, Jack had promised himself, he was taking a harmless stroll.

The woman was reading a newspaper. Jack thought her eyes looked tired; lines around them betrayed that she was used to laughing, but deeper grooves around her mouth told him she had not even smiled for a while: misery dictated her mood.

He understood the plethora of papers and the open doors. She was lonely and unconsciously was inviting guests. The grey man in the portrait was dead. Grieving, his widow was struggling with the household admin that was his legacy. Nothing for Jack here, although she might welcome his company.

The woman was jotting something down from the article. Jack stepped closer, but could only see three letters in the head-line. They spelled 'The'. He saw the photograph beneath and stifled a yelp. Stella. Jack could just see the byline: Lucille May. He shivered. The widow was reading about Stella. This was a sign. But of what?

Something struck him on the forehead. He had banged his head on the glass pane. He flung himself flat against the house wall. If she came outside she would see him. He heard clicking: her shoes on a wooden floor. She was coming. He shut his eyes, then snapped them open and cast about. There was nowhere to hide.

Jack broke cover. He leapt across the band of light from the sitting room and bounded along a path that skirted the lawn. He found himself by the outbuilding. He risked looking back. The woman was still at her desk.

He was surprised to find the outbuilding was not a shed, but a circular business of white-painted brick with a domed roof. He tried the door; it was locked. He peeped through a glass porthole, out of sight of the house, and saw only a sweeping white wall. It was empty, yet she had locked the door. A sense of peace overwhelmed him and it was all he could do not to return to the flagged patio and slip inside. He could stay here happily. Jack's justification for night ramblings was to find men who killed and to stop their work. He must not choose places that made him feel at home. He had promised Stella to stop, but in truth as soon as he stepped on to the lawn he had broken this promise.

Jack did up his coat and, out of the sightline of the camera, returned to the gap in the pyracantha and thrust himself back into the alley.

He jogged along King Street towards Hammersmith Broadway and swore that from now on he would keep his promise.

Jack had reached the Lyric Theatre when he realized he didn't have his *A–Z*. It must have fallen out of his pocket. He retraced his steps, scouring the pavement.

He crossed Ravenscourt Road. A dark object lay on the pavement outside the gates of the park. He increased his pace. As he did so a figure stepped out of the gloom and picked it up. Jack was close enough to see the white of the cover. It was his *A–Z*. He stopped. He could not ask for it back. It was his policy on his journeys never to speak to anyone. He must not be seen or remembered.

The figure was consulting his atlas as if they had lost their way, slowly turning the pages. Jack could not tell from here if the person was male or female: they stood just outside a circle of lamplight. They wore a coat similar to his, with the collar up. Jack went cold. The person was tracing his journeys, page by page. They could see into his mind. Jack had walked every page of the atlas, treading on unyielding pavements. He knew London's streets by heart. He avoided high buildings and sprawling concourses where the wind whipped around pillars as they made him feel exposed and robbed him of intent. Instead he went out of his way – all ways were 'his way' – to use subways and tunnels where he felt at home. He had completed the journeys traced on the pages in the book last year, but he kept the book with him. It was his companion as he took routes not marked on his map and went where the signs pointed. Without the book he was lost. This person might as well possess his soul.

The figure closed the book and began walking smartly across the road as if a decision had been made. Jack slipped behind a parked van and watched through the side windows. His heart thumped so loudly he had the crazy idea it would be heard.

He had forgotten his shift! Horrified at this lapse he checked his watch. Thirty-nine minutes before he must pick up his train at Earls Court. He should go to the station.

The woman had gone. Jack broke into a run, now heedless of being seen. There was no sign of her. No sign. He darted around a building on the pavement. It had been a public toilet – the words 'Men' and 'Women' were inscribed above the doors. It was now a café and was closed. She was not there.

To his right were the wrought-iron gates of a mansion he had passed often, but ignored. They were secured with a chain. A notice was fixed to one of the gate pillars:

Mallingswood House
Pre-Prep and Prep School for Boys
Five to Thirteen Years

Through the curling design on the gate he saw a flicker in the forecourt beyond the gates and the figure detached from the shadows of a tree and trotted – a woman, he was now sure – around the gravel turning circle. She went up broad steps to a glassed-in porch and in the muted street he heard her key scratch in the lock and the door shut.

Jack felt a jolt of foreboding. She was not a Host – his name for the killers who unwittingly had him as a guest in their homes – yet something disturbed him. She had too readily pocketed his street atlas.

In front of the gates stood what would once have been a splendid circular stone drinking fountain with a lower trough for small animals. Jack hid behind it; mounting the plinth he edged around it to survey the school.

A substantial square construction that had fallen victim to two extensions either side, the mansion had lost architectural balance. Once obviously a grand family home in parkland that would have stretched to the River Thames, it was stranded between two roads. The wall – bricks charcoaled by fumes – was spiked with broken glass weathered smooth but still vicious. A prefab structure with grilled windows and a scrubbed-out graffiti tag on one panel had been erected as an overspill classroom beside the porch. Despite the dilapidation, the school had pupils.

Jack counted eleven windows on the three floors and seven more in the attics. All dark: the boys would be tucked up and asleep. The coping was chipped and a smattering of roof tiles was missing. A cast-iron gutter had snapped at the joint and beneath it the stucco was streaked with rust and in places had cracked or fallen away, exposing crumbling brick.

There was a carriage mounting block to the left of the porch; it was identical to another block in a bleak quadrangle where plane tree leaves were ripped from branches by a searing wind. A seven-year-old Jack had climbed those steps, slippery with slimy moss: they led nowhere. The harsh weather had expressed a systematized unkindness that infected the boys. He felt his heart clench and straightened. If this was like his old school it should be easy to find his way in.

Jack whispered another verse – to soothe himself, not from joy:

'The king was in his counting house,
Counting out his money;
The queen was in the parlour,
Eating bread and honey.'

He would have to decide on a room with care. He had only once stayed in a place with children and then he had slept on the roof. Children knew how to hide and how to find those that hid. And in this day and age he didn't want his motives misunderstood.

He was staring at a lens. A camera was fixed discreetly to one of the pillars of the porch. Jack had forgotten about CCTV; he was out of practice. He had to hope it held no film or was rarely monitored. Whatever the case, he could not do any more tonight, he must prepare for his visit properly.

He took a last look at the mansion. The woman was different. Most would have discarded the book, tatty and out of date with every page marked. But she had kept it, just as he had when he had found it – in an empty carriage. She had a mind like his own. Like him she would not imagine herself anonymous in a world of strangers, but would expect a random stranger to choose her life to track and her home to live in. She would expect Jack, or someone like him, and she would literally watch her step. The person who had taken his *A–Z* would know what harm was possible. Yes, he must prepare properly.

Three numbers were carved into each of the pillars: '231'. Jack felt the ground swoop. He pulled his duty book from his coat pocket; like his street atlas, it went everywhere with him. On the cover was an image of the front of a District Line train; the protective plastic had scuffed, making it seem the train was emerging from a fog. Rainwater had swelled pages already frayed with his frequent thumbing. He ran a finger down the left-hand column of minute figures.

231 was the set number of the train he was to pick up at Ealing Broadway and stable in a siding at the depot at Earls Court. In

fifteen minutes. He was never late. Everything was out of kilter. Jack noted the letters 'ETY'. The pick-up would be empty, a ghost train. Another sign.

The numbers that Jack encountered on his nightly meanderings through London or while driving an Underground train were, as he had once made the mistake of telling Stella Darnell, signs that gave him direction and opportunity. Luckily Stella had not believed him.

Jack did not lead a double life, he explained to Stella under his breath as he strode to Ravenscourt Park Station, an explanation he couldn't give in real life. This was part of him. Seeking out Hosts was integral to his life. If he saw evil he could not stand by. A trait they shared, he pointed out to her. Now he had to get back what was his. Jack convinced himself that Stella would understand.

On the eastbound platform at Earls Court, he watched the empty train approach, its windows dark. The set number was propped in the cab window: 231. It told him that tomorrow he would move into Mallingswood House.

When he inserted his driver's key into the control panel and closed the door, Jack began to sing:

> *'The maid was in the garden,*
> *Hanging out the clothes,*
> *Then came a little blackbird,*
> *And snapped off her nose.'*

Six

Stella trawled the streets around Barons Court Station. On her third circuit a car was pulling away outside her mother's mansion block. With a spin of the steering wheel she slotted her Peugeot into the tight space between a Range Rover and a pizza delivery scooter.

When Suzanne Darnell and her seven-year-old daughter had moved into the top-floor apartment just before Christmas in 1973, parking had been plentiful. Few residents, including Suzie, owned a car. Now kerbs were clear only if the road was being dug up by one utility company or another. Fierce parking restrictions were enforced by slow-pacing wardens whose proximity was heralded by the chatter of their two-way radios.

It was past ten o'clock at night, but the district was in full swing. Pedestrians jostled on pavements, huddled outside cafés under heating lamps, eating, smoking, drinking. Conversation and laughter mingled with the revving engines of traffic on the Talgarth Road. At intervals could be heard the rapid clatter of Underground trains in the tunnel beneath the street. The bustle, a contrast to unpopulated pavements on Terry's cul-de-sac and his empty house, confounded Stella. On autopilot after her experience in the basement, she turned off the engine but did not move.

Flashing signs advertising a foreign-currency exchange, beacons on waiting taxis, a rolling screen of properties in the window of an estate agent's and the glow of shop fascias tinged the interior of the van with flickering colour. A late-night super-market, goods displayed outside on sloping crates and draped with fake grass, was doing good trade. In the 'Family Butcher' by Suzie's mansion block, gleaming metal trays awaited the next day's cuts of free-range organic meat. The intimacy of the shop's name belied the transience and anonymity of the neighbour-hood. Stella could not remember being happy here.

Suzie Darnell was the only tenant who had lived in the Edwardian red-bricked block for over ten years. With a lease over thirty years old and her low rent protected, her presence in what had become a top-flight property was the managing agency's albatross, she was fond of boasting to Stella. Periodically she glee-fully rejected cash offers to vacate. Indifferent though she was to her apartment and its surroundings, she had no better idea of where to live.

She was unmoved by the inexorable gentrification around her. It was what she had been used to before she met Terry, she would archly inform her daughter, as if her marriage had caused her to slip down the social scale. Since Suzie was the daughter of a prison officer, Stella knew this was untrue. Her mother was gratified that the sooty brickwork had been brought back to salmon pink and the doors and window frames painted or replaced. But she did not visit the cafés selling fresh ground coffee and or applaud that the local shop now sold Earl Grey tea and Prosecco. She did care that the Tesco Express would not deliver ad hoc packets of cigarettes or sliced bread but she refused to shop online. If she wanted toast she called her daugh-ter. Getting out of the van, Stella decided that the telephone calls for help had increased.

She skirted a bicycle chained to a lamp-post, droplets of dog's pee jewelling its wheel, the saddle stolen or removed to prevent it being stolen. She toed aside a bag of rubbish slumped by the entrance. The musty foyer was lit by a chandelier blurry with dust and already brown walls were darkened with a film of grease. Stella's soles clacked on the grimy tiles and, loath to touch, she dragged aside the grille to the lift with her fingertips. The hollow clang further dampened her spirits. She steeled herself against the ominous swaying whenever she got in the cramped lift. She punched a brass button for the top floor and regarded herself in the grainy mirror while the apparatus shuddered upwards. Tonight the dull light was flattering and showed off the glossy new haircut that did indeed accentuate the shape of her face. Her suit did do the trick, Stella decided; she looked quite the sharp businesswoman. Cheered, she stood straight. Jackie would urge: You're lovely and tall, make the most of it. Almost immediately, Stella's shoulders slumped: it was late, it had been a long day and it wasn't over. She pictured being in her bedroom in her mum's flat, sipping the Horlicks Suzie would insist upon and then falling into a deep sleep. The lift jerked to a stop and Stella dismissed the image.

On the landing she was greeted, as always, with the absolute hush that never failed to unnerve her; somehow, it was worse than the silence in Terry's house. The carpet was thickened by a patina of grease and balls of fluff like miniature tumbleweed. A shadow of dirt lay on the windowsill, the glazing bars and along the wainscot. The infrequent cleaning was intended, Suzie Darnell insisted, to flush her and the other 'low-rent' tenants out to make way for 'adolescent bankers and other such types'. Stella suspected these 'types' included herself. Stella had considered pitching for the cleaning contract, but was fairly sure that the weekly letter Suzie sent the landlords detailing the parlous state of the common parts would not stop if her daughter were responsible for the cleaning. Suzie was right, the landlords were trying to lever her out by letting the building deteriorate. It was the wrong approach. If something was wanted of her, Suzanne Darnell moved mountains to avoid giving it. She generally got her way; her disappointment was that she never liked what she got.

Tonight, as on other nights, outside her mother's flat, thoughts of Horlicks vanished and Stella wanted only to take the stairs to the street, go to her office and do her emails in the out-of-hours quiet.

'It's me, Mum.' She squeezed inside and, sweeping her hand over the wall until she found the switch, clicked on the light. It spread bleak illumination over a narrow hallway, made narrower by piles of newspapers and cartons, reaching higher than Stella's six feet, that threatened to topple when, moving crabwise, her rucksack in her arms, Stella inched along.

She paused at her old bedroom. There were the boxes of carbon-copied reports from when her mother worked, magazine recipes, bank statements, postcards and letters awaiting Suzie's attention; they must not be thrown out. A box in the doorway had 'Mum' scrawled on the side. Stella's grandmother's knitting patterns, needles and odd balls of wool spilled out. It being there gave Stella scant hope her mum was sorting it at last, but more likely she had, on a whim, been prodding about for the pattern she would knit when she 'found the time'. She would not throw it out, it would be 'killing her mother all over again', she said. As if she had killed her the first time. Sometimes the way Suzie talked reminded Stella of Jack.

Stella's bedroom had been Clean Slate's office and like her room at Terry's held no evidence of her childhood. The day Stella started at the 'big' school, Suzie had announced she was grown up. Stella had been pleased by this but when she had got home her toys, her wool rabbit, her puzzles, her Sindy doll and the glass tube of sand from the Isle of Wight holiday – the first without Terry – had gone to charity. Preoccupied with the complexities of new teachers, noisy children and so many classrooms, Stella had not thought she minded.

Despite her cleaning only yesterday, the air was cloying with cooking smells overlaid with cigarette smoke. Suzie insisted she had given up; Stella knew this was a lie. Her mother lied about many things, or maybe she could not distinguish the truth.

Stella paused outside the living-room door. Despite knowing Suzie was in there, Stella felt that she could be alone – so unlike her impression that Terry was present when she was in his house.

A semblance of domestic comfort signalled by a standard lamp with a fringed shade was cancelled out by clutter. More newspapers behind the door, a plastic laundry bin full of the umbrellas her mother insisted she had taken by accident. A gate-leg table took the weight of serving dishes, jars filled with buttons, paper clips, bus tickets and the other objects Suzie collected indiscriminately. There were two more tubs of mini chocolate biscuits, her mother's latest food fad.

The serving hatch was of no practical use: it was partially obscured by piles of books and a sofa blocked access to it. A cracked plastic Adidas holdall lay on the path to the kitchen; Stella recognized her old games bag and wondered with a sinking heart why her mother had got it out. Beside it was a green glass fruit bowl spilling over with bars of staples, packets of screws, a bulb of garlic, a root of stale ginger and the used jiffy bags Suzie had asked her to bring from the office two days ago. Stella had cleaned the room only yesterday; none of what she had achieved was evident.

One item dominated the chaos: a threadbare wing-backed armchair upholstered in red velvet. Stella was uncomfortably reminded of Mrs Barlow's recliner. She snatched up the fruit bowl and wedged it between two shoe boxes on the table and made her way across the room. A television Stella had fitted into an alcove by the gas fire was back on the kitchen chair with the broken strut that Stella was forbidden to take to the dump because it had been 'Mum's favourite'. Laying siege to this were more jars with coins, scraps of material and stamps. The flickering screen increased Stella's impression of instability and she tripped over a mound of tea towels by the sofa.

Suzanne Darnell was small-boned and, in contrast to her tall daughter, barely over five foot. Disappointment and dissatisfaction had not eroded the beauty that had captured Terry Darnell years ago. Her shoulder-length blonde hair – one of her outings

44

was to the colourist – was tied back with a succession of brightly coloured ribbons. Curled in her chair, a cushion hugged to her chest, legs tucked beneath her, she was lost in her ex-husband's fisherman's jumper, a favourite. Stella had noticed that, unlike herself, her mother achieved chic even when scruffily dressed. Her careless pose implied a girlishness that belied her sixty-six years. Her neediness, on the other hand, could add a further twenty years to her age.

Her mother was glaring at the television screen on which a man was being given cardiac shock treatment. Suzie kept the volume down in case of shouting or raucous background music; she hated surprises. She continued to gaze in the direction of the screen when Stella stepped into her line of vision.

'Where have you been?' Corncrake asperity broke the quiet. When she spoke, Suzie's fingers tapped the patchwork cushion.

'It takes a while to get here from—' Stella stopped. Terry's death had not stemmed her mum's waspish remarks about his shortcomings. Meant, Stella used to suppose, for her to pass on to her father. Growing up, Stella had side-stepped this tacit intention; now she found odd comfort in her mother's sniping: while Terry was found wanting, he had not gone entirely. She avoided mentioning Terry's house. If Suzie demanded to visit Stella would not know how to prevent her.

'Even at this time there's traffic,' Stella finished.

'So you say.' Suzie laid the cushion flat and tapped it. Her hand stilled and she rested her head against the back of the chair.

'What's the problem?' Stella had not meant to sound harsh; she could see no sign of an emergency, which was a relief. Then she bit her lower lip: a scorch mark on the arm of the chair was new; her mum must have fallen asleep with a cigarette in her hand. She could see no sign of a stub or flecks of ash.

'Lucky you turned up out of the blue.' Nestling deeper into the chair her fingers busied themselves briefly again on the cushion.

'You asked me to come.'

Suzie shook her head. 'I didn't.'

Stand-off. Both women turned their attention to the television where the heart monitor now showed a flat line.

It seemed to Stella that she could hear the continuous signal without the volume. She looked away. 'You did.' Instantly she regretted pursuing a battle she could not win.

'I didn't.' The fingers tapped. 'Watch closely, you'll see a pulse. No one can play dead for long.' Her mother waved a hand as a sheet was pulled over the man's impassive features.

Stella went to the kitchen. When she had lived there, the hatchway meant she was not alone in the lounge when her mum was cooking and her mum would chatter on. Now, jammed with objects, there was no connection with the adjoining room.

The bin was empty only because Suzie persisted in dropping rubbish into a plastic bag hung from a cupboard knob. This was bulging, the plastic ripped by a foil tray. The sink and draining board were heaped with dirty dishes from which there came the acrid odour of stale tomato sauce and possibly nicotine.

Stella relaxed. She could clean.

She looked for the rubber gloves she had left by the tap. Her mother must have thrown them away; her hoarding instincts did not apply to what Stella brought to the flat. Suzie didn't seem concerned that disposing of these things could 'kill' her daughter. The idea in this context seemed less absurd to Stella, because finding that the cleaning agents and equipment she had stowed in the under-sink cupboard had disappeared could well be the death of her.

She delved into her rucksack for her emergency kit: gloves, a sponge, a cloth and a vial of anti-bacterial cleaner. Within minutes she had restored order. She returned to the living room with the sealed bag of rubbish.

'Let me see.'

'It's the rubbish, Mum.' She should have hidden it behind her back.

46

'Get newspaper and lay it out properly. If a job's worth doing…'
The fingers pattered furiously over the cushion.

It was pointless to resist what was coming; Stella fetched a newspaper from the tower near the door.

'Not from there. I want those!' The drumming on the cushion was intense.

Stella went into the hall and snatched a newspaper from the top of the highest pile, steadying the rest in case the paper – *The Sun* – by some quirk of balance was keeping the whole thing upright. She spread it at Suzie's feet. It was dated 12 June 2008. Suzie hopped out of her armchair and knelt beside Stella. The delicate scent of her mother's perfume wafted around her: Suzie had asked for Givenchy's 'Very Irresistible' for her last birthday, a change from the Elizabeth Arden Terry used to buy her which she had worn for all of Stella's life.

Suzie grimaced at the picture of Myra Hindley on the front page. Hindley stared back. Beside the iconic 1960s mug shot was the headline: 'Myra swamped by fan mail'.

'He never caught her.' Suzie's fingers tapped the crinkled paper.

It took Stella a moment to understand. 'Dad was in the Met, he didn't work that case.' Every unsolved case, every criminal injustice, every police error was Terry's fault. Suzanne Darnell had no fear of logic.

Stella undid the knot she had tied in the neck of the bag and, cross with herself for not anticipating this regular sifting of the rubbish, tipped it out, moving it over the sheet to evenly distribute the contents. Myra Hindley vanished beneath sodden tea bags, used tissues, bread crusts and a congealed half-eaten lamb chop. Stella clambered on to the sofa and reaching through the hatchway unhooked a fork from the carousel. The tines caught the light of the lamp as she teased through the detritus, lifting, pushing and raking it. Suzie was rapt with attention.

'It must be there somewhere,' she said eventually.

'Don't think it is,' Stella replied, not knowing yet what 'it' was. It didn't do to jump the gun, as her mother called it.

'It's the only present Terry gave me.' Her voice was tiny, her fingers relaxing when she subsided into silence. 'They're my favourite earrings. If one is lost both might as well be.'

'When did you last see it?' Stella knew the answer: 30 August 1978, they had looked for them many times before. Had they been looking for Suzie's Parker pen, lost six months ago, there was a chance of uncovering it somewhere in the flat, but most of the objects Suzie had her hunt for had been mislaid long ago in Terry's house. They would not discover them in the rubbish here. The pearl earring had come up in the searching after Terry died; Jackie said it was symbolic and was her mother's way of handling grief. Stella was sceptical: Suzie had left Terry and had not seen him since Stella was old enough to travel to see him unaccompanied. Whatever the reason, the forensic unpickings of the bin were a waste of time; nothing was ever found.

'I took them out after the parents' evening when they said you were bossy to that boy, ridiculous to-do. The limp lettuce should have stood up for himself. I was on my own. Terry had been called out as per.'

Stella forked through the mush and Myra Hindley reappeared, blotched with stains. At last she convinced Suzie, and by now herself too (because once involved in the process she forgot its futility), that the earring was not there. She refilled the bag and put it in the hallway.

When she returned to the living room, she said brightly, 'I wondered if you fancied a trip? Maybe to Richmond Park?' This was where Terry had taken Suzie on their first date. After they moved to Barons Court, Suzie would take Stella there for tea and a slice of coffee cake.

'It's bedtime.'

'I don't mean now.'

'Then why mention it?'

'It would be something to look forward to.'

Suzie gave a vague shrug. She got to her feet and brushed her jumper down. Her attention returned to the television on which were images of a sparse parched landscape that might be Australia. Or Africa. Stella roused herself.

'If you don't need anything more, I'll get going, Mum.' Again the thought of tucking into her bed next door flashed through her head.

'Are you rushing off to solve a case? I never fail to see the irony in the attention paid to dead people compared to those of us who are alive.'

'Mum, I'm a cleaner, not a detective.'

'You could do better. Get a bigger office, hire more people. Do less cleaning.' Her fingers tapped out a well-trodden refrain.

'One step at a time,' Stella said mildly.

'All the boys wanted me for their reports. I was the best in the pool. Fastest shorthand and typing speed with no mistakes. PC Darnell was happy to have me spend nights deciphering his handwriting and correcting his English so he could swarm up the greasy pole.'

'Not now, Mum.'

'Never now. Always later.' Suzie moved about the room straightening objects, adjusting jam jars. 'You get going, that business won't run itself.'

Sometimes Stella couldn't tell if her mother was being sarcastic.

'How is your nice friend?' Suzie was fiddling with her cuticles now, pursing her lips with the effort.

'What friend?' Stella had no time for friends unless she counted Jackie. Perhaps she did count Jackie.

'That young man. He was a charmer.'

'Mum, I don't know who you mean. I'll give you a ring tomorrow to see about Richmond Park. Otherwise maybe pop out for a paper or fruit? Not cigarettes. Get some fresh air?' Stella intonated everything as a question to avoid an accusation of bossing. Her mother kissed her palm airily at her and headed for the kitchen where she would undo all Stella's work.

In the hall Stella gathered up the rubbish, holding it away

from her suit, although after the cistern business and Terry's basement it would need dry cleaning.

Suzie never mentioned men other than Terry. Since Terry's death her mum had changed: new perfume, more rubbish hunts. Maybe Jackie had a point about grief.

The bins were in a yard kept in permanent shadow by a wall at the rear of the mansion block. Barbed wire discouraged residents from climbing over and falling on to the railway tracks below. Today, the rumble of a train coming out of the tunnel made her think of Jack. He had the Dead Late shift on the District line so would not be driving yet. She heaved the bag up into the nearest bin.

The 'charming young man' was Jack Harmon.

She hurried out to her van. Her mother, who recently had been forgetting so much, had not forgotten Jack. In his thirties, he was hardly young but he could be charming.

One evening, over a month ago, Stella had been at Jackie's desk in the office perusing the latest figures submitted by the bookkeeper when two things happened. Jack returned the van keys after a shift and her mobile phone rang. Seeing it was her mother, Stella ignored it, but Jack had not.

'It says "Mum". You should answer it.'

He had a thing about parents, probably because he didn't have any. To top it off, this time Suzie had a genuine emergency. She had slipped and cut her arm on the door of the oven. Stella rushed out the office and Jack had come too.

Jack had been charming. Ridiculously, he had given a bow and then knelt at Suzie's feet with a washing-up bowl of warm soapy water to sponge the graze on her arm. He had dressed the wound with gauze and cotton wool from the first-aid kit from the van and bandaged the whole of her forearm. Stella had been tasked with sifting the rubbish for Suzie's reading spectacles, lost when Stella was ten. Jack had assured Suzie that if the specs were there Stella would find them. He had meant well, but set her up for failure because they were not.

For the first time in decades Stella spent a night in her old bed – Jack didn't think Suzie should be alone after the shock. Unable to sleep, she had traced the pattern of luminous stars, stuck on the ceiling by her dad when they first moved in, as she used to do before falling into a sound sleep.

Suzie appeared to take Stella's presence for granted and when Stella was leaving, had suggested they go to Richmond Park.

A horn sounded. A driver wanted her space. Stella swished down the seat belt and pulled out into the night-time traffic.

She found herself driving into King Street instead of taking the flyover to the Hogarth roundabout, the quicker route to her flat. She was accidentally following the route to Terry's. Stella remembered that the last time she had seen Jack, when he had popped into the office a week ago, he had asked when she planned to sell Terry's house. Stella had changed the subject because she didn't know.

She hit a snarl-up outside Marks and Spencer's. Jack would be the perfect cleaner for Suzie. He would amuse her and she might pay attention to his suggestions, which when it came to cleaning were all sensible. Jack seemed good with older women. She let the handbrake off and drifted the length of a car and then came to another stop. A witness appeal board was propped by the kerb, secured by sandbags. Jack once pointed out they looked like piglets. He felt sad for them lolling by the side of the road. He could also be absurd, she reflected. Jack and her mother would egg each other on. In the light from passing headlights, Stella suddenly saw what Jack meant – the two piglets hung over the metal strut of the notice board as if they had passed out. If he cleaned for her mum she would eventually find fault with Jack and Stella didn't want that to happen. To stop the jangle of this problem she switched on the radio.

'... a hit-and-run incident in which a seven-year-old boy was killed this afternoon in West London. Joel Evans chased a football across King Street in Hammersmith while out with his grandmother and was hit by a car travelling from the Broadway. He was killed instantly. The driver failed to stop. A workman on Chiswick High Road reported a man checking his vehicle soon after the time of the accident. He walked around it before driving off. The car may have been a Ford Fiesta and was white or a light blue. The police believe the incident may have been caught on the camera of a 27 bus and hope to identify the number plate of the car. They are appealing to the driver to come forward and to anyone who witnessed the incident to contact them...'

Alert, Stella edged the van up to the notice and sure enough it referred to the same incident: '16.32 p.m., 23/4/12'. In the gap between her van and the lorry in front her headlights cast a wash of light over a muffled sandy shape. It resembled the outline of a sprawling figure. It must be a trick of the light; the police would not have traced the boy's outline on the road. A torn strip of blue and white police tape fluttered from a lamp-post. She took her foot off the accelerator and the van coasted past the notice. She needed to get to bed.

With Joel Evans on her mind, Stella knew how easy it would be to speed, so she did not go above twenty-five miles an hour all the way to Brentford. The van's sensor opened the automatic gates to her estate and she accelerated up to her apartment block. Although the development was protected by steel gates and CCTV, here, as at Terry's, the lighting was faulty, working during the day and going off at night. Unwilling to park by the dark garages, she put the van in a visitor bay near the foyer.

Stella keyed in the security code, heaved on the door to override the closing mechanism and pushed it shut. A sharp ping made her jump. It was the lift. She had not called it. The door slid open and a shaft of light cut across the marble floor. She waited. No one got out. Cautiously she approached; the interior was empty. Along with the outside lights, the building's smart controls often went awry and the lift would move without anyone operating it. Stella berated herself for succumbing to frayed nerves and stepped inside as the doors shut. Her discovery of the photos of herself in Terry's basement had rattled her: all those faces smiling at her. No, not at her, at Terry. She could not smile at him now.

The sparse tidiness of her flat tended to be a relief after her mother's. Tonight it was not. Stella was alive to the hermetic silence and, with so many flats unsold, to the likelihood that she was utterly alone on this floor. She dropped her keys in a vase in the living room – a policeman's daughter, she never left them in sight.

In the bathroom she splashed her face with cold water and cleaned her teeth. The battery-operated brush ran down because she had forgotten to leave it on charge. She found a manual brush in the cupboard. Suzie's muddle was catching.

It was not until Stella was in bed that, disturbed by gripes in her stomach, she remembered that since a hurried hoisin duck wrap from the mini-mart below the office that afternoon she had eaten nothing. She was getting like Jack, who never ate properly. Jack. She did not want him to clean for Suzie: it would lead to complications. She would do it herself. Her mum had asked if she was busy on a case. Perhaps her muddle had extended to mixing up her ex-husband's job with what her daughter did.

This reminded Stella of the blue folder in Terry's basement. He had taken fifteen photographs of roads and filed them according to a number order. Everything Terry did was for a purpose, so the pictures must be for a case. Although Terry had retired from the police he had not stopped being a detective.

Stella sat up in bed. She would find out what the case was. Then she and Jack would solve it.

Seven

She stood up on the pedals and made them go faster. The wind in the chestnut tree filled her ears and everything flew by. Her dad said it was the wrong time for conkers when Michael asked. Michael was stupid for not knowing and she had been right to tell him that. It had not been right to be told off. Mary did not say that she did not know when conkers were. She did not care about conkers.

She whizzed around the bend in the path and skidded to a stop, her brakes squealing. She looked behind her and saw Michael and her dad huddled by the flower bed. Perhaps they were hiding from her. She grew hot. They had not noticed she was missing.

'Crocuses!' Michael had shouted when they got to the park and he had pointed at the hyacinths. Daddy did not say he was wrong because he was unscrewing the stabilizers from Michael's birthday bike. Michael was trying to stop him taking them off by saying flower names.

Now Daddy was doing something at the back of Michael's birthday bike, but she could not see from here. Michael had got back on and was wobbling on the saddle, which was set too high, making his frog-legs stick out. Mary held her breath; she knew her brother was scared without the extra wheels. It made her tummy ache and she let out a squeak when the wobbling got worse. Daddy was tall in his brown weekend trousers and his blue and white chequered shirt blew out like a balloon in the wind.

She decided he was more like a cowboy with his sleeves rolled up and she wished that he was a cowboy so they could canter off together on horses as if he were her real daddy.

They hadn't seen her do her skid. Mary twisted the bike around and mooched over the handlebars, her chin on her fists. Daddy was teaching Michael to ride his bike properly the way she could, although he hadn't said that. It was a secret, one she had decided to keep, that Michael did not like his new present. He'd told her he had wanted a microscope. She actually did think that would have been a nicer present for him and was sorry for him, especially as the bike was too big. All Michael's things were too big: his trousers, his new blazer, even his shoes. He was supposed to grow into them. What if he didn't?

Michael had refused to have lessons off her, so now he was being punished because lessons with Daddy were worse. He had to pretend to be big and brave, which he wasn't. He was too scared to tell Mummy and Daddy that he was frightened stiff of falling off. To them Michael was brave and courageous: their little soldier. They didn't know he was terrified of everything.

Mary Thornton had tried to prevent Bob and Jean Thornton knowing how frightened their son was of climbing trees, playing football or riding a bicycle. At six that morning he had sneaked into her bedroom and asked her to finish the bedtime story their mother had been reading to them. Mary agreed because she knew he lived in fear of the rattling attic door in the corner of his new room. Then he annoyed her with questions about her new name, so she had sent him packing. When Bob Thornton announced he was taking Michael round to the square to get him used to his bike without the stabilizers, Mary had ignored Michael's pleading stare and said nothing.

At the park she had ridden around with no hands partly to take Daddy's mind off unscrewing the wheels and partly to show him she was highly skilled on her bike. But the plan had not worked because he carried on as if she were invisible. He ignored her suggestion that she do things on her bike to show Michael how to do it. He did not see her lift up her front wheel and mount the hump on the path like a cowgirl on a horse and now he had missed the best skid she had ever done. Mary eyed them dolefully from across the grass.

After a bit, she let the wheels meander along the slope to the statue of the Greek Runner.

The statue had no clothes on. Mary was not interested in penises – Michael had one – so she didn't bother with the nude man and scooted her bike around and around the base. On the last lap she stole another look at her father and brother. Their heads were still close together. Secrets. She was inflamed. Michael was helping her daddy with the wheels. Traitor! Boys will be boys, her mum said. 'Leave them to it, Mary.'

Her dad arched backwards and stretched. Michael was like a statue. He was staring at the ground, which wouldn't help him balance. Mary was startled by her dad's shout: 'Ready, steady ... go!'

Michael tried to stand in his seat as she had done. Despite her worry for him Mary was outraged that her daddy was keeping his hand on the bike rack and running along with Michael, help he had not given her. It meant Michael would never learn to ride by himself.

As if he could read his daughter's mind, Bob Thornton let go of the rack and ran on for a few more paces beside the bike, his hand out as if still gripping the rack. He dropped back and slowed to a stop and, hands on hips, watched Michael cycle away along the path.

Michael had seen Mary and was coming right at her, his eyes fixed on her as he had done when he was learning to walk and was made to cross the room to her. She felt panic. He did not know Daddy had let go and he was going too fast. She started to climb off her bike. She must reach him before he realized this. He was treading too hard on each pedal, making the bike sway. The front wheel went first one way then the other; each time it got closer to the grass.

Mary dropped her bike and hurtled towards Michael. She was the Greek Runner. It was like running in a dream; her legs would not work properly. Michael seemed to get no closer.

The little girl would never forget this fleeting impression.

Michael Thornton looked back to where his father's face had been. It was like flying, he was going to say, but there was only sky. He kept going. His sister was watching him. He was like her; he was just as good.

The front wheel jack-knifed and the boy truly took off in flight. He landed belly first on the tarmac.

An aeroplane droned above, a momentary gleam of sunlight flashed off the colours of British European Airways. A pigeon flying much lower might have been crossing the flight path. It alighted on the topmost branch of the chestnut tree that cast a thin shadow over the two children.

Mary got to Michael before her father and dragged him to his feet. Her baby brother was not crying, but he would not look at her, which was a bad sign. She followed his eyes to where he was looking and saw white houses with ravens above their doors.

'You stopped holding,' she accused her father. She smacked dirt off the front of Michael's jumper. A trickle of blood came out of one of his nostrils.

'I dropped this.' Their father pulled a handkerchief from his pocket. 'Here, lad, use this. Buck up!' He handed it to his son. Mary snatched it and clamped it to Michael's nose.

'The main thing, Michael, is you went by yourself.' Bob Thornton folded his arms. 'Keep practising, son, you'll soon be the best.'

'Did you see?' Michael's voice was muffled through the fabric now stained crimson.

'Not properly,' Mary scowled. 'Tip your face back.' She wanted to tell her daddy that she was the best.

Bob Thornton went back across the park and Mary saw him pick up her bike. He did not need to; she would have got it. He knew where to find it: perhaps he had seen her do the skid.

'He didn't drop his hankie.' She kept her voice low.

'Yes he did.' Michael eyed her warily.

'He let go.' She stepped away from him as if he were a bomb set to explode.

'You said you didn't see.'

'I saw him let go.' Mary was firm.

'So did you see?'

'You shouldn't have stood up.' She persisted: 'He lied to you.'

'He didn't.'

'He did.'

'You're not Mary!' Michael's widening eyes betrayed that he was aware he had plunged into treacherous waters. He snuffled into his father's handkerchief although the bleeding had stopped.

The sun went behind a cloud and a chill fell like a mantle over St Peter's Square. The breeze intensified pushing the branches of the chestnut tree violently.

Rooted to the spot, Michael Thornton watched with growing panic his sister stalk off along the path.

Mary took her bike from her father and scooted it, standing on one pedal; then she swung her leg over the saddle, like a cowboy. She rode around the park and out of the gate.

'He didn't lie,' Michael repeated to himself, with less certainty.

Eight

Monday, 23 April 2012

She leant shut the front door, her shopping bag in her arms, and conjured up the reassuring aroma of overcooked vegetables, disinfectant laced with the collective body smells of a hundred boys. She imagined so many innocent souls, their hopes and dreams before them, sleeping soundly above her.

At this time of the evening, Reception, a partitioned area built before her time, was closed and she would be in charge of greeting the few visitors; a time she liked best.

At the turn in the staircase something made her pause. She surveyed the cavernous hall below. Everything looked in order.

Her shoulders bowed, the woman's silhouette on the expanse of green gloss wall had no head; distorted further by her shopping bag, she could have been the minotaur.

She wended her way upwards in the school where for decades she had been a trusted housemother. At each landing she extinguished lights behind her, leaving darkness in her wake. She did not wince at the weight and awkwardness of her bag, or the long climb. The effort was a price of existence. It must be paid. She focused on the step in front of her, unblinking. It was the way she approached her work and her life, unstinting and unswerving.

The crêpe soles on her lace-ups expressed stolid reliability. Despite her heavy tread, she knew no one would hear her on the frayed linoleum. She never disturbed the boys: growing children needed sleep.

Three floors up she did stop. She liked this window. It had fascinated generations of boys because, cut across by the stairs, it disappeared into the floor. The architectural necessity fascinated her too. It was possible to see through the gap to the stairs below where a boy was waving. James, William, Nicholas, Mark, the long list of boys had over the years merged into one lovely boy with all of their best qualities. A boy with the aura of an angel. She pressed her face to the glass.

The car park was dark and deserted; no staff or parents here tonight. She observed without pleasure new leaves on the plane tree. They would screen off the school from houses in Weltje Road. She resented nosy parkers. Soon the weather would be warmer. She liked cold days shortened by dark nights when she could wear clothes that covered her body. She held the bag to her chest and resumed her climb.

On the top floor, opposite a long unlit passage, was a door. Through shamrock-petal-shaped holes carved out of the upper panels a faint light sent elongated shamrock shapes along the low ceiling. These did give her pleasure. She flicked another switch, but the strip lights above did not respond. She left her bag by the door and felt her way along the passage, her shoes sponging on the linoleum. Six doors, three each side, had the same shamrock holes, dark outlines in the wood with no light beyond. She opened each door, ducked her head into the room, withdrew and closed the door. At the last door she went in.

The room was dark but for orange light washing in through a window. She retrieved a rubber-covered torch from the top of a cupboard by the door and, keeping the beam low, revealed three iron bedsteads. A paperback book lay open on the tumbled blankets of the window bed, spine up. She folded down a page to mark the place and shut the book, laying it on a bedside cabinet next to a leather-bound travelling alarm clock. She gave the book a stroke as if to underline the action.

She lifted a pillow that hung over the foot of the iron frame, plumped it, averting her face from a cloud of dust and then restoring it to the bed. Tutting, she pulled up the blankets and batted out creases. A bundle of material was jammed against a bed leg. She got down on her hands and knees and dragged out a shirt, no longer white. She struggled to her feet and, in the wardrobe, unhooked a hanger and draped the shirt over it. Throughout this procedure, one apparently familiar to her, she was quiet as a mouse. The perfect housemother, she was fond of reminding herself. She closed the curtains, aligning the fabric so that the pattern of a trellis twined with flowers with red petals was unbroken. Sleep tight, don't let the bugs bite. A whisper on the breath, she pit-patted out and closed the door.

She returned to the stairs and reached a key down from the lintel above the locked door.

'I'm home.' Despite the sing-song gaiety in her tone her expression remained impassive. If she was concerned by the lack of response she did not betray it. Two strip lights with frosted plastic casings spotted with dead insects cast a bland light on a corridor with a vermilion runner along its length.

In a bright utilitarian kitchen she unpacked shopping with the efficient air of fulfilling a routine, lining up her purchases on a blue Formica table: a tin of dried milk, two boxes of frozen ready meals, baked beans, a jar of chocolate powder, six pork sausages, a box of tea bags and the London *A–Z* street atlas. Apparently no longer mindful of being quiet, she stowed the groceries away, banging cupboard doors and opening and shutting a large fridge and freezer. Now she appeared to want to draw attention to her presence. She secured the bag on a hook behind the door and straightened a yellow apron hanging there to reveal a yellow smiley face. When she spoke, in a confiding voice, it might have been to the apron. 'I told you I wouldn't be long.' The intention perhaps not to reassure, but to be proved right.

Carrying the street atlas, she went down the passage to a room like the boys' dormitories, furnished with an iron bedstead, a plain wardrobe and bedside cabinet. Here the bedding was immaculate, a wool blanket tucked so tightly that only a

61

cardboard figure could have comfortably slipped in between the starched white sheets. The woman shrugged her coat off and arranged it on a hanger in the wardrobe using the same spare movements with which she had handled the shirt. She regarded herself in the wardrobe mirror and shifted her rayon top so that it did not bunch around her waist. She smoothed a hand over a swollen stomach: not a promise of new life, but the bane of middle age. She gave a perfunctory brush to one leg of her black cotton trousers and a pat to her hair – a serviceable style demanding the minimum of effort. In the hallway, head up, shoulders back, she approached a door at the end.

Her hand on the knob, her determination seemed to falter. She straightened her jersey needlessly and, the *A–Z* in one hand, tapped on the door. Rat-a-tat-tat, the jaunty tattoo at odds with her stony demeanour. No sound came from within and after a moment she opened the door.

'There you are.' She addressed a spacious room in which she seemed to be the only one present. It reeked of adhesive and paint. She grabbed a long pole resting against the door jamb and, thrusting it upwards, slotted it into the fastener of a skylight and hauled open the casement.

'Let's have some fresh air,' she told the pole.

'You're late.' A disembodied voice.

Darkness obscured streets and tiny lights twinkled on the shimmering surface of the river. They lit up rooftops, exposing missing tiles here and there and chimneys prickling with aerials; signals, traffic lights and scraggy trees sent shadows over the roads. Hammersmith Bridge dominated the scene.

'The river looks as good as new.' She put out a hand towards the model but then withdrew it as if commanded not to touch. She waved it over the blue and grey painted plaster of Paris. Stiffened peaks and troughs moulded to illustrate the wash of a passing boat beneath the looping span of the bridge. The water level had lowered with the ebbing tide. Figures hurried along tiny streets. A trapdoor in the river dropped down with a bang and a skulled head emerged, grey eyes venomous behind thick glasses.

'Got it?' The working jaw straining parchment skin hatched with lines. Fluffy brown hair tufted like a young bird's in a fringe around the tonsure.

'Of course.' She held out the book.

He dipped into the hatch and, scuffling, reappeared by the side of the miniature cityscape. He was shapeless in a baggy mauve tracksuit, the jacket zipped up to a neck corded with veins; over this he wore a wool dressing gown, the cord trailing.

'This is second-hand. I want a new one.' His voice was querulous. He leant on the structure and the frame creaked.

'I found it. We save money.'

A stain ran down the man's trouser leg. Shambling along the boundary of the streets, he left a spatter of droplets on the floorboards, smearing them with his leather slippers. Even with the skylight open, the stench of piss and solvent was strong. He opened the paperback and, licking a finger, consulted the pages.

'There's no airport terminal, the A13 isn't here and you've scribbled on every page. What have I told you about spoiling things?' He directed a bony forefinger at a house in a Georgian square, the curling wrought-iron balcony fashioned from fine wire and painted black. In the centre of the square were two rectangles of green washing-up scourer and between them, on a grey painted path circling a patch of moulded soil, stood a miniature ceramic figure fashioned in a running pose. 'That house has been rebuilt since this book was printed.' He blew at dust on the roof of the five-storey house, whiter than the others in the square.

'They don't put houses in the A to Z, just streets.'

He pulled at the waistband on his trousers and lurched towards the door. 'This edition is 1995, it's older than the one you lost.' His voice subsided to a whine. He thrust the book at her and proceeded out to the passage.

She skimmed the atlas. The pages were marked with lines

traced along the streets with a ballpoint pen. They made shapes that made her think of letters.

'I'll get you a new copy tomorrow,' she called and then blurted out to the empty room: 'I didn't do the writing, it wasn't me.'

He knows that.

She paused for a moment as if acknowledging the words. She noticed the drops on the floor and went after the old man.

'Shall we change your trousers, Dad? They must be horrid.'

The man shambled off into another room along the passage without replying.

From a cupboard in the passage, she lifted out a fresh pair of pyjamas. She was too late to stop her father sitting on his bed-spread, sodden trousers around his ankles. He did not help when she lifted his feet up and slid the damp material clear. It was hard to believe that the boys would end up like this.

Not all of them.

She hefted the frail man to his feet and gripped him by his tracksuit jacket to stop him falling. Her eyes averted, with the other hand she eased up his pyjamas and, holding his weight with her body, deftly knotted the cord.

Once he was propped up in bed, all tucked in with the travelling alarm clock set for his early start, she returned to her room and fetched her coat and car keys.

'Sleep well, Dad.' She hovered in the doorway. He was leafing through a colourful hardback book, the cover depicting young men racing in canoes. It occurred to her that his reading matter was now the same as the boys.

She was certain that no one saw her leave by the back door and get into her car.

Nine

Monday, 25 April 1966

At five to eight in the morning few in Ravenscourt Park had time or leisure to sit in contemplation on one of the benches by the floral beds or winding paths. There were children, many with harried parents in tow, and commuters cutting through to the station. Suited men with briefcases, shadowy in trilbies or bowlers, macs draped on arms against forecast showers, strode along the avenue. Most were breezily oblivious to the carpet of blossom softening their tread or fluttering down like out-of-season snowflakes. If a petal landed on a Crombie-coated shoulder it was whisked off with an impatient hand.

Beyond the candyfloss canopy of cherry trees were tennis courts and the flawless verdure of the bowling green. Swings in the empty playground hung motionless from chains, the sandpit was pocked with little footprints and a moonscape of collapsing castles. Still mid spring, the paddling pool had not been filled and pigeons and sparrows pecked at crumbs blown from picnic lunches on the blue surface.

Pedestrians were funnelled on to a path darkened by a mesh of oak branches on one side and the District Line viaduct on the other leading to a gate between two stone pillars topped with stone spheres.

Mary and Michael Thornton walked at a slower pace than the other children, still strangers to them. The ten-year-old girl gripped her seven-year-old brother by the hand. Neither spoke; each was grappling with the business of starting at a new school halfway through the year where the other children would already have made friends.

Their mother had left earlier than usual for her job because she had a longer journey involving two buses and a walk at the other end. Mary was in charge; she held on to her brother's fingers for dear life.

At the road they hung back. Children bunched up at the kerb, teetering and shoving while a car rolled by and then a motorbike. In their wake, the group swarmed across the road and, shouting and jostling, pushed through the side entrance into the primary school. Michael and Mary followed. Michael paused; pulling on Mary's hand, he pointed through a mesh fence.

'It's all mud,' he breathed. 'It's not a real playground.' He clutched the mesh with his free hand.

'It is.' Mary swung his hand up and down as if the action would convince him that the obvious was not true.

'I don't think I like it,' Michael confided.

'Yes you do.' She tugged him forward, but paused by a board in the middle of the mud.

Ravenscourt Gardens School
Headmistress: Miss B. M. Crane BSc (Hons)

'That's a bird,' Michael announced. 'Cranes eat rats and toads.'

'Hurry up!' Mary jerked his hand and then looked down at him. 'Did you read that?'

Michael nodded, dwelling on his sandals.

'You can't read.' Mary was firm. It was she who could read.

'Do you think she looks like a crane?' He brightened.

'Of course not.' Mary set off again, forcing Michael to fall in step.

The siblings straggled along paving beside the soil, the clamour of children's voices getting louder. Rounding a low building they found themselves in a playground. There were two entrances flanked by raised brick flower beds. Mary pulled her brother closer and, batting off invisible crumbs, adjusted his jumper. She tucked his shirt into his shorts with such energy she lifted him on to his toes. He tottered when she let him go.

'You're an infant. You go through there.' She indicated the word engraved in stone above the doors: 'Infants'. This information appeared to surprise Michael.

He gaped at her. 'Aren't you coming?'

'Of course not, I'm a junior. See?' She gesticulated at a corresponding sign above the other entrance. 'I'll meet you there at home-time.' She nodded towards a chrome drinking fountain fixed into the wall by the Infants' door. 'Don't be late. I shan't wait. I've got the tea to make.' She spoke sharply, evoking their mother. She grabbed Michael and gave him a rudimentary hug. They clung together. Then Mary pushed her brother off and propelled him through the doorway.

Mary Thornton watched children file into the Juniors' entrance. After a bit, she drifted over to the doors and looked inside. A row of shoe racks and coats hung from hooks. There had been a cloakroom at her old school too. She had no cause to go into this one because, furious at being made to mind Michael, she had ignored her mother's instructions and not worn her coat.

'Mary Thornton?'

Mary wondered if there was a hook with her name in this cloakroom like there was in the other school. Was her name still on the hook by the window there? Perhaps they had scribbled over it as they did to Arthur Madden's when he left. She had been next to Jean Bryan, whom she wished were her friend. Now that she had left, Jean would never be, not that Mary cared, she told herself.

'Mary Thornton!'

She could go in and find her hook even without her coat.

'Did we wash our ears this morning?'

A hand clamped the back of Mary's neck so that she could not turn her head.

'What?'

'"Pardon", dear, not "what".'

A woman in black and white zebra clothes fastened with huge black buttons was above her. The hand stopped Mary escaping.

'You must be Mary Thornton, our late arrival in Class One.'

Mary could not make her mouth move and she darted a look at the Infants' gate. It was too late to run away; they should have done it in the park.

'I'm Miss Crane. The headmistress. Welcome to Ravenscourt Gardens School. I am going to take you to your teacher.'

All Mary thought while she trotted beside the tall, thin lady along a brown corridor that smelt nasty was that Miss Crane did look like a crane. She wanted to tell Michael.

She was taken to a room with a glass wall. Out of the light floated another lady, smaller and crosser than the Crane Lady, who pointed at a chair at a table on which lay a blue exercise book and a pencil that someone had chewed. Mary wedged herself on to it.

Later in the day Mary Thornton would see that the wall was not glass, but made up of windows with metal frames. The design, innovative in its day, ten years earlier, was intended to give the children a long view and encourage creativity. Perhaps it did in the summer but the unremitting sunlight warmed the crates of milk and in the winter despite the radiators a draught made the rooms permanently chilly. All of this Mary had yet to discover. Allowing her new landscape in bit by bit she registered a playground with goal posts and, away from the school, the railway viaduct that her father travelled over to get to his new job. She gazed longingly at it.

'Children, this is Mary.'

Mary whipped around and without considering the horror of speaking in front of the class said, 'I have to be called Mary.'

'Yes, dear, that's what I said,' the teacher snapped.

Everyone was staring and not one was smiling. Perhaps after all the new job and the new name was her fault.

Michael was not by the fountain. Mary sat on the brick flower bed, running her fingers through the nasturtium petals. The flowers were familiar. She had grown nasturtiums at her old school. Some girls she remembered from her new class went by without noticing her. One of them was the nice girl with plaits who had taken her to the dinner hall and asked if Mary would like her to sit with her. Mary had said no because she was sure the girl with plaits did not mean it. Now she wished she could think of her name so she could call to her. She prepared a smile, but the girl didn't see her. Mary pretended to busy herself with her satchel buckle.

There was a bang. She looked around. Everyone had gone. The Juniors' door was blowing back against the wall. Bang. The noise gave her a bad feeling in the pit of her tummy. She heard a train, but from where she sat couldn't see the station. The train didn't stop, which she knew meant it was on the Piccadilly line. That was blue on the map and went to Caledonian Road to where she used to live.

The little girl ran back to the Infants' door. It was shut. She grabbed the metal bar and, leaning on it, dragged the door open. She decided it was all clear and squeezed through the opening.

The corridor was identical to the Juniors' corridor except it stank of stale dinners. Mary hated the smell but now it reminded her of her old school so it gave her the courage to creep right in. She popped her head into the cloakroom. Michael wasn't there. All the coats had gone. She risked a peep into the boys' toilets. She could hear a plinking like pebbles dropping into water and, about to leave, spotted that one of doors to the stalls was shut. She was drawn forward despite her unease and she pushed it with one finger. The door swung slowly open to reveal a toilet with no lid and a brown smear inside. The urinals behind her began to flush, one after the other. Water rushing inside the pipes suddenly gushed out along a ceramic gutter into a drain. Mary fled.

Michael had gone back to the new house without her. Or, worse, he had run away on his own.

She rushed back the way she had come and turning the corner came upon a man in a grey overall. Behind him the lino shone like ice. He waved a string mop before him like a scythe sweeping a crescent of wet on the floor. She tried to sneak away but he had seen her. He leant on the mop handle, squeezing out dirty water into a bucket.

'You wanting to walk here?' He sounded cross but he was smiling. He ground the mop into the bucket.

'No,' Mary said promptly.

'You look lost.' He resumed his cleaning. Back and forth. Back and forth. Coming towards her.

'It's all right. I can go this way.' Mary gestured behind her.

'How're you going to get out? I can't see your wings from here.'

Mary wished she did have wings, like an angel. Wings would change everything.

'It's locked. You'll have to sleep here. Detention!' He laughed and sloshed the mop around in the bucket. 'Oh, go on. I've hardly started. Careful not to slip.'

Mary tiptoed past. Once outside she was about to run, then remembered Michael. He was not by the drinking fountain. She had been given a watch for her tenth birthday, but was not allowed to wear it to school so had to guess that it must be after four o'clock. She could go without Michael. No, she could not.

She heard voices and was immediately frightened because there was only the man with the mop to save her. She edged around the side of the building and stopped.

Michael was crouched by the dug-up soil with two other boys.

'What are you doing?' Mary stormed towards them. Michael let out a cheer and a boy shouted:

'You're the champion!' None of them had noticed Mary.

'Get up,' she ordered. 'You are filthy.'

Michael sprang to his feet. The other two boys chased through the gate and away under the railway bridge. 'See you tomorrow, Mike,' one, his jumper knotted around his waist, yelled.

Michael made to go after them. Mary grabbed him.

'What were you doing down there?' Her voice was level. At their feet was a drain covered with a grille, the bars the thickness of a pencil, the spaces between them the same width. Mary scrunched up her nose although there was no smell.

'I won all seven marbles.' Michael opened his palm.

Mary counted the cluster of gleaming glass marbles, three coloured with a twist of red glass, one with blue and three light green. 'Where did you get these?'

'I just said. I won them.'

'You didn't have any marbles in the first place.'

'Paul gave me one of his and then I won with it so I gave it back. Then I won another and another and another.' His voice got louder and higher.

'Sssssh! Who's Paul?' Mary asked gratuitously, not caring.

'My best friend.' Michael was firm. 'Tomorrow he's going to put me on his football team, because I'm the best.'

'You can't play football.'

'I can.' Michael was matter of fact.

'Give me your marbles.'

'No.'

'Now.'

'I'll swap some with you,' Michael offered.

'You don't have anything to swap.'

'You can have my nature collection instead.' Michael gave a little jump as the facts dawned. 'I have the marbles to swap. What have you got?'

'Why would I want a load of twigs and leaves?' Mary yawned, tiring of the exchange. She took her brother's hand. They trotted into the park, past the tennis courts, in tetchy companionship. Michael skipped to keep up.

'Myr— um… Mary?' Michael gave Mary's hand a pull.

'What?'

71

'Daddy stops people being dead, doesn't he?'

'You are a nitwit. How could he do that?' Yet Mary was unsure. She did not understand what her dad did for a job beyond calling it 'insurance'.

'Paul asked and I said he was the Life Insurance Man.' Michael uttered the words with the veneration of an incantation. 'Paul said, does it mean he stops people being dead.' Michael hesitated then added sheepishly, 'I said yes.'

'You were lying. Daddy can't do that. No one can, except God.'

'What does he do then?'

'He gives "insurance" to people in their houses, that's why he goes out at night so that they're indoors when he calls.'

'What's insurance?' Michael was losing interest.

'If you don't know by now, I'm not telling you.' Mary had a hazy belief that insurance was sticky like toffee and came in wrapped packets, but wasn't going to risk saying so.

They continued on in silence towards the railway arch. Mary said, 'Michael, I've decided' – she gave his fingers a squeeze– 'we will do our Plan. You remember? We'll go back to our real school and fend for ourselves.'

'It's better here.' Michael batted at the air. 'It's good you made us come.' He wrenched free of Mary and galloped down the path, his satchel bouncing on his back, one shoelace trailing.

'We are going tomorrow. On the Underground.' Mary caught up with Michael and shoved him against the tennis-court fence. 'I didn't make us come here. Stop saying it! '

'Mummy said. They gave you a new name and we had to have a new house.' Michael wriggled from her grasp and dodged back up the path.

'Dad got a new job, you idiot, it's miles from our old house.' She waited. Michael would have to come back.

Michael meandered towards her, chinking the marbles in his shorts pocket. The avenue of blossom trees was deserted. A crow cawed from a branch above their heads. The trees and the viaduct prevented sunlight from penetrating and made the air cool. Mary turned on her heel towards the arch where a sign proclaimed: 'Children's' Playground'.

She had strict instructions. 'Go through the arch, follow the path by the flower beds to the gates, turn right – the hand you write with – on King Street. Cross at the zebra by the post office. No dawdling.' She must bring Michael straight home and make the tea. Mary had promised she would.

'Let's have a go on the slide,' she said.

Michael hung back. 'We're not allowed.'

'It's up to me.' Mary was finding being her mum made a lot of things possible. She snatched at Michael's jumper, pulling it out of shape, and hustled him along to the next arch where, gleaming silver in the chill shadows, was the highest slide either of them had ever seen.

Children were clustered at the bottom of an iron ladder. Far above was a pretend house with a pointy roof and a chimney. Her eyes adjusting to the gloom, Mary saw the girl with plaits; she was climbing up the ladder.

'Can I go first?' Mary pushed through the group.

'Before me?' The girl looked down at her.

'We're in a hurry.' Mary grasped the metal: it was cold and rough like the skin of a snake. She placed her foot on the first rung beside the girl's plimsoll.

'OK then.' The girl got down. 'Watch out, it's very steep.'

Mary let go of Michael's hand and grabbed the other metal handrail. She had not expected the girl to be nice.

She scurried up the ladder and stuck her head out of one of the windows in the pretend house. She was aghast to see Michael coming up after her. He was going up the rungs as he did stairs, leading with one foot, looking at the ground, which was the worst possible thing. He did not seem to hear the children shouting from below for him to come back.

'Stop!' Mary signalled with the flat of her hand.

Michael climbed doggedly, his breath laboured.

'Look up!' she whispered and looking through the slats she

saw the concrete below, a dizzying drop. Mary forgot about her brother and crossed unsteadily to the slide. She leant out through the doorway. The slide tapered downwards.

She got astride the flat end of the slide and the cold metal was a shock to her bare legs. She adjusted her skirt and shuffled to the edge. There was nothing to grip, and each scoot brought her nearer to the chute. Her body grew lighter as gravity took hold and, kicking her legs, Mary plummeted out. Skimming metal burned her skin as, gathering speed, she tumbled against the shallow sides. She snatched fruitlessly for a hold, her duffel bag slipped off her lap and swung over the edge, it pulled the string tight around her neck cutting into her skin.

At the foot of the slide Mary shakily got up. She smoothed her skirt and then whisked around the structure for another go.

There was a commotion. The children, six in all, were arguing and wrestling at the ladder. Two boys and the friendly girl with plaits were blocking the bottom rungs. The girl was persuading the boys to climb down, but they ignored her. Mary saw why no one had followed her down the slide. Michael was in the opening of the house. There was room for more than one child on the platform, but no one could get up there because he was in the way. Mary heard the girl with plaits call to him that it would be all right. She knew her brother would not be able to hear because he was scared. Someone threw a tennis ball at him. It missed, but he flinched. If he fell he would die.

'Michael!' She heard her own voice as if from far off.

Cissy. Cheat. Baby.

Mary barged through the group, elbowing and punching her way to the front.

'You won't be in trouble,' the plaits girl was saying.

Mary stared up. When he saw her, Michael flung his legs through the rail as if he might leap into her arms.

'Don't move!' She must not look at him for fear of what he would do.

'He's scared,' the girl explained and touched her shoulder.

'No, he is not! My brother is never scared. We have to go, that's all. We are in a hurry.' She shook the girl off and risked a look. 'Michael, come here now!'

Michael's eyes were strange, as if he didn't know her.

'Get him off there.' A voice in her ear. The boy was sturdy with sprouting-up hair and a bright white shirt tucked into grey shorts. Mary could smell Bazooka Joe bubble gum. She knew his name. Clifford Hunt had a silver snake buckle belt and had given her a brand-new pencil.

'Michael is stuck.' She felt herself grow hot.

Clifford Hunt leant on the handrail and rested his chin on his fist as if her point was worth considering. 'He's your brother,' he declared. 'He'll do what you say.'

Mary squeezed past the children. She felt fingers beneath her sandal when she put a foot on a rung and began the climb. Halfway up she hesitated; the girl with plaits was called Jacqueline, but it didn't matter any more. They would not be friends; Mary and her brother were leaving tomorrow.

Michael was a lump and Mary could not get around him on to the platform. Out of view of the audience below she pushed him but he didn't move. He was the most petrified she had ever seen him.

'Mike, face the other way round and go into the house.' He stayed where he was. She nudged him in the chest, but it made no difference.

'I'll give you sweets.' Mary crossed her fingers behind her back so that he couldn't see she didn't mean it.

Behind her the ladder shook. The children were coming. The house began to shake but Mary was steadfast: they were in the way; no one could get in. Suddenly Michael scrambled backwards until he was cross-legged in the centre of the platform. Mary wedged herself in the entrance, resisting the pressing behind her.

'Sit on the slide,' she commanded in a low voice.

Michael crawled to the slide and obediently sat on it. He

gripped the sides so tightly his knuckles were like chicken legs. Mary saw two marbles roll out of the pocket of his shorts and trundle along the gap in the planks until, the gap widening, they dropped through. Michael was very still.

'Keep back,' Mary snarled over her shoulder when someone jabbed her shoulder blade. She dived forward and joined Michael on the slide and, her legs either side of him, held him around the waist.

The platform drummed and rattled when the children clambered up. Shouts and whoops bounced off the bird-slimed walls of the brick chamber.

'There's too many up there,' a man's voice thundered. 'Get down!'

Mary wedged her heels against the lip of the opening and pushed with all her might. Bricks zipped past. Michael was flung against her chest. She felt a jolt on her arm that made her teeth clack together so she bit her tongue. She careered off the slide on to the concrete with Michael on top of her. When she tried to get up, a smarting pain in her wrist prevented her.

She rolled on to her other side and struggled up. She grabbed her brother and pushed him out of the arch.

They ran helter skelter up the path. Under the arch, past the flower beds, through the iron gates. They turned right on the main road and did not stop until they reached the zebra by the post office.

'I rescued you,' Mary panted. Michael's face was chalk-white, the freckles on his cheeks like pencil dots. He had shrunk; the jumper their nan had knitted was baggy, his socks rumpled around his ankles. His elbow was bleeding.

He looked at the blood. 'We should have gone straight home.'

'We are.' Mary set off down the street. 'Pull your sleeve down.'

When Mrs Thornton came into the kitchen her children were scraping the remains of beans on toast off their plates and draining glasses of milk. She did not notice the bruise on Mary's wrist and only found the plaster on Michael's arm at bedtime. He had hurt it playing football, he declared, adding that he had scored a goal. The first statement was the only lie Michael Thornton ever told his mother.

As she often did when she kissed her son goodnight, Mrs Thornton told him he was her little angel.

Ten

Tuesday, 24 April 2012

Stella Darnell started her domestic and commercial cleaning business the day after she left school, aged seventeen, ignoring the application form to join the police her dad had given her. She did the cleaning herself, but when the jobs grew and she was threatened with turning away new clients she gave in to her mother's advice and recruited other cleaners. She continued to clean and, bleary-eyed from late-night and early-morning shifts, clacked out quotes, invoices and receipts on a second-hand electric golfball typewriter into the early hours.

One night Suzanne Darnell appeared in the bedroom now serving as a makeshift office, in her silk dressing gown and black-out shades pushed up on her forehead, with two mugs of tea. Stella accepted the tea but, licking and stamping envelopes, had no time to chat.

Her mother pulled out carbon copies of letters and invoices stuffed in a bulging concertina file. 'Spacing's wrong and only put "yours sincerely" if you know the recipient's name.' She sat on Stella's bed. 'You haven't given a payment due limit. Put "immediately" or you'll waste time chasing payment and have cash-flow problems. You must look professional or customers will decide you won't do a good job. You need a name – Stella Darnell won't do. Clients will always ask for you.'

'I've had no complaints.' Hunting and pecking at the typewriter keys, Stella had tried to shut her ears to this advice.

'You don't know how many clients you have lost. Hop up.'

They swapped places. Suzie's fingers flew over the keys, the juddering machine sounding like sustained gunfire. She churned out error-free letters, proposals and contracts until there was nothing to do and the vinyl record storage case serving as a filing tray was overflowing. The dawn chorus began and the indigo sky was streaked with pink as the last envelope was sealed.

Suzie grabbed the mugs. Pausing by the door, she said: 'Clean Slate.'

'What?' Stella squared off the envelopes for posting.

'That's the name of your company.'

For the next year Suzanne Darnell handled the administration for Clean Slate. She visited second-hand shops for a filing cabinet, a waste bin. She brokered deals for cheap stationery. She set up a system – a tower of trays: 'in', 'pending' and 'out' – filed client accounts in folders and locked them in the cabinet.

Stella had to clean less, drum up new business. Suzie devised new packages and joined her in recruiting cleaners; they rarely disagreed about whom to employ. Suzie insisted they trial the cleaners in the Barons Court flat and that everyone wear Clean Slate polo shirts to reinforce the message that they meant business.

Jobs increased, in size and quantity. Banished to the 'office', Stella kept to herself that she enjoyed cleaning more than anything.

One blustery rainy night, soon after Clean Slate's second anniversary, Stella arrived to clean the premises of her first commercial client, an employment agency over a Spar supermarket on Shepherd's Bush Green. Months before, the manager, a Mrs Makepeace – late twenties, snappily clad in a suit with shoulder pads – had haggled a knock-down price for the Silver Interior package. Suzie objected, but was mollified when Mrs Makepeace secured Clean Slate contracts with three companies. Stella did the employment-agency shifts and modelled herself on the older woman. She bought a suit for meetings and was nicer to people.

Despite Suzie's warning to maintain a line between staff and clients, over tea and biscuits after sessions Stella confided to Jackie – they had quickly moved to first-name terms – her plans for Clean Slate. She switched to Jackie's trusted suppliers and absorbed tips on client handling.

That stormy evening there was no tea or biscuits while, her voice raised above the lashing rain and wind buffeting the windows, Jackie Makepeace told Stella the agency had gone under. Her employer had emptied the bank account and disappeared. Clean Slate's invoice would not be paid and nor would Jackie, although she made little of this. Surrounded by the trappings of an efficient office, she admitted she had completed the filing after hearing the news, although everything would be incinerated, the equipment sold for a song and the lease given up. Jackie was relentlessly optimistic; it was the one time Stella saw her close to crying.

Stella made the tea and, running down to the mini-mart, bought two packets of Rich Tea biscuits, Jackie's favourite.

By the time she left, Stella had appointed Jackie her office manager and decided to take over the lease of the premises overlooking Shepherd's Bush Green. Her mum fretted that Clean Slate was too big for Stella's bedroom, so would applaud her professional response to a crisis; she need not consult her.

Suzanne Darnell did not applaud any of it: she disliked Shepherd's Bush and, without meeting her, disapproved of Jackie. Once a client always a client; besides, Mrs Makepeace must have had a hand in the collapse of the employment agency. Suzie had relished her role in Stella's business; she was horrified by the abrupt redundancy, but could not say so.

Soon after this Stella rented a bedsit over the dry cleaner's next door to the office and left the home she had shared with her mother since she was seven. Suzie showed no further interest in Clean Slate; or much else.

In 2011, on her accountant's advice and responding to Jackie's concern that she was living on the job, Stella bought the corner apartment of a gated development by the Thames in Brentford. Stella still held to the rule that clients and staff should not be friends; she forgot that it was Suzie's rule.

When Stella reached the office the door was open. A man was balancing on his haunches fiddling with the lock.

'What the hell do you think you're doing? Stand back with your hands above your head. The police are on their way.' Stella backed away from the door. She had frightened herself.

The man flung himself to the floor, his arms over his head, his hands over his ears. In the brief quiet Stella became aware of a mewing sound. It was the man.

'What on earth is going on?' Jackie appeared, holding a tray of tea things. Stella jumped. Jackie just kept her grasp of the tray.

'I've caught a burglar.' Even as she said the words Stella had a creeping suspicion this was nonsense.

'Duggie has put in a new door. The lock broke. I couldn't make my key turn. So I took the opportunity. The freeholders have agreed.'

Stella watched the man get to his feet. She guessed he was one of what she dubbed Jackie's lame ducks. If Jackie had no problems of her own she solved other people's. She and her husband Graham often had waifs and strays staying or popping in for supper – friends of their sons, a school friend of Jackie's whose husband had died – and every Saturday Jackie shopped for three old people. Stella did not understand how she found the time.

The man pushed back thinning grey hair with both hands and began screwing a mechanism into the side of the new door. Stella muttered an apology as she stepped past. After David Barlow she had burglars on the brain.

As she dumped her briefcase on the floor by her office door and paused to leaf through today's post, Stella considered that she herself might count as a lame duck or stray.

'It does mean that if someone comes in off the street, they'll keep going up the stairs.' Jackie nodded at Stella. 'Duggie will make this place a fortress.'

Stella had requested – in person, in emails and on laminated notices – that the insurance company above keep the street door locked to ward off casual callers. Her requests were ignored. A stream of deliveries came and went from Keyhole Securities and, not having an intercom, their staff did not want the bother of the two flights of stairs. Instead the leather-clad and helmeted couriers bothered Clean Slate. Lying awake at night, Stella worried over the likelihood of a burglary.

'I'll call off the police, shall I?' Jackie indicated the phone, eyebrows raised.

'That was just to frighten him.' Stella looked out of the window. It was eight o'clock in the morning and Shepherd's Bush Green was log-jammed. It was not helped by a slow-moving street-cleaning vehicle. Through the ill-fitting sash, she distinguished the hiss of the water spray, an unsettling sound that made her think of *Doctor Who*.

'Speaking of police, did you ring Hammersmith Police Station?'

Slatted sunlight through the Venetian blinds warmed Stella's face. She thought of David Barlow's conservatory. She would rather be cleaning there than reading through the proposal for the new database.

'That nice policeman rang again.'

Stella's attention was caught by staff contact forms on Beverly's desk awaiting scanning for the database. Jack Harmon's was on the top. Jack had walked into the office early one morning when the downstairs door was open. He had typical left-hander's writing, slanting backwards. Had Stella seen his application without meeting him it might have hit the reject pile. But in January last year, after Terry's sudden death, she hadn't been with it. Not that she regretted her decision: Jack was her best cleaner. He was more than that, she admitted. He had helped her solve the Rokesmith murder and refused credit for it. Stella had known Jack for over a year but actually didn't know him at all. Yet she wanted him to work with her on another case. Somehow she trusted him.

'Calling Stella?'

'Sorry?'

'Martin Cashman has left two messages. Beverly did say. Wasn't he the bloke who was kind when Terry died?'

Stella must phone Jack. 'I'll call him.' She picked up the form looking for Jack's number. Jackie gently took it from her.

'It's ringing.' She handed her the phone.

Stella had not spoken to Detective Superintendent Martin Cashman since Terry's funeral. It would be about Terry; she wasn't sure she wanted to know. '

'Cashman.' The voice was businesslike and not for the first time Martin Cashman, who was about the same age as Stella, reminded her of her father. Recently everyone was reminding her of Terry; he was haunting her. Again she thought of David Barlow, although he was actually nothing like her father. Younger, for a start.

'Stella Darnell. You called me?' Stella caught Jackie frowning. 'How are you?' She tried for more warmth.

'Hey! Stella, great stuff. How are you?'

Detective Inspector Cashman had been promoted to Terry Darnell's post of Detective Chief Superintendent at Hammersmith Police Station after Terry retired. Obliquely and without logic, Stella viewed him as having usurped her dad.

'You left a message.' She caught Jackie's eye. 'Fine, how are you?'

'Ageing by the minute. Crock of the Walk, that's me!' The microphone picked up Cashman's breathing. Like Terry he sounded fresh from jogging, which would not be the case. 'I want your company.'

'I'm sorry?'

'I've terminated our contract with the cowboys we were using. They went through every office leaving the dust intact.' He laughed uproariously, then was conspiratorial. 'I've had the go-ahead from the powers that be to commission direct. Clean Slate ticks all the boxes. No one else in the frame. We want you to clean the station.'

When she was fifteen Stella decided to give the police a wide berth. Her dad, overtaken by the Rokesmith murder, saw little of his teenaged daughter and she blamed the police. If Jackie had not been monitoring her call, Stella might have refused the job. But Jackie was right, Cashman had been kind after her dad's death and it was not in Stella's nature to turn down work.

A Mrs Marian Williams, Cashman's civilian administrator, would email Jackie the details. Stella agreed to start the next morning at six with three shifts a week.

Jackie poured hot water from the kettle next to the photocopier into four 'Clean Slate' mugs. 'You'll need at least three operatives.'

'I'll do it.' Stella was unwrapping the Rich Tea biscuits.

'Ask Jack.' Jackie fished out the tea bags, squeezed them and dropped them into a plastic takeaway tub. She added milk to each mug – more in Stella's.

Clean Slate always had a staffing crisis – the work exceeded those available to do it and Jackie always found a solution. Since last year, her solution had been Jack Harmon.

'He's driving a late-night train.' Stella congratulated herself on her prompt and plausible objection. Then she wondered why she had objected. She didn't want to clean the station; there, more even than in his house, Terry would be hovering, highlighting her mistakes. Yet she had an objection. What little she did know about Jack warned her to think twice about letting him loose in a police station.

Beverly, the admin assistant, arrived and, ignoring the pile of work on her desk, settled down with her mug of tea. The day got under way.

Stella was still at her desk at six-thirty that evening when her mobile phone rang. She snatched it up, thinking of Jack; she had not phoned him.

'I want a cleaner.' Her mum had rung Clean Slate forgetting it was Stella's company.

'Mum, it's me. Stella. Don't worry. You're confused.'

'I'm not worried or confused. I want a cleaner. That's what you do, isn't it? Clean?'

'Yes, but—'

'When can he start?'

'Who?'

'Jack.' Recently Suzie had been forgetful; it astounded Stella that she had total recall about a man she had met once.

'I don't think that's a good idea.'

'He did a super job last time. He got everywhere.'

There was no point in Stella saying that it had been she who had cleaned that evening because if it had been Jack he would have done a better job. She couldn't remember why she hadn't wanted him to go there and now, distracted by an email, this time she agreed.

As she was driving past Marks and Spencer's on King Street Stella saw the witness appeal notice again and thought of the boy who had died there the day before. Joel Evans; she even remembered his name. It had rained heavily since then and the sandy stain on the camber had washed away.

Eleven

Mary made a grab for the chain and pulled with all her might. Water thundered around the toilet bowl. She shrank back against the door, horrified by the crumpled lavatory paper dashing around and around. The water was rising and coming closer to the lavatory lid. The paper was still there. She shut her eyes and, her lips working rapidly, prayed to be saved. Her prayer was answered. With a hideous gurgle the water drained away and Mary pattered forward; she was relieved to see that the paper had disappeared. A new panic arose. Playtime was over. She was late.

She pulled at the bolt but it was stuck fast. She used both hands but could not get a grip; the sharp metal cut into her skin. She cast around the tiny cubicle for something to knock the bolt with but there wasn't even a toilet brush like at home. The thought of home made things worse. She had no home.

The water was coming back. Mary shut her eyes and opened them. She was making it up. No, it was higher. It would stop, Mary told herself. It must stop. It was creeping to the top and not stopping. Mesmerized she fixed on the toilet as if she could work a spell. The words 'Armitage Shanks' were under water, the letters waving. The water was moving as if someone was stirring it with a giant spoon. It was getting closer and she couldn't swim.

Mary reached up to pull the chain again, but then thought better of it because it would make more water. Her stomach churned. She teased Michael about his terror of falling down the toilet; now it was happening to her. She pulled and tugged and pushed on the bolt but it didn't budge.

She heard a sound that chilled the heat in her cheeks. Liquid was spilling on to the tiles. It welled up to the rim of the toilet and seeped through the gap between the bowl and the seat. It took its time and gradually a puddle collected in a dip in the tiles and imperceptibly lapped towards her feet. Mary was helpless and when it touched the toes of her sandals could only stand on tiptoe, her back against the door.

'Help! Get me out of here. I'm trapped. He-lp!' Her shouts escalated to a scream.

Unlike Mary the water could escape. It flowed smoothly under the door like a snake going about its business. The toilet paper she had used when she peed floated out of the bowl and slopped down, soggy and twisted, one end like a fishtail in the gentle current. It shamed her.

The sibilant sounds of the cistern began as a whisper and then built in intensity.

'I'm stuck!' Her cries subsided and, defeated, she watched the veil of water slide over the rim.

Mary's trance-like state was shattered by a hooter. She covered her head with her hands; the water was washing around her ankles.

Shouts from the playground. She had forgotten about the fire drill. First thing that morning, their teacher – Mary still did not know her name – had told the class that after playtime an alarm would sound and instead of filing back to the classroom, they must 'congregate' in the Sunken Garden for the register.

She heard guns and cannons; the booms and cracks were coming this way. If they peeped under the door they would see her sandals: she could not stand on the toilet. An explosion made her jump. Someone was thumping on the door.

'Mary Thornton?'

She screwed up her eyes and didn't answer.

'Who's in there?

'Me,' she admitted in a small voice.

'Come out now!' the voice ordered.

Mary grasped the bolt. It slid aside. Miss Crane, the headmistress, stood by the roller towel, water creeping towards her shoes.

'So this is where you are hiding.' She made a sweeping motion with her hand. Mary slunk out of the cubicle, treading through the welling tide.

'I wasn't hid—'

'This is disappointing, Mary. The fire drill means we all do as we are told. You are the only one who has not. What if there had been a fire?'

'I couldn't get out.' Mary spun around, splattering the woman's tights. Water had reached the sinks and was stealing under the doors of the other cubicles. 'I would have burnt alive,' she said.

'Don't be rude.' Miss Crane ushered her towards the door. 'What a story. No trouble getting out when I called, I see!'

'It's not a story! It happened.'

'Please don't answer back.' Miss Crane propelled Mary with a hand on the back of her neck. 'Given that you are new, I'll draw a line under this incident.'

Mary shrugged the hand away. 'It happened.'

'Everyone has been looking for you, wasting their time while you were hiding.'

'I wasn't.'

'What did I say about answering back?' She made an arch with her arm by the door. 'You have caused enough trouble. Go on back to your class.'

'You're answering me back.' People had to answer if someone spoke. Mary stood immobile on the puddling floor.

'That's enough!'

Miss Crane yanked her around and swooped close with peppermint breath. 'If it wasn't for your sweet brother, I might consider asking your mummy and daddy to remove you. This is not a school for liars.'

I am not a liar!

The scene was in Technicolor. Mary grabbed at the bun and got a chunk of grey hair in her fist. She hauled Miss Crane to the overflowing toilet – the wet floor made it easy. Her legs stuck out of the cubicle like a doll's. Mary jammed Miss Crane's head into the toilet and pressed hard into her neck, keeping out of the way of the kicking doll's legs. She stuffed toilet paper around the doll's head and pulled the chain. Miss Crane was flushed away.

'Blimey, what's gone on here?' Mary recognized the man with the mop. 'I should have brought me rubber ring!'

'I'm afraid we've had a flood.' Miss Crane kept her hand on Mary's neck.

'The stopcock'll have gone. I said they all need doing. 'Fraid these will be out of order for the rest of the day.'

When she edged out past him, he winked at Mary.

'Miss Crane, it's County Hall.' The woman from behind the typewriter was waving a note. Miss Crane took it, read it and walked away down the corridor with the woman. She must have forgotten about Mary.

The little girl waited until both women were out of sight.

The man came out of the toilets. 'You OK?'

'I was locked in.'

'Those bolts are a devil. There's a knack: lift as you slide.'

Mary's sandals squelched on the floor, leaving a trail of damp footprints. Her plan was taking shape.

Twelve

Stella left the van in St Peter's Square to avoid Terry's neighbours, although in over a year she hadn't met one. The petrol gauge was on empty; she would fill up at the garage on King Street on her way to her flat. She was parked outside a house that had belonged to a client who had died last year. The area was peopled with ghosts; not that Stella believed in them. She observed with disapproval that the new owners had replaced Mrs Ramsay's 1960s black and white curtains in the dining room with wooden blinds. Jackie had suggested Stella drop a leaflet in for the new owners but Stella was not keen to clean a house when she had known the previous occupant. Jack had said this was because she was fond of Mrs Ramsay. To prove him wrong, Stella resolved now that she would return with a leaflet and put it through the brass letterbox, which even from the street she could see was in need of a buff.

She punched in Terry's alarm code; the beeping stopped and she caught the chimes of the church clock striking ten.

She opened the basement door, this time switching on the light and, feigning confidence, stomped down the stone steps.

She avoided the photograph wall but still had the conviction that her many faces were watching her. She was haunting herself.

The blue folder was on the table where she had left it. This mildly surprised her, as if Terry might have filed it away in her absence. She sat down and directed the lamp down. She properly examined each photograph. Some were of roads stretching away.

She had already fathomed that photographs labelled for example with '3a' or '3b' were of the same road as the first photograph labelled simply with a '3'. They were close-ups of features in the same street: a tree trunk, a telegraph pole. There were only two prints in the file with one number, these were '1' and '4'.

She could see nothing new and was beginning to think there was nothing to see when on the photograph labelled '5b' in Terry's handwriting she spotted something by the kerb. She looked closer and made out a witness appeal notice. It was an older version of the one in King Street marking where Joel Evans had been killed, but like that one it was anchored by sand bags draped over the cross bars that, with the poor quality printing, looked even more like Jack's piglets. She tried to read the writing on the notice, but it was too small.

She flicked through the photographs but found no others with boards or anything that gave an indication of the date the picture was taken. It was late and she was cleaning the police station in the morning; she should go back to her flat. Yet she was sure she was on to something. Jack was the one person who she could be sure would be awake at this hour. She had to hope he wasn't driving his train or he wouldn't answer. In the subterranean chamber there was no signal. She gathered up the folder and ran upstairs to the hall. In the thin light from the intermittent lamp-post across the street, vaguely aware of Terry in the shadows overseeing her every move, Stella dialled Jack Harmon's number.

Two rings and then it went to voicemail. The abruptness of the switchover made her suspect Jack had cut the line. Had he broken his promise about his night-time business? This was why she didn't want him anywhere near a police station. She was about to hang up when she changed her mind and left a message: 'Jack. Me. I've got a job for you.' She paused, then added: 'A cleaning job.' She grimaced; she liked to see a person's reaction when she was talking to them. She had forgotten to tell Jack about the case.

Still holding the blue folder she went out and double-locked the door. She hurried around to St Peter's Square and clambered into the van. She turned on the engine and glanced up at Mrs Ramsay's house – she would always think of it as Mrs Ramsay's – and thought of Jackie's idea about the leaflet. She opened the glove box and found the stash of flyers kept in all Clean Slate vans. She was startled by her phone blaring through the van's speakers. The caller's name flashed up on the dashboard screen.

Jack Mob.

She pressed the 'pick up' button on the steering wheel. She loved her new van's gadgets.

'You've got a cleaning job for me,' Jack said in a hushed voice.

'Why are you whisp— Oh, never mind. Yes. No.'

'Great that you're clear. I love that.'

'I mean it's not cleaning.' She paused. 'It's a case.'

'A detective job?'

'Probably nothing.'

'But you think it's probably something.' Jack's voice was hardly audible.

Stella stuffed the flyers back in the glove box and picked the blue folder up from the passenger seat. 'Yes. I think it is,' she said, opening it at the first photograph.

'See you in the morning, then.'

The light on the dashboard went out.

Thirteen

'Hurry up, Michael. We'll be late and it won't be you in trouble.' Mary used her mother's imperatives.

'Are we going to the park?' Michael wrestled his arm from her grasp. 'Let go, you are hurt-ing me. I'm com-ing any-way.' His *Lost in Space* robot voice.

'No. We are going home.' Mary snatched at Michael but he broke free and hopped and skipped about in front of her.

'All-firm-ative', he croaked, in hazy imitation.

Mary snatched his flapping shirt-tail. There was the sound of ripping fabric and both children were brought up short.

'You've torn it,' Michael wailed.

'It was your fault, you should have behaved.' Mary could not see Clifford Hunt; if he was not at the swings she had lost him. She pinched Michael's arm. 'Keep up.'

'This isn't the way home.' Michael pointed back towards the first railway arch. 'It's that way.' Then, 'I'll have to tell Mummy about my shirt. She'll see.'

'You did it playing football.'

'Then I'll be in trouble.'

'Carry on like this and we'll be late and Br'er Fox will get you.'

This silenced Michael. Mary's truncated telling of Tar-Baby, an Uncle Remus story read to her class at her old school, had instilled in Michael the vivid possibility that like Br'er Rabbit he would be stuck to his teddy bear coated in strawberry jam and be gobbled up by the fox. Mary knew to use the threat sparingly to maintain potency.

There was no one at the swings. She yanked Michael past the paddling pool and the sandpit where some younger children were playing: all girls, no Clifford. One of them shouted out Michael's name and he waved enthusiastically at them. Mary pushed him on and veered down the dark path beneath the railway arches.

'You said we weren't going to the slide.' Michael spoke more to himself than his sister.

Clifford Hunt wasn't at the slide or on the roundabout. He was too old for roundabouts, but Mary had seen him there with older boys in black blazers, smoking cigarettes. The last arch was closed off with a gate. A ring of plastic barriers was in the middle of the path. It surrounded a patch of drying concrete on which was engraved a heart pierced with an arrow. Mary's own heart was thumping. Letters had been carved into the heart: 'M. T.' Clifford had done it. The letters looked new, so he must be hiding in the bushes. She felt the fizzing in her stomach that happened on Christmas Eve or every leap year on her real birthday.

Clifford loved her as much as she loved him.

Michael broke her reverie. 'Those spell my name.'

'What?'

'M. T. means Michael Thornton. That's me.' He squeezed between the barriers and before Mary could stop him was scrabbling at the 'M' with his fingers. The concrete had hardened so he made little impact. He grabbed a twig and managed to dig at the 'M'.

'Leave it.'

The little boy jumped when Mary shook him. 'You've ruined it.'

Michael stared up at her in astonishment. 'Did… you… write… it?' He got the words out between shakes.

'It's for me.'

'Who would do that?' Michael asked the question without malice.

'They will be very angry when I say what you did.' Mary stalked back up the path, sure Clifford Hunt was watching. She did not turn at the sound of footsteps or when she felt his hand on her bare arm, but to her horror she felt herself blushing.

Michael put his hand on his sister's arm. He felt sad, but did not know why. He knew that the girls in his class had drawn the heart; it was like the one they did on the classroom window. He had not known that Mary's name were the same letters as his; he had hazily supposed that he had his own name and his own letters. He wished that the heart did belong to Mary.

Mary stared at her brother with hatred, then as quickly as it had come the feeling went. Clifford had put a heart in concrete for her. The heart would be there forever and ever.

Fourteen

The house was a rectangular monolith with little to recommend it in terms of elegance. The spindly lamp over the porch wanted a jet of gas to cast light on the sweep of drive, once a turning circle for barouches and phaetons; weeds flourished through the gravel. Jack spotted an alarm box on the wall, although nothing signified it was active. This time he kept out of the range of the camera, although he doubted it functioned either.

Mallingswood House had a tired air. Jack was familiar with boys' boarding schools that limped along on a shoestring, dependent on parents who, saddled with unwanted children or living abroad, were perhaps less concerned about educational standards than with snatching at privilege. His father had deposited him in just such an establishment.

He had walked from the Great West Road and was on the south side of Weltje Road. His rucksack, packed for his stay with his new Host, was light. She wasn't a proper Host; he would be her guest only for as long as it took to get back his street atlas. He had been tempted to go in from the front: a bold move, certainly, but people seldom saw what was under their noses. His most effective hiding places had been in plain sight. Except that the woman who had picked up his book had seen what was under her nose. He walked slowly back along Weltje Road, looking for a means of entering without breaking.

The back was even more featureless than the front. The few windows were in darkness; trade gates, warped on their hinges, were secured by a chain. He looked again and found the chain was looped around a bolt: he could just unwrap it. Casual intruders might be fooled, but not him. His Host had issued him an invitation. He hitched his rucksack on to his shoulders and eased open the gate; then he replaced the chain exactly as it had been.

Jack found himself in a dark concreted yard and, wasting no time, flitted over to the building and immediately found his point of entry. The putty in a rotting box sash came away in strips when he ran his hand along it. Methodically Jack arranged these on the ground in order like a jigsaw. Gently he levered the pane out and rested it against the wall.

In one movement he vaulted on to the sill and, twisting, insinuated himself through the opening. Inside, he took a moment to gauge whether he had been heard. Nothing, but he would not make himself at home yet. Efficiently, his movements economical, he lifted the snib on the door. Outside he replaced the glass and the putty, regretful that his Host could not appreciate his care. He retrieved his rucksack and slipped inside, closing the door. He could come and go as he pleased.

His torch revealed a long passage, the ceiling lowered by tracking that supported heating and water pipes; he dipped his head to avoid them. He passed closed doors either side, which he would explore once he had his bearings.

One door was open. Jack crept inside and, certain now that he was alone on this floor, tried a switch by the door. A warm comforting glow from a yellow fabric shade gave all the feel of a friendly sitting room but what he saw was mundane. A black plastic bin bag, cardboard boxes spilling out brown and white envelopes of different sizes. One step and he kicked a stack of filing trays; one cracked when it hit the stone floor. He turned off the light and went behind the door and counted to ten.

When no one came he risked the light again and saw a plastic crate filled with cellular blankets like the ones at his school, the initials MHPS stitched along a hem. The room swooped. Jack grabbed a swivel chair and kept his balance. He was a seven-year-old boy devising his escape in the basement of his school.

The air was still and deathly cold; sunlight never reached this room. Jack was an Underground train driver: he preferred the tunnels, bricks coated with centuries of dust, to the daylight. But here a sense of evil was suddenly palpable. He forced himself into the present and, keeping to the wall, stole along the passage.

The heating was not on or the pipes above his head would be hot. Basements in institutions generally housed the generator and the boiler and were stifling and stuffy. Mallingswood House was saving on heating bills; this too was familiar.

At intervals a green 'Fire Exit' sign affixed to a cross beam confirmed his direction. The silence was unremitting and Jack almost wished to hear some sound, even if it signalled danger.

At last his torch picked out a flight of steps. The trick was to enter the bones of the house and build up an affinity that made it more likely he would be invisible to his Hosts. He had noticed that however alert they were on the street, even they tended to relax in their own homes. On the top step he was enveloped by a smell he knew well: stale rice pudding and polished parquet floors. He was surprised to find it reassuring.

There was the front door of studded wood. The diamond lights that framed it projected shapes across black and white tiles. To his left rose a grand staircase not diminished by worn brown lino. A curving balustrade ended with a volute newel supported by six balusters thickened by layers of faded cream gloss paint.

The bottom three stairs had been spared the lino and a sleek sheen of marble lessened the institutional grip on the Victorian mansion. However, the once magnificent hallway was compromised by a boxed enclosure, with 'Reception' above a grille on which a wooden notice was slid to 'Closed'.

He peered through. A swivel chair was half turned from the hatch, a cushion on its seat moulded by some absent sitter. He tapped the counter. One. Two. Three. 'Come out, come out wherever you are,' he whispered.

No one came.

A notice was stuck on the glass to his right, he shone the torch on it. Term dates for 2011–2012. Summer term was due to start on Monday, 7th May, boarders returning on the 5th. This was even later than his own school.

He swept the light up the staircase to the balustrade on the half-landing – where a debutante would have been marvelled at by the crowd below before making her stately descent to the party. He was certain that no one was there now.

He felt a vibration in his pocket; the accompanying buzz, while inaudible in most places, was insidious in this hollow space where there was no other sound. Stella had left him a voicemail. He listened to her message and decided to call her in the morning. Then he changed his mind: he had once before delayed a call to Stella and had regretted it; he would not make that mistake again.

'You've got a cleaning job for me.' His face was in his sleeve to muffle his voice.

'Why are you whisp— Oh, never mind. Yes. No.'

'Great that you're clear. I love that.' He risked teasing Stella.

'I mean it's not cleaning.' She went silent and he was just about to check she was still there when she said: 'It's a case.'

'A detective job?' He forgot to whisper. He had been disappointed that after last year Stella had played it safe and concentrated on cleaning. He wanted to shout with joy.

'Probably nothing.'

'But you think it's probably something,' he breathed.

'Yes. I think it is.'

'See you in the morning, then.' He turned his phone off and put one foot on the marble step. He held his breath and tuned in to the creaks and sighs of the house in which so many inhabitants slept. Far above he heard a door closing, then footsteps, a purposeful tread. As he had hoped, he was not alone. Jack twisted off the torch and began to climb.

Fifteen

Monday, 2 May 1966

'I hope those two never breathe fresh air again.' Mrs Thornton snapped shut her purse and wrote a note on a spiral pad. 'They should suffer as much as that poor little girl.'

'Four pints and six yogs'. She tore off the paper and, rolling it into a spill, poked it into the neck of one of the empty milk bottles on the draining board.

'Shame they weren't doing it a couple of years ago. We could have hanged them.' Bob Thornton was tying his shoelaces. He got up and took his briefcase from the boiler and added: 'The ink's hardly dry on the law. They should bring back the death penalty just for them, although the rope's too kind.'

'How can a rope be kind?' Michael wriggled on his chair.

Bob Thornton mussed his son's hair and blew a kiss at his wife.

'Don't be late back for tea with your brother,' he instructed his daughter. Mary was assiduously scooping up the last corn flakes floating in too much milk in her bowl. She made a noise with her mouth full.

'Say goodbye properly.' Mrs Thornton poured water from a plastic jug into a pot of geraniums on the sill.

'Goodbye properly,' Mary piped.

Mrs Thornton tutted. 'I don't know what's got into you.'

The front door slammed, making the windows vibrate.

'Dinner money for you and your brother.' She slapped a pound note in front of Mary and snatched up the Corn Flakes box. 'Put that in your satchel safely and hand it straight to Mrs Jones. She'll give you a receipt which you must hold on to or I'll be very cross.' The threat was uttered without conviction; Jean Thornton had moved on to other morning duties.

She put the bottles out on the front step and then wiped the table in busy circles, pushing Mary's elbows off the Formica to gather up toast crumbs and driving the dishcloth through a ring of milk. Mary held the crisp pound note up to her nose: it crackled and smelled of her dad.

'Myr— Mary! Stop dreaming and clean your teeth. Michael's waiting.' Mrs Thornton sluiced the cloth under the tap, squeezed it out, and draped it over the dish-rack. Mary observed this procedure wistfully; it had happened in their old house. She allowed herself to imagine that everything was the same.

Mary had conjured up a spell that worked. She kept her eyes on the table while she ate and, blinkered like a horse, was in the old kitchen. Fixing on her cornflakes, she saw the lemon-yellow walls, the speckly lino and the geyser with the friendly flame in the middle of the night. The spell worked until she lifted her head.

Hampered by her longer journey to work, Mrs Thornton was relying more and more on her daughter to look after her young brother. Mary had been intrigued at the idea of being a grown-up until Michael said she had to mind him because she had been bad. Although she told him this was not true, in her heart of hearts she suspected that it was. She felt bad all the time. The night before last she had left the key in the front door. Anyone could have got in, her mum had said, and stolen everything – or worse. Mary had brought her Everyday Diary home from school and forgotten to take it back. Grown-ups did not make mistakes, she decided. They wrote notes for the milkman, lists for the shops and carried briefcases and handbags with everything safe inside. She would never be a real grown-up.

During the few days she and Michael had been at their new school Mary had made no enemies, but nor had she made friends. She had shunned the helpful overtures of Jacqueline, the girl with plaits, because she had seen her laughing at something with Clifford Hunt. She would not join in games at playtime. Most children struck Mary as stupid; they were not grown up like she was. At her last school there had been a sort of friend, Linda, whom no one played with. Mary did not much like her, but trailing around the playground with her, through a mix of guile and patronage, she had gained a modicum of authority. With the move to the new house she made up her mind she didn't need friends.

Michael Thornton was immediately popular. Every evening after school, since that first day when Mary had found him winning marbles over a drain cover, she had known where to find her brother after school. He was at the centre of a gaggle of boys and girls, making them laugh, weaving around tackles with a football or handling jacks like a juggler or winning marbles crouched over the drain. His marble collection grew along with his popularity. Although Mary could not articulate it, her little brother had become a bargaining asset. If she were to be visible it would be because she was Michael Thornton's sister.

She dreaded the walk through Ravenscourt Park on school mornings and would slow their pace, meandering between the beds, pretending interest in newly planted flowers or a name on a bench. Michael said this made him look a 'cissy'. She told him she was a grown-up and knew best what was good for him. Both children knew it was to stop Michael joining his friends and when they arrived at the tennis courts Michael would pluck up the courage to escape. Mary tried not to hear their shouts – the passing of urgent information and childish jokes – and feeling ever more alone, she plodded on down the shaded path beside the viaduct. Michael never believed that she would tell their dad he had left her. He didn't believe anything she said any more.

On this particular morning, they met two small boys before they reached the railway arch and Michael was soon out of sight. Mary scuffed her heels along the ground, refusing to give chase or shout. Ahead were girls from her own class; there was Jacqueline, who had found her a colder bottle of milk at yesterday's morning playtime. She was with Clifford Hunt again and three boys Mary didn't know. Clifford looked behind him, but did not seem to see her.

At the gate Mary brightened. Michael was there; he had obeyed her instructions. She darted forward to tell him they would have their dinner together and she would get him seconds of ice-cream.

Michael called out: 'No cars. Now!'

His gang gathered around him and it seemed to Mary that her brother was carried over the road. Sharp metal caught her shin as prams and pushchairs rattled past, with children shouting and mums scolding; the pain was distant. She went and sat on a low wall outside a house. In the glare of spring sunshine, the warmth of the bricks seeped through her dress and made her drowsy.

The voices stopped. There was no talking, laughing or yelling, no legs and satchels or shoving. The paving sparkled in the sun and made her eyes water. She would not cry. Mary looked up and down the road; there was nothing coming. She got up and trotted past the park entrance, past the school gate and under the cool shelter of the bridge. She was startled by the clatter of another train. The wheels clunked over the rails above her head. In time to the beat of the carriages Mary quickened her pace and went into the station.

The concourse was vast, bright with diffused sunlight through a glass roof. It was too wide an expanse for the little girl to manage. She was momentarily paralysed and stood stock still. She steeled herself and made for the ticket windows.

'Caledonian Road, please.' She unbuckled her satchel and, straining up, poked a crisp pound note though the opening.

'Single or return?' Without looking at Mary, the woman licked her finger and leafed through the pages of a bulging book.

'Single.' Mary's plan took shape.

The green slip of cardboard between her teeth, Mary scooped the torrent of change into her palm and tipped it into her satchel. A threepenny bit slipped from her grasp, bounced on the ground and rolled under a ticket machine. Mary pretended she didn't care.

She went up the stairs. With each heavy step her skin prickled with the expectation of hearing her name: either name. Miss Crane was telling her off for wasting money or for letting her brother cross a road without her. She couldn't hold all the reasons for a ticking-off in her mind – there were too many – and as she paused on the platform and looked down the steps, a small corner of her wished for Miss Crane to appear. She divined there was no turning back.

By the sweet machine was a Tube map. She stretched up and traced her finger along the green line from Ravenscourt Park to Hammersmith to the blue line that would take her home. Mary was surprised by a train sliding into the station behind her. As soon as the doors opened, she leapt on board with a giant step. A man and a woman were sitting by the door and to avoid them Mary went to the other end of the carriage. When the doors rolled shut she settled on her seat, her toes just touching the ground and her ticket in her fist. Knees together, she pretended that, like a grown-up, she did this every day.

The train gathered speed and the carriage swayed; Mary had trouble reading the names on the strip of map above the windows. Hammersmith was the next station. She struggled up before the train stopped and wrapped her arms around a pole in the centre of the carriage and only let go when the doors opened.

At some point Mary Thornton changed her mind about travelling north to Holloway. She simply did not cross the platform to the Piccadilly line. If she had boarded a train all she'd have had to do was stay on it until Caledonian Road and walk the few yards to her old house. Instead, she toiled up the exit staircase, handed in her ticket at the barrier and walked out of the station. With no traffic lights, Hammersmith Broadway was a gigantic roundabout, four lanes of weaving vehicles going for pole position. It presented many opportunities for collisions or pedestrians to be run over.

Baffled by the tumult, Mary was a tiny timid figure beneath the Underground roundel.

'You look lost, lovely.' A man with carious teeth smiled.

Mary was polite. 'I'm on my way home.' The man's jacket filled her view.

He scratched his bristly chin. 'Where's that then?'

'Up there.' She tried to point, but could only see the inside of the man's jacket.

Sixteen

Tuesday, 24 April 2012

At the first landing a corridor stretched off in each direction, doors either side. Jack went left, because he was left-handed. He tested each step; a groan from seasoned wood could be his undoing but he might have been a ghost for all the sound he made.

He must establish where his Host slept because that was ground zero.

The handle on the first door turned smoothly so he would not need to oil it. Jack felt a stab of dismay. This might mean his Host already had a guest who had paved the way and taken precedence. He dismissed the idea: he should not torment himself with such fancies. Besides, he just wanted his book back.

He switched on his Maglite. The room was spacious; two windows faced on to King Street. At three corners were iron bed-steads. Jack had been so taken up with fretting that his Host had a guest that he had forgotten he was in a school and that behind each of these doors boys would be sleeping. It only took one to detect his presence and give him away. He waited for his heart to calm down and crept into the room, the torch low.

There was no one in the bed by the window. He wheeled around. None of the beds had occupants. The blankets, like the ones in the basement, were tightly tucked in, starched sheets folded over on which were the letters: MHPS. On a cabinet stood a glass and a copy of the *Beano*, its pages curling. He opened the cabinet and ran his hand over the shelves. The cupboard was bare. He sat on the bed, perversely gratified when the springs jingled in the cold stillness. It was identical to the one he had slept in at his boarding school twenty-five years ago. Everything was the same.

Jack shone the beam at the glass: no water. No one was here. It was the last week of the Easter holidays. He had his Host all to himself. He had not brought a sleeping bag, unwilling to admit he was staying and breaking his promise to Stella. He had to stay, he told Stella, just for a few days, and to minimize fuss he would sleep here. Jack assured himself that Stella would understand.

He caught a flash of white above the bed-head. Colin. He read the label.

'Thank you, Colin,' he whispered. 'Who's been lying in my bed?'

At the foot of each bed, against the wall, was a wardrobe – like a coffin, Jack remarked to Colin. It was the wrong thing to say to a seven-year-old boy who had nightmares and wet the bed. Inside the wardrobe was a row of wooden hangers; below, drawers for underwear and a rack for shoes. Perfect.

If she had approved this visit, Stella would insist he wore latex gloves to avoid leaving fingerprints. Jack was not bothered about leaving fingerprints because he left no clue that he had been there.

He hid his biscuit tin of treasures at the back of wardrobe. Tokens to remember his Hosts by, he explained to Colin. On top of this he laid the book, sad that he could not leave it in plain view on the bedside cabinet. He was rereading *Howards End*, he told Colin.

He ran his light over the other beds. They belonged to 'Jimmy' and 'Steve'. Jimmy was halfway through *William the Conqueror* by Richmal Crompton, but Steve didn't read, unless you counted the well-thumbed book of logarithms, which Jack did. Steve's compass in a brass casing said that out of the window was south. Jack knew this but, although fond of imparting facts, he kept it to himself.

The other dormitories were unoccupied, the beds neatly made. The names on the beds offered him company of a sort: 'Chris', 'Bob'... Only two beds lacked a label and there was no glass on the side cabinet. The informality of the names surprised him; his own school had disapproved of diminutives and nicknames.

His Host did not sleep on this floor. If this was like his boarding school, customs from when the house had been a family home would linger and staff would sleep in the attics. His Host was staff. On the upper floors the staircase narrowed to a plain set of treads with a handrail. There were more passages and dormitories off the landings. He paused on each floor but did not sense the presence of a single soul. No seven-year-old boy remained dispirited at the school in the holidays, sitting listlessly on his bed writing brave and upbeat letters to his mother that he never sent.

At the top there was a corridor to the left, but opposite this was a door with a lock. Feeble light defined three shamrock-shaped holes carved above the panels, perhaps for ventilation. Ground zero.

He took his wallet from his inside coat pocket, flicked out his bank card and swiped it down the crack between the door and the jamb. He teased and shifted it with minute movements to locate the end of the bolt. Jack had never opened a door with a credit card before and was relying on having seen it in films. It didn't open.

He returned the card, pocketed the wallet and, determined his Host would not defeat him, risked the torch. He was rewarded by a glint above the lintel. He lifted down a silver Yale key.

The door swung silently inwards to a passage like the others, but with a thick carpet. He put back the key where he found it, stepped inside and shut the door. He must rely on his wits. Jack felt truly alive.

The air was warmer and he smelled recently cooked food, something fried; he imagined egg and chips or fish fingers, typical school food. He had a rush of saliva; he had forgotten to eat.

He turned off the torch. He must familiarize himself with the house through touch, smell and acute listening. Ahead, as his eyes adjusted, Jack saw a blurred line of yellow. Someone was in the end room. He felt every nerve in his body as he crept towards the light.

He recalled a door on his left and felt for the handle. Inside he switched on his torch. Instead of a spartan dormitory he was in a kitchen with chessboard lino tiles and pale blue cupboards and Formica surfaces. A table was draped with a plastic cloth patterned with sumptuous blooms in seventies colours of oranges and browns. A yellow roller blind was up and looking out he could see shops on King Street and in the distance the railway and the dark mass of trees in Ravenscourt Park. No more trains tonight; the colleague he had swapped driving shifts with would have stabled the last train in the Earl's Court depot an hour ago.

There was a noise. He switched off the torch. Too late to hide behind the door; there was nowhere else to hide. Jack moved stealthily away from the fridge which, an ethereal pale figure in the dark, would reveal him in silhouette. It happened again. He placed it. Rain. Gusts of wind swept drops against the glass – like a smattering of gravel thrown at the window. A storm was forecast for dawn. It was early. Jack breathed and put his torch back on.

Brown crockery was stacked in a wire-framed dish-rack; the cloth draped over the mixer tap was still damp. He tipped the lid on a rubbish bin: crushed packaging for fish fingers – spot on. He opened one of two free-standing fridges and light blazed into the room. After the bedside cabinets, he expected the shelves to be bare, but they were stacked with blocks of cheese, pork pies, an open packet of bacon, milk and orange juice and a bowl of congealing baked beans. One of the packets of pork pies had been split; two were gone from the pack of six. Jack hesitated, his mouth watering. He shut the fridge. He did not eat the Hosts' food, it was impolite and as they had a mind like his own they would miss it and he would have to leave. Or worse. He brought his own provisions when he came to stay; tonight he had been too eager and had not thought of food. Never mind, he'd find his book and be gone by the morning.

The next room was furnished like the dormitories: there was the coffin wardrobe and iron bedstead and a cabinet on which there was a glass; this one was full of water. The wardrobe was not shut. He hooked it open with a finger. Pleated black skirts hung beneath starched white shirts with knife-sharp creases on the sleeves alongside two black jackets. An unofficial uniform intended not to cut a dash but to make the wearer invisible: the perfect attire for a Host. But the woman he had seen in the street had not struck him as a Host. He prided himself on knowing straight away.

On the rack were two pairs of pristine lace-ups, fringed tassels dangling. Substitutes for when her present shoes wore out. She was person of practical mind like Stella, who always wore the same sturdy boots. Only his keen eye knew they were not the same boots.

The cold truth sank in. The woman had access to his secrets. She might have known he was watching. He had not followed her here. She had lured him.

Jack was alive to the trap: everything was precision-placed to show the slightest change. By her bed were no books, magazines or newspapers. Few Hosts were readers: they acted out their imaginings. A cream plastic clock – the kind that came free with a stationery order – was three minutes fast. Something else. Jack shone the torch. A framed photo. A young family squinting in full sun at the camera. A gawky-looking couple, the man slightly out of focus as if he had rushed into the shot, his pose typical of a photograph snapped on a timer. The woman, conversely, seemed anxious to be off, perhaps to make tea or put sun cream on her pale children. Some maternal task had been delayed for the sake of freezing a perfect moment in time.

His Host was not in the photograph. Hosts didn't have

families; he should know, and Jack had glimpsed enough of her to find no connection between the gamine, hawky-featured child standing by the father and the dolorous middle-aged woman whose bed this was. There could only be one reason why this picture was here.

It was a trophy.

All of Jack's daytime selves – the man Stella Darnell thought could clean better than any operative or the skilled driver who taught novice drivers on the District line – had gone. This night self took risks, with emotions dulled and senses electric. A stranger to those who knew Jack's other selves.

A voice warned Jack to return to his home with the owl door knocker, get into his own bed and sleep until the morning sun warmed his face.

He turned the handle and opened the door.

He was high over a city. He took in office blocks, terraces of houses, shops on high streets, some bisected by winding crescents and long straight roads. He saw dead-end streets, the sprawling acreage of a municipal park and a half-full gasometer on the horizon. He came lower and saw pedestrians crossing at zebras or dodging cars and buses. Traffic halted at lights and lorries clogged up an arterial road. A river wound through the middle of the conurbation, past a water tower, the blues, greens and metallic greys of the water intimating murky depths and the reflected sky.

Jack tuned into humming, intermitted by clicks. Out of a tunnel came a silver train. It clattered over a section of crisscrossing tracks and slid into a station. Mechanically Jack moved a closed fist towards him, coaxing the lever, bringing the cab to a halt at the correct place on the platform to allow the passengers off.

The attic was the width of the mansion. Jack recognized the metal cone shade from his own school. Like those, it cast an insidious circle of light that dampened the spirits. Now it mimicked the sodium glow of a London sky at night and revealed the largest architectural model Jack had ever seen.

A hatch was raised in the river and an old man, homely in a wool cardigan over a flannel checked shirt, rose like Poseidon. With bony fingers, he adjusted wire spectacles and bent to see the train – on the Piccadilly line – pull out of the station and journey off to the west; the whine Jack had heard earlier rose when it gathered speed.

Jack felt queasy. He shrank into the shadows and willed himself into the cab. He did not drive Piccadilly trains.

'She's running late, should be at Acton Town by now but there was an earlier hitch. Some fool couldn't stick it and bailed out. "One under", they call it. Life is to be treasured. Agree?'

Jack's veins ran cold; the man knew he was there. 'Ye-es,' he managed.

'The infrastructure's under pressure, needs maintenance.' The old man dipped back into the river and reappeared at the far end of the model. Precariously straightening, he continued, 'Tunnel's perishing. Foundations require shoring up.' He spoke in rasping breaths and leant on a ledge at the perimeter of the model.

'I could take a look?' Jack stepped into the light. 'I know a bit about tunnels.'

The man nodded. The train was at the limits of the model, a space painted black like a void. He began a slow shamble around the cityscape. Jack smelled piss and his own father flashed into his mind; then, just as quickly, he was gone.

The model, on a base just over a metre high and perhaps five metres square, filled the attic. The base was boxed in, Jack was impressed to see, with drawers and cubbyholes labelled with materials for redevelopment and repair. Beneath a work table on the other side of the room were stacked cardboard, ply, tin, lengths of wire and panels of MDF. Bags of sand were piled like a flood defence. Sacks of cement and plaster sagged beside a rack holding sheets of glass. Small pots of enamel paint on a shelf were gradated in order of colour, white leading down to black. The old man had everything needed to maintain a model of such size and detail.

Jack found a trapdoor beneath the model; he scooted along a crawl space on his hands and knees, trying not to inhale the odour of ammonia or consider why his hands and trousers were damp. Between a bundle of wiring clamped with a plastic strap he found a hatch; he pulled down the door and stood up.

To the east was a looping span bridge and to the west an outcrop of land that would become an island when the tide came in. Chiswick Eyot. Jack felt a stirring of excitement. He was down-river from the Bell Steps in Hammersmith and could climb the slippery stairway to Hammersmith Terrace and walk along Black Lion Lane to the subway tunnel under the Great West Road. He shut his eyes and breathed in the warm air, heavy with slick river mud and heard an aeroplane heading for Heathrow and the honks of geese flying in a 'v' down river.

It was the London Borough of Hammersmith and Fulham. The model was not for architects or engineers, trees were not circles on sticks, buildings were not blocks of white folded card-board, perhaps with windows and doors pencilled in. It did not rely on symbolism to get the point across and nor did it provide the bland specificity of the planned developments exhibited in town hall foyers to ignite the imagination of those who would inhabit or use the proposed buildings. This model was a precise imitation of life.

There were lights in some houses; residents were still up at this late hour. A van like those used by Clean Slate was travelling along King Street where a miniature witness appeal notice signalled a traffic accident. Soon the van would pass Mallingswood House where a light in the attic dimly glowed. Grass in Ravenscourt Park was of different greens, diagonal browning strips detailing the desire paths of short cuts. Coarse weeds, nettles and buddleia sprouted from concrete ballast supporting the riverbank on the south side below St Paul's playing fields. Jack picked out road markings, a granite drinking trough for horses, a yellow salt bin: faithful renditions of street furniture. From his *A–Z* journeys Jack knew their positioning was accurate. There were buses, lorries, tankers and vans. Some of Stella's fleet. The only exception to the veracity of the miniature urban landscape was the cars. They were all family saloons and they were all grey.

The sides of the tunnel by Barons Court station were crumbling and when he peered inside he saw sifts of plaster dust on the track, the rails lit by a sprinkling of light from the pock-marked roof.

'How old is this?' Jack enquired.

'Companies don't honour contracts.' The man was fiddling with the mesh fence around the tennis courts in Ravenscourt Park. Again Jack thought of his father, who in his last years neglected personal hygiene. He had let him help with his work, what little there had been of it.

'It's wear and tear. We could repair it, but the plaster of Paris is perishing so will undermine the work. You're better off demolishing it and reinstating with new material. More trouble, but worth it.'

'Good lad.' The man rubbed his hands. 'Get on with it then.'

Jack had won the contract. He ducked out of the model and went over to the work table. He contemplated the tools hung from hooks at its side. All he needed was here. He returned to the model and lightly ran his fingers over roads, the points of parapets and turrets, feeling the solidity of rounded kerbstones and the roughness of the tarmac. He tackled the tunnel mouth with an exploratory tug; it held fast. From the hooks, he selected a scout knife with an ivory handle. 'We must excise this without damaging the surrounding area.' He teased at the plaster with the tip of the blade.

The old man was tightening the nets in the tennis courts; he must trust Jack.

The blade was sharp. Jack caught it on his thumb and broke the skin. A bead of bright red blood welled up.

A key scratched in the lock of the door at the other end of the passage.

Seventeen

Wednesday, 25 April 2012

Stella clasped the brass knocker – an owl with a puffed chest and a cross expression – and rapped it on the strike plate three times. The reverberation died away. Most people would resent a caller at six in the morning. Jack was not 'most people'.

She confirmed there was no one on the pavement and against her better judgement raised the letterbox and looked in. A draught of cold air greeted her. She gave a succession of dog-like sniffs: beeswax furniture polish and soap. It might be early, but she didn't think Jack was there.

Her mobile phone was ringing. Jackie.

'You're up?' Stella was glad she had rung; the world was turning as it should. She returned to the road, reluctant for Jackie to know she was outside Jack's house because then she would ask why and Stella, unable to lie to her, would have to explain about the blue folder, and then – going into 'lame-duck' mode – Jackie would say it was grief for her dad and offer to help Stella clear his house.

'Beverly diverted the calls to me instead of the answer machine. I was woken by a new client demanding a job urgently. She's not properly new; it's that Mrs Hampson. Ring a bell?'

'The one who sacked us for using bleach instead of tea tree?' Such a woman would ring at all hours although this was a new record.

Stella had parked the van outside Terry's house. Phone in one hand, she unlocked the door and got in to avoid waking up the street.

'That's her. She made no mention of it, but I had a feeling so plugged her into the new database and three years ago there she was!'

'Did you refuse?'

'I was cagey but warm and no, I didn't.'

'We don't want a customer who tells us how to clean.' Stella was nettled. Mrs Hampson had been no loss.

'Blimey, Stell, then we don't want customers! Mrs Hampson was the woman whose husband was killed. You can go weird when someone dies.' Jackie added quietly: 'I said we'd find her someone appropriate.'

'Does that someone exist?' Stella generally appreciated Jackie's 'can do' approach; saying 'yes' when Stella wanted to say 'no' had meant that in a recession Clean Slate was gaining clients.

'Shelley takes no prisoners, but her hands are full with her mum and that nursing home. Wendy has no more hours in her life and while Donette would be perfect she's on the police job and there's her grandchildren. I thought Jack Harmon.'

Stella closed her eyes. Everyone wanted Jack. Where was he? Last night he had said nothing about being away. 'I'll do it,' she decided. 'When does she want it?'

'Today, but thanks to me, you're lumbered with that peculiar deep-cleaning work for Mr Barlow in Aldensley Road. Stella, you are the boss. Someone has to steer the ship, you're doing a lot of clean—'

'It's not peculiar,' Stella snapped. A lot of cleaning was how she liked it.

'Speaking of the police, their admin woman rang. No grass grows there. She's sent the contract and wants it signed yesterday.'

'I'll call Jack about Mrs Hampson.'

'I have. He's going in this afternoon. I'm calling you because I thought it would get your day off to a good start knowing this.'

'Did he answer?'

'Of course he did.'

Stella was driving past the petrol station on King Street when she noticed again that the petrol gauge was on empty. She was due at the police station in twenty minutes: she risked being late. She pulled on to the forecourt.

In her haste she pressed the option to pay in the shop instead of at the pump. There was no one else about, so at least there would be no queue. She squeezed the handle on the nozzle, leaning away to avoid the fumes when diesel spurted into the tank. She urged the numbers on the pump to roll around faster.

An orange Ford Fiesta drew up on the other side of the pump island while Stella was replacing the fuel cap. Horrible colour, she thought fleetingly as she ran into the shop.

There was no one on the till. She dumped her bag loudly on to the counter and jumped when a shadow fell across the rack of chocolate beside her. She turned in time to see a man, balding with strands of flyaway hair, by the snacks section, pulling apart a box that had contained crisps. He looked vaguely familiar, but a lot of men looked like him. Nondescript.

'Just petrol?' He spoke so quietly that had she not guessed what he must have said, she would not have got it.

'I'm in a hurry.' Stella's purse was not in the usual compartment in her rucksack. She looked up to apologize. The man had vanished. He reappeared by the till as if in a magic act and, leaning forward as if shackled, switched on the till with a key attached to a plastic coil around his neck.

'Take your time, it will be there,' he said helpfully.

'I always have it on me.' Stella shook the rucksack and plunged her hand into the pockets again. No purse. It was on the dining table in her flat. Last night she had cleared out her receipts and shredded stuff she didn't need. So much for efficiency.

'Stella! Can I help?'

Stella wheeled around. Clean-shaven, dark glasses, immaculate hair swept back from proverbially chiselled features. In his lounge, overtaken by the opportunity to deep clean, Stella had not properly appreciated how good-looking David Barlow was even so early in the morning.

'Oh hello,' she said. 'I've forgotten my purse and—'

'Do let me.' He opened a wallet bristling with plastic cards and approached the till.

'No, really...' Stella began.

'That won't be necessary, sir.' The man was chalk-white and beads of moisture pricked his forehead. He stared at the sweets stacked in front of the counter.

'Are you all right?' Stella tried to dredge up her first-aid training. She glanced behind her, but other than David, there was no one in the shop.

The man nodded. 'You can charge it to your account.' He addressed the Twix bars.

'I don't have an account.'

'You do.'

'If she says she doesn't—' David Barlow interjected pleasantly.

'Jacqueline Makepeace opened one for Clean Slate six months ago.' He blinked quickly at Stella.

'There must be a mistake. How do you know where I work?'

'I'm happy to cover this lady's costs. She can confirm later if there is an account with her office.' David Barlow had a credit card in his hand.

The attendant looked at Stella. 'Your company name is on your van.' He might have been imparting a secret. Rapidly he tapped at the till. A receipt ground out of the top, he tore it off and passed it to Stella. 'Jackie will tell you.'

'I'm sure you're right.' Stella made a mental note to use the newest van in the fleet, still plain white; Jackie wouldn't approve, but she didn't need people knowing her business. Literally. She needed to get on, but after his kindness, thought she'd better wait for David Barlow. 'Thank you,' she said when he joined her outside by the logs and throwaway barbeques.

'It was nothing. Man's a nervous wreck – drinker probably. His hands were shaking when he took my card. He could have taken your details, account or not. It happened to my wife; she hates – hated to fall foul of the law.' He looked at her over the top of his sunglasses. 'Do at least let me buy you a coffee – or breakfast?'

The yellow wool scarf knotted around his collar complemented the soft brown leather of his jacket. David Barlow had an air of precision; he would not forget his wallet.

'I'm late for work.' She was surprised to note a twinge of regret.

'Since I retired, I forget others have jobs to go to! A drink one evening perhaps? Or if you don't mix business—'

'It would be a pleasure.' Stella was startled by a horn. The forecourt was busy; a car was queuing for the pump.

'Tomorrow night? There's a pub by the river – oh, I'll see you later today!'

As she drove off the forecourt Stella tried to corral a swoop of worries. The point of Clean Slate's details being on the vans was to be noticed, yet Stella was uneasy when they did. She had agreed to dinner with a client she didn't know, who must after all be trawling for a new wife. Jackie had dubbed the job 'peculiar' and she was never wrong. Barlow had retired early; he could do his own cleaning. In her rear mirror she saw David Barlow getting into the orange Ford Fiesta. Out of Stella's concerns, the colour of his car disturbed her the most.

Stella had forgotten she kept her watch three minutes fast, a trick of Terry's, so when she parked in the station compound she was bang on time. Metres away stood Wendy, Clean Slate's first recruit, now in her fifties, and Donette who, though tall like Stella, seemed small beside a huge horse in Metropolitan livery being led out from the stables.

By the time she had helped carry the cleaning gear into the station Stella had decided she would tell David Barlow she was busy so couldn't meet him. He had caught her on the hop; she should not have accepted.

She trundled her cleaning trolley to the door of what was once

Terry's office and out of the blue recalled Suzie's request for Jack to clean. Her mum would need a reliable cleaner. Martin Cashman's name was on the door. Hardly a surprise, yet she was taken aback. Staring at it, Stella admitted that around her mum she wasn't reliable. She cancelled her if another job came up. Jackie was right: Jack was reliable. He would handle the difficult Amanda Hampson and he would handle Suzie.

Despite the nameplate, when Stella pushed open the office door it was Detective Chief Superintendent Darnell that she expected to see.

Eighteen

Monday, 2 May 1966

Voices crackled on the car radio; the words were mangled and made no sense. Mary gazed out of the window at street after street that she did not know. The policewoman in front was talking into a thing on a telephone cord. Mary caught 'foxtrot'. It was about Br'er Fox. She was stunned. Instead of Michael, Br'er Fox was going to eat her.

'... we're ... Mary Thornton ... to the parents ... in Hammersmith. Arriving now...'

Mary's eyes smarted; she was not going to die. The police car swung off the main road and she saw the sign for the new street: British Grove.

The policewoman pulled her out of the car. Mary's satchel fell into the gutter, the strap around her ankle. She banged her head on the door, but acted like she hadn't. The nice policeman who had given her a biscuit and orange juice was walking up the path.

'Police Constable Terry Darnell, I'm happy to report that this little one's as right as rain...'

Her mum hugged her so tightly she was lifted up and reached the house without moving her feet. She watched from the living room to see the nice man wave. He had told her his wife was having a baby. He would be a dad like her dad. He said he would be very sad indeed if it was a little girl and she ran away from him. Mary didn't say that her dad liked boys best, that he wasn't really her dad or that she wouldn't run away from the nice policeman. No one called her little – that was Michael. She wished they did.

Mary gave a tiny wave when the police car moved off, but he was talking to the policewoman and didn't see.

She discovered that she was not in trouble. She and Michael had beans on toast and a glass of milk for tea and her dad behaved as if they had both come home from school. Her mum watched them eat like she used to in the old house. Everything was back to normal.

Mary was three years older than Michael and since coming to the new house her bedtime had been promoted to eight o'clock, an hour later than his – a source of triumph for Mary and dismay for Michael. That evening neither child commented when they were put to bed at seven.

Mary submitted to the routine of washing, burrowing into her nightdress, cleaning her teeth and kissing goodnight. The point when Jean Thornton shut the door would be a signal for Mary to switch on her torch and read under the covers. Tonight she lay stiff as a board, staring at a spear of moonlight on the ceiling.

After a while, she could not have said how long, she saw her bedroom door handle turn and the door jerked open.

Michael was on the landing, hair sticking up, his pyjama jacket collar half turned in with one trouser leg bunched up. He waited until Mary struggled up to sit with her knees under her chin and then scampered into the room. He stopped and, returning to the door, shut it carefully without letting the latch click. He launched himself on to her bed. The springs groaned under his weight and something under his jacket rustled.

'I brought you this,' he confided in a hoarse whisper.

His sister did not move.

'Mrs Berry gave it to me.' He pulled out a bar of Cadbury's milk chocolate from his pyjama jacket with the flourish of a hankie from a hat. It had been opened and the foil was folded inadequately over the exposed chocolate. 'Because I was very good when Mummy and Daddy were with the police. She told me not to give any to you. I have to have it all to myself because it's mine.' This information was uttered in a rasping hiss. Mary leant closer to catch it. 'She made me have some of it with her looking.'

'Who is Mrs Berry?' Mary forgot to talk quietly.

'She's our new naay-bore.' Michael pronounced the word with some pride.

'Why can't I have any?' Mary already hated Mrs Berry. She aimed her torch at Michael.

'Because of what you did.' He sounded uncertain of the facts and brandished the bar under her nose. 'I said I would save it for later. That was a good trick.' He beamed.

'Why did you say that? You never save things.'

'So that you could have some. We always share and I would have told her, but I don't think she would of let me keep it if I had of.' He pivoted the bar on his sister's knees; it see-sawed when he shuffled up the bed to her.

Mary took the bar and sat cross-legged beside Michael. She peeled back the foil. The chocolate had softened from being next to his skin. She tore off a soft segment, covering her fingers with chocolate, and handed it back to Michael. 'Don't get it on your pyjamas.' She ripped off a smaller bit for herself.

The children munched ruminatively. They looked out at the rooftops beyond their new back garden. A light was on in one of the windows. A woman was sitting there. Every now and then she put up a hand and then lowered it. The square of light could be hanging in space.

'She's reading,' Mary murmured.

'How do you know?' Michael breathed in her ear as he strained to see.

'She does it every night.'

'I think she might be painting a picture.' Michael spoke seriously.

Mary handed him more chocolate, but did not take any herself. She had not liked to tell Michael she did not want it, that she had no appetite and the beans were still there, lurking like enemies. She tucked the rest into the foil and slipped it within the paper sleeve. She placed it beneath her pillow.

'That's for tomorrow night.' She wiped her mouth with her hand.

'Shall I come at the same time?'

'What is the time?'

'I don't know.'

'Come when you hear the television go on.'

Michael clambered off the bed and, scuttling over the rug, sneaked out of the door with exaggerated determination. As he was about to shut it he stopped and regarded his sister, still sitting on top of the bedclothes.

'Mary?'

'What?'

'I'm glad you didn't run away after all.' In the dark room, the moonlight made Michael pale, less substantial.

'Come back tomorrow for the rest.' Mary hopped under the blankets. The chocolate paper rustled when she repositioned her pillow. 'Thanks for sharing.'

The door closed.

The following night, mechanically eating her way through the rest of the bar, Mary decided that the woman in the window was painting a picture.

Nineteen

David Barlow was on the doorstep when Stella arrived at Aldensley Road. She preferred clients to be out while she cleaned but, maybe because she was deep cleaning, today she did not mind. She would put off telling him she would not meet him until she had finished; she wanted to enjoy the shift. When David Barlow offered to carry in her brand-new room sanitizer, she let him.

'Here are details of the pub I suggest, I've put in the post code so your navigation system can find it and my number should you have to cancel. I am crossing my fingers that you won't have to.'

Stella took the note, in fact a sheet of Basildon Bond writing paper, the sort on which Suzie had made her write 'thank you' letters when she was little. This memory and the trouble that David Barlow had taken confounded her and she could not think how to reply.

'I'm going out. I need to go to the cemetery, tend her grave.' He lifted up a bunch of flowers from the hall table. 'The place is yours.' He looked about him, seemingly impressed by Stella's equipment lined up in the hallway: the floor scrubber-drier, carpet cleaner and the Planet vacuum cleaner. He added, 'Please clean absolutely everywhere. No stone unturned!'

'Of course.' Stella felt a stirring of excitement.

'A fresh beginning.' Barlow brandished his bouquet and, stooping down, hauled up a plastic tub from beneath the table. 'No more delaying. I must do Jennifer proud.'

'Creating Life from Glass': the tub contained twenty kilos of 'Festive Green Aggregate (Jade)'. Stella started to lift it, but it was too heavy.

'Let me.' David Barlow swung it up. 'For the grave. Saves the time spent weeding.'

A great one for saving time. Stella vaguely thought weeding was good for grief. She was starting in the bathroom. She gathered up her equipment bag, which bulged with boxes of disposable gloves and aprons, antibiotic wipes and disinfectant scented with woodland pine to dissolve all grease and banish germs.

On the half-landing she noticed that the layout was the same as her dad's house. Typical Victorian terrace with one door on the first landing, two on the second landing, the far one was probably Barlow's bedroom, as at her dad's house it had been his. Again she remembered the time she had gone to her dad's house after his death. Stella shivered and gripped the disinfectant. She had no time for ghosts.

She knew from scoping the job that this bathroom, unlike Terry's clinical white, was a mix of sickly colours like the orange Ford. No doubt it was the dead wife's taste. Stella recoiled again at the scalloped suite, the shell shape echoed in the 'sea-bed' pattered shower curtain. Pink tiles offset custard yellow walls. Only the ceiling was white. Stella suspected Jennifer Barlow had ruled the roost. She did so from beyond the grave soon to be decorated with jade aggregate. He might regret his invitation to supper; it was too soon. Stella would leave a note letting him off the hook.

She wheeled in the floor scrubber and stopped. On her last visit she had not noticed the coved flooring. A mandatory feature in hospitals and other hygienic environments, she had never seen it in a house. She considered David's pristine appearance, his specific efficiency; the coving would have been his idea. He was serious about hygiene.

So was Stella. She set to work.

The next two hours passed blissfully. She tackled the tiles, bleached grouting and scrubbed in corners, crevices and grooves.

She washed the walls and the ceiling and ran alcohol wipes down cords for shower, the light and the roller blind. This she dismantled to clean at sluice temperature on her own machine along with the shower curtain. She boiled kettle upon kettle of water, suspecting the tank of dead birds. There was little dirt. Stella began to suppose she was not the first to deep clean here. This was disquieting; if she was liable to jealousy it focused on those who had cleaned before her.

Had she been one to reflect, Stella would have agreed with Jack Harmon that the measurement of time was necessary only for punctuality and invoicing. Otherwise it got in the way. The afternoon shift was drawing to a close, but she didn't want to stop.

Stella's previous deep-cleaning client, Mrs Ramsay, had made her clean under the bath and in other places no one saw. David Barlow hadn't specifically requested she include this in the itinerary. Yet she would. Stella unscrewed the bath panel and slid it out. Here at last was dirt. The panel was streaked with cobwebs and furred with muck. She washed it over the bath. Soon water in the bath was grey; she let it out, pinched out strings of cobwebs clogging the plughole and tossed them into her rubbish bag. She switched on her torch and turned her attention to the cavity under the bath. Usually rational, Stella had been affected by Mrs Ramsay's fervid imagination and had dreaded discovering an animal, putrid and rotting, or worse, a human corpse. Now she banished the possibility from her mind.

She saw something. Her heart pounded.

Her fingers grappled with a stiff mound and she was grateful for the latex protection. She found purchase and hauled it out. It was a man's jacket. She laid it on top of the bath panel. The garment had been folded as if for sale in a shop, the sleeves crossed over the chest. Stella shivered; the jacket's pose and its rictus-like state did make her think of a dead person.

The fust of years pervaded the room. She gave several dog-like sniffs – her sense of smell was acute – and detected a faint suggestion of hair oil. Gingerly she unfolded the jacket. It had narrow lapels and the material could be seersucker. Engrained with grime, it was the grey of the bath water, but beneath the lapel the material was a pale blue. Stella didn't know anything about the history of fashion, but Suzie had grumbled that when she met in him in 1965, Terry was a Mod, trim in his suit and two-tone winkle-pickers down the Hammersmith Palais on a Saturday night. In natty outfits and free with his wages, Terry had hoodwinked her because after they married the dancing stopped. Stella resisted reminding her mother that weeks after they married she was born. Nights at the Hammersmith Palais would have been a rare treat.

The jacket had been under the bath a long time. It wasn't David Barlow's; he would be careful with his clothes. It would belong to a plumber or someone. She slipped it into a bin bag and replaced the panel, leaving slack in the screws should he ask her to clean there again. She trundled in the ultra-violet sanitizer and programmed it to run for half an hour.

David Barlow had not returned by the time she had finished. Stella was irritated; how much work did a grave need? Mrs Barlow had only been dead a few months. Stella had opted to have Terry cremated. She had no grave to tend. Or to visit.

She hesitated over whether to pop the jacket into the dry cleaner's by her office, but doubtless Barlow would throw it out. She left it out for him to decide.

She loaded up the van. No sign of his orange car. She would have liked him to see her work, to confirm it was what he wanted. She drove out of Aldensley Road. Driving down Shepherd's Bush Road, Stella realized she hadn't left a note cancelling dinner. Perhaps after all she would meet David Barlow.

Twenty

'Mrs Hampson.'

'Clean Slate?' A sharply dressed woman in her forties held the door of a 1960s house in Kew half open.

Jack Harmon lifted the plastic card around his neck on which 'Clean Slate' was written in blue. The woman looked familiar. But he had noticed that this happened more and more. He saw a lot of people.

'I was expecting a woman.' She was stern.

'People often do.' Jack let the card drop. He was happy to leave it; his new Host had left the school early that morning and, delayed by Jackie's call, he had lost track of her. She had taken the A–Z; it wasn't in her bedroom.

'You'd better come in.' Mrs Hampson let go of the door and went inside, saying over her shoulder, 'Don't do my meditation temple, it's circular so doesn't attract dirt.'

Jack collected up the Henry vacuum and heaved in the cumbersome green and blue bag of materials. There was no sign of Mrs Hampson. His job sheet stipulated he begin in the kitchen so he snapped on his blue rubber gloves and got started.

The room had a modern Scandinavian feel: light wood and a bright open aspect, helped by a large window that framed an overgrown lawn. He pictured walking across the springy turf and felt a tingling. Mrs Hampson must be in the house, yet there was a profound quiet not unlike that in the school. A quiet he had learnt not to trust.

At first glance he couldn't see what needed doing, surfaces gleamed in the afternoon sunshine. But when he got to work on the sink, he found scum around the plughole and the taps, streaks of grime on the stainless-steel splashback and a greasy residue on the hob. A veil of dirt shrouded the room. This was the years of accumulation that Stella relished. No wonder Jackie had circumvented her in favour of him. Stella would never run the business if she did jobs like this. This reminded him that Stella had talked about a case. Odd she hadn't been around to his house first thing. He wrung out his cloth and groaned. Stella would have knocked and got no answer. She would ask where he had been and he could not tell her.

It was half past four; he was on schedule with just the sitting room to clean and the house to vacuum. He would stay longer than an hour if necessary. Jack felt vaguely that this would make amends to Stella for his night-time activities. With the vacuum in his arms he padded along the hallway and opened the sitting-room door.

'Oh!' he exclaimed.

Mrs Hampson was seated at a desk by the French doors, staring at papers strewn over the surface.

'Did I frighten you?' She did not look up, a pen poised.

'I didn't expect you to be here.' Jack lowered the vacuum cleaner. 'I thought you had gone out. This room's on my list, but if you'd rather...'

'I would hardly leave you alone.' Mrs Hampson flung down her pen and swung around to face him.

'I can do the vacuuming first.' Jack understood his unease in the kitchen and what was wrong now.

He had been here before. He had stood on that patio outside two nights ago. This was the room he had seen through the glass. Mrs Hampson had been where she sat now.

On the wall above the fireplace was the man in grey. Jack saw that while a smile played over full sensuous lips, the eyes were cold. The painting, or rather the photograph scanned on to canvas, was no less life-life up close.

Jack did not choose True Hosts at random. He could come across them by chance. That he knew them on sight was due to intuition. He spent time following them before he accepted a tacit invitation to stay. Those who risked cutting along a secluded towpath or dark alley must have a mind like his own. He divined that they had either done a dreadful deed or were planning one. True Hosts spread unease at best and misery at worst. Jack styled himself a saviour. Detectives finds murderers because only by the flip of a coin are they not a murderer themselves. Jack believed himself of the same cast as his Hosts and dreaded that one day the coin would flip again and he would become a Host. Until last night he had kept his promise to Stella to stop looking for Hosts, he had assured her it was over. That he found himself back here was a sign.

'That's an imposing picture.' Jack broke Stella's cardinal rule about commenting on clients' possessions or their homes. If she knew what other rules he had broken this would seem paltry.

'It's my husband.'

Mr Hampson was a Host. 'He must be pleased with it.' Jack gave the frame a flick with his duster. It came away thick with dust.

'He's dead. Didn't they tell you?'

'I'm only told what I need to know for each job.' Jackie had told him and of course he had guessed the other night. Jack got more out of people by feigning innocence.

'You need to know Charlie has been dead three years.' Mrs Hampson stood up. 'Did you use bleach?'

'Tea-tree concentrate.' Jack was prompt.

'He was killed at some time after eleven on the evening of Sunday the fifteenth of March, 2009.' She came over and, putting out a hand, stroked the frame, seeming not to notice that her finger came away blackened.

'I'm sorry.' Jack set down the vacuum cleaner. He resisted telling her that he had been thirty-two on that day and could remember what he had been doing.

'He was due home at seven. He was area sales manager and did ridiculous hours driving around his territory – West London, Surrey, some of Hampshire – and on a Sunday, poor love.' Mrs Hampson looked sharply at the portrait as if she sensed contradiction. 'He rang me at six saying something had come up and he would be late. We were going out, the table booked for eight. He said, "Don't cancel, get the last sitting." He would not have done it.'

'Done what?' Jack was glad Stella was not there to see him crash through the rules. 'Let clients talk. Do not engage them in conversation on personal matters. Keep cleaning throughout or afterwards they will blame you.'

'Killed himself. Suicide. Took his own life. Took it where?' She sat down at the desk. 'They insinuated Charlie was having an affair and couldn't cope. "Dumb wife blind to what's under her nose" was written all over their faces. Meetings on a Sunday; all men tell lies to unsuspecting spouses. He'd completed expensive dental treatment only days before. Why would he do that if he planned to be dead? Sodding waste of money since his head smashed through the windscreen.' She snatched up the pen again, holding it above the papers on her desk as if about to pounce.

Jack regarded Charles Hampson. The man's chilly smile revealed flawless teeth.

'At first they were sorry for me. You get sympathy if you lick your wounds and go quietly. Then I came out fighting and, boy, did that put them off!'

'Who are "they"?' Jack pulled the flex out of the vacuum but then stopped; it felt inappropriate to clean, even though that was why he was here.

'The boys in blue, the sickly coroner, our so-called friends and my family – such as they are. Two motley cousins. "Don't fool yourself, Amanda dear, face facts." I couldn't stand it and now I don't have to. No one invites "the Widow" to dinner – not even to a party. They pretend I'm dead too.'

She had the low, cracked voice of a heavy smoker, although Jack couldn't detect smoke on her or in the room.

'I told the policeman, "If you won't get to the truth, I will."' She stirred the papers on her table with the pen.

'What do you think happened?' Charles Hampson had a portentous air. Beringed hands clasped, he could be peeing.

'Not what I think.' Mrs Hampson grabbed some pages and rattled them at Jack. 'I know. Charlie's car came off the road. I called him at ten past eleven and couldn't get through. That was normal, he turns his phone off for meetings but I was fretting. I had the table until midnight – if it had been anyone but Charlie they would have let it go, but people did anything for him. I was calling him for the umpteenth time when the doorbell went.'

In the pause, Jack imagined he could hear the bell ring. 'Don't feel you have to—'

'He died instantly. They assured me he felt nothing – as if that was consolation.'

'Wasn't it?'

Mrs Hampson shot Jack a look. 'Of course it was, I don't want him to have suffered. But suicide? The man was happy. Why kill himself?' Mrs Hampson reached for a plastic carrier bag by the desk and brought it on to her lap. She pulled out a newspaper and, unfolding it, jabbed at the print, motioning to Jack.

She had been talking for fifteen minutes. Jack would not finish on time; the job was slipping away from him. He joined her at the desk.

It was a copy of the *Fulham & Hammersmith Chronicle* and was dated Thursday, 19 March 2009. Mrs Hampson prodded an announcement about a forthcoming Japanese Garden Party to be held in the borough. Jack was puzzled until underneath he saw the piece reporting a fatal car accident the previous Sunday on Phoenix Way on the Phoenix Industrial Estate. The driver was Charles Hampson, aged fifty-four, a sales manager for AVCOM Technology. Mr Hampson was dead on arrival at Charing Cross Hospital on the Fulham Palace Road. His BMW, a brand-new vehicle, the report stated, swerved off the road, glanced against a tree and finally smashed through a wall.

'His teams were exceeding targets. He was due a whacking bonus and had promised me a Lexus. His car was a week old. Had he wanted to do something so fucking stupid, it would not have involved his beloved Beemer.' She glared up at Jack. 'It was not suicide.'

'It was an accident.' Jack nodded, at a loss as to how to resume cleaning without appearing crass. Mrs Hampson seemed to have forgotten why he was there. Soon she would remember and demand a refund for dawdling.

'It was not an accident!' She leapt up and barged past him, stopping by the sitting-room door.

'What do you think happened?' Stella's rules had never seemed more sensible.

'I know what happened.' Mrs Hampson pointed a jabbing finger at the portrait. 'Charlie was murdered.'

Jack stowed everything into the van. He opened the driver's door and with a sigh got in.

'You're running late.'

With a yelp he scrabbled at the door, his instinct to jump out and scream for help.

Stella was sitting in the passenger seat.

'We need to talk,' she said. 'Go round the corner.'

'I won't charge overtime.' Jack turned on the ignition and took the van unsteadily down a little road on their left. He stalled the engine before he could brake.

'Yes you will, don't be silly.' Stella twisted around and leant back on the door facing him, her rucksack on her lap. She rummaged in it and produced two flasks; she passed one to Jack. 'There's hot milk and honey in yours. I've got tea.' She busied herself pouring tea into her cup.

After a sip of the hot sweet liquid Jack brightened: 'What do you know about Amanda Hampson?' He did not mention he had seen her before. It would involve him confessing how he came to be there.

'Ex-customer come back to haunt us after three years in the wilderness. We lost the job over using bleach. Did Jackie say?' She raised her eyebrows. When Jack nodded, she went on. 'Husband dead. Cancer, I think. Tell me there were no hiccups.'

'He was killed in a car crash. Mrs Hampson says he was murdered. She's trying to get the police to reopen the case. They're not interested.' Their drinks had made the windscreen steam up so he rubbed a porthole in the glass. 'I'm guessing they think she's potty. She swears Hampson had no enemies and was popular at work. He sold process software of some kind.' He blew on the hot liquid.

'How did he die?'

'Car accident. I just said.'

'Literally.'

'He hit a tree and then a wall, he must have been going fast.'

'I'd say so. What's the problem, does she think the brakes were tampered with?'

'The car was new. She has no evidence for murder.'

'Sounds far-fetched. Was the verdict "Accidental Death"?'

'No, it was "Narrative" – a catch-all for when nothing else will do. She is sure they think it was suicide. She said he would have left a note.'

'Not if he'd wanted her to collect on the insurance.'

'I doubt Charlie-boy would be that considerate.' Jack pictured the ice-blue eyes of the man in grey. 'Hampson told his sister three weeks before he died that he was furious at losing a sales pitch, but Amanda Hampson says that's nonsense, he was on top of his job and his sister is, quote: "a stirrer". They don't get on.'

'She can't accept it was an accident. She said we used bleach on purpose.'

'Perhaps she was right,' Jack said without thinking. Seeing Stella was about to protest, he added: 'It is a mystery why Hampson left the road. It was straight with no parked cars. The only thing was the weather. That night it was foggy.'

'Was he drunk?'

'No, and there's no mention in his diary of the meeting he

said he had. Although he told Amanda it was last-minute, which could explain that.'

'He was lying.'

'He was lying to someone. She says he always told her the truth. Oh, and there was no CCTV.'

'He was having an affair and drove too fast to get back in time.' Stella drank her tea. 'People assume their partners tell them the truth, erroneously usually.'

'You have to assume a level of trust or you go mad,' Jack countered. Stella was cynical about relationships.

'People are blind to reality if it suits them not to rock the boat. It means they don't have to have sex, but get companionship; they keep the status quo and the lifestyle. Some people would rather live with betrayal than be on their own.'

Jack poured more milk into the flask cup and breathed in the steam. She had a point there.

'It's a pact with the devil,' Stella said. 'Those people keep a clean house.' She sipped her drink in silence as if digesting this idea.

'Amanda Hampson would have clouted me if I had hinted her husband was meeting someone,' Jack said at last.

Stella screwed the cup back on her flask. 'It's open and shut.' She could have been meaning the flask.

'Anyway, she likes my work and wants me every week.' Jack drained his cup. 'Because, as she put it, I "understand".'

'We'd better allow two and a half hours: she'll want to chat on to you about her "murdered husband".'

'I'll try to avoid it.'

'Make allowances. Tea-tree and sympathy: that's what you can offer!' Stella sniffed at her pun.

'You don't make jokes. What's happened? Is this the case you mentioned last night?'

'Will you clean for my mother for two hours twice a week? If you go in the late afternoon it will give her time to make a mess and lose stuff for you to fail to find.' She stuffed the flask back in the rucksack.

'Yes of course.' Jack looked at her. 'And the case?'

Stella reached into her rucksack and produced a blue plastic ring binder.

'See what you make of that.'

Twenty-One

'Your brother's crying. He wants you.' A red-faced boy rushed up to Mary Thornton. She ignored him, her attention on a boy waiting by the wall. In the two playtimes that day, Mary had lobbied for children to meet her by the drinking fountain in the playground after school. She was methodical, her Brooke Bond cards – Trees of Britain – were arranged in ascending numeric order, bound by an elastic band. Even outside, they gave off a whiff of tea leaves. Mary had several swaps.

Only Douglas Ford was here. A head shorter than Mary and painfully thin, the boy had knobbly knees and eyes that blinked when he spoke: easy pickings for teasing. He had forty-seven cards stuck crookedly on to the flimsy pages of his album.

He wanted Mary's Yew (Number 9) and Sycamore (Number 13). With these two swaps he would have forty-nine and only needed the Holm or Evergreen Oak (Number 43) to have the set of fifty. Mary had thirty-six. Douglas was offering her the Holly (leaf and berries), which she didn't have, and the English Elm, which she did. Her dream of being the first in the class to fill her album was slipping away. She was holding him off, hoping for more comers.

'He's asking for you right now.' The smaller boy ran on the spot.

'Is this all you've got?' Mary demanded, waving the album at Douglas.

'Michael's hurt,' the boy persisted.

'You could swap the Elm with someone else,' Douglas replied helpfully. 'Could I at least have the Yew in return for the Holly please? It's a bit more rare.' He twitched, his eyes shutting. His album was firmly in the new girl's possession; one hand fluttered impotently towards it.

'Michael wants you.' The smaller boy tugged at Mary's sleeve.

'It's rude to interrupt.' She shook him off. The Holly would add to Mary's collection, but would give Douglas Ford a terrible lead. The sun was hot on her bare shoulders. She eased the straps on her sundress.

'Michael says to get your mum.'

Mary came up with the perfect deal. 'Meet me under the last railway arch in five minutes.' She nodded to Douglas to confirm it was an order not a suggestion. She slipped the elastic band from her fingers on to her cards and dropped them into the ample pocket of her dress.

Douglas's eyes were screwed tight shut. 'I'm to go home. Nan'll kill me.'

'Don't answer back.' Mary was Miss Crane. She drew herself up: 'It's either that or no Yew for you.'

'You have to come now!'

Mary looked down at the boy at her elbow. 'I don't have to do anything.' She pulled her satchel strap over her head, arranging it across her chest. 'Where is he?'

She did not hurry. The boy rushed off around the corner to the Infants' playground. Mary sauntered behind. The boy tore across the asphalt, dodging the last of the infants straggling out of the gates to waiting parents and stopped by wide shallow steps that led to a circle of grass which Mary had learnt was the called Sunken Garden. Becoming an instant signpost, the boy pointed at a forlorn figure in baggy shorts and scuffed Clarks sandals hunched in the centre, his bright red pullover pulled over his knees. Mary trotted down the steps and over the grass. Michael had one arm around his crooked knees. His other arm hung limp as if it did not belong to him. He watched his older sister impassively.

'What's the matter?'

Fresh tears brimmed and the little boy dashed at them with a grubby palm.

'I fell over.'

'You tripped, you mean.' She stood with her hands on her hips. 'You look all right. Come on, it's late.'

'It hurts.' Michael cradled his right arm in his left hand. 'I can't write.'

'You can't write anyway and you don't need to now because it's home-time.' Mary grabbed her brother's right wrist.

He blanched when she swung his hand up then down and let it go. Silent tears flowed in earnest and he sniffed miserably while Mary peered at the dimpled arm. The skin, brown from the sun and dusted with dirt, was otherwise unmarked.

'Don't fuss.' She tossed back her hair, her voice low like Miss Crane's. 'There's no blood. Don't be a baby. Go on home, I'll be along.'

'What? Why? Where are you going?' Astonished at the new arrangement, Michael stopped crying. 'You're to get our tea.' He had learnt to rely on the newly established routine of his sister looking after him after school, however prone to sharp jabs and illogical tellings-off it was.

'You can get your own.' Mary was brisk. The idea that she did not have to look after her little brother every day was gaining momentum. 'You're seven now.'

'You've got the key to the house.'

She hesitated. If she gave Michael the key he might lock her out or lose it and then she would be in trouble. It was better that he wait on the front step for her.

She hauled him to his feet by his good arm and squeezing his hand led him out of the gate nearest to the Sunken Garden. This exit was by the sweet shop.

Mary spent the last of the change from last week's lunch money on a half-pound bag of Fruit Salad chews. This was more chews then either of them had ever seen. She resisted taking some for herself. Miss Crane did not eat sweets. Michael was not grateful and, irritated, Mary summarily stuffed the bag into his satchel.

By Ravenscourt Park station, Michael slowed to watch a newspaper vendor fix the latest headlines into a display case. The man smacked smooth the paper and snapped it behind the grille.

Moors Murderers Get Life.

Michael was behind with his reading as well as his writing, but he did recognize the 'M's in the headline as being from his and Mary's names. About to point this out, he was engulfed by a wave of nausea when his arm swung out. He concentrated on not being sick and stumbled along beside Mary.

Mary stopped by the park and bashed at her brother's blazer, brushing it down. 'When you get to the house, sit outside and have some sweets. Not too many, save your appetite. I won't be long,' she added more kindly and, sorting his collar, combed back his hair with her fingers.

She hurried into the park. On the other side of the viaduct tiny patches of sunlight penetrating the foliage looked like gold leaves scattered on the path. From the tennis courts came the pock-pock of rackets hitting balls; from somewhere else came girls' laughter. Mary saw no one but knew they were laughing at her.

At a break in the bushes she glimpsed the sandpit and paddling pool and faltered. She should have made Michael play there. She continued, reassuring herself that she would not get into trouble with her parents, for she had the perfect plan. Nothing could go wrong.

The arch with the slide was dark and silent: no children. The slide gleamed, tempting her inside, but she did not give in.

Under the next arch was the roundabout where she had seen Clifford Hunt smoking. A little girl was perched on it, going slowly round and round. Mary thought she was alone but then saw a lady, who kept still until the girl got near when she gave the roundabout a push. The girl saw Mary and twisted to keep looking at her until she was facing the other way. Before the lady saw her, Mary hurried on.

She hesitated by the next arch in case Douglas had got her instructions wrong and was here. Metal railings stood in front of the opening through which she counted lawn mowers, trimmers, rollers and tins of white paint, which she guessed was for the lines on the tennis court and football pitch. There were ladders at the back and a barrow for collecting leaves. Douglas was not there. The last arch was screened with sheets of corrugated iron but, as she expected, the door was open a tiny bit and she crept inside.

The walls were streaked with bird slime and snakes of moss where rainwater had got in. At Mary's feet lay fir cones and leaves. Sweet wrappers betrayed that other children came here. She smelled exhaust fumes and dog's mess and wrinkled her nose. She was alone.

Douglas Ford had disobeyed her. She charged towards the door and collided with something warm. She heard a gasp and reeled back.

Douglas cowered by the opening, his bag across his shoulder. Goose pimples on his legs disgusted Mary. She tugged at the hem of her dress, trying to conceal her own fear. He had been hiding in the bushes to scare her. It had worked.

They were a stone's throw from the playground and close to the high street, yet Mary Thornton had come to believe that they were far away from anyone. For a moment she understood she had set in train a misdemeanour more serious than running away. If she shouted, no one would hear.

'I don't have other swaps, only the Holly. I told you.' Douglas took out his album of cards and held it against his chest like a shield. Mary knew he wanted to make her jealous so she would give in.

'You can see under my dress.' She was businesslike.

Douglas blinked.

'Did we wash our ears this morning, Douglas Ford?' A pitch-perfect Miss Crane.

'See what?' Fixed on Trees of Britain, Douglas Ford was slow to comprehend.

'My knickers.'

'Oh.' He clicked the heels of his brown lace-up shoes together as if brought to attention.

An animal or a bird scrabbled in the foliage outside the arch.

'I've seen girl's knickers before.' Douglas was equivocal.

'Not all of it, you haven't.'

Douglas gripped the booklet and backed into the corrugated iron with a clang. Both children froze at the noise.

'And touch? With fingers?' He pursed his lips as if the words had escaped unbidden.

'No.'

Neither child moved.

'All right, but be quick.' Mary was her mother allowing ten more minutes before bedtime.

Douglas hesitated.

'Give me the cards first, stupid.'

'I don't have any to swap. Only the Holly,' he whispered. He was translucent pale in the dim light.

'You have the Common Lime with leaf and seeds, the Rowan, the Crab Apple, the London Plane, the Hawthorn without leaf and seeds, the—'

'They're stuck in. There's only my Holly for your Yew.' Teetering on the verge of the unknown, the boy stuck to the facts of life with which he was at home.

'Then you shan't see a thing.' Mary folded her arms. 'This is very disappointing, Douglas Ford, but I will draw a line under the incident.'

A twig snapped.

'How many?' Douglas spoke thickly, sensing a possible compromise.

'You give me all the cards I haven't got, that's fourteen including the Holly (leaf and berries).' Mary knew her collection off by heart.

Overhead a helicopter clattered. The ground trembled; the sound beat around the brick after the machine had passed overhead.

'All right,' Douglas breathed into the quiet.

Mary was a forbidding supervisor, while one by one Douglas tore each card from the page. Page after page. He made a hole in the paper when he ripped out the Hawthorn, and he stopped and looked pleadingly at Mary. She was steadfast. On he went with the painstaking task. On the back of each card, framed in blue, was the number in the series with a paragraph about the tree. Mary was saddened to see words blotted where Douglas had spotted glue; she preferred her cards to be clean.

It was the happiest feeling in the world when she lifted a new card out from among dry tea leaves in the packet and saw she did not already possess it. Recently she had not had this feeling. She had it now.

A rapid sum told Mary Thornton that she would have forty-nine cards and that even with her Yew and Sycamore, Douglas Ford would be nowhere near. It never occurred to Mary to take possession of the boy's book intact and swap it for her own. Perhaps that would have exposed the stark reality of her arrangement.

She retrieved her swaps from her dress pocket and slipping off the elastic band, slotted the new cards into the pile in number order. She stowed the fat bundle in her satchel. The entire procedure had taken no time at all so she would be home before her mum and dad. It had worked in two ways: she had not had to look after Michael and she had got more cards without needing a packet of tea and or having to find swaps.

It did not occur to Mary that Douglas Ford would not start a fight or tell anyone if she did not keep her part of their bargain. She had got what she had come for and could go. Perhaps her pragmatism did include a personal code of right and wrong.

She moved into the shadows of the far wall and whipped up her dress. Dull light illuminated her sturdy body and showed off her bright white knickers dotted with minute pink roses. Douglas gaped. With one hand, Mary caught at the elastic in her knickers and tugged them downwards. She shimmied them to her knees.

The gate in the barrier creaked and a face appeared. Mary yanked up her knickers. In one movement, she dragged her brother inside and backed him up against the wall. Michael's scream was shrill, cutting the air. She clamped her hand over his mouth.

Douglas crammed his depleted album, the denuded pages ripped and flimsy, into his bag. 'That wasn't enough time... could I have some cards back?' He was tremulous.

The ground vibrated with a rumble that grew louder and louder.

'You were spying!' Mary shook Michael. He was sheet-white, his arm limp, his body flopping with each jolt like a doll.

Michael's teeth chattered. 'It hu-uh-urts.'

'His arm looks funny.' Douglas took a tentative step forward. 'Actually, it might be broken,' he ventured. 'I broke my arm last year, a greenstick fracture.'

Neither sibling appeared to hear. The vibration made the corrugated iron hum.

Michael broke free of his sister and lurched towards the gate. He stopped and abruptly threw up; a torrent of multicoloured gloop smattered his sandals and spattered over the dusty ground.

Mary stared at half a pound of hastily eaten Fruit Salad chews.

The rattling bounced off the bricks like machine-gun fire. A Piccadilly line train hurtled over the tracks above the children. The noise was tremendous; it was not scheduled to stop at Ravenscourt Park station.

Michael had gone.

He would tell. Her mum would take his side. Mary snatched up her satchel and gave chase. Although her brother had a head start, she had longer legs and had not just been sick or hurt her arm. She knew which way he would go and that he would not have the gumption to hide. His red jumper gave him away. She slowed to a trot. She would catch him because he was running in that funny way of his that made it look as if he had a limp. He scampered across the 'Do Not Walk on the Grass' area and out of the tall gates on to King Street.

There was no need for Mary Thornton to chase Michael; he was going to the house. But she was livid that he had not done as she had told him and could not let him get away with it. He was running faster than she expected. She caught at his pullover and the seam ripped. She let go.

Michael gained the kerb and swerved out of her reach. He did not stop to look right, left and then right again but plunged out on to the road. A car was going too fast to stop.

It was Mary's lasting impression of her young brother that, when he flew up into the air like an angel, he looked at her with his bright blue eyes just as he did when he was waiting for her to decide what game they would play. Then his body thumped on to the bonnet and rolled beneath big black wheels.

Mary carried on down the street and into British Grove. She let herself into the house, scooped up the post from the hall mat and laid it on the table. This was Michael's job. She smoothed the shock of green hair on her troll key ring and dropped the key safely back in her satchel.

Alone in the house, the competent ten-year-old filled the kettle and set it on the stove. She lit the gas ring with the lighter which, as in the old house, was kept by the tea and coffee. She checked the tea caddy. Her mum would have to buy some more tea.

She lifted down Michael's plastic Mickey Mouse plate and a grown-up china one from the cupboard for herself. She laid his baby knife and fork each side of his plate, and proper cutlery for herself. She opened a tin of baked beans and spooned them into a pan, which she set on the hob on a high flame.

Mary Thornton was counting out slices of Mother's Pride bread – 'two for Michael, two for me' – when her mother opened the front door. She came into the kitchen and dropped her string shopping bag on the table.

'Look at you, doing the tea! Since you've been such a good girl, see what surprise is in there.' She handed her daughter an unopened packet of Brooke Bond Tea.

Mary gave the beans a quick stir and then pulled up the flaps on the box. She used her fork and fished among the leaves until she caught a glimpse of white and blue. With nimble fingers she lifted the card out and held it up.

Holm or Evergreen Oak (Number 43).

She had the full set.

Mrs Thornton had been home five and a half minutes when, for the second day since they had moved in, PC Terry Darnell knocked on the front door.

Twenty-Two

The stench of stale tobacco smoke was mitigated by a wafting of lavender and a hint of bleach. When she entered her mother's hallway that evening Stella was dazzled by light. A high-wattage bulb shone on to the newspaper towers. She moved crab-wise past them and outside the lounge heard a low rumbling tone and then a raucous laugh. She could not think when Suzie had last laughed. Slowly she opened the door.

Jack sat cross-legged on the mat, like a small boy engrossed in a game. The 'game' involved raking through the rubbish. Suzanne Darnell was leaning over the arm of her chair, chattering happily to him; neither was aware of Stella.

'... he would have got away with it if it hadn't been for me because no one had spotted the anomaly. Their filing system was a mountain of Xerox boxes stored in the basement. Call yourself a detective, I told him.'

'Sometimes it takes another eye.' Jack stirred a lump of soggy tea bags about with a forefinger. He delicately parted them, then pushed them to the far reaches of the newspaper.

'Another eye? Terry never paid attention in the first place, he was always somewhere else,' Suzie Darnell retorted. 'Terry used to say my legs could win Miss World,' she said apropos of nothing.

'Ah ha!' Jack exclaimed.

Stella, still by the door, watched with distaste as he sweep aside the cellophane from a pork pie and the packaging of a ready meal of liver and onions.

'Is this it?' He balanced on his haunches, steadying himself on the armchair.

Suzie made a darting motion like a bird; their heads came together like conspirators.

'Yes!' She clapped her hands and looking up saw Stella. 'He's found my ring! Your clever Jack has found my ring.'

'Your engagement ring? The one you lost in 1980?' Stella was disbelieving.

'What? I didn't get engaged. My view was if you're going to do it then just do it. No, my eternity ring, I lost it… oh – when did I lose it?' She appealed to Jack, her hands fluttering over the cushion on her lap, fingers tapping away.

'Last night.' Jack bundled up the rubbish.

Jack had found the needle in the haystack. Stella ought to feel pleased. She looked about her. The room was transformed. When she tidied, she picked something up only to put it down again because there was no place for it. If she threw anything out, her mother might not miss it, but months later it would feature in the rubbish search. Suzie maintained she had lost a black glass necklace that Terry had given her when Stella was born. Stella found a similar necklace in an antique shop in Kensington and bought it, put it in the bin and then feigned its discovery. Her mum claimed never to have had such a necklace and didn't want the one Stella had found because it had been in the rubbish. It sometimes occurred to Stella that her mum might be getting early onset dementia, but then she would refer to something insignificant that Stella herself had forgotten and she would dismiss the suspicion.

Stella had become resigned to simply keeping her mother's chaos at bay, but Jack had gone further. He had rearranged the furniture to give the electric fire focus. By placing the sofa under the window, he had forged a pathway to the serving hatch. She hoped the knick-knacks had been disposed of, but spotted her mother's horrible china figurine of a maiden with a basket of blooms propped on her hip dancing towards the toy guardsman with the movable arms that Suzie had refused to give to Stella when she was little. Jack had put them together.

'We need to get going.' Stella jangled her keys. There had been no spare van. Jackie had dropped Jack at Barons Court and Stella had come to collect him in the van that had not yet been sprayed with the logo. She wanted to discuss the blue folder.

'What a marvellous job.' Suzie Darnell's hands fell still on her cushion.

'Until next time.' Jack tied up the handles on the rubbish bag.

'Jack will come next week at the same time, Mum.' Stella was harsher than she had intended.

'I want him before that.' Her mum sounded sad.

'He has other work. We'll see.' Stella moved the dancing maiden to the middle of the shelf. She had forgotten that she had decided Jack should come twice a week but would not admit her mistake.

'She was perfect there.' Her mother's fingers were frantic on the cushion.

Stella slid the figurine back. She walked over the newly exposed carpet and pecked Suzie on the cheek.

Jack was leaning on the handle of the steam cleaner by the lift, surrounded by cleaning materials. Stella felt bad for her behaviour upstairs; her mum had the knack of bringing out the worst in her. Clumsy at small talk, she told Jack about finding the jacket under David Barlow's bath to lighten the strained mood, but Jack said nothing. She couldn't read his closed expression. They walked out of the flats in silence.

A paper flapped behind the windscreen wipers on the van. Stella had a parking ticket.

'I forgot to put money in the meter!' Unbelieving, she folded the ticket into the map compartment. Was it she and not Suzie who was losing her memory?

'What do you think?' Jack asked when they were beating traffic in the outside lane of the Talgarth Road.

'It looks good.' Stella had worried that Suzie would find fault with Jack. A worry that was nothing in the face of her mother turning him into a god.

'Not the flat, the pictures in this file. The streets.' He had the folder on his lap.

Stella signalled left and rounded the Broadway. She exited on to King Street and slowed down by Marks and Spencer's.

'A boy was killed here on Monday afternoon. He was called Joel Evans.'

Jack craned around to see the witness appeal notice. 'See how like piglets those sandbags—'

'There's one like that in one of the pictures. I think they're scenes of an accident,' Stella interrupted.

'I can't meet tonight.' Jack was genial. 'Actually, if you could pull over by the school here on the left. Oh… OK, too late.' He patted the blue folder.

'Be careful with that,' Stella warned. 'Why, what are you doing?'

'Oh, nothing that can't wait.' Jack settled back and began leafing through the photographs.

Stella accelerated towards Brentford.

'You said it used to annoy you that Terry took pictures when he was with you. Suzie seems exercised by that too.'

'It did, but I was a kid. Dad wasn't a tourist, he was following a hunch or a lead. He's numbered the pictures, but not said where they are.'

'More than one accident. These are different streets. Do you think he suspected a crime?'

'I'd say he'd spotted a pattern.'

'Question is, what is it?' Jack scratched his cheek ruminatively.

It was a year since they had solved the Rokesmith murder – using the case files Stella had found in her father's attic – and she missed the work. Jack said that detective work was like cleaning: it restored order to people's lives. Stella had not thought of herself as a detective, but perhaps Terry had. Suddenly she knew this was true. Terry was a tidy man; he put things away. He had died of a heart attack, but must have felt ill for a while and had sorted out his affairs. Her dad had left the blue folder out for her. It was another case. Stella bit her lip to stop herself smiling.

Twenty minutes later Jack and Stella were side by side on her plush white sofa, Jack in his coat despite the effective central heating. Stella clasped a mug of tea; Jack was neglecting his hot milk and honey on which a skin was forming. She trained the table lamp on to the folder.

Jack examined the witness appeal board on the kerb in the labelled picture. 'This is not the accident you pointed out just now in King Street.'

'Of course not, that happened this week.'

'Silly me. You might be on to something with the accidents.' Jack leafed through the folder. 'Was Terry ever in Traffic?'

'Don't think so.'

'Suzie will know.'

'Don't tell her.' Stella spilt her tea on the file. She hastily wiped the plastic. 'She'll get in the way. I mean, she'll confuse things.'

'You underestimate her.' Jack nibbled the arm of his reading specs. 'Where did you find this file?'

'In Dad's darkroom. I think he wanted me to see it.'

'Ah, you made it to the basement. Well done.' Jack pinched the skin off his milk, draped it on the edge of the mug and took a gulp.

Stella ignored Jack's remark. 'On the other hand he was always taking pictures so maybe there's no significance.'

'Could be like an artist's sketchbook: Terry's collection of hunches.' Jack lingered on the picture of a car on a forecourt with two legs sticking out from under it. 'A man mending a car. It's numbered one in the series which could be significant, or then again not.' He turned the pages. 'Your mum's had quite a life, hasn't she?'

'Hardly. She did the same secretarial job for years and since retiring has done nothing.' Stella sank back on the sofa. This was why she didn't want Jack to clean there. Suzie was now a paragon of virtue.

'She was telling me she used to type up your dad's reports. She was a secretary for the police and once solved a murder case.'

'She made that last bit up.' Stella was peremptory.

'I'm not so sure.' Jack sipped his milk.

'She was a secretary. It's how she met Terry.'

'She said he caught her speeding on Holland Park Avenue. He was off duty and she was doing forty miles an hour in a Mini Traveller. He promised to let her off if she went on a date with him.'

'That's not true!' Stella struggled up from the sofa and took her mug into the kitchen. She called back, 'Terry would never have broken the law.'

'He told her it was love at first sight and got her the police job, which she loved. When she divorced him she went to work for the council. I get the feeling everything stopped for your mum after that.'

Stella stowed the mugs in the dishwasher and rinsed out the milk carton and tossed it in the recycling bag. Jack had finished her milk, which meant black tea in the morning. One cleaning shift and he was the expert.

When she returned, Jack was examining the blue folder. 'We need to identify these roads, then find out what happened there. Shame Terry didn't label them. I suppose he thought he had time.' Jack got up. 'Let's look on the internet.'

Stella used the third bedroom as an office. It overlooked the landscaped slopes at the front of the gated development. Night had fallen; the glass reflected only Jack and Stella sitting at the desk.

Jack slipped the photograph with the witness appeal board out of the plastic sleeve and aligned it on the scanner. Stella pressed 'Scan' and the image appeared upside down on the screen. She rotated it 180 degrees.

'Zoom in on the board,' Jack murmured. Black print filled the screen. Although fuzzy and pixelated, Stella read:

WITNESS APPEA
FATAL ACCIDEN
2002 at HOUR
CAN YOU HEL
Telephone 080 8246

'We know the time.' Stella jotted '20.02' in her Filofax. 'That's not much help.'

'From the position I think it's the year: 2002, which actually limits it. Let's assume it's Terry's borough.' Jack typed 'car fatalities Hammersmith 2002' into the search bar. It returned eight possibilities between 2003 and the 2012 all linked to the *Hammersmith & Fulham Chronicle* website.

'I think you mistyped,' Stella said.

Jack did it again and got the same result.

'Not all answers are here.' He sniffed steepled hands. 'OK, let's go with it.' He clicked on the top link and brought up the newspaper's web page. Amongst brightly coloured adverts was a postage-stamp-sized piece about a fifty-three-year-old man who had crashed his car into a telegraph pole on Marquis Way in March 2003. In the habit of capturing every scrap of information, Stella jotted down 'Harvey Gray' along with the details in her Filofax.

Jack took the photograph out of the scanner. 'We should check out back copies in Hammersmith Library.' He contemplated the picture in his hand, frowning. 'Could it be as simple as Terry was thinking of moving house and these streets are contenders?'

'Nothing is simple, you're always saying that.' Stella did not want this to be the explanation. Surely Terry wasn't planning to move from the house in Rose Gardens North? It had been her home for the first seven years of her life.

Jack sat down again. 'You know we could shortcut this by you asking that mate of your dad's to buzz through their database.'

'No.' Stella took the picture off him and slipped it into its sleeve. 'The police are clients.'

'You're working for the police?' Jack's voice fluted on the last word. He turned to look at her.

'Not working for them. We're cleaning the station.' Stella was mild. She worked the mouse and panned the image until the entire street was visible.

'How is you cleaning not working for them?' Jack looked at the laptop. 'Wait a mo. What's that grey blob?' He tapped the screen. 'Go in a bit.'

'Careful of the plasma,' Stella barked. She enlarged a square shape beside the kerb until it took up the lower quartile of the screen.

'A horse trough!' Jack pronounced. 'I love those. They were a wonderful idea. Practical and yet considerate.' He folded his arms and tipped the chair back. 'Bit like you, Stell!'

The trough stood at an angle from the kerb. Faint lettering was carved in the stone. Stella scribbled down what she could read: 'Be ind a d rci ul To Ou Ani a s'.

It was like an anagram in one of her mother's crosswords; despite having all the letters Stella could never get them. Her mum took seconds to find the sentence.

'"Be Kind and Merciful to Our Animals"'. Jack contemplated the trough. 'The Metropolitan Drinking Foundation and Cattle Trough Association was a charitable venture set up in the late nineteenth and early twentieth century.' He leant forward. 'I'm sure I've been to that street.'

'That narrows it down nicely.' Stella preferred not to think about where Jack went at night. He had promised to stop his nocturnal jaunts, but this morning when she had knocked on his door he had not been there.

Jack grabbed the mouse from her and brought up Google. With one finger he laboriously pecked out 'horse troughs London

Borough of Hammersmith and Fulham'. Of the links listed, most referred to the borough, to horses or to troughs.

Stella snatched at his cuff: 'Go to that one.'

Jack clicked the penultimate link on the page and brought up an Excel spreadsheet. 'Voilà!' He clapped his hands.

The document listed the location of all horse troughs, drinking fountains and other 'items of statuary' in London. The last entry was numbered 1006.

'This will take forever,' Jack sighed. 'This trough could be anywhere.'

'We're focusing on Hammersmith,' Stella reminded him. 'Let's assume it's there.' Privately, Stella too was dismayed by the immensity of the task. She looked at Jack: 'Might you recognize a street name? From your walking...'

'I don't bother with names unless they are a sign. I get a feel for the direction, the paving, the light, chewing-gum shapes on the pavements...'

'OK, so what about the pavements and the light? Anything strike you?' Stella went with Jack's methods, off the wall though they were.

Jack yawned and scrubbed at his hair. 'No, can't say it does. We need to find out what happened in Hammersmith in that year.' He stood up. 'Actually, I have to go.'

Stella was taken aback. Jack's use of 'actually' was a bad sign – speaking of signs; he was up to something.

'If you did talk to your guy he might at least tell you—'

'No.' Stella addressed the grainy grey of the granite trough. 'And he's not "my guy".'

'Fair enough.' Jack did up his coat. 'Shall I come at the same time tomorrow?'

'What time was that?' Stella scrolled the spreadsheet up to the first entry.

'I'm not sure.'

'Come when you finish work.'

Stella heard the front door shutting. She should be used to

Jack Harmon going off without warning, not responding to messages or being home when she called. He was reliable when he wasn't going AWOL. Jack was not like other people and generally she liked this, but tonight she was uneasy. Jackie said knowledge was power, yet Stella suspected knowing more about Jack wouldn't help at all.

The spreadsheet belonged in her world. Jack lived by numbers, light and pavements. He saw signs and portents everywhere, which dictated his decisions. At work, Stella spent hours compiling or combing spreadsheets. She collected and cut data according to an objective, analysed it, drew a logical conclusion and made a rational decision.

She put her worries about Jack to one side and applied herself to the task. She chose the 'filter' tab in the header, pressed 'sort' and keyed in 'horse troughs'. Within minutes she had isolated six streets in Hammersmith with horse troughs. She printed off the list and opened Street View. Jack had told her that before he went on walks in London, he rehearsed the route on Street View. Stella was dubious about the motive for his 'journeys', as he called them, but saw sense in a reconnoitre of the task. She rather thought that Jack's approach was why he was the best cleaner she had ever known.

The hours passed. Stella worked on.

Some troughs sported displays of blooms, others were unofficial litter bins. One of the locations – on King Street outside a prep school – turned out to be a drinking fountain with no horse trough to be seen.

Stella sniffed success with a trough by the kerb as in Terry's picture, but this was dashed when she saw it was on a corner. Terry's trough was on a straight road with no side turnings.

She reached the last entry on the list. The picture on Street View jerked into focus. There was a trough by the kerb on a long road. There were shops and traffic and the pavements were busy with pedestrians. The trough was outside a pub. Dead end. Either the horse trough had been removed since the Terry took the photograph so wasn't on the list or the list was incomplete. Or both.

Later in bed, Stella remembered Jack's suggestion that she ask Martin Cashman. While it made sense, she would not cadge a favour. She had never told Jack that she had approached Cashman during the Rokesmith case and got her fingers burnt. Terry could have asked him but had not. The witness appeal board gave them a year: 2002. A big window but, like deep cleaning, laborious forensic work was Stella's forte.

She pulled the duvet up over her chin, shut her eyes and willed herself into a dreamless sleep.

Twenty-Three

'Shut your eyes and don't look till I say.'

Clifford Hunt blocked Mary's view of the Infants' gate. She would miss Michael coming out. She screwed her eyes up tight.

'... *commit his body to the ground, earth to earth, ashes...*'

'Hold out your hand,' Clifford said. 'It's a surprise.'

Mary had a fleeting image of Clifford slapping her palm with a ruler as Mr Sparrow had done to him for talking. Clifford hadn't cried. Mary would not have cried either. Nor would she have been caught talking because she had no one to talk to.

She splayed out her hand and felt a butterfly land on her palm. She heard footsteps, but she did as Clifford said and did not peep. After a very long time she said 'I like surprises'. Although she did not.

Birds twittered in the plane trees by the viaduct. More moments passed.

'Could I please see?'

She heard laughing and dared to open her eyes. A group of girls was clustered around the Infants' gate. They were in Michael's class and treated him like a doll, brushing his hair and sticking up for him when she was in charge. Michael was not with them.

'... *In that it has pleased our heavenly Father, who loaned these little ones to us for this short time, to take them back to Himself...*'

She looked down at her hand, still outstretched. There, face up, lay a Brooke Bond tea card with a picture of two brown circles like squashed conkers and a branch with leaves. She turned it over. Number 42.

The Sweet Chestnut cannot in any way be confused with the Horse Chestnut...

The voice in her head was Michael's even though he couldn't read.

Clifford had given her a card that she already had. She could not swap it because there was no one to swap with.

'Cliff's escaped.' One of the girls sniffed through giggles.

'Mind your own business.' Mary said.

... its flowers are attractive erect catkins, conspicuous for the bright yellow anthers of the male...

The girls took off. Satchels swinging and bumping against their backs, they scattered past the Sunken Garden where Michael had sat, past the drain cover where Michael was marble champion and out of the gate to Ravenscourt Park.

Mary was pleased that Clifford Hunt had remembered her birthday but cross that he had not asked what she needed. She pulled out the Trees of Britain album from her satchel and flicked through it. She did not need the Holm or Evergreen Oak: Number 43. She had the full set, he only had to ask.

She looked again at one of the pages in her album: there was a space. It was for number 43. Mary couldn't make sense of this. She flicked through the pages. It must have fallen out. She knelt on the ground and tipped out her satchel but it was not there. A feeling crept over her. It started at the back of her neck and went to her tummy. There were back-to-front words in the square for number 42. Mary could do mirror writing: ...crown is heavily and densely leafy, giving a deep shade...

The card Clifford Hunt had given her was not the brilliant white and dark blue of the brand-new cards in the tea leaves. It was bent and the writing missing on the card was there in reverse on the album page.

Mary dropped the card into the album and slipped it into her bag next to her pencil case. Michael's voice chattered gaily at her.

He's given you what was yours anyway!

Mary rushed out of the school gate. The faster she ran the less she could hear Michael. He stole it from you. She stopped at the kerb – nothing coming – she belted across the road into the park.

He didn't get you a real present. He knows your name's not Mary.

A train rumbled above but the sound did not block out Michael.

Mummy said you have to make our tea.

The rule about Mary making tea had disappeared since the day she swapped cards with Douglas Ford. 'I can do what I like,' she shouted at Michael and ducked along the path by the arches.

The girls from Michael's class were on the slide.

It's only me having tea, and I don't care. She marched over to the ladder to wait her turn. To her astonishment all the children stood back.

'You can go next.' It was Jacqueline, the kind girl with plaits.

No one moved or argued with Mary. Maybe they liked her after all? Mary looked up at the pretend house at the top of the ladder. Michael wasn't there. She slipped her satchel around to her back and placed one sandalled foot on the first rung. She expected someone to shout that she had pushed in, but it was quiet. Everyone wanted to see her perform her incredible feat. She climbed fast and clumsily, banging her knee on the metal. She would not cry. From the doorway of the house she looked down. The girls had gone.

Mary stood alone in the little house where her brother had crouched with chattering teeth and trembling knees. He had held her tight around the middle. She touched her tummy. His hands had gone. Without Michael the slide would be easier, but she still wished he were there to see her.

She would go head first. She lay on her tummy and with a swimming motion propelled herself over the edge and pitched downwards.

Everything was at top speed; the skimming metal burned her

legs. She went faster and faster and jolted to a stop at the end of the slide, her head hanging over the side and the ground close to her nose.

Mary rolled off the chute and trotted out of the arch. The girls were up ahead at the end of the path. She wanted to run away, but they would know she was scared so she kept going. They were looking at her heart in the concrete. This gave her courage; she would tell them that Clifford had done it for her.

'What are you lot doing?' Mary tried to sound cheery, but her voice was shrill. She looked at the heart. The concrete had set hard so the 'T' was clear, but where Michael had dug at the 'M' the letter could have been anything.

A girl shoved her. 'You spoilt it.'

'We hate you.' Another voice. More shoving.

The girl with plaits wasn't there.

'What have I done?' Mary retreated and trod on someone's foot. She felt a sharp kick on her leg.

'You don't care about your brother.'

'He's not your real brother. You don't have a daddy!'

A girl with long blonde hair was pointing at the heart as if Michael was under there. For a moment this seemed possible, but no, Mary knew where he was.

'... *to the ground. Looking for that blessed hope; when the Lord Himself shall descend from heaven with a shout, with the voice of the archangel...*'

She had told her parents that Michael had gone to his bedroom while she was making tea. He must have run out to get sweets. Mary could believe this had happened.

'Michael hated you.'

Mary stared at the heart, uncomprehending. 'He hated you.' It was a chorus, the words flying around her ears. More kicks and punches.

'No he didn't.' Mary got down on her knees. The letters were cold and hard as stone. Her fingers tore at the concrete; her nails split. She made no difference.

'Michael wanted to rub it out because you made him a cissy. He hated you!' A fireball rose in her chest.

'You should be dead, not your brother!'

Mary clawed at a girl's neck and rubbed her face into the heart until it and the girl crumbled to dust and ashes and there was nothing left.

Pigeons cooed in the arches; the sound might have been in her head along with Michael. Mary warily traced along the groove of the heart. Where Michael had tried to scrub out the 'M' was a lump of cement she could not break off.

'... *our Saviour Jesus Christ who shall change the body of our humiliation and fashion it anew in the likeness of His own body of glory...*'

Michael had gone for good.

Clifford Hunt had not done the heart for her. Mary wandered along the path. At the arch where she had done the deal with Douglas Ford she pushed open the corrugated iron sheeting and went in. If the girls came back they would not find her.

There was no sun today; the curving brick was like the inside of a chimney. She crouched on the dusty ground. Dimly she knew it was tea-time. She wasn't hungry. She wanted to sleep but it wasn't bedtime. She unbuckled her satchel and drew out the Trees of Britain album. The red cover was crimson like blood and heavy with the weight of the cards. She licked her finger the way her dad did while he read his insurance reports. She flipped to the page with the spaces. She decided the card Clifford had given her had fallen out. He had found it and given it back, which was the same as a birthday present.

Your birthday is not till 29 February 1968. Soon I'll be as old as you.

You will never be as old as me.

You only get a birthday every four years. I will catch up.

At her feet was a congealed mess stuck with flakes of bark and dead leaves. It was Michael's sick. Leaning against the wall was a bundle of canes. She drew one out, like a sword from a scabbard, and poked the end into the crusted mixture. She drew an 'M' in the sick and unearthed smeary bright pink streaked with orange. Michael had gobbled up the Fruit Salad chews. Her daddy had found the crumpled bag in Michael's shorts with one sweet left. She would have liked to have it. The bag proved Michael had gone out to buy sweets, she had said.

How could my sick be here when I have gone?

Don't be stupid. But she didn't know. How could the concrete heart with Michael's crossings out be there when he was under the ground?

Mary Thornton brushed her cheeks dry with her sleeve and fitted the stick back with the others. Her bag swinging, she returned to the path and went under the arch to King Street as she and Michael had been told. Certain nothing was coming, she crossed at the zebra. Today she was not having a pretend birthday; because of Michael her mum and dad were not making a fuss.

'I'm doing fish fingers and baked beans,' she confided to Michael. 'Your favourite.'

Twenty-Four

Thursday, 26 April 2012

A fierce wind blew through the sixteen spans supporting Hammersmith flyover and the clouds massing were the grey of the obdurate structure. Traffic noise was amplified to a discordant roar that drowned out the reproachful call of pigeons sharing cavities with electricity cables and the heating pipes that were an innovation in their time. Birds finding tenuous perches on the spalling surface made the paving around the supports viscous with excreta.

Stella tried to put out of her mind the rumour, which she supposed she had got from Terry, that criminals of London's underworld were entombed within the units of pre-stressed concrete.

The Hammersmith and Fulham Archives were housed in a nondescript building without signage in the shadow of the flyover at the west end of the Talgarth Road.

Stella had left the office after lunch, intimating to Jackie that she had an appointment with a new client, without actually saying so. She hadn't told Jackie about the blue folder, and in particular hadn't admitted she was going out with David Barlow this evening. Jackie was keen for Stella to meet 'Mr Right'; she was always saying Stella must give people time, get to know them, dare to trust them. While she might approve of David Barlow's looks and considerate manners, her judgement would be clouded by the deep cleaning and him being a client, a transgression of Stella's rule.

Ten minutes later Stella was untying the string from a roll of film that held editions of the *Fulham & Hammersmith Chronicle* for 2002 and clumsily feeding the intractable end around a series of rollers on a microfiche reader. When she attempted to spool it forward, she twiddled the dial the wrong way and the strip of celluloid whipped from the casing and smacked against the glass plate. The librarian, whose help Stella had refused, glanced up from her desk with raised eyebrows, silently renewing her offer. Stella shot her a grim smile and began the process again. At last she mastered the sensitive controls and, as she tentatively turned the dial, the film jerked forward.

Optimistic of success, Stella drew a grid in her Filofax with columns headed 'Date', 'Street', 'Accident' and 'Victim'. She put in seven rows, because, not counting the numbers with letters, there were seven streets. She squeezed in an extra column for the picture number.

She had forgotten how unsettling a local newspaper could be. The murders, muggings and accidents that befell people in the ordinary course of their lives – house fires, more than one murder in an abandoned church or a bedsit, robberies and accidents at work and in the street – were so frequent that, if they read the paper, residents of Hammersmith could be paralysed with fear.

After two hours she had only reached May 2002 and found two fatal traffic accidents. An elderly man – Harry Pickering – hit by a motorbike and a young man who, the article reported, had yet to be identified, crushed by the 272 bus on Shepherd's Bush Road, not far from Stella's office. He had died later of head injuries. This story intrigued her because a man arrested at the scene was not the bus driver, which inspired further questions. Who else could be responsible? Was he pushed in front of the bus? She trawled through the following weeks but found no answers. She was getting distracted. Terry would keep strictly within the limits of the case. There was no mention of a horse trough.

Her back ached from sitting on the hard chair and a headache from staring at the poor resolution screen was nagging at her temples. She went to the lavatory.

She was drying her hands – on a towel whose hygienic properties she mistrusted on principle – when she saw what had been under her nose. She hurried back and pulled out the blue folder from her rucksack; she flipped to the street with the witness board (number 5b) and there they were. Two horse chestnut trees – she had learnt about trees at primary school and could still identify most species in the British Isles – their bare branches black lines against a white-grey sky placed the season of the photograph as late autumn or winter. Stella was safe omitting the months between May and August from her search.

She opened the cabinets housing film dating back to the 1960s, eased out 'September 2002' and loaded it into the machine. By now she was operating the clunky apparatus with the breezy skill of an expert and arrived quickly at Thursday, 5 September, the day the paper came out. No accidents reported for that week. A woman was found dead in her bed of a paracetamol overdose. A nurse in the renal department of Charing Cross, she had stopped work to care for her father and after his death was diagnosed with depression. Stella believed that keeping busy was the best cure, not that she had looked after Terry. She whizzed the film on and accidentally skipped a week. Reversing it, she found no fatal accidents.

Another hour passed and she was at the end of October. Her headache was worse; she could do with a handful of paracetamols herself.

She was about to give up when she found it. Date: Thursday, 14 November 2002, above an advert for Woolworths in King Street.

Hit and Run Man in Fatal Collision

By Lucille May

A man who was given a suspended sentence of two years for causing death by dangerous driving and leaving the scene was killed when his Peugeot RCZ hit a tree on Britton Drive W6. James Markham was taken to Charing Cross Hospital on Sunday night where he was pronounced dead.

The smash is known to have occurred after 11.30 p.m. when DS Terence Darnell, an off-duty police officer, drove down the street and noticed nothing unusual.

James Markham, 36, of 1 Glenthorne Road, was married with a two-month-old son. On 2 January 2002 Markham caused the death of seven-year-old Christopher Mason, who ran out in front of his car on Shepherd's Bush Road. Mr Markham failed to stop, but reported the accident at Hammersmith Police Station that evening. His widow Sasha Markham told us: 'Jamie was thrilled to be a father and was rebuilding his life.'

Anyone who witnessed the incident or who has information should contact Hammersmith Police Station quoting reference P103/1900/12.

Incredibly Terry had given the accident a time frame. Trembling, Stella pressed 'copy' and the photocopier by the librarian's desk sprang to life. She called up Street View on her iPhone and dabbed Britton Drive into the search box. She had expected a fiddly, careering perambulation along the streets as the controls on the phone were clumsier than on her laptop – but there, set back from the kerb and framed by two sweet chestnut trees in full leaf, was a horse trough. Street View takes pictures in the summer when it is meant to be sunny; these were taken in June two years ago. Like the trees in Terry's photograph these were sweet chestnuts. Stella knew not to confuse them with horse chestnuts. More evidence, if she had needed it, that she had found one of Terry's streets. Stella sat back in her seat, her arms folded to contain her excitement. If she needed proof that the pictures in the blue folder were clues to a case, this was it. Sometime later, years later even, her dad had returned to Britton Drive and taken his own record of the accident spot. Why?

Her phone rang. She fled back to the toilet because a notice at the reception instructed users of the library to turn off their phones and, reluctant to obey instructions other than her own, Stella had ignored it.

Suzie. She would be complaining about Jack's cleaning. Stella did not answer.

Twenty-Five

Jack did a check on his dormitory. Nothing had been touched; it hadn't even been cleaned. They were cutting costs. Outside the flat, he waited a moment. No sound. He retrieved the key from above the door with the shamrock holes. If it took a while to finish the repairs, he would make a copy.

Jack had forgotten he was there to get back his street atlas and get out.

The old man was a hazy figure in the poor light; he hovered godlike over his streets, his breathing stertorous. He gave no sign of knowing Jack was there. Jack manoeuvred along the tight gangway between the model and the wall that had served so well as a hiding place the other night. The man was wiring one of the signals outside Hammersmith Underground station. He gestured at the work table.

'You're late.'

'Yes, sorry. I...' Jack's father had hated excuses. He measured out the powder into a bowl, trickled in water from a pint bottle and stirred until the mixture was a thick malleable consistency. He cut squares of gauze with a scalpel, soaked them in the plaster and then laid them out on an artist's palette. Holding the palette and a flat-bladed knife he worked his way along the stuffy crawl space to emerge in the middle of the Thames.

'Did you mention I was here the other night? To your daughter?' He regretted the question instantly. The old man would not have mentioned him, he trusted Jack. His question fractured that trust.

The man was mumbling something.

'Pardon?' Jack leaned out over Hammersmith Flyover.

'She's not my daughter.'

'I'm sorry, it's not my business.' Jack's hands trembled as he draped the plastered gauze over the wire frame he had exposed on his last visit, careful not to drop any on to the rails. He did not apply too much or the roof would sag and lower the height of the tunnel. Practised at constructing tunnels, Jack knew how to spread the load and keep the height for the rolling stock.

The old man behaved as if he had not heard Jack speak.

Preoccupied with his mistake, for the second time Jack did not hear his Host return until she opened the door to the flat.

She paused at the second flight to get her breath; once upon a time she had run up and down these stairs, carrying bags, trays of hot drinks, laundered blankets. She sniffed the air; there was an infinitesimal change. She put down her bag and padded along the corridor to the first dormitory.

Everything was as she had left it. Or was it? Colin's bed was made, yet she didn't recall smoothing the blanket and he wouldn't have made it himself. Before term started she would collect up the glasses and give them a wash. Jimmy had dropped his book on the floor – he was a one for reading after lights out; she bustled over. She had to guess his place from the way the book fell open. No bookmark, silly boy.

How often she had stood in the doorway listening to the boys' breathing, ready to catch the culprit who had been up to mischief and was feigning sleep. She had always hated the holidays when beds were empty.

She heard his voice as soon as she entered the flat, conspiratorial and secretive. It twisted her stomach. She went to the kitchen and decided to find a tasty snack for him. He'd like that.

He was flicking at a rooftop with her pastry brush. She stumbled in and leant on the Chiswick boundary. He eyed her over his glasses. He didn't like being disturbed at work, but he was always at work, she had no choice.

A District line train left Hammersmith station and rattled along the viaduct down to Barons Court where it stopped to let passengers alight and get on board. She watched it disappear into the tunnel. The plaster was a brilliant white; he had repaired it. Perhaps he would let her paint it.

Twenty-Six

Thursday, 26 April 2012

Stella had not read David Barlow's directions. She had forgotten all about the date. She found the folded note in her anorak when, having done all she could do at Terry's, apart from eat the shepherd's pie, she was looking for her van keys. Even allowing for her watch's extra minutes, she was due at the pub in ten minutes. The sloping capitals were like Jack's handwriting. She should have stuck to her initial instinct and refused the invitation. Except her initial instinct had been to agree. She read the directions and caught her breath. The Ram, by the Bell Steps leading to the River Thames, had been Terry's local. Maybe a drink was just what she needed.

Outside the subway tunnel Stella checked her appearance in the distorted reflection of the convex safety mirror. She fluffed up her hair. The style was meant to be messy, but not this messy; it kept falling over her eyes. She would have to do.

On time, she pushed open the door of the nineteenth-century pub on the corner of Hammersmith Terrace and Black Lion Lane as Terry must so often have done. She wondered briefly if he had ever spoken to David Barlow.

Stella saw him at once because he was in the seat near the fireplace. She had chosen that seat the only time she been here before; and, it being out of the way, she had been heading for it again now. That night she had been avoiding a man whom she had dumped. This memory made Stella feel bad.

'What do you fancy drinking?' He was by her side.

'Let me,' she countered.

He shook his head, so she gave in and requested a ginger beer.

When David Barlow returned, he sat opposite her and they clinked glasses.

'Cheers!' They said it together and laughed. Stella relaxed.

'The grave looks good with the headstone. Tidying took me a while, but done and dusted now.'

Stella could not think what to say. Jackie had offered to take her to Mortlake Crematorium on the anniversary of Terry's death to see the Memorial book open on the page with her message. 'To Dad, love Stella.' Stella had been on a twelve-hour shift and besides, she said, the crematorium had a website, she could see it online anytime.

'Do you miss your father?' He was looking searchingly at her.

'Yes.' Stella gulped her drink and the bubbles made her cough. She hadn't properly considered this before. She was suffused with heat although the fire was not lit and, unlike the previous time she was here when it had been snowing, the door was propped open, letting in a cool evening breeze.

'You were close. That's nice. When I was a boy me and my dad were like that.' He clasped his hands together. 'But we grew apart. Jennifer wanted me to make something of myself. My dad didn't fit her bill. He was a mechanic – he could have built a car from scratch – but Jennifer didn't have time for cars that needed mending. I miss him for the wrong reason. Too many regrets. The newspaper article said your dad was proud of your success.'

'Don't know how they knew that.' Stella gripped her glass. 'Amazing you kept the newspaper.' While pleased at the PR success, Jackie had thought this peculiar.

'To be honest, the newspaper was lining the bottom of the wardrobe. I found it when I was disposing of Jennifer's shoes and what not.' He rolled up his shirt sleeves, smoothing the material at each fold. He ran a hand over his arm, up and down. Stella found herself picturing doing the same. His skin would be smooth, yet muscular. 'I thought that if you could give your dad that send-off you'd be principled. Our parents launch us into the world; we owe it to them to see them out. I reckoned Clean Slate would be like you.' He took a draught of his beer.

Jackie had predicted that readers of the article would think that. When Stella had been horrified that Terry's funeral had made the front page, she had said it was great publicity. Her comment had surprised Stella since Jackie discouraged her from always taking a business perspective. 'Sometimes it's good to think with the heart,' Jackie said.

Stella tried to think with the heart. 'You must miss your wife.'

'Would it shock you to say I miss my dad more?'

Stella had cleaned for too many households to be easily shocked, but shook her head, deciding it unwise to voice this. Clean as if you can't be seen. What you see, never say, she had penned for the Clean Slate staff manual. Thinking of this reassured her.

'Jennifer and I weren't right for each other. We met too young. Since we didn't have children, these days we might have gone our separate ways. But I hold store by loyalty and she was not a woman to give up.'

'Like school friends who remember the person you want to forget you were.' Stella was not in touch with anyone from school and supposed this was why.

'That's exactly right!' He drained his pint glass and wiped his lips with the back of his hand. 'Why do we go to school reunions? Jennifer's death is hard because, if I'm honest, it's a relief.'

Stella thought of her manual: Listen and nod; keep cleaning. The client is not interested in you, only that you agree. Suzie talked about Terry as if they had stayed together for the last forty years. 'If you had divorced it might not have helped,' she pondered.

'I'll never know.' He got up. 'Another?'

Stella's eye caught the blackboard chalked with the evening's menu and remembered the shepherd's pie. She had planned to return to Terry's after the drink to eat it, but she was hungry now.

'Do you have time to eat? I thought perhaps...' She hated eating with other people. 'Although if you've eaten...'

'Great! We'll keep off death, is that a deal?' He beamed, his blue eyes bright. 'What'll we have?' He turned to the board. Stella went for the ham and eggs; it was what she had eaten the previous time here. She was vaguely gratified when David chose the same.

While he ordered, Stella cast about for conversation topics. Men had limits on hearing about new cleaning methods however technical she could be.

The pub was busier than it had been on the snowy night last year. While he queued, David was chatting with three young men perched on stools, coordinated in light suits, brown hair cut short and gelled back. They laughed uproariously at something he had said. Stella recognized them from last time and this made her wonder again if Terry too might have chatted with David while waiting at the bar. Her phone was ringing.

'Please could I speak to Stella?'

'Obviously you are. Hello, Jack.'

'I called your home and got no answer. Aren't we meant to be meeting?'

Another appointment that Stella had completely forgotten.

Jack didn't wait for her to reply. 'Where are you?'

'I'll meet you at Terry's in half an hour.' Stella hadn't told Jack that she spent every evening at her dad's because he would ask why and she didn't know. Or worse he would know and tell her.

'I'm at Terry's now. I can see your van.'

'OK, I'm on my way.'

'Guess what?'

'What.'

'Go on, guess!' Jack sounded cheery.

'I can't.' David was shaking hands with one of the men at the bar.

'I know the name of the street!'

'What street?' David was making his way towards her, holding the drinks carefully to avoid spilling them. Her evening had slipped away.

'Marquis Way.' Jack seemed astonished that she could ask.

Jack often continued conversations broken off days before and expected her to keep up, but this time Stella had started the conversation. Ever since her visit to the library she had been impatient to tell Jack about identifying Britton Drive, but after she had sorted Terry's house and remembered her drink with David, she had forgotten. 'Yes. So have…' she tailed off. Jackie would advise she didn't trump others' success with her own. David was handing a glass of ginger beer to her. She took it and mouthed a thank you.

'I had a hunch about Marquis Way, I'm sure it's near the front of the file. Like I said, I've walked there.'

'That's great.' Stella spoke in a monotone. David tilted his glass against hers in a silent toast. Their fingers brushed. She pressed the phone to her ear to cut out the background chatter.

'Where are you? Sounds like a pub. It's past eight. I need to get to… I need an early night.' Jack's voice was jerky; he was walking, his breath across the microphone was like the roar of the wind. With sudden clarity Stella knew that she couldn't tell him about David. There was nothing to tell.

'Where are we going?' She reached around the back of the chair for her anorak trying to think of an explanation for David.

'Marquis Way, of course!'

Twenty-Seven

Saturday, 18 June 1966

She urged the bike forward and went faster until the bushes and leaves were a whizz of green and brown. She stood up on the pedals and, her feet working furiously, she leant into the bend.

Michael and her dad were timing her from the other end of the park, but she didn't need the stopwatch to know she would break the land speed record.

There was a dreadful grinding and the bike shook. Even though she pedalled harder she did not go any faster. She pressed on the other pedal and the scraping got worse. The bike tipped and Mary somersaulted on to the path. Hot pain rushed up her leg and she knew that, like the man in the Bluebird, she was going to die.

A whirring as if she was winding down. She opened her eyes. A pedal was spinning; it slowed and stopped. Silence. Above Mary was a blue sky with no clouds.

She sat up and stretched out her leg. Beads of blood dotted it like the dash of a red crayon. She twisted around. Michael and Daddy had gone.

Mary got out of bed and in her nightdress pattered across the matting and squeezed through the door, keeping quiet as a mouse. Michael's bedroom door was shut. If he came out she would send him back to bed. She scurried along the landing and down the first three stairs from where she could see the hall.

Her dad had on the black suit he'd worn for Michael's funeral. He was combing his hair at the mirror; it was shiny and Mary imagined stroking it. He lifted up his briefcase and gave her mum a quick kiss. Mary hadn't seen her because she kept still, just as she did when Mary kissed her. Daddy opened the front door and went out.

Her mum stayed where she was. Mary knew she was not waiting for her dad to come back, but for Michael. She waited in the hall a lot now and only moved when Mary's dad returned from his insurance visits – since Michael had died he even went out on Saturdays. Mary had tried to get her upstairs once and her mum had looked at her as if she were a ghost.

Mary wouldn't try now. She ran back up the stairs. Outside Michael's bedroom she listened. She couldn't hear him. She glared at the door, doing the magic spell that worked with corn flakes in the kitchen, but instead of wishing herself back in their old house, Mary wished that her brother were fast asleep in his bed.

Twenty-Eight

Thursday, 26 April 2012

'Be Kind and Merciful to Our Animals.' Balanced on the edge of the drinking trough on the ill-lit road, Jack was caught in the glare of the van's headlights.

Britton Drive was long and straight and desolate, its bleak aspect unmitigated by the tall sweet chestnut trees. The wind whipped their faces and pushed at budding leaves on the branches. Stella had told Jack about Britton Drive and since it was closer than Marquis Way, they had come here first. She had not told him about her abortive date with David Barlow. David had encouraged her to leave – for a member of staff in crisis – and invited her to go for a walk with him by the river the next evening and have a meal to make up for the one they had missed.

'Not much here.' Jack patted the trough. 'According to your list, this is granite and was erected in 1935.'

Putting David to the back of her mind, Stella fished out her torch from her anorak and focused it on the blue folder. She turned to the picture with the witness appeal notice. Jack leant forward.

'Is that a tree behind the trough?' He directed Stella's gloved hand to light the lower part of the picture.

'I think so.' Stella looked up. Although she had left the headlights on and there was a solitary lamp-post some metres away, Britton Drive was dark and unsettling. A horrible place to die.

Industrial units were set back from the road, many with broken windows or boarded up and smothered with jagged graffiti. Even when occupied the buildings must have been shoestring-shabby, their occupants one step ahead of the receivers. Stella knew the sort: fly-by-night outfits that paid only the bills that kept them trading. She read a nearby fascia that proclaimed in blistering letters: 'Gray Shoes Fa ory Outle at Amaz g Pr ces.' It gave her a dull sensation in her solar plexus. She had not experienced commercial failure, the trick was keeping overheads low. They would not move to a bigger office, they would stay put until the economy picked up.

Jack lifted a Coke can out of the trough and stuffed it in his pocket.

'What are you doing with that?' Stella was appalled.

'I'll put it in your recycling bin. This isn't a rubbish bin, it's for horses.'

'Don't expect many horses pass this way.' As she said this, Stella hoped she was right. The area had an air of despair, of hopes shattered and of life long gone. No place for a horse. She shivered. Or for them either.

The warped 'To Let' sign on an imposing stone building with arched windows that had been an electricity substation suggested it had been available for a long time.

'That's in the photograph, behind the appeal sign,' she pointed at a plastic salt bin near one of the trees. As she reached it she saw the indented logo: 'Gina-Ware'. Since discovering the company was owned by the daughter of her late client Mrs Ramsay, Stella came upon their products everywhere. Jack would say it was a sign.

Jack jabbed at the photo. 'There's a crack in the paving here. I missed that.'

Stella had not noticed the meandering crack under the witness appeal board. If she had she would have dismissed it as insignificant.

'This is a working crack,' Jack announced.

'Meaning?' Stella asked.

'Meaning it's more than three millimetres, so is moving and is open to intrusion from water which freezes then expands, so widening the crack.' On his knees Jack traced a finger along the crack. 'A priority for street maintenance, but no doubt this has fallen off the council's list. Who's going to trip here?'

'This is private land. Businesses have to pay.' Stella looked around her at the abandoned buildings. 'Or not. Let's get on with it. This place is like a dead zone.'

'It is a dead zone.' Jack gave her a look. 'See how the crack's lengthened since Terry's picture? We could have used it to guess the year if we didn't already know.' He sounded disappointed.

'You think it caused Markham to crash?'

Jack jumped up and ran to the middle of the road. 'These appeal boards are placed to alert motorists coming either way. Where did it happen?' He darted over to the salt bin and, holding the file out like an offering, he tightroped along the pavement, one foot in front of the other. Every so often he gave a hop, avoiding the breaks in the kerbstones. Stella had hoped Jack was improving.

Far off a siren whoo-whooped, dipping and soaring and then fading away.

'James Markham smashed into a tree.' Stella flapped the photocopy of the newspaper article. 'Since these are the only trees we can assume...' She marched over to the nearest tree and, kneeling, shone her torch at the trunk.

Jack joined her. He ran his hand over the bark carefully, as if the tree were a person.

Stella allowed her mind to wander briefly. David Barlow had said he would stay at the pub to eat his supper; wistfully she supposed he had left by now.

'There!' Jack nudged her. 'This is where he died.'

A gash cut into the tree two feet up from the ground. Over the decade since the accident, the exposed wood had spotted with grime and moss. They wouldn't have seen it had they had not been looking. The bark was closing over the scar.

'Trees are two-thirds below ground, a substantial tree like this would have held fast when Markham hit it, even at speed. A wall might give way. Wait a minute, what's this?' Jack scrabbled in the earth around the roots. One by one he placed little chips of stone on the pavement.

'Stones.' Stella got up and stamped about to stop the pins and needles in her right foot. 'Not everything's a sign.' She swung the torch out along the road; it fell short of a shape fifty metres away. A rubbish skip, although in the dim light it was hard to tell. 'Let's get out of here.'

Stella had forgotten to lock the van and had left her phone in view on the seat. It was glowing. Jackie had left a voicemail. Sitting at the wheel, Stella listened. 'Can Jack go to Amanda Hampson's at eight o' clock tomorrow morning as well as Tuesdays? Of course she's taken to him!' Jackie enjoyed telling Stella they had more business. Stella wished they had spoken; she wanted to make up for leaving at lunchtime. While she hadn't actually lied to Jackie, she hadn't told her the truth. This didn't sit comfortably with her.

Jack was still by the tree. 'Jack, come on!' She gesticulated through the windscreen. Jack waved, but didn't move. Without asking him, Stella texted Jackie that he would be there. Jackie would see she was working. More deceit. Stella huffed in her seat. It was no good. She would return the blue folder to Terry's basement and attend to her business.

'This is a wild-goose chase,' she declared when Jack finally joined her. 'So what if there was an accident here? Terry took the picture because he was there that night.' She started the engine. 'It's a souvenir.'

'You don't believe that.' Jack was businesslike. He was jingling something in his palm. 'Was Terry in all the streets? Life is rife with coincidence, but this seems implausible.'

'He was a police officer.'

'Not on Traffic. I asked Suzie.'

Stella pulled out into the road.

'Your lights are off.' Jack examined his cupped hand.

Stella flicked to full beam. 'What was that?' She rubbed a porthole in the fogging windscreen.

'What was what?' Jack dropped whatever was in his hand into his pocket and clipped on his seat belt.

'I saw something.'

'A fox probably.'

'This place gives me the creeps.' There, she had said it.

'A man died here, that's why,' Jack replied amiably. He tilted his head back against the cushioned rest. 'His ghost is here.' He was matter of fact.

Further along the road, Stella remembered the dark shape. They must have driven past it. She looked in her rear mirror and saw the sweet chestnut trees silhouetted against the sky. Ghosts indeed. She had imagined the car and the fox. Nevertheless she confirmed the central-locking switch was activated.

Jack pulled on the gloves that Stella had found in Terry's jacket pocket after he died and had given him. The brown leather accentuated his long slender fingers. The folder, still open at Britton Drive, lay on his lap. 'I should imagine Terry was puzzled how it was that Markham came off the road. It's as quiet as a grave here.'

'It would have been thriving ten years ago.'

'Not in the middle of the night.'

'Maybe he suspected suicide, unless the guy fell asleep.'

'Or murder.'

On Britton Drive it had seemed the dead of night. But Uxbridge Road was bright and noisy with cars and late buses. Teenagers and returning commuters bunched outside late-night groceries and off licences; knots of tardy smokers sat at pub picnic tables nursing last orders as if for warmth. Glad of the bustle, Stella didn't resent braking when a man wove his way in front of the van. She wasn't a detective, she ran a cleaning company and should be in bed now. She jumped when Jack batted the dashboard.

'That was Marquis Way.'

'Not tonight. It's late.'

Twenty-Nine

Friday, 27 April 2012

'I'm off to the police station. You can manage without me, can't you?'

'I'll try.' Jack screwed the cap back on the toilet cleaner and smiled at Amanda Hampson. So far she had hardly spoken to him. If she was going out, he would finish on time although he found he was disappointed not to hear how her investigations were going.

'Jack. Darling. We shall celebrate.' She stamped her foot, clutching a book and a pink plastic wallet garish with yellow and red flowers. 'I shall force them to reopen the case!'

'I see,' Jack said in a neutral voice. He squirted a stream of yellow scouring cream around the sides of the bath.

She sighed. 'Don't you be sceptical. I rely on you. And that so-called journalist, she's next in my firing line.'

He gathered himself. Although he had only known Amanda Hampson a short while, he was drawn to her energy. She was indefatigable in her quest, however ill-judged it might be.

'Which journalist?'

'Lucille bloody Ball. I love Lucy, I don't think. Making sheep's eyes at Charlie even when he was dead. She's got me to answer to now!'

'What have you found?' Jack tried to keep Amanda focused. He suspected this was how it had gone wrong with the previous cleaner.

'They can all sit up and listen.' She did a dipping motion on the landing. For a split second Jack expected her to ask him to join her in a dance. He would accept.

'Charlie was pursuing compensation.' She brandished the book, which Jack saw was a history of racing drivers.

'Was Charlie a racing driver?' he tried carefully.

'What? Don't be a twerp. Charlie killed a child. Poor lamb, horrible in general, of course, but a dreadful business for him.' She did another dip.

Jack put down his scourer. 'What happened?'

'It wrecked our lives. Stephen thingummy… name's gone… chasing a ball or a pet. God knows. Charlie never stood a chance. He got blamed anyway and damn near lost his job. They don't think of the drivers. It's not only the victim's family that suffers. Do you read?'

'Do I what?' Stella would have no truck with this, even without knowing about Amanda's body-scan meditations in the temple by the lawn.

The telephone began to ring. Amanda swooped off to her bedroom extension. Jack could not hear the conversation. He snatched the chance to finish the bath. Rinsing away cleanser, he pondered that she was not well. Perhaps when her husband was alive Amanda had been a lot of fun, if unburdened by principles, but now her indomitable spirit could atrophy in her quest to prove wrong was right. The grey man in the portrait was a Host. Cold and ruthless and self-serving. He would stop at nothing. He had stopped at nothing. Charlie Hampson would dub a dead child an irritant.

Amanda was back.

'Dentist. They ring to remind you of your appointment, as if you forget.' She clacked her teeth together. 'I must fly. Hold on until next time for the next episode. Wish me luck, Jack my sweet. No, wish them luck!

'Inspector Whatsit will bloody listen.' She tapped the file. 'I have the missing jigsaw piece. The murderer has underestimated me. *Ad mortem!*' She went down the stairs.

'Good luck.' Jack was ashamed at his surprise that Amanda knew Latin.

Charles Hampson had killed a child. This made suicide more likely. It would be hard to live with causing the death of a child even if it was the boy's fault. Doubtless the police thought so too. 'To the death' or not, Amanda might be home sooner than she intended.

Jack's arm ached with scrubbing at the film of grease. Something nagged. He dredged his mind, but nothing came to light. What with the old man and the model, his *A–Z* and Stella's blue folder he had enough to nag at him.

Jack leant against the curving external wall of Amanda's meditation temple and rolled a cigarette, enjoying the warm sunshine. Amanda's lawn needed cutting. He fished in his pocket for his cigarette case and found his job sheet. He hadn't filled it in. He wandered back up the crazy paved path to the sitting room, avoiding several jutting stones.

On his way out to the garden Jack had been disappointed to find the room had reverted to a pickle. Papers strewn on the bureau, over the dining table, piled on the carpet and on the chesterfield. It had given him an inkling of how Stella felt when she visited Suzie.

He found a biro by a newspaper on Amanda's desk, tested it in the margin of his job sheet and then scribbled in his hours and dashed his signature under 'Operative'. He placed a cross where Mrs Hampson should sign if she approved his work. Stella had designed a clearly accessible form, but Amanda would be too distracted to make sense of it.

He was looking for a prominent place to leave it when a photograph on the newspaper caught his attention. It was the article Amanda had been reading when he saw her through the window that first night. It was no coincidence that Amanda had called the office. Scrawled next to the photo of Stella at her desk were the words 'call first thing'. Amanda had rung at sunrise.

Underneath were two newspaper cuttings. One showed another funeral. A mound of floral tributes spilled over a kerb, dotted with teddies, stuffed lambs, giraffes and other cuddly animals. Cards were slipped in plastic bags to protect the messages. Inset was a close-up of one: 'For Stevie, Mummy's little angel. Sleep tight. xxxxx'.

Heart-stopping, but it was not the words that caused Jack to rush out of Mrs Hampson's house still holding his job sheet.

It was the photograph in the other newspaper clipping.

Thirty

Monday, 20 June 1966

Mary saw the Angel from a long way away; her white gown shimmered through the yew trees (Number 9 in Trees of Britain). She headed towards her but the Angel dodged out of sight as Mary zigzagged along rutted tracks and clambered over fallen headstones.

The Angel's wings were folded behind her back and she was very tall, as tall, Mary told her brother, as the Scots pine (Number 3), the cypress trees and the thin larches (Number 1) that were all around. Mary shivered when the sun dipped behind clouds.

Today she was eleven. The thing about being born on 29 February was that she was allowed to choose the date for her birthday for three years out of four. When she had told Clifford Hunt that her birthday was today he had given her a pear drop, but did not say 'Happy Birthday' as if he didn't believe her.

He knew you were lying, you can't have two birthdays.

Her mum and dad would be doing a surprise so she must not spoil it by sneaking in as Michael had done when he was seven.

Mary could not make up her mind about Michael being dead. There were good things: more food and no one bothering her. But the bad things were bad. Her mum let her go to bed when she was tired instead of at her new grown-up time. Michael was not there to be jealous so there was no fun in staying up. Her dad went out on insurance visits every night and never came to the park to see her perform astonishing feats. Before he had missed

190

the feats because Michael got in the way, but Michael was not in the way now.

The Angel stood on the hole where they had put Michael.

IN LOVING MEMORY OF
MICHAEL
AGED 7
15TH MARCH 1959 – 6TH MAY 1966
BELOVED CHILD OF
ROBERT AND JEAN THORNTON
'WHO IS LIKE UNTO GOD'
'BONNY AND BLITHE AND GOOD AND GAY'

Mary turned and ran. She crashed helter skelter through the foliage and along the paths to the high stone wall. All around were dead people with plastic flowers or flowers that were brown and drooping. The trees crept closer when she wasn't looking, like Grandmother's footsteps. She had run for ages but the Angel was still watching her.

Mary let herself into the silent house. She found her mum in the kitchen frying fish fingers.

'Where's Daddy?'

'At work.' Her mum slid the fish fingers on to a plate heaped with beans. When Mary did the tea, she made it neat for Michael. His chair was tucked in tightly at the table.

'Wash your hands. After this, go and play in your bedroom.'

When she was drying her hands, the towel stiff and rough on her skin, Mary understood something impossible had happened. Her mum and dad had forgotten it was her birthday.

Thirty-One

Friday, 27 April 2012

Stella backed into the administrator's office, pulling her cleaning cart after her, and was disappointed to find a woman seated at the desk. It was empty the last time she cleaned and at half-seven in the morning she had presumed it would be today.

'Would you rather I returned later?' Stella apologized to hide her annoyance; she preferred to clean alone.

'I'll still be here when you do,' the woman said, coming around the desk, 'Say when you need me to move.' She put out her hand. 'You must be Stella. Marian Williams. I'm so pleased to meet you at last. I used to work with your father. I was at the funeral, but naturally you were taken up with so many people.'

The woman's grip was stronger than Stella expected.

She let go. 'Have you got what you need?'

'Yes thanks.' Stella rattled the cart. 'If you don't mind me being here?'

'Carry on. I'll be too busy to notice.' As if on cue, her telephone rang. Marian Williams took up the receiver and, guiding the flex around her computer, sat down again.

Relieved that Williams was reasonable – it made her job easier – Stella began taking files from the shelves and stacking them on a row of cabinets. Although not actively listening, she could not help hearing Marian Williams's conversation.

'... Yes, forgivable. I've done the paperwork. Joel's mother is on tranquillizers. Mr Evans has hurt his hand.' She paused. 'He punched the wall when Paula and Phil broke it to them and broke a finger. I took them to the site. She came over faint, had to take her into Marks to recover. Breaks your heart.' Another pause. '… No, they have an older girl. Poor love was a shadow …'

Joel Evans was the boy killed by a car on King Street. As an executive officer, Marian Williams had to process road traffic accidents and, from the conversation, Stella guessed her duties included liaising with the bereaved parents.

'Let me know if you get the Nominal.' Marian Williams ended the call.

Stella thought back to the news bulletin: a man had been seen checking his car on Chiswick High Road. From Williams's conversation, no one had confessed.

The woman caught her eye. 'I've been at this for years. It never gets easier.'

'Sorry?' Stella assumed an expression of distraction.

'FATACs. Fatal accidents. Collisions, we call them now, because frankly there's no such thing as an accident. Reckless motorists think they own the road and a child is so much flotsam. The excuses I read in the report books the officers fill in at the scene. You'll know from your dad.' She waved an orange booklet at Stella. 'This one is a hit and run so no driver statement, but I've lost count of the ones who bleat it wasn't their fault. They don't come out and blame the pedestrian, but they're itching to. Did you hear about Joel Evans?'

'Yes.' Stella was glad she had. Ignorance would have counted against her. For Marian Williams the death of a child outweighed everything. While her manual didn't encourage conversation with clients, it did advise that operatives took interest if engaged in chat. 'Have they found the driver?'

'He will have washed his car and had the bodywork repaired with cowboys who don't ask questions. No qualms that a young life is wasted and a family destroyed.'

'It isn't only the victim who dies.' Stella heard herself echo Terry. She rummaged in her cart for the beeswax polish.

Mrs Williams might remember James Markham's crash on

Britton Drive. Perhaps she had gone there with the wife and son. She could imagine Mrs Williams being unsympathetic about Markham; she'd think he deserved it.

Williams's phone rang again.

'Hello, Detective Chief Superintendent Cashman's office… What? Martin's not here. Tell her to make an appointment, not that he'll see her. Thanks for the warning, or rather no thanks. Next time keep that portcullis shut.' Marian Williams slammed down the receiver. All her good nature gone.

The door burst open and a woman in a tightly belted rain mac, long blonde hair streaming over her shoulders, marched in on sharply clicking high heels. Her handbag, threaded through an epaulette, swung from her shoulder and she waved a plastic wallet as if clearing a path before her. Stella retreated to the shelves and began rearranging the files. Marian Williams stood her ground from behind her desk.

'I have come to see Detective Chief Superintendent Darnell.'

No one moved. The words took on horror-movie proportions in Stella's mind.

'DCS Darnell promised that if I found him fresh evidence he would reopen my husband's case.' She smacked the brightly coloured wallet down on the desk. 'My name is Amanda Hampson. My husband was Charles – yes, I see you remember me – his file is in that lot.' She gestured at the box files heaped on the cabinets and saw Stella. She addressed her: 'Now they have to listen.'

'Can we go outside?' Marian Williams moved swiftly to the door and held it open. 'Please!'

'I am not going until I see the Chief Superintendent. No offence, but I won't be fobbed off with civilian staff this time.'

Marian Williams was clearly flustered and Stella guessed it was because the scene was being played out in front of the cleaner and because of who she was. For her part she wasn't keen to meet her newly returned client. She grabbed her cart. 'I'll come back,' she mouthed. The administrator nodded.

Stella trundled the cart to the stairs and sneaked back to the door. Not one to eavesdrop, she had to know why Mrs Hampson wanted Terry. It might have a bearing on the case, she told herself as she dusted the skirting board.

'Mrs Hampson, DCS Darnell has left us. His replacement is DCS Cashman but he is not here and no one else is authorized to consider this case.' Although the voices were muffled, Stella could hear.

Stella didn't think the last point was true but had little sympathy for Mrs Hampson, what with the business of the tea tree and now her lying about Stella's dad asking her to return. Terry would not have done that; he hated time-wasters.

She heard a sliding sound and then a thump, like a body falling, and for a wild moment thought Mrs Hampson had attacked Marian Williams.

Then the administrator spoke: 'Leave those, I'll deal with them.' She was close to the door. Stella fled up the corridor. Two uniformed officers were coming down the staircase but paid her no attention. The administrator's door did not open. Stella risked returning to her listening post.

'You've been kind.' Mrs Hampson sounded defeated; she might even be crying. Marian Williams, it seemed, was an excellent gatekeeper. Stella felt a little sorry for the woman who, after all, had lost a husband. She hoped Marian hadn't said she was DCS Darnell's daughter.

Marian Williams was speaking briskly – the equivalent of sweeping up – and in a minute she would have got rid of her. '… although I doubt much can be done after all this time.'

'… once I've explained it you'll …' Mrs Hampson was saying. Stella strained to hear but her words were mumbled as if into a hankie; then she blew her nose. She was leaving. Stella bounded back to her cart and pushed it into the next office.

When she went back to finish off, Mrs Hampson had gone and Marian was frowning at her computer. She did not acknowledge Stella.

'Thank you for that.' Stella squirted polish on the shelves. She was running late.

'For what?'

'For not introducing me to Mrs Hamp— to your visitor.' She'd rather the administrator did not know Mrs Hampson was a Clean Slate client.

'I had to puncture her hopes. It shows how little she knew her husband.' Williams punctuated this with a stab on her return key. 'She had just discovered he had passed his advanced driving test and told me this proved his crash could not have been an accident. I had to tell her: police officers pass that test and it doesn't prevent them having accidents. Rare, I grant you.' She tapped the keyboard and a printer by the window came to life. Still sitting, she wheeled her chair over and caught the page as it tipped into the tray.

'I see.' Stella was not surprised Mrs Hampson had not known about the test; many of her clients knew little about their partners.

Marian Williams had been more patient with Mrs Hampson than Stella would have been if faced with irrational behaviour. Indeed, she had not been patient and it had led to Mrs Hampson cancelling the contract. People like Mrs Hampson must be par for the course at the station. Even if they were grief-stricken and could not accept that an accident was just that, an accident. Terry must have appreciated that his executive officer kept them at bay.

Marian Williams would take her time passing Mrs Hampson's message to Martin Cashman and Stella did not blame her. She did not envy Williams her job.

A young constable knocked on the open door. 'Hey, Marian, something to make you smile. The Nominal who mowed down the kiddie has only gone and walked into the lobby. He's given himself up. Paperwork's on its way. Brace yourself, you're going to love him!'

'Name?' The administrator wasn't smiling; her fingers hovered over the keys.

'Matthew Arsehole Benson.'

She nodded grimly. 'Was he sorry?'

'Gutted.' The young man slapped his palms in a rhythm on the door jamb. He stopped when a frisson of annoyance passed over Marian's face. 'Gutted there was a camera above Marks and Spencer's. He knew we'd get him so he pipped us to it. He's crying so get your tissue box out.' With a cheery wave, he was gone.

Stella folded and refolded her cloth: 'Just like you said.'

Mrs Williams did not reply.

Thirty-Two

Tuesday, 21 June 1966

The sand stung her face and a grain got in her eye. She kicked blindly with her feet and sent a spray of damp sand across the play area. When she peered through watery slits she saw the three boys from Michael's class running away. A train on the bridge above drowned out their shouting.

Mary's plimsoll was ripped and both shoes were stained orange from the sand. They were ruined.

She sat on the tiled lip of the sandpit and wrenched them off without undoing the laces. She pulled her sandals out of her duffel bag, slipped them on and did up the buckles. She picked up the plimsolls by the laces and dropped them into a rubbish bin outside the playground.

'Here's your tea, Daddy.' Mary lingered on the step, gripping the heavy mug with both hands. She hoped he would take it off her soon because her fingers were stinging from the hot china. 'Can I help?'

'Nothing you can do.' Her dad often said this.

'I made the tea.' This was a lie. Her mum had made it and said yes when Mary had asked if she could take it to him. It was Monday, so she had been surprised to find him in the garden cleaning Michael's bike when she got home from school. At their old house, and before Michael went underneath the white Angel, her dad would have ticked her off for being a 'clever clogs'. Maybe he believed she had made the tea.

'Put it on the wall.'

'Please.' She wished she hadn't said it but luckily he hadn't heard.

Nuts, cogs, a chain and other bits were laid out on newspaper. Oil splodges had landed on a photograph of policemen in coats and helmets walking in fog. Mary saw the words ...it was October 1965 when Saddleworth Moor first became a grisly household name... Stepping around the paper, she balanced her dad's mug on the mossy wall. In the middle of the garden Michael's swing looked bigger than ever and she imagined sitting on it. In the sunshine it looked especially colourful.

Dad will tell you off. Michael was here all the time now.

'Myr— Mary, there you are!'

Her mum was holding the door as if it would fall off. She held on to things wherever she went: hedges, fences, cars, handles and walls as if she were on a ship in a stormy sea.

'I can't find your new plimsolls and you need them for PE tomorrow. Please fetch them.' Her mum did not stand back to make room for Mary to pass. 'And wash your hands for tea.'

'What are we having?' Although they had stopped expecting Mary to make it, teatime was now her least favourite part of the day.

'Fish fingers and beans as a treat, but only if you get your plimsolls.'

This was not a treat. Mary did not like fish fingers; they were Michael's favourite. She didn't know how to pluck up the courage to say she had thrown away her new shoes. In the bathroom she assiduously washed her hands to make up for there being no plimsolls. She sat at the kitchen table, her hands folded on her lap, hoping that her mum had forgotten. She had not.

'What did I just say?'

The back door opened and her dad came in. He stood on the mat drinking his tea.

Say they got stolen by robbers!

'I lost them,' she mumbled so he wouldn't hear.

'What do you mean?' Her mum whirled around from the cooker, a plate of food in her hand.

'They were stolen by robbers.'

'Don't talk nonsense,' her dad said.

'Do you mean someone has stolen them?' Her mum was concerned.

Mary waited for her brother's help.

'Who took them?' Her mother put the plate in front of her. The fish fingers were burnt and the beans were stuck together so Mary couldn't see each bean.

'I had to swap them for Hawthorn, Number Twenty-four, and Sycamore, which is Number Thirteen.' Mary filled her mouth with a forkful of beans and chopped a fish finger into four pieces like a train for Michael.

'What are you talking about?' her dad demanded.

Jean Thornton retied her apron, bringing the ribbon around to her front and tugging it into a knot. 'It's cards from the tea leaves.' She sounded enormously tired.

Mary kept her eyes on her dad. He put his mug down on the draining board and wiped his feet on the mat, although he had already walked on the lino and his shoes were clean.

'She's swapped expensive plimsolls for two blinking cards.' He shook his head.

He made you do it.

'He made me do it.' Mary spat out a fish finger by accident. 'He gave me his swaps though I don't need them. I've got fifty.' She could not hide her pride.

'How did you manage that? Last thing I knew you… Oh never mind…' Her mother mopped her face with her apron. 'Bob, you need to go up to the school and sort this out.'

'Who made you swap?' her dad asked, swallowing his tea.

'Douglas Ford.' Mary was prompt. She sat up straight as the facts presented themselves. 'He steals things. He was going to bash me up if I didn't give him my plimsolls. He made me have the Sycamore and the Yew even though I didn't want them.' She spoke without drawing breath.

After that the matter was taken out of Mary's hands. Bob

200

Thornton would see Miss Crane the next day. The kid would be punished and the shoes returned.

Mary had never gone to school with her dad before. She demonstrated her hopscotch skips on King Street but did not lead him over the grass with the sign: 'Do Not Walk on the Grass'. She was taking her dad to school and not the other way around. She knew the way and he did not.

She was triumphant when they passed Michael's stupid friends. The girls and boys would see how tall and strong Daddy was and wish he was their dad. She hoped they had not seen him tug her across the road, even though she liked holding his hand.

At the entrance to the Juniors' he let go of her. 'Which one is Douglas Ford?'

At that moment, like magic, Douglas came round from the drinking fountain doing his strange pony walk, his blotched pink knees knobbling over his Cubs socks. He had his duffel bag for football. Mary pictured her brand-new white plimsolls hidden under his football boots.

'That's him!'

'Go and get your shoes back,' her dad commanded.

'Aren't you going to go to Miss Crane?'

'I'm not your daddy. Time you fought your own battles.'

Mary caught up with Douglas Ford in the cloakroom. 'Give me back my plimsolls!' She had not meant to shout; everyone stopped taking off their coats.

'What? I haven't got them.' He went red.

'You have and my dad's come to get them back off of you. Hand them over and it'll be all right.'

Douglas appealed to the other children: 'I don't have her shoes.'

He is a scaredy cat.

'I won't ask again, Scaredy Cat!'

'What's going on here?' The real Miss Crane appeared. She stooped to retrieve a cap from the floor, read the label and passed it to a boy who was strait-jacketed half in and half out of his windcheater.

'Douglas stole Mary Thornton's plimsolls and Michael's dad is here.' The voice was echoed by others, keen to relay the available information to the head teacher. Keen to state the facts.

Clifford Hunt came and stood next to Mary, his arms folded.

'Is this true, Mary?' Miss Crane was severe but sounded concerned and Mary felt a glow of pleasure.

'He made me give them to him.' She sniffed. She was truly on a ship with nothing to hold on to and the land was receding. Clifford Hunt smelled of salty sea.

The morning went faster than any school morning ever had. Mary's dad went with Miss Crane to her office. Douglas Ford's mother was called away from work and told of her son's crime. He no longer had the shoes. He claimed he had never had them and his mother believed him. Bob Thornton said the one thing about his daughter was she never lied. The father of a dead child had the last word. Douglas was given detention and made to shake hands with Mary. He had to say sorry loud enough for all the adults to hear. Mrs Ford – there was no Mr Ford – would pay for new shoes.

The day ended happily for Mary. Clifford Hunt had stuck up for her and this made the other children nicer to her. Her dad collected her from school and got her Fruit Salad chews from the sweet shop where the woman serving remembered her from when she came in with Michael and asked if she wanted half a pound. Mary gave her a funny look as if she had never seen her before. She kept close to her dad and Michael, wherever he was, kept quiet all the way home.

After her mum had said goodnight, Mary waited until she was downstairs then jumped out of bed and opened the curtains. The lady that Michael said was painting was in her room. The room was like a lighthouse, the bright window suspended in the dark. The lady was looking out of the window so Mary gave a wave and imagined she waved back.

Please could I have a chew?

'You are dead.' Mary climbed back into bed, satisfied it had turned out well in the end. Douglas Ford had stolen her plimsolls. He had made her swap for the Yew and the Sycamore. Mary had the cards to prove it.

Thirty-Three

Friday, 27 April 2012

Kew Bridge was pinkish grey in the evening sunlight. The Thames, choppy from rowing boats skimming under its arches, was a mix of dancing lights and shadows. Above the drone of traffic could be heard the hoarse shouts of a man cycling along the south towpath, holding a megaphone; he kept pace with a boat cutting through the water near the shore.

Stella paused until the man had passed and then, hurrying along, she spotted David Barlow further up the path. He was gazing down at the fast-flowing current, his hands in the pockets of his leather jacket. Light sleek sunglasses complemented prominent cheekbones. He cut a striking figure. Stella noticed two women in their thirties, jogging side by side towards the bridge, see him and share a glance. Despite herself she was gratified it was her he was waiting for.

Her phone rang. It was Jack. She didn't answer it. She wouldn't abort a second date with David

'You found it,' David murmured, turning from the river as if he'd known she was there.

'I came here as a kid.' The memory came out of nowhere. She had cycled behind her dad from the Ram pub, over Hammersmith Bridge, back along to Kew and then past Strand-on-the-Green. Her mum had said it was far too much for a child.

'I often see children with their fathers here.' He led them away from the bridge. 'It can make me feel envious.'

'You don't have children?' Stella was spiked with heat at her temerity and then at her forgetfulness. David had told her he didn't.

'Jennifer had a miscarriage soon after we got married and what with one thing and another that was it. I might have liked to be a dad.' He was briefly wistful.

'Children are a lot of work.' Stella appreciated the idiocy of the comment, but fortunately David Barlow went on:

'What bad parents we would have been. No child should live with two people quietly at war with each other. My own home was happy until Mum died. I was eighteen and already engaged. What was your childhood like?'

'My parents divorced when I was seven. My mum wanted it, but she complains about my dad as if they're still married. I think she wanted him to fight it, but if someone asked him for anything he did it. Mum got her way and has been unhappy ever since.' This unexpected insight was obvious now she had said it. Stella thought of telling Jack.

'Maybe she wanted him to make her feel loved?' David was keeping up a fast pace that suited Stella's long legs. 'Don't we all. Oh no!' He swerved into Stella, holding her shoulders briefly to steady her, then he ran over to the edge of the bank.

A small dog was making its way along the water's edge. It was unsteady on its legs and perilously close to the river, which Stella saw was rising. Oblivious to danger, it batted and snouted at an overhanging branch above its head.

'Bloody thing!' David Barlow flung off his jacket and handed it to Stella.

'Dogs are sure-footed. It'll be fine.' With a shock Stella watched David Barlow shuffle and slither down the steep bank, finding foothold in the merest of indentations in the soil. Stella knew nothing about dogs, but she did know people died trying to rescue them while the dog survived. Going by the speed of scum and flotsam racing by, the current was strong.

'It's a puppy, it has no sense.' He spoke through clenched teeth as he grasped a clump of groundsel. He anchored his foot in a gap in the concrete ballast.

Stella was relieved he wasn't wearing the Italian loafers of her first visit. Grasping another branch, David whistled at the animal. The puppy cocked its ears and looked around.

Stella cast about either way along the towpath. They were alone. The sun had gone in and a breeze whipped over the water, sending ripples across the grey-blue surface. Deep in conversation and walking fast, they had come a good way and the bridge was out of sight. There was no one to help.

'Here, Bubsy.' He clicked his tongue. The dog gave a sudden spring into the air and landed facing the other way, its hind leg in the water. To Stella's horror, a sparrow flew out of nowhere and alighted between the dog and David. The puppy stared at it with liquid brown eyes. It lifted a front paw and held it bent.

'If the bird flies off, he's going to try to follow.' David spoke in a crooning tone presumably intended to placate the dog rather than herself. He undid his belt buckle. 'Pull it, Stella.' Still in the soothing voice.

Stella didn't move.

'Quick!' he gasped, the effort causing him to slide closer to the water's edge.

Stella put a tentative boot on the mud-slicked stone, dizzied by the sheer incline. She caught the thin leather and gave it a tug. David shifted on the slope. She stopped.

'I'm OK.' He nodded curtly.

She pulled again and the belt whooshed out of his trouser loops. The buckle whacked her thigh.

'Do it up around that branch, on the last notch so the noose is wide.' He indicated the branch near her with a tip of his head. 'Don't fall in.' He gave a short laugh as if the idea was absurd rather than likely.

The leather was warm from being around his waist. Stella did as he had asked. Slowly, keeping his balance, David felt with his hand behind him and caught the loop. He thrust his arm through and hitched it under his shoulder.

The sparrow, a twig between its beak, shot upwards into the leafy canopy above. The dog launched itself after it, paws flailing, flying over the rushing water, David caught it by the belly and pulled it against his chest. It struggled. He did a pirouette on the bank, dangling by his belt. Then he lost his foothold. Stella grasped at his shirt.

Everything slowed. Sounds were muted. The cloying odour of river mud filled her nostrils, cut with the tang of David's aftershave. She was pushed backwards and landed heavily on the bank, her palms stinging. Strong hands dragged her to the towpath. The fragrance was stronger now. David's jacket smothered her. She struggled up. David was crouched in a ball beside her. Two button eyes glared at her through the crook in his arm. His white shirt was streaked with mud and needle dots of red.

'You're hurt.' Stella croaked. A cut ran from his little finger's knuckle to the base of his thumb.

'I'll live.' He sucked it.

Stella's phone rang. Jack again. She turned it off.

David helped her to her feet and, clasping the dog, retrieved his belt from the bough. Still with one hand, he rethreaded it through his trousers. Stella looked away as if the action was intimate.

'You could have died,' she said eventually. 'There's a plaque on Hammersmith Bridge for a man who drowned saving a dog. It could have been you.' She contemplated the dog: scrawny, with matted fur; it was hard to tell the colour.

'There are worse ways to go.' David Barlow did up his jacket and finger-combed his hair back. 'He's a poodle. They're intelligent animals. We'd better take it to the police.'

Stella's heart sank. She did not fancy turning up at Hammersmith Police Station with a poodle, with anything.

'Someone's dumped this little lad. No collar, see? He's been fending for himself. Let's eat first. We can't take him into a restaurant. Are you OK with a takeaway round at mine? Unless that call means you have another mercy dash.'

'It wasn't important.' Stella linked arms with David Barlow and strolled back with him along the darkening towpath.

Thirty-Four

Friday, 27 April 2012

Jack slotted the glass back into the basement window, impatient to get to the streets in the attic. He had been stuck in a tunnel outside Hammersmith Broadway for an hour while a broken-down Richmond train was towed to the depot.

He didn't consider the miniature cityscape a model; it was another dimension of reality. He knew from his nocturnal journeys that the buildings, roads, alleyways and even the trees were faithful renditions of Hammersmith. He didn't understand how this was possible. The old man could hardly walk and never left the house.

Jack had divined that the woman, because she had kept his street atlas and had the photograph of the family in her bedroom, was a Host. Yet she didn't fit the profile. He couldn't sense evil in her eyes or in her aura. She appeared to show no interest in the streets in the attic and rarely lingered there. She had no idea he was there and, emboldened, he stayed longer working with the old man in companionable silence, as he had with his father. He would not ask about the *A–Z*; he didn't want his motive mistaken. They repaired roofs and camber, replaced straggling trees with pollarded versions to clear the way for buses and other high-sided vehicles. The old man went to bed at ten and Jack left for his driving shifts. He compiled for Jack a list of alterations and repairs which, returning in the small hours and working by the light of a lamp strapped to his head, Jack completed for when the man started the next morning.

Jack was there under false pretences. He should try to retrieve his *A–Z* – once he had it, he must leave. Lured by the attic streets, he was losing his touch. If the woman was a True Host, capable of killing and feeling nothing, and the photograph by her bed suggested this, he should take action. Yet he did not.

He stopped off in his dormitory. He froze. The difference was minimal: most would miss it; the book that had been on Colin's bed open and spine up was now closed and by the bed. He should pack up and leave. Stella would be appalled if she knew. In fact he'd been so keen to get here he had forgotten to call her after leaving Amanda's. She believed they were a team; he was letting her down. He crept over to his bed and, squatting down, punched in her number.

'Stella Darnell. Please leave a message…'

Jack ended the call. Leaving the dormitory, he went to the stairs and continued upwards.

'You're late.'

'Got held up.' Jack gathered up the skirts of his coat and ducked into the crawl space.

'Test the tunnel walls. You made them too narrow. A train was stuck there.'

Jack surveyed the tunnel he had been stuck in. He did not explain about the faulty Richmond train: his father had hated excuses. He depressed the button on the console and set the District line train in motion. It clunked along the track, the sound a replica of life. Jack gripped the lever, the curving brickwork sliding up and over his cab. The dusty yellow headlamps lit the silver rails. The train took the bend outside Hammersmith Broadway and on to Barons Court where Stella's mother lived. The man was repairing a gas leak on Fulham Palace Road near the hospital. He was wrong about the width of the tunnel, but Jack knew better than to say. His father didn't brook criticism. For good measure he pared at the walls, careful to avoid puncturing or ripping the gauze.

After this he set to work on the road by the brewery leading down from the water tower. Undergoing conversion to flats, the tower was caged in scaffolding as it was in life. Jack repaired a freeze-thaw crater in the tarmac and meandered down to the Eyot. Here the tide regularly flooded up to the opposite pavement. It was out now, so he cleared away debris washed up from the riverbed: twigs, takeaway cartons, lengths of twine. Using a toothbrush he scrubbed at slime on the kerbs. This time, in tune with the school, he heard the front door shutting far below.

'I have to go.'

The old man did not reply.

Even before his Host had mounted the stairs, Jack was in his dormitory. He gazed out of the window at the orange-tinted sky noting her step was slower tonight. As he expected, she paused on the landing, but still he tensed. The repositioning of the book told him that, a good housemother, she checked the dorms.

He heard her go on up the stairs and, opening his door, crept along the passage to the landing. Her head was bowed, her breathing stertorous. Jack had learnt to hide with scant cover. Most people looked in obvious places like attics, cupboards and wardrobes in spare rooms and did not consider shallow alcoves or pools of shadow. Jack hid in what amounted to nowhere, where not even a True Host with a mind like his own thought to check.

Her shadow receded on the wall; the angle of the light made her monstrous, the curving shadow of the balustrade providing a backdrop as if she was caged.

There was a bang and then a knocking. An object shot down the stairwell and bounced against a banister. It skittered on to the tiles in the hall below. Jack melted into the black of the corridor and flattened himself beside the open fire door. She made her laborious way down the stairs. He knew enough about his Host to perceive that tonight she was untypically clumsy.

She was talking; he couldn't catch the words. His mouth went dry. There was someone with her. Surely he would have felt their presence. She had dropped her telephone and the banister had broken its fall. He glided down the stairs and stopped at the turn in the staircase before his own shadow projected on the wall.

Her voice dropped, Jack only caught snatches: '... sorry ... full diary ... Cheltenham ...' Her soothing tone implied a lover. True Hosts rarely had partners.

She said goodbye. Jack took the stairs and gained the landing ahead of her. She was wheezing and he was tempted to race back down and lend her his arm. From his vantage point by the fire door he watched her pass by, her phone in one hand and a book in the other. He imagined she was a ghost, condemned to wander the corridor of the building forever. She stopped. She sensed him.

Jack had forgotten to switch his own phone off. He got few calls: from London Underground and from Stella. Both could ring anytime. He willed it to stay silent. If he reached for it she would feel a shift in the air. From two metres away she must hear his heart smashing against his ribs. She was fumbling with a book, fanning the pages as if she had lost her place. His London *A–Z*. She was writing something in a flipover pad like a police officer's.

Jack saw why she went out at night. The woman wasn't following him. She used his street atlas to collect details of London to report back to her father so he could adapt or change buildings, signs, minor details on his model. She had probably walked every street in Hammersmith. Jack felt an oblique envy. His Host's journeys had tangible purpose.

She switched on the landing light. All she had to do was look to her left and she would see him. Jack was paralysed by thrilling fear. She knew where he went; she had his journeys.

Upstairs she would quietly confirm her suspicion that her father had received a visitor. In absolute control of events, she would turn back her father's bed, lay out his incontinence pads, boil a kettle for his nightcap. She would bide her time.

It was pitch dark when Jack eased into bed. He wrapped his coat close; it crackled. He felt in the pocket and found the newspaper cutting he had taken from Amanda Hampson's house that morning. He had not told Stella his suspicions about Charlie Hampson: she would be annoyed he was, as she would put it, 'up to his old tricks'. He must ring, or she would wonder where he was.

Jack dipped under the blankets and for the second time that night dialled her mobile. He imagined Stella pottering about her father's house inventing tasks, reasons to stay. She was unable to move into or to sell Terry Darnell's old home.

'Stella Darnell.'

'It's Jack,' he breathed.

'Please leave a message after...' It had gone to voicemail, almost as if Stella had cut the line. She wouldn't have done that.

He lay back on the unyielding pillow. Last night when he called, Stella wasn't at Terry's, nor when they met had she said where she was. He felt creeping unease. Softly he began to sing to himself:

'Mary had a little lamb,
Little lamb, little lamb,
Mary had a little lamb,
Its fleece was white as snow...'

Jack fell asleep without finishing the first verse.

Thirty-Five

Monday, 30 April 2012

Marian Williams's office was empty, but a steaming mug of coffee on her desk meant she wasn't far away. A green faux-leather handbag hung from the back of her chair and an open manila file that Stella saw from the label had been signed out of the General Registry lay beside the keyboard. She frowned; when clients left valuables out, it made her and her staff vulnerable to accusations of theft.

Stella was about to leave and return once the administrator was there when she noticed a black and white photograph half out of the folder. It was of a street. Stella ignored an urgent voice in her head commanding her to clean at the other end of the building. She checked the corridor and set her cleaning cart outside, blocking the doorway.

She snatched up the photograph. Her hunch was on the nose. It was a road in one of Terry's pictures, but it looked different. Shot by a police photographer, it showed the aftermath of an incident. A cordon of police tape was in the foreground; behind was a car, its bonnet crumpled against a tree, which Stella identified was an ash. Jack was right about trees holding up: the trunk was unscathed. Forensics in white jumpsuits examined the wreckage. A case number code was stamped in the corner. Stella had read two digits when she heard a footstep. She slipped the picture back in the file, too late realizing she had put it flush with the other documents. Marian Williams would notice.

She bounded to the window and swished her cloth over the

heating vent, an eye on the door. Two women in plain clothes passed; one glanced in. Stella flashed a tight smile. They were police; they would see her guilt.

She should get out while the going was good, but instead pattered back to the desk and tweaked off the closing report from the top of the pile. On red alert she ran a finger down the text. 'Paul Vickery, aged forty-three, crashed his Triumph TR7 in North Hammersmith on Monday, 16 March 1977.' She swept up a block of sticky notes from the desk, grabbed a pen, snapped it on and scribbled: 'Accident at approx 11.30 p.m. Victim thrown clear of vehicle, suffered broken neck and fractured skull. Died on impact.'

She was startled by the dead man's address: 42 Primula Road. The street where Terry had grown up. A coincidence? Could have drawn his attention to the collision. Traffic incidents were not Terry's remit.

Someone was coming. She shoved the report back. A green form floated to the floor. Stella had no time to return it. The cart rattled; her ruse had bought her seconds. She stuffed the paper into her trouser pocket.

'It must have moved,' Stella panted. She pulled the cart clear. 'I have literally just arrived.' She was no good at this stuff. Nor did she want to be. She should not have listened to Jack.

'You carry on.' Marian Williams trotted past her. Trailing behind, Stella gave the desk a wide berth and wheeled her cart to the window. She pushed the form deeper into her pocket.

Stella moved robotically around wiping and polishing while Mrs Williams, sipping her coffee, tapped at her computer. She showed no sign of leaving.

Any minute now she would consult the folder and miss the form. She would make Stella empty her pockets. Stella tipped the contents of the waste bin into a sack hanging from the handle of her cart. She missed and scattered rubbish all over the floor. Scooping it up, she saw too late it would have been a chance to have appeared to come across the form.

When Jack called, Stella had run out of anything to clean and had no reason to stay in the office.

'I thought it was on silent,' she muttered in apology to Marian Williams. 'It's a member of my staff. Would you mind?' She hoped Marian would mind. She couldn't talk to Jack; he would know she had stolen the form.

'Not at all, go ahead.' Marian Williams got up and swung her handbag on to her shoulder. 'I'm popping out. If you're gone when I get back, have a good rest of the day.'

Stella answered the phone. 'I'm at work,' she barked into the mouthpiece.

'I've been trying to get you. Where have you been?'

Not answering his phone was what Stella found exasperating about Jack. She could not tell him she had been helping David Barlow rescue a puppy from the river or that she had been out with him each time Jack had called. She didn't know why she was reluctant to tell him. Of course it was none of his business whom she went out with and anyway it wasn't going out. In fact it had been staying in. All of this meant she had not called him, but none of it could she explain, to Jack or herself.

She went on the defence. 'I only got a couple of messages.'

'So why didn't you answer one of them?'

'I'm answering now.'

'I've found another street, but if you're not interested…'

Stella clamped the phone to her ear to prevent his voice carrying into the room. 'Me too.'

Marian Williams gathered up the manila folder and slid it into a drawer in her desk. With a jangle of keys she locked the drawer and dropped the keys in her handbag. She didn't trust Stella. Five minutes ago Stella had wanted the file locked in the drawer, now she was dismayed she couldn't get to it.

'You talked to your policeman?'

'No.' Watching Marian Williams fussing at her desk, Stella was unprepared for what Jack said next.

'We might have Terry's pattern. Amanda Hampson's husband killed a child.'

'What do you mean? He …' Stella stopped. The word 'murdered' would get Marian Williams's attention. 'He used bleach?' she finished lamely.

'What? Oh, OK, you can't speak.'

'Yes. I mean no.'

'Charles Hampson killed a child months before his own accident. He was driving too fast. This is why I was calling you.'

'Try a different astringent.' At last Marian Williams snapped shut the clasp on her handbag and left. 'How do you know?' Stella asked Jack.

'I found an article about Charlie Hampson's death among Amanda's stuff. He ran over a boy called Stephen Parsons. I have the cutting here. It was the eighth of January 2009.'

'That's stealing.' Stella wiped her hand over her face. She had a green form belonging to the Metropolitan Police in her pocket and had rifled through a confidential file. She had evaded telling the truth about why she hadn't returned Jack's calls. She was not in a position to bandy ethics about.

'Amanda won't mind. She's treating me as a sounding board over this business.'

'What does it say?'

'Hampson died on Phoenix Way – the name's a little ironic, no rising from the dead for him – and I'm sure it's in Terry's blue folder. Hampson was done for causing death by careless or inconsiderate driving. He got off with a six-month suspended sentence and was banned for a year. Amanda thinks the punishment disproportionate. Indeed, one might say it was – too little. What you got?'

'I'll say when I see you. Did you go to the street you found, Marquis Way?'

'Not without you.' Jack was firm.

'Let's go tonight. Meet me at Terry's at nine-thirty. I'm cleaning there,' she added, knowing Jack wasn't fooled.

'Pick me up on King Street. That school, Mallingswood House, near Ravenscourt Park Station.'

'Why not the Tube?'

'Nine-thirty sharp,' Jack stipulated.

Stella rang off. Jack was sulking about her not returning his calls. He was up to something or he would have commented on her being at Terry's house. She thought of the form in her pocket and pulled it out. Dated Sunday, 17 October 1976, and headed 'James Harrison – Deceased', it outlined the facts of the fatality of a six-year-old boy in a road traffic accident at 3.30 p.m. He was hit crossing a zebra opposite Latymer Upper School on King Street by a Triumph TR7 that, according to witnesses, was travelling at speed.

Scrawled on a slip stapled to the corner was: 'Driver: Paul Vickery. Deceased Marquis Way W10. 16/3/77'. Stella had known the handwriting all her life: DCS Terence C. Darnell.

Terry had signed the addendum slip on 13 August 2008. One day after her birthday and the year before he retired. He had cross-referenced it with the Vickery file, now locked in Marian Williams's desk. Both incidents were over a quarter of a century old. Terry had signed the James Harrison file out of the General Registry four years ago. He would have given a reason, probably fresh evidence. If only she could see the file. But at least she had some information. They were getting somewhere.

As executive officer, Marian Williams's job was to process traumatic information and handle shocked and bereaved families. They didn't need Cashman to help with the photographs. However, with the green form burning a hole in her pocket and her conscience, Stella would not push her luck.

Outside in the station compound Stella fitted the completed job sheets at the front of her Filofax and flicked to her grid. She put in Jack's information, relieved she had retained the name of the boy and the date he had died, and what she had learnt from the police file and the green form.

Now proficient on the Street View app, Stella checked Phoenix Way on her phone. Jack's photographic memory was accurate: the road matched the street in the last picture in

Terry's blue folder. She noted down Terry's references – two photos for Phoenix Way – on her grid. Jack might be right about a pattern. Two of the drivers had knocked over children. Stella added extra columns, one for 'Child' and another with the date of child's death.

Pic. No.	Date	Street	Accident	Victim	Child	Date
1						
2(2a)						
3 (3a & 3b	16th March 1977	Marquis Way	Crashed car	Paul Vickery	James Harrison	17th October 1976
4						
5 (5a & 5b)	10th November 2002	Britton Drive	Hit a tree (car)	James Markham	Christopher Mason	2nd January 2002
6 (6a)						
7 (7a & 7b)	Date of death? Ask Jack	Phoenix Way	Hit a tree (car)	Charlie Hampson	Stephen Parsons	8th January 2009

They had identified streets for nine of the fifteen pictures. Stella was parking the car in a street behind the office when she thought again about Mrs Hampson confiding in Jack. Women had a soft spot for him. It was mutual. However irksome this was, Stella had learnt – within limits – to trust his judgement. Maybe Terry had also listened to Hampson – she was a good-looking woman – and had encouraged her to bring him anything new? A rash offer: Amanda Hampson would come with the flimsiest of clutched straws.

By going out with David Barlow – not that she was – Stella had crossed a boundary with one client, so hanged for a sheep… The next time Jack cleaned for Amanda Hampson, she would tag along and introduce herself as the detective's daughter.

Thirty-Six

'Fifty yards, turn left.' The satnav voice broke the silence. 'You have reached your destination.'

Stella drove a little way along Marquis Way and, stopping, leant over the wheel and peered out at the darkness. Like Britton Drive it was poorly lit. She left the headlights on full beam. Jack said it was better to be here at night – when Hampson, for one, had died – to recreate the scene. She knew this to be true.

Jack was right about atmosphere. Marquis Way was deserted. Stella questioned the wisdom of the decision: she was about to suggest that they come back in daylight when Jack jumped out of the van. He sprinted over to a high fence fixed into breeze blocks on the other side of the road. Clinging to the mesh, he peered through. A sign to his left read: 'Guard Dogs Patrolling'. Beneath the words was a cartoon drawing of a slavering dog.

'Jack, I think we should...' The words died on her lips. Jack wouldn't listen. Instead Stella joined him, this time bringing her phone. She switched on her torch. Surely there was nothing to guard in this sprawl of wasteland? Scraps of rubbish were caught in the wire and banked up at the base of the fence. In the midst of the levelled ground stood a hoarding on which was a mock-up of a 'modern office unit' featuring sleek cladding and plenty of stainless steel and glass. A banner declaring 'Affordable Prices!' cut diagonally over the picture beneath which was more sales blurb about square footage and Wi-Fi. Nettles and brambles, weeds and sycamore saplings dotted amongst the rubble suggested that the 'unique opportunity to acquire a unit within a landmark development' was some way in the future. The saplings would be trees before the diggers arrived. Stella scanned the street; again like Britton Drive, it was derelict, victim to the recession.

She had met Jack by a drinking fountain on King Street. She told him the photograph of Phoenix Way in Amanda Hampson's cutting was the street in three photographs numbered 7, 7a and 7b in Terry's folder. This made him annoyingly happy – he loved it when apparently disconnected facts and events were linked. Jack was a magnet for coincidence, signs that he took for instruction. Life wasn't like that for most people, Stella would say. She told him about the Paul Vickery file, avoiding how she knew. He was so excited that they had proved three photographs in the file were of streets where a collision had occurred he didn't ask how she got the information about Vickery and James Harrison.

Marquis Way lay on the outskirts of Hammersmith and Fulham, bordering Acton. Like Britton Drive it was long and bleak and penetrated deep into a dilapidated industrial estate. Opposite the wasteland was a row of four prefab units, with tar roofs peeling and fascias askew, that Stella dated to the eighties. They looked abandoned but for a sack of rubbish placed by a door and a dull blue light glowing from behind the wired glass in a window. Only one building proclaimed its business, 'Luxury Imports' spelled in vinyl letters stuck on the window. The last prefab had blinds drawn down, two slats were bent, leaving gaps through which someone could be watching. Stella's body flooded with adrenalin; if they were attacked no one could help. She checked her phone. There was no signal.

'This is a feeder road. It's not a short cut so there will be little traffic.' Not for the first time Jack seemed to read her mind. 'You'd only be here on purpose.' He leaned against the fence; it gave slightly with his weight. 'It's not on Street View. We are off the map!' He seemed pleased by this.

'We are off our heads. Let's go.' Stella turned to the van. Jack spent as much time on Street View as on real streets.

'Not now we're here,' Jack replied illogically.

'How do these places exist in a wealthy capital city with land at a premium?' Bringing Jack back to reality, Stella indicated the prefab with the blue light.

'Probably zombies.'

'What?'

'Companies earning enough to meet interest payments, but the bank won't lend more so they can't develop. They are in stasis, unable to live or to die. The walking dead of capitalism.'

So much for reality. Stella took a few steps along the road. She shone the torch up a driveway and picked out what looked like an old chapel. The drive continued down the side to what must have been the door for collection and deliveries. The paint on a sign was gone, leaving a ghostly outline: 'Wilkins Laundry'. The words 'Established 1868' were carved at the apex of a tiled roof. Buddleia and bindweed grew around the door and sprouted through cracked window panes. This business was properly dead. It belonged in a horror film. She retreated.

'This is brilliant. Come on.' Jack hurried up the track. Stella kept pace in case he did something stupid. Something else stupid. Jack tried the door handle at the back of the laundry. It was locked. Stella brushed her hand on a clump of tall nettles and stung her knuckles.

Jack was checking the fastenings on windows either side of the door. These too were shut fast.

'This is trespassing, we should go.' As soon as she spoke, Stella heard a noise. The low drone of a car engine. Someone else had a reason for being here and it was unlikely to be legitimate. She switched off her torch. Silence. Either the car had passed by or had stopped. The road was a dead end. It was out there. Alive to every sound, Stella heard a creak, a door opening. Her knuckles tingled as if her fear had located itself there.

Treading carefully, as if over a minefield, Jack took her hand and led her around to the other side of the laundry. This was an alley with no way out. Halfway down was a wheelie bin from which came a smell that Stella didn't want to trace to its source.

This was no hiding place if the driver of the car looked properly. Jack stood in front of Stella, shielding her. She stopped breathing, willing herself to disappear.

She heard a sound: the measured tread of a person intent on hiding their presence, keeping to the nettles where the ground was soft. Had she not heard the car she would not have known someone was there. Stone grinding on stone: they had reached the rubble at the back of the laundry. Jack's shoulders were rigid. Two more metres and that was that.

Stella could not bear it. She would rather confront the man. The only thing stopping her was that he might be armed.

Then she heard an engine and a throaty acceleration receded to nothing.

'He's gone.' Jack pushed aside the bin.

'Let's go.' Stella was overwhelmed by another rush of adrenalin. Her tongue was rubbery; the nettle sting was vengeful. If only nettles were all she had to worry about.

'We haven't found what we came for. Shine your torch here.' Jack's voice sounded loud in the intense quiet. He was by a tall spreading tree, the one live thing in the area. Stella's hand shook; the beam wavered. He took the torch from her and trained it on to the trunk.

Stella made her way over the remains of a low wall, stepping over a slab of bricks that had fallen away from it and lay, almost concealed, by grass and thistles.

'This is where Paul Vickery died.' Jack indicated a faint mark in the rough patina.

Stella let out a breath. 'He must have rammed straight into it.' Suddenly anxious, she scanned the road for the car they had heard. Far off a lamp-post spread a dull cone of light too weak to be effective. All was long shadows and patches of dark. 'Let's go.'

'Two minutes.' Jack spread out the article on the pavement and pulled the blue folder from his capacious coat pocket. He opened it at the photographs prefixed with a three. Like the Hampson pictures there were three: 3, 3a and 3b. In the newspaper picture the tree was possibly smaller, the wall outside the laundry intact, as it was in Terry's black and white photograph.

'Terry took his picture before this collapsed,' Jack shone his torch on the remains of the wall, 'which judging by the bricks was some time ago.'

'This is an ash tree.' Stella peered into the dark of the leaves above her. 'What's the connection between these deaths?' Her voice rang across the deserted space. She turned round, but Jack was heading off along the street and soon merged into blackness.

She got up, fear coiling, and ventured forward, keeping within the van's headlights. From the wasteland beyond the fence she fancied she heard breathing; perhaps dogs actually were patrolling.

Jack was squatting by a telegraph pole. He had set the torch on its end and the uplight gave him dark eye sockets and gaunt cheekbones. Stella would not have liked to encounter him unexpectedly on a bleak and desolate street after dark. He wasn't reassuring her now.

'Recognize this?'

'No.' She fought off panic; ridiculous, she wasn't easily frightened.

Jack flipped through the photographs. 'We've established that Marquis Way covers the photos numbered with a three, but look.'

Judging by the angle of the sun, Terry had taken the two pictures early in the morning. A metal fence gleamed in piercing light blurring a spindle that Stella recognized as the telegraph pole. It was the same street as the pictures of Vickery's street with the ash tree, but these – only two this time – were numbered with a six.

'You know what this means?'

'Jack, it's too late for a quiz.'

'Someone else died here, see these grooves in the wood. The pole withstood the impact or they would have replaced it.' He scrabbled in the earth at the bottom of the pole.

Terry's gloves were smeared with soil. Stella resisted grousing that he should look after them; she had given them to Jack, so he could do what he liked with them.

He held out his hand. For a moment Stella hoped he was asking her to clean his glove. She looked into Jack's open palm. 'More stones.' She quelled a sigh.

'Yes! Like the ones where James Markham was killed on Britton Drive. They're not stones, they're chips of broken glass. Money on we find more at Vickery's tree next to the laundry and on Phoenix Way where Charlie Hampson was killed.'

Stella went cold. 'I do think we should leave.' This time she turned on her heel and hurried towards the van.

'Jack.' She stared at the van, its headlamps cutting into the dark of the long avenue. 'That man must have seen the van. He knew we were there.'

'That's why he went.' Jack was unruffled. 'Scared him off.' He walked back to the laundry and ferreted around the base of the tree. Stella believed that Jack's tenacity, a quality she relied upon, might tonight be their undoing. 'Maybe we've prevented a crime,' he called cheerily.

Stella wiped her hand down her face. If she wanted to prevent crime she would have joined the police. She climbed into the driving seat. At any minute the man might come back, and with a gang. She tapped a tattoo on the steering wheel until she began to remind herself of her mother and stopped.

At last Jack joined her. 'Just as I guessed.' He was triumphant. 'I found more under the tree.' He began decanting the glass chips into two plastic bags.

'Oh no!' Stella bashed the wheel. 'They'll find me. Clean Slate's details are all over this bloody thing!'

'Not this one. You swapped it after that chap in the garage clocked you, remember?' Jack stuffed the bags into his coat pocket. 'Every cloud, Stell, every cloud. I do believe we are getting somewhere, just not sure where.' He leant forward and reprogrammed the satnav to the street where in 2009 Charlie Hampson's life had abruptly ended.

Just inside the Hammersmith boundary, Phoenix Way was bounded by Hammersmith Cemetery on one side and Mortlake Crematorium on the other. Long and bleak like the other roads, here too street lighting was sparse – not helped, Stella noticed, by two of the lamps being out. She rolled the van on to a verge of grass between the pavement and the road. The tree that had killed Charles Hampson was an oak, tall and flourishing; thick roots had lifted the flags around its base. Stella reckoned it was over a century old. The odd car smashing into it now and again would be small fry. Again Stella reckoned that this was a reason why she liked trees. They weren't affected by petty concerns.

Like James Markham's tree, the trunk had sustained a deep gash. Hampson's fatal incident had only happened three years ago so the wound was still raw, the exposed wood a blurred shape in the darkness.

This time it was Stella who spotted the glass pieces, they were embedded in the soil between the roots. Jack tipped them into a bag.

'OK,' she conceded. 'They could be significant.' She took the bag from him and pointed her torch at it. 'Perhaps relatives leave them instead of flowers?' She peered through the plastic. 'There are seven. How many in the others?'

Jack produced the bags from his coat pocket.

In a lull on the main road, the faint sound of the bells of St Nicholas Church by the river striking quarter past eleven carried on the night breeze.

'Seven,' Jack said at last. 'A sign. It can't be family or why are there always seven and always green?'

'Maybe it's someone who knows all the victims?'

'Seven's a special number,' Jack mused. 'There're seven notes in the major scale, seven Roman emperors; if you divide any amount under seven by seven you get the same six digits always in the same sequence—'

'That's too clever.' Stella cut in. 'It must be simpler – days of the week or a lucky number.' Terry said start from the simple and work up. Start in the corners and clean outwards. It was important to keep to the process.

No car had passed. Although it was late, Stella doubted that Phoenix Way ever got many pedestrians. The reason would be to attend a funeral and few would walk. Why was Charles Hampson here? She contemplated the glass bits. 'These are familiar.'

Something moved. She whisked around. The road was empty. In the cemetery she heard an owl hoot, or a pigeon. Whatever, it decided her. 'We're leaving!'

Perhaps at last Jack shared her anxiety because he immediately came back to the van with her and when they were inside pressed the central-locking switch. Stella turned the ignition key; the engine fired and stalled.

'I shouldn't have left the lights on,' she groaned, flooring the accelerator. The starter motor whined; the engine coughed then died.

'The engine's flooding. Let it rest.' Jack examined the latest bag of green chips.

Stella heaved a sigh. It was not completely dark and through the railings pale headstones looked unattached, ghostly. One moved. Stella shuddered. It wasn't a headstone. There was someone in the cemetery. Dressed in white, they drifted beyond the line of yew trees.

She fumbled with the key, the motor caught and she bunny-hopped the van off the kerb without checking her mirror. She looked over at the cemetery. The white figure had gone. She was tired. So much for evoking atmosphere; they had evoked phantoms and in her case a headache.

Jack rattled the bags of glass. 'Four dead men.'

'Four?' Stella tried to summon up her grid.

'Paul Vickery, James Markham, poor old Charlie Hampson and a mystery driver who tangled with a telegraph pole. Someone or some people wanted them dead,' Jack murmured.

'You think they were murdered?' She was very grateful to join the South Circular where the lights worked and there was still plenty of traffic.

'I don't think they were accidents.' Jack weighed the bags in each hand, tossing them back and forth. 'And nor did Terry.' He stamped on an imaginary brake, 'Turn right here.'

'It's not the way to my flat.'

'You said you wanted to meet Amanda Hampson.'

Thirty-Seven

Monday, 30 April 2012

It was nearly midnight when they reached Kew. All the lights in the two-storey house were blazing. Jack was right: Mrs Hampson was still up. A lamp over the porch lit a gravel path to the door.

'It's open.' Jack made to step inside.

'We can't just walk in.' Stella reached around him and rang the bell. The sound pealed like a fire alarm. She preferred David's Big Ben bell. She was meeting David tomorrow.

No one answered.

'She must have forgotten to close it. People are always doing that,' Jack said.

'How do you…? Oh, never mind.' Stella pushed the button again. The sound was difficult to miss, she thought.

'Come on.' Jack pushed the door wide and they were greeted by a bluff of warm air. 'Mrs Hamp-son?' he called cheerily and when he got no reply, 'Amanda?'

'She must be here, the heating's on full blast.' Stella undid her anorak and followed Jack into a brightly lit hallway.

The kitchen was large. In the centre was a hexagonal island inset with a six-ring hob.

'We shouldn't be here. Clean Slate has upset her already. Using bleach will be nothing to wandering about her home uninvited,' Stella said.

'We should secure the house. She's gone out and forgotten to lock up.' Jack did not say that he too was keen to leave. He was used to occupying Hosts' houses in their absence, but this felt different.

Droplets of water clung to plates and dishes in the draining rack. Jack felt the kettle: it was warm. The oven emitted a gentle heat when he opened the door. Amanda Hampson had cooked, eaten and washed up her supper things. She had started taking care of her newly cleaned home, but then had gone out, leaving the door open. It didn't add up.

'Maybe's she's in bed,' Stella whispered.

'She says she never sleeps.'

'She must sleep some time.'

The sitting room was the hub of Amanda's quest for the truth about her husband's death. Here too it was tidier than Jack usually found it. Amanda had stacked her papers into piles and placed them on her desk and on the dining table. Cushions plumped in their corners on the sofa were as he had left them.

Charlie Hampson smiled down, sardonic within his gilded frame.

Jack trod heavily up the ladder-style staircase to warn Amanda, but she was not in any of the rooms.

He stopped. 'Look in the bathroom.'

'Why me?'

'If she's fallen asleep in the bath, it's better you wake her than me.'

'Hardly.' Nevertheless Stella pushed the door open with a finger. She stepped back on to Jack's foot.

'Ouch!'

'She's not there.'

They retreated to the sitting room.

'She might be at the station.' Jack was hopeful. 'Maybe she got an appointment with Martin Cashman after all.'

Stella shook her head. 'At this time of night? Besides he's on holiday.'

'Wait a minute.' Jack flicked one of the piles with his gloved hand. 'She's taken her file.'

'What file?'

'The pink one she took to the police.'

'I saw her with that.' Stella looked around.

Jack glanced behind him and Charlie Hampson's eyes met his. Amanda Hampson would never leave her house unattended. On his first visit she had not trusted him to be alone there.

'We're being dense. Call her. You have her number.' He nudged Stella.

'I don't. Jackie does, but obviously she's at home now.'

'Ring her.'

'At home asleep. Most people are at this time, Jack. Besides, she won't have the number there.'

Jack stirred the papers on the desk and unearthed a fat leather wallet. 'She hasn't taken her Filofax.' He felt a creeping unease. In the event of loss, please return to… Amanda had filled in her name, address and home telephone and at the bottom in different ink was her mobile number. 'Got it!'

'She will be cross that we're here.' Stella peered out of the French doors at the garden.

'Let's ring her and see.' Laboriously Jack keyed in the number on his phone. He counted the rings. 'Come on, Amanda.'

'Ssssh. I can hear a ringtone.' Stella put her finger to her lips.

Jack shook his head. 'She's on voicemail.'

'Try again.' Stella was fumbling with the door handle.

Jack pressed 'redial'. 'That's weird. I can hear ringing.' He joined Stella.

'It's out here.' Stella heaved on the doors.

Jack stamped his foot. 'The meditation temple!'

'The what?'

'She's doing Yoga Nidra!'

Cool air wafted in from the garden. Jack plunged on to the path. He hissed at Stella. 'You stay here. She hates being disturbed, but she knows me.'

'She's not expecting you in the middle of the night. You could scare her witless.'

Jack trod on something. He looked down. The light on the crazy paving was Amanda Hampson's phone, its screen glowing with a missed call.

'Jack.' Stella grabbed his coat sleeve.

Amanda Hampson lay face down on the threshold of her temple. Jack took some moments to comprehend that the dark spreading pool around her head was blood.

'She's dead.' Stella dabbed at her phone and rapped out. 'Police. And ambulance, although it's too late.'

The springs on Colin's bed were painful, but Jack didn't care. He stared at his hands. Long and slender, his mother said they were the hands of a pianist. His fingers tingled as if they still rested on Amanda Hampson's neck – her skin had been warm – feeling for a pulse. He buried his face in the pillow. The bed was meant for a child so he had to bring his knees to his chest. Tonight the position suited him: he felt small and lost. When he was at school he had lain alone in the dark, missing his home and his mummy. Time had telescoped.

Until he had found the glass on Phoenix Way, Jack had rather assumed that Amanda Hampson herself had been driven off kilter by her husband's death. In the grip of an obsession, she wheedled at every bit of evidence to make it corroborate her conviction that someone had killed him. Tonight Jack had planned to apologize and say he believed her. But Amanda was dead and the police were treating it as suspicious.

He swung his legs over the bed. He would go back to the house and examine it properly. He slumped forward; of course he could not. The bona fide detectives were there; he had no right. Amanda was not a relative: he had no rights at all.

The front door clicked shut below. His Host was back. He should hide, but he was tired and tempted to let matters take their course. He could share these thoughts with her, two minds were better than one and her mind might serve him well. He went into the corridor and took up position in the shadow of the fire door.

She paused for breath on the staircase. Again Jack experienced the certainty that she was aware of him. This time he crouched low; most people expect intruders to be the height of an adult so rarely look down. His Host was not 'most people'.

She went on up the stairs without looking right or left.

She was as much a stranger to him as on the day he had encountered her. He loved working on the streets in the attic – the work was a secret he shared with the old man about which his Host clearly knew nothing – but he could not afford the indulgence. Tomorrow he would get his book back and leave. He and Stella had a murderer to catch.

Jack Harmon climbed back into bed and burrowed beneath the blankets. In the woolly darkness he pictured Amanda Hampson, alive and executing flighty dance moves on her landing. Softly, the way his mother did, Jack sang himself to sleep.

> 'I had a little pony,
> His name was Dapple Gray;
> I lent him to a lady
> To ride a mile away.
> She whipped him, she slashed him,
> She rode him through the mire;
> I would not lend my pony now,
> For all the lady's hire.'

Thirty-Eight

Tuesday, 1 May 2012

Early the next morning Stella pushed her cart along the corridor of the second floor of Hammersmith Police Station, the wheels spinning on the varnished wood. She parked it by the ladies' toilets, unhooked the mop and bucket wringer, grabbed the floor cleaner and, complete with latex gloves, shouldered inside.

Four cubicles took up the left side of the tiled room; doors ajar, they faced a matching number of sinks with mirrors. The sinks, dating from the thirties, were generous in proportion with flat rims on which lay blocks of soap. The porcelain was riven with cracks, darkened with time and impossible to clean properly. Stella eyed them like enemies while she massed her equipment in the echoing chamber.

She had not slept. Unlike Jack, who had remained cool at the sight of Amanda Hampson dead and bleeding, her eyes blankly staring, it had been all Stella could do not to pass out on the floor of what Jack kept calling a temple. Perhaps he had been affected, because on King Street, as they were passing the drinking fountain where, in what seemed another life, she had picked him up earlier, he had bundled out of the van without saying goodbye.

Even after a shower and a hairwash the metallic odour of blood clung to her. She had lain all night stiff and inert as a corpse until the dark sky resolved to grey, when she gave up on sleep and took another shower. It was then she had remembered Terry's trick of dabbing eucalyptus oil under his nostrils. She found a bottle in the bathroom cabinet and smeared it liberally around her nose. It stung and had not eradicated the metallic odour. It was in her mind.

With Jack gone, the milky eyes staring up unseeing were only more vivid, even when, stopped at traffic lights, she could shut her eyes, she could not obliterate the image. Stella had doubled back to invite him to sleep in her spare room, but he was not on Weltje Road or King Street or walking along the Great West Road. He had not had time to go into the subway to the river. She drew up alongside the drinking fountain, her eye drawn to the wrought-iron gates of the prep school. Jack had vanished. She worried that he was up to his old tricks. She had hoped solving the Rokesmith murder would have sorted it. On top of finding Mrs Hampson, this worry had contributed to Stella's lack of sleep.

Now, alone in the police toilets, she scowled at her reflection in one of the mirrors. She tucked a lock of hair behind her ears and grimaced to relax her facial muscles, a trick of Jackie's. She glanced past her reflection and froze. One of the cubicles was shut. She whipped around.

There was someone inside.

She heard a groan.

'Hello?' she faltered. The doors were fitted from the ceiling to the floor; the only way in was by smashing the lock.

'Can you hear me?' Stupid. Only a dead person would fail to hear her. Stella shook her head at this idea. 'I'll get help,' she quavered.

The bolt slid slowly. The door jerked open. Marian Williams staggered out and toppled into Stella's arms. Shorter by many inches than Stella's six feet, and well built, Stella had to rest against a basin to keep her balance.

Eventually Williams let go and tottered to a sink. Stella steeled herself against the possibility that the administrator was going to vomit. This she could tolerate less than a corpse.

The woman twisted on the tap and ran water over her hands and mopped her brow. 'Thank you.' She didn't look at Stella, she returned to the lavatory and came out patting her face dry with a wad of toilet paper.

'What happened?' Stella leant on the handle of her bucket wringer set.

'Everything went black. I fainted. Next thing I heard you.'

Stella snapped into action. 'I'll get help. Someone must do first aid here.'

'That's me.' Marian Williams pushed the sodden paper into a swing bin by the door. As she did so, her cardigan sleeve rode up.

'You're hurt!' Stella jerked the mop handle at a dark bruise that merged into a graze on the administrator's forearm.

'It doesn't hurt.' Williams regarded the wound as if it was not her own.

'It's shock.' Stella was brisk. 'Come back to your office, I'll get you a cup of tea with sugar.'

They sat either side of Marian Williams's desk with hot drinks that Stella had fetched from the canteen. Marian Williams rested her injured arm on her lap and drank unsteadily with her left. The bruise was livid crimson, overlaid with darker marks in a row that made Stella think of fingers.

'That was some knock. You were lucky not to break it.' Despite herself Stella was relieved she had not cleaned the toilets before the accident, it cleared her of responsibility. Core to Clean Slate's induction was a warning to staff not to over-polish floors or leave them damp without a warning cone.

'Lucky not to break what?' Detective Chief Superintendent Cashman breezed in.

'Mrs Williams fell in the ladies' toilets.' Too late Stella realized the woman did not want Cashman to know. Tugging at her sleeve, she was concentrating on her computer screen.

'It's nothing, sir. I'm fine, thanks to Ms Darnell.'

'Let me be the judge of that.' Cashman towered over the desk. When Marian Williams rolled up her sleeve he gave a whistle. 'You are going home, no argument.'

'It looks worse than it is.'

'I insist.' He rocked on his heels. 'It is as bad as it looks. What happened?'

'I thought you were on holiday.'

'I was hauled in last night. A fatality – as Stella knows: she called it in. Did you do that here?'

Stella wondered if he was thinking about compensation, but Cashman was old school like Terry, he didn't work that way. What you saw was what you got.

'It was my fault.' Marian Williams shook her head. 'What fatality?' She frowned at Stella as if she were responsible for his curtailed holiday, which, in a way, she was. Marian Williams had not heard about Amanda Hampson's death. Stella was suddenly sure that the woman did not like to be a step behind. Especially if the one in front was the cleaner.

'It's on Surrey's patch,' Cashman said. 'Near Kew station. They got me in because we know the victim. It's that Mrs Hampson who, I've just heard, you handled like the pro you are last week. Stella and a colleague had the nasty experience of finding her.' He sniffed and glanced at Stella. 'Actually Stell, I never asked what you and your friend were doing there, better tick that one off!'

Stella felt her brain empty of words. She should have anticipated this, but despite her misgivings about the police she did rely on Cashman treating her as one of their own and so had not prepared an answer. Her rescue came from the least expected place.

'Were you passing, perhaps?' Marian Williams wheeled herself to the printer where a paper lay in the output tray. She did not look at Stella.

'I was, yes.' Marian Williams had inadvertently saved her. 'My colleague does – did her cleaning and he noticed lights on and the door was open. I didn't know her myself.' Marian would wonder why Stella hadn't mentioned this after Mrs Hampson's visit to the office.

'It'll need processing.' Marian Williams snatched up her mouse.

'Go home, Marian!' Cashman clapped his hands. 'We're on it.'

Stella broke another cardinal Clean Slate rule and questioned a client – and it was the police – about their business: 'Any idea what happened?'

'No suspicious circs. It's looking like she tripped on the path. Money on the tox report says high blood-alcohol levels. There was an empty whisky bottle in the bin and a tumbler with whisky dregs that had lipstick on the rim. No sign of an intruder. As you know, Stella, the door was open. Neighbours heard nothing. One said it wasn't the first time she'd forgotten to lock up. Another implied she wasn't the full shilling, but that was based on that temple thingy in her garden.' He was pacing the room; he stopped by the door. 'Marian, before you shoot off, can you give me the heads up on what Mrs Hampson wanted when she came?'

The administrator was staring at her screen, showing no signs of shooting off. If Stella were her, she would disapprove of Cashman involving the cleaner. Cashman behaved as if she were an extension of Terry. Stella found herself liking this notion.

'She had found out Hampson had his advanced driving licence. I said we knew.'

Cashman puffed out his cheeks. 'Got to feel sorry for her. She was scraping that barrel.' He rocked on his heels. 'Suicide's not ruled out, though there's no note.'

'What about Joel Evans's killer?' Marian Williams got up from her desk. 'Matthew Benson has to be expedited. I'm fine now.'

Stella had sympathy. Jackie had once packed her off to the dentist in the middle of a crisis. Work was the best cure.

Cashman strolled to the filing cabinets and leant on one. 'Benson's going nowhere: we've got his passport. You are! Watch rubbish daytime telly and return fresh as a daisy.' Cashman thrust his hands in his pockets.

Marian Williams turned to Stella and said formally, 'Thank you for your help.'

'It was nothing.' Stella squeezed her empty tea beaker until it cracked. 'I hope you feel better soon.' Marian had gone.

'She's a diamond.' Cashman pushed away from the cabinet. 'Here week in, week out. Marian's missed one day in the last twenty-five years.'

Stella whisked her cloth at the vacated desk. 'I suppose you need Marian to keep up with processing traffic-accident figures.' This was the nearest she would go to asking Cashman outright about Terry's streets. And then, conscious of the non sequitur: 'Like that boy Marian mentioned.'

'I wish! We don't analyse traffic incidents. They're a second cousin to crime. Even if we did, we don't have the resources to follow up. That was one of Terry's beefs.' Suddenly he was efficient; rubbing his hands together, he crossed to the door. 'Stella, you manage people. Did she look OK to you?'

Stella didn't think of herself as managing people. 'Yes. Well, apart from the fall.' So Terry had been bothered about traffic incidents.

'Lucky it was you that found her. Terry's daughter can do no wrong! Your dad was a god to her. I'm a poor substitute!'

Alone in the office, Stella could not wipe away the sight of Mrs Hampson bleeding on the stones. She should call Jack. Terry would have checked on his team after a trauma. Martin Cashman had sent a key staff member home because of a bruise. Stella had no idea about managing people.

When she returned to the toilets it was after eight and the station was busy. She wouldn't clean with women coming in and out; clients resented their privacy being disturbed.

She did not know what made her go into the cubicle where Marian had fallen, lock the door and sit on the closed toilet lid. Her knees were an inch from the door, the tiled walls close to her shoulders. There was little room to move, what with a plastic bin for sanitary towels, another Gina-Ware product. The porcelain toilet-paper dispenser was inset flush into the tiles. It had not caused the injury.

Marian Williams was not a small woman so it was freakish that she had hurt herself in the tight space. Bad luck that she got such a drastic bruise; she must bruise easily.

Someone entered the adjacent toilet. Stella hurried out, wheeling the bucket-wringer ahead of her like a child's toy.

At the lights on Shepherd's Bush Green, Stella recalled Cashman's prediction that Mrs Hampson's death was an accident fuelled by alcohol. It was as unlikely as Marian's injury. Terry said there was no such thing as an accident. For once he was wrong. Odd things did happen.

The lights went to green. Mulling on Jack, Stella concluded that if she rang to offer him support, he would be embarrassed. She would be.

Some things were best unsaid.

Thirty-Nine

Tuesday, 1 May 2012

The electronic Big Ben clangs were strident. Stella had seen David Barlow three times now and on each occasion his manner had been warm and understated. The doorbell must have come with the house. But he had said he had lived here for over thirty years. The chimes must be his wife's choice. She jumped at the click of a latch behind her.

'Come this way, Stella.'

David held open the side gate. Lit by a strip of afternoon sunlight, he appeared taller while oddly less substantial. Something was draped over his left arm. Stella shifted her equipment bag on her shoulder and crunched over the gravel to him.

The 'something' was a small apricot dog. It took Stella a moment to recognize the stray from the riverbank. Washed and brushed, it had come up a lighter shade with ears brown and sticking out as, rapt with attention, it pinned its gaze on her. The dark brown unblinking eyes suggested attack if she got too close.

'You kept it.' Stella avoided contact with animals; she passed clients with pets to her staff. Such clients had a lower standard of what she considered clean.

'He had no microchip or collar. The vet reckoned he'd been dumped because the owners couldn't afford the upkeep. No reports of a lost poodle. The vet thought he'd been living rough a while.' David Barlow lifted the dog's paw. 'Stanley, meet Stella!'

'Stanley?' Stella tried to sound neutral. She was uncomfortable with giving pets human names; it made the boundaries fuzzy.

'My father was called Stanley.' David Barlow ushered her down the side passage of the house.

Stella could not name a dog after Terry. It would be as if Terry was the dog. Jack believed that when people died their energy was redistributed, he would probably approve. That pets caused mess and fuss was one thing she and her mum agreed on.

She stepped on to the lawn and relaxed. A flawless green – not a weed or a bare patch – with the grass cut so short it propelled her along.

'Watch.' David lowered his hand and the dog sank to the ground. It flicked looks at Stella. She glared at the whites of its eyes.

'Stanley?' The dog shot around, tail pert. 'Ssssit!' He raised his hand, palm up. It rose to a sitting position. Despite herself Stella was impressed.

'Poodles are smart.' David scooped up the dog. Paws hanging like bagpipes, it contemplated Stella's equipment bag. 'We never had dogs. Jennifer didn't like animals: too much mess. I'm suspicious of anyone who doesn't like animals.' He jiggled the dog in his arms. 'Aren't you?'

'I'll get started.'

'Let's have tea out here first. Though if you are going somewhere later...'

Stella was due at Terry's house, but at no particular time. Terry wouldn't be there. When he was alive, she often rang to say she was running late.

'That would be nice.' David wasn't like a client, she told herself.

'Hold him while I bring everything out.'

'I'll do it.' Stella knew where the dog had been.

'He likes you.' David Barlow lifted it into Stella's arms.

Stella stood on the lawn, the poodle lolling on her forearm, paws spilling. She held her breath against a doggy odour, but when at last she inhaled only caught David's aftershave. She sniffed properly. Warm clean wool and the invigorating fragrance that she had yet to identify. Her sense of smell was laser sharp and she divined something else pleasing. David. Jack said that if you didn't like a person's body odour you could never be close to them even if you liked them. Stella had supposed he meant her. She made sure to smell of nothing personal. She wasn't close to Jack. She patted the dog. Pat. Pat. It whisked around and licked her knuckles. Stella snatched her hand away.

'I knew you'd have a way with him.' David was passing with the tea tray. 'Come on, dog whisperer!' he laughed over his shoulder.

A green wrought-iron table was set beneath a matching umbrella at the end of the garden, screened by a trellis trailing with red roses. Stella blinked away the crimson of Amanda Hampson's blood coagulating on pale limestone. She squeezed the dog; it licked her hand again. She didn't wipe it dry.

David had been sitting here: his notebook and pen were on the table. A letter with the logo for the insurance company Terry had used for his car lay open. There were three chairs. Wildly she envisaged Jennifer Barlow joining them. Jack said ghosts were everywhere. She pulled herself together and sat carefully on the nearest chair, supporting the dog.

David unpacked the tea things. Another cake. Stella expected the dog to leap over to him when she sat down, but instead it turned around on her lap twice, flopped down and, head tucked into its chest, went to sleep.

'Just got that.' He indicated the letter. 'We're not getting anything for the burglary.' He slipped it back into the envelope. 'Police found no signs of forced entry, no proof of a crime. They're not accusing us outright of making a false claim, but…' His good mood seemed to have evaporated.

'They find any excuse not to pay up,' Stella agreed. She was discouraged by his use of 'we'. Her first instinct had been right: Barlow still loved his wife. Stella would not be a substitute. She regarded the third chair. Someone, Jack probably, said that dogs sensed the presence of ghosts. She looked at the sleeping poodle. No ghosts here. Still, she would eat the cake, do the cleaning and go.

'Jennifer insisted I report the break-in to the police. She made me go every week to see if they'd got anywhere. Of course they hadn't. Then she died. I only submitted the claim a month ago. More for her sake. I'm guessing they found the time lapse of four months suspicious. I'm not sorry. The burglars were welcome to all of it. Its value was sentimental, more to Jennifer than me.'

'Odd they didn't take any electrical goods.' Stella heard that she sounded suspicious. 'Specialized thieves target what they can fence.' She stopped. David had risked his life to save a dog. He would not make a false insurance claim.

'Spoken like the daughter of a police officer!' David slotted the letter into his notebook and laid it on the grass. '"God is watching you," she'd say, "he sees all our transgressions." She promised she'd be watching me too. Absurd!' He gave a wry smile and poured the tea.

It wasn't absurd. Over the last year, eating shepherd's pies in Terry's kitchen, and cleaning his house, Stella felt Terry watching.

'This is her seed cake. Are you OK with almonds?'

Stella smiled, reluctant to eat anything made by a dead woman.

'By the end Jennifer could hardly speak or walk, then three days before she died, the Tuesday, she was her old self. A miracle, she said. "God has given me a day to spend wisely."' He thrust the point of the blade into the sponge. 'Her voice was strong, she could walk – with a frame – even dress herself. She baked seven cakes. She often did that, for fairs, charity or whatnot, but these were for me. "Keep me in your thoughts," she said. She put them in the freezer saying she'd know if I gave them away. This is number six.'

'Why wouldn't you eat them?' Stella was too late to stop David tipping a large slice onto her plate.

'Call me unfeeling.' He gazed over the dog. 'Life has to be about more than being obedient.' He talked between mouthfuls of cake, dabbing his mouth with his napkin. 'That dog is pure joy.' He gave her a shy smile.

Stella, concentrating on restoring order and keeping surfaces spotless, had not thought about life in these terms.

'We were unsuited. By the end it was a loveless relationship. Got so you never knew what was around the corner. There, I've said it!' He stopped eating. '"Grab life while you can," to quote Stanley Barlow! Dad didn't take to Jennifer, said she was "starchy". He'd approve of ... of me starting again.' He cut himself another piece.

Stella didn't mention Terry's shepherd's pies, not that Terry had cooked them or insisted she eat them. Besides, she had bought them herself when they had run out. Once the freezer was empty she would sell the house.

A thought occurred: 'Did you find the jacket?' Distracted by the dog, Stella had forgotten the jacket behind the bath panel.

'I did. More cake?' He held up a piece balanced on the blade.

Silly question, of course he had. 'I'm fine thanks.' He was no longer smiling.

'I'd better get on.' She gathered up the dog, still in a ball, and stood up. She shouldn't have mentioned the jacket. Cleaning is our business; what we find is their business. The sun had gone in; the air was cooler.

'I shall take this little lad out for a walk.' David Barlow scrambled the plates and cups on to the tray.

Only a third of the cake was left. Despite the disparaging comments, he must like it. Stella had never baked a cake. Nor would she.

They walked across the lawn to the house. The dog struggled up on to Stella's shoulder. David put the tray on the kitchen table and came back outside.

The silence was broken by a drawn-out mewing sound. The dog smacked his lips and nuzzled into the crook of Stella's neck.

'He's yawning!' David tickled the dog under the chin and the back of his hand caught her cheek. He was looking at her, smiling again.

'Stanley's my second chance. You too,' he murmured. 'I'm not a believer in God, nor do I hold with things being meant, but hanging out like this, it's OK, isn't it?'

'Yes.' David didn't care about the jacket. It must have belonged to whoever lived here before. His wife had died four months ago, he respected her memory, but he had been honest about the relationship. Everyone deserved a second chance.

When she handed him the dog again, Stella caught David's smell on the animal's coat. It could be possible to get on with a person with that smell.

After David had gone, Stella lugged her bag into the downstairs bathroom that he'd had installed when his wife couldn't get upstairs. He'd done a lot for a woman he didn't love. She snapped on rubber gloves. Another bath, another bath panel.

She liked David Barlow. They could have tea and then she could clean. No demands, no promises. Suzie said that Stella's trouble was she didn't know what she wanted even when it was under her nose. She might have a point. Jackie kept saying Stella needed to trust people more. She trusted David.

Forty

Tuesday, 1 May 2012

'Ring when you get this. Tell me how you are. No, come round and we can catch up. Take stock,' she added. Jack would not come if it was only to tell her how he was. She rang off and finger-dabbed up the last of the shepherd's pie, a habit her mother had disliked when Stella lived with her, but now did herself. Jack had not been in touch all day; she would rather he was sulking than was upset about Amanda Hampson. She couldn't shake the idea, either, that he somehow knew about her tea with David. So what if he did?

Jack was not the only man who hadn't called. Nor had David. She checked her messages again although she hadn't missed any. It was five and a half hours since she had opened the bath panel and, squatting on her haunches, stared unbelieving into the dark space.

A treasure trove. Three crucifixes and five pictures. One of a golden sunset; another of an electric blue sky, the sun obscured by dark clouds with bright edges. Something about Faith being the Light of the Soul was printed along the bottom. One showed a long-haired Jesus holding a child on his lap, a dove fluttering top right and red roses in the foreground. Blood red. Sickened, Stella had sat back on the floor, her back to the toilet. Unlike the jacket, she had no doubt these belonged to the Barlows. The objects, stacked beneath the bath – the panel was screwed tighter than the one upstairs – were what David Barlow had claimed was stolen in the burglary. Had literally claimed.

She started to put back the panel when she considered that David Barlow expected her to remove vents, panels, move furniture to get everywhere. He wanted a deep clean. He would know she had seen behind the panel and what she had found there. He would know she had said nothing. She was implicated; her silence complicity. He was right about the silver: the crosses were plated and worth little. The pictures were crude depictions of spiritual and religious moments; 'creepy', he had called them. Stella came across them in some clients' homes; they were not her taste but she didn't judge. She was not one for pictures at all. They gathered dust.

She thought back to what Barlow had said about not being religious. He had wanted rid of them but couldn't bring himself to throw them out. When his wife made him go to the police station to report the theft, he must have feared they would find them and charge him with wasting their time. He had talked about prison. When his wife died he had claimed for goods that were not stolen. This afternoon she had seen how annoyed he was that the company wouldn't pay out.

The pictures were arranged against the back wall and propped on the pipes. The crosses lay in order of size on the cement floor. The bath cavity was a shrine.

Yet it didn't add up. Barlow had been obliged to claim because the police had given him a crime number. When he asked her to deep clean he knew she would do under the bath. If he hadn't known, he would have been alerted when she found the jacket. Stella got it. The burglars were interrupted. They had hidden the loot under here, intending to return. She must warn David.

Stella had arranged the crosses and pictures on David's kitchen table. She was tempted to restore everything to their hooks in the lounge, but she had wiped away the dusty outlines so would have to guess their positions. David hadn't liked them; he would probably only take them down again. She had tried to call him, but like Jack his phone went to voicemail. She had waited beyond the time of her shift – she would rather tell him in person, but by six he had not returned or responded to her messages. Stella needed to get to Terry's; she was late. She wrote David a note and placed it next to a picture, her eye catching the words:

... while we were yet sinners, Christ died for us...

David would call when he read her message. 'Call any time, I'm here.' She had not said where 'here' was.

In the harsh electric light of Terry's immaculate kitchen, his white china gleamed. Stella washed his plate, knife and fork and slotted them on his draining rack. She had trusted David. Jackie would approve of her for taking a risk. Still no call. It was half past nine. Surely not too late for David to call. Odd type of burglars who in a rush made time to stow everything away neatly. She would be that kind of burglar herself, but that was not the point.

Now distinctly uneasy – David couldn't still be walking Stanley – she set the kettle to boil, popped a tea bag in a mug from the box of Brooke Bond Choicest Blend, noting there were five tea bags left. She would buy more. She had resolved to sell Terry's house after she had exhausted his cupboards. Jackie had warned this wouldn't happen if Stella kept renewing the contents.

She had not told Jack about David because he would work out that she had been with him when he rang on Friday evening and had cut his call. She could explain that she couldn't interrupt another date with David, but then Jack would realize it was the second date. So what? Not that it was a date. Stella gave up; most problems disappeared if you ignored them.

The kettle boiled. She dunked the tea bag and stirred in the milk. The pint should last a week and then she would think about selling the house.

Perhaps David had gone to tend to his wife's grave. She felt a stirring in her gut. He had not told her. She pulled out the bag before the tea got too strong. If she was the jealous sort, she would mind. After finding Mrs Hampson's body by her temple, coming across Marian Williams in the police station toilet that morning and, this afternoon, discovering the stuff under David

Barlow's bath, she could do with his company. She wouldn't even mind the dog.

In the brooding silence of Terry's kitchen, Stella got the blue folder out of her rucksack, unclipped the spring binders and extracted the photographs. She laid them on the table in number order and sat sipping tea contemplating the fifteen images. The mug was hot so she rubbed her fingers on her trousers. The bruises on Marian Williams's arm were fingermarks. Four fingers gripping so hard they bruised.

Marian had not fallen. Her husband or partner was violent. She worked in a police station; she could easily have him charged. She must be afraid her colleagues would find out. Ashamed even. Stella had seen enough of Marian Williams to guess that she would keep her troubles to herself. She must have been mortified that Stella had found her. Stella decided that when she saw Marian next, she would act as though it had not happened.

She heard a tapping. An irregular drip. The kitchen tap hadn't dripped since she replaced the washer. Stella ignored it and rummaged in her rucksack for her Clean Slate sticky notes. She flicked through her Filofax to the grid. Jack had found a second collection of glass in Marquis Way, but had no idea who, if anyone, had died there. She filled in the line for the photograph indexed six and wrote 'Marquis Way' in the 'Street' column, then scribbled 'Hit a telegraph pole' in the same line. She printed each street name – on sticky slips and fixed them to the photographs. She was a detective.

All the men had died in crashes, most of them into trees. At each crash site they had found seven green pieces of glass.

No such thing as an accident.

The dripping was insistent. Two clicks then two close together in a steady beat. No leaking tap did that. Stella got up and crept down the passage. Her heart tumbled in her chest. A shape filled the frosted glass door panels. The letterbox flap lifted slightly and dropped. Her back to the wall, Stella edged along the passage. A neighbour would press the bell. Someone was trying to frighten her. They had succeeded. Her body was liquid with fear. Call the police!

Stella flung open the front door.

Forty-One

Jack was dog-tired, but he couldn't stop dwelling on Amanda. Her death had astonished him. She was misguided and obsessed, but sure of herself and so determined. To die in such a prosaic, even ridiculous way was more than he could bear.

He was in his dormitory when he heard the door to the flat upstairs open and close. He ran down the stairs and hid in an alcove behind the staircase by the basement steps. Opposite was a door with a sign saying 'Dining Hall'. He had to assume that at this time of night his Host had no reason to go in there.

Her shoes made no sound on the linoleum. Up until now Jack had relied on intuition to detect her proximity. He was alert to minute changes in temperature, a stale odour of food from the kitchens when she opened a door or the car fumes she brought in from the street. His luck must have run out. His Host was preparing to act and he must save her and her victim. After a week as a guest in her house, Jack had not got his book and did not know where she went at night. Tonight he would forgo working on the streets in the attic and concentrate on the Task.

By the time his Host reached the hall, Jack was racing along the warren of concrete passages in the basement. He was rewarded for familiarizing himself with the topography because the luminous fire-exit signs guided him now.

He was about to run up the area steps into the yard when he saw her. She could move faster than he expected from her bulky frame. She was by the back gate. He heard the clink of the chain when she locked it behind her.

Jack ran to the end of the alley between the house and the street to where an ancient twisting apple tree grew up the wall, the branches gnarled and bunched. He pulled himself up and, flailing an arm, hoisted himself on to the wall, avoiding the shards of glass sunk in the mortar. His Host was nowhere to be seen. She had not had time to disappear so effectively, so she must be hiding. It was a trap.

He belted up Weltje Road and looked up and down King Street. Nothing. He doubled back down to the Great West Road. Something brought him up short. He wheeled around. At a topmost window of the dark mansion was the silhouette of a figure.

The old man was watching him. Despite the distance and the dark, the man – he had not learnt his name – knew it was him. Jack had missed their appointment. This was not how it should be. He should follow his Host as if attached by a thread, invisible and at home in the night streets. But it was the old man who had him in his thrall. Jack retreated along the Great West Road and stopped. She was by St Peter's Church. She was willing him to follow. He did as she wanted.

Jack considered the statue of a reclining woman a friend. Draped in loose cloth, she was sculpted from concrete by Karel Vogel in the late 1950s as a commemoration of the extension of the Great West Road. 'The Leaning Woman', her arms folded, body tipping forward, reflected the curve of the six-lane road. Nowadays daubed with graffiti, her surface pitted by the weather, she was screened from the road by thick foliage. She no longer signed a warning to motorists speeding into London from the West and was a secret known only to locals. Jack touched her gown. His Host was not there.

There was no one on Black Lion Lane or walking towards St Peter's Square. The simple portico of the church was in shadow. The time on the clockface above was twenty past nine. The gate was ajar. Jack eased through and mounted the wide steps. She was not behind either of the Palladian columns. He felt an icicle chill; he had ventured into the open with nowhere to hide.

He edged around the church to the graveyard. Wedges of lamplight broke through the branches. Shadows flitted and shifted, giving him the crazy impression of figures dancing.

She was by a grave in the far-most corner holding something in her arms. It looked like a baby, but could not be. Jack hurried back to the street and took up position by the subway entrance to watch for when she left the church.

She did not come.

He broke cover and, keeping in the shadow of the trees, dodged across grass planted with cherry trees, their blossom ethereal in the lamplight, to the church. She wasn't in the graveyard. That was impossible, there was only one way out. He stumbled over to where she had stood.

STEPHEN PARSONS
20TH JANUARY 2001 – 8TH JANUARY 2009
'A LIFE TOO SHORT, OUR LOVE ENDURES'

The name was familiar. But Jack collected many snippets of information, so many facts. There was a Derek Parsons at work; he had a son, possibly called Stephen. When Jack drove the Wimbledon route he passed through Parsons Green.

He felt a sick lurch. Murderers returned to the graves of their victims. This death was relatively recent, there were fresh flowers beside the headstone, and the grave was well maintained.

He felt a prickling at the back of his head. His Host had not left. She was here somewhere.

Jack flung himself on to the ground. Damp seeped through his coat. He crawled forward on his tummy. There was a crackling. He had squashed a bouquet of flowers placed on a grave. He fluffed them up and gingerly snaked around to the rear of the church. Here the darkness was absolute. There was an alley between the church and the next-door house; halfway along he realized that he was doing what she expected him to do. He stopped. Stopping was what she anticipated too. Whatever he did he could not surprise her. He had met his match. He had two choices: she would expect him to go part-way and double back, then think again and go forward. He returned to the cemetery.

He zigzagged between graves to the street. The gate was as he had left it, but he felt sure she had passed this way and was ahead of him, not behind him.

He skirted the bushes, shielding the Leaning Woman and darted through the cherry trees to the tangled bushes that formed a boundary to the scrap of leftover land. He pushed through the branches, his coat protecting him from thorns. He vaulted over the railings and found himself in Rose Gardens North. He was opposite the house where Stella's father had lived. It was in darkness and although he could not see Stella's van, Jack was positive she was inside. He crept up the path to the house. Dustbins at the right of the bay window were an inadequate hiding place; he was taking a risk. His Host didn't take such risks; this was his advantage.

Through the bars of the gate he caught sight of her by the subway moving briskly towards the Great West Road instead of following his path through the trees. She was returning to the school. Jack felt a flicker of disappointment: the game of cat and mouse was over before it had begun.

Her singing was soft and lilting. She was in the street. How had he missed her? Jack could bear it no longer and put his hands over his face. Despite the threat, the tune, a song of the sirens, filled him with peace and caressed his cramped, stiff body.

'Mary had a little lamb,
Little lamb, little lamb,
Mary had a little lamb,
Its fleece was white as snow.

And everywhere that Mary went,
Mary went, Mary went,
And everywhere that Mary went,
The lamb was sure to go…'

The singing was louder as she passed his hiding place. The church bells chimed ten o'clock.

Jack crept up to Terry's front door. He tilted the flap on the letterbox and let it go. Once, then quickly two more times so that Stella did not mistake it for movement caused by the wind.

'… And so the teacher turned it out,
Turned it out, turned it out,
And so the teacher turned it out,
But still it lingered near.'

The singing grew louder still.

Jack lifted the flap and it took all he had not to bang it and scream out for Stella. He tapped again and pressed his face to the cold glass.

'"Why does the lamb love Mary so?"
The eager children cry…'

*

The door opened and Jack pitched forward. He put hands out blindly in the darkness and, grabbing the door, silently closed it.

'What the—'

'Sssssh!'

Stella felt herself propelled along the hall. She stumbled on the step into the kitchen and lost her footing. A fusty cloth smothered her; everything went black.

'Keep still and don't speak.' More a breath than a whisper.

Her pulse was racing. There was trembling that was not her own. 'Jack?'

'Sssssh!' The trembling increased.

The chill of the floor penetrated Stella's polo shirt. She could not move: Jack was lying across her and his coat was smothering her. This was not why she could not see. The light was off. Beyond her heart's feathery beat, Stella heard the letterbox. It was lifted. It did not go down. Someone was looking through.

Jack was shaking. He was scared.

The letterbox shut. Stella strained for the slightest sound and heard the Terry's gate click shut.

'OK, safe to move.' Jack did not move.

Stella felt the length of his long frame along her body. His soft coat brushed against her cheek. It smelled of Ecover non-biological and Jack. She let herself relax.

Abruptly Jack was up and she was dazzled by the overhead strip. Stella struggled to a sitting position and collapsed against the dresser, rubbing the back of her neck to ease the numbness.

Jack was sitting at the table. The shadow of a beard was stark against his ashen features. His fringe flopped, hiding his eyes. With his coat collar up, he looked like an overwrought hero in a black and white film.

'What was that about?' Automatically Stella took down a mug from the pine dresser.

'Nothing.' He was fiddling with the photographs on the table.

'Funny nothing.' Stella flicked on the kettle.

'Please could I have hot milk with honey?'

Stella poured the remainder of the milk into the mug – so much for it lasting a week – and placed it in the microwave. 'Jack, what is going on?' She wasn't sure she wanted to know.

'Thought I was being followed.' Jack straightened the row of prints. 'Terry is numbering these chronologically. That second crash on Marquis Way was more recent than the first one in 1977 when Paul Vickery died. He's numbered the two shots as '6' and '6a', which suggests it's later than the Markham crash which Terry's numbered with a series of fives.'

'I wish you wouldn't walk about at night, there's all sorts out there.' All sorts included Jack. The microwave bleeped. 'You're lucky I opened the door.'

'Weren't you expecting me?' Jack asked reasonably.

It was true, Stella had asked him to come, but he hadn't said yes. 'I said come to my flat, at around eight,' she said firmly, unsure this was true.

'I'm glad I didn't then.' Jack peered at the pictures.

Stella had seen him distracted like this before. It was due to Amanda Hampson. 'Would you like more shifts?' He needed structure.

Jack scratched his cheek, leaving marks down his cheekbones like a Red Indian. 'I'm fine.'

'Why did we have to keep quiet?' She glared at him. 'Who is out there?'

'I told you, some weirdo.'

'Actually you didn't say they were weird. We should call the police.'

'This is London. It's nothing.' Jack swallowed his milk down the wrong way and was overwhelmed by a cough.

'Promise me you'll be sensible.' Stella had no right to exact anything from Jack and he would say so. Nor would he be sensible.

'I promise,' Jack said.

Stella joined him at the table and tried again: 'Are you OK after, you know, after Mrs Hampson?' Saying her dead client's name brought back the smell of congealing blood.

'Yes. You?'

'Me? Definitely.'

They scrutinized the roads stretching into the distance.

'I've been wondering what Amanda wanted to tell your dad,' Jack said finally.

'We know. She told Marian Williams her husband had passed his advanced driving test. Naïve to suppose that prevented him having an accident, as Marian pointed out.'

Jack sipped his milk. 'She wasn't naïve. She wanted to save her nugget of gold for Cashman if she couldn't tell Terry. I think

Amanda was fobbing her off, she didn't want to waste it on a lowly civilian employee.'

'She got that wrong,' Stella huffed. 'Marian is hardly lowly. Her job is vital and she takes pride in it. She's Cashman's gatekeeper so that tactic meant Mrs Hampson didn't speak to him.' Stella saw something of herself in the rigorously organized administrator.

'Are you sure she didn't say anything else to the clerk?'

Stella told Jack about Marian's arm and her own conviction that Marian was a victim of domestic violence. She had appreciated Marian's tact in not telling Amanda Hampson that she was Terry Darnell's daughter. Luckily Hampson had paid her so little attention she had not noticed her Clean Slate uniform or the bleach issue might have come up.

'Bruises don't darken that quickly,' Jack agreed, sipping his milk.

Stella mimed wiping milk off her upper lip but Jack appeared not to notice.

'Any more thoughts?' He gestured at the photographs.

'The streets look the same.'

'We know they're not because we've been there.'

'But they are!' Stella pulled her chair forward. 'They are the same kind of street.' She jabbed at the second shot of Marquis Way where Paul Vickery had died. 'They have no bends or side roads and are long. No houses. All of the three streets we have been to were in a no man's land – clapped-out industrial units and businesses shut up or run down, cemeteries. No ordinary person would go there after dark.' She glared at Jack. 'That man at the laundry would have called out if he was there legitimately. As you said, he legged it when he saw the van.'

'You're right.' Jack traced his finger along Marquis Way. 'There are no cameras. CCTV didn't exist in 1977, but it did in 2002 when James Markham slammed into that horse chestnut on Britton Drive.' He spiralled a lock of hair and said ruminatively, 'It's terrible for the tree. No one thinks of that.'

'Sweet.'

'Thank you.'

'It was a sweet chestnut, not horse.'

'Fancy you knowing that!' Jack brushed back his fringe. 'What a dark horse, or dark horse chestnut you are!' He eyed Stella gleefully over his mug.

Looking at her grid, Stella saw something that should have been obvious. 'Every man drove into a tree!' She put down her tea. 'Jack, there's no way these are accidents.'

'You're right!' Jack slumped back. 'How do you make three and possibly four men, if we count the telegraph pole, die on impact? Law of averages means it's not possible.'

'That's the "how". Let's keep to the "why" for now.' Once Stella knew why there was a stain, she knew what had made it and could decide what agent to use to remove it. 'There were no cameras on Phoenix Way where Charlie Hampson died either. So for each of these incidents there was no CCTV and no witnesses.'

'Amanda saw the Collision Report Book for Hampson's accident. Weather conditions were dry, but there was thick fog. The police told her it's likely he got disoriented.'

In the beat that followed, the fridge sprang to life, its hum loud in the hushed quiet. Again Stella had the sense Terry was in the room with them. If David's dog was here, he would know. She picked up her phone. No message from David.

'Where's your back-door key?' Jack got up.

'Terry hides it in the fork section of the cutlery drawer. Why?'

Jack rattled around in the drawer and found the key. He unlocked the door and went out on to the patio. 'Lock up after me.' He buttoned up his coat. 'A small thing: when you leave, try to look normal.'

'How else would I look? Where are you going?' Stella was dismayed.

'To bed.'

Jack scaled the garden wall and melted into the night.

Stella waited on the patio, half expecting him to reappear. Eventually she turned the key in the lock and returned it to the drawer. She washed up Jack's mug and, casting about for her own, saw the notes she had stuck on the photographs.

Charles Hampson was killed on 15 March 2009. She had written '15/3/2009'. Seven digits counting the zeros, and seven for '16/3/1977' for Paul Vickery. Jack said seven was a special number. Seven was number of stones he had found at each crash site. Seven was the number of cakes Jennifer Barlow had made for her husband before she died.

Stella reached for her mobile to call Jack. The date for Jamie Markham was 10/11/2002. Eight digits. She put down the phone. Dead end.

There was a message.

Fancy a meal at mine with Stanley and me? Sat eve after last sesh of dp clng? Dx

Yes, she wrote and was about to add a kiss, but decided against it. Then, before she pressed 'send', she changed her mind and typed a lower-case x. David was right, it was the last deep cleaning session, she would make the most of it.

Stella had planned to go to Richmond Park with Suzie on Saturday. She would cancel.

Forty-Two

'This will be nice and tidy when we finish, Daddy,' piped Mary. She was helping pack up Michael's room because her mum would not come in there. Her daddy was using two gigantic boxes. If Michael was there and she was not grown up, they would have hidden inside them. Instead she was doing as she was told and filling them with Michael's comics and cars, his toys and his Andy Pandy books.

Mary had expected to enjoy the task. Michael would be cross she was touching his things and even crosser that they would be given away. But being dead he couldn't spoil it and stop her. She kept forgetting all the things that being dead meant. Some of them were not fun. She did like helping her dad. She would do anything for him, and was waiting for the moment to say so.

She heaved Michael's shoebox of lead soldiers out of his toy cupboard. A headless sentry fell on to the floor. 'He was broken already,' she said quickly. 'Where shall I put it for mending?'

'In the box, no need to mend it.'

Michael's marbles filled an enormous glass sweet jar to the brim. Mary grasped the jar and lifting it, staggered to the boxes. The jar slid from her grasp and crashed to the floor. The afternoon they had moved in she had dropped a box and broken china and glass.

The jar landed on Michael's sheepskin rug and did not break. The lid burst off, scattering marbles among the tufty wool. Her dad had gone. Mary tiptoed to the window. Grass grew around the legs of Michael's swing. She stepped on a marble and, stooping, picked it up. It did not have the pattern of the others – single twisting leaves of blue, white, red or yellow. This one had fiery orange snakes coiling around each other. It was Michael's champion marble. She had confiscated it from him. He must have stolen it back from her. She heard voices and ran to her place on the landing.

'Jean, we have to get it done. The room's a mausoleum.'

'You never wanted her.'

'Don't go over this again.'

'You blame me.'

'That woman said it, the one you allowed in and blabbed away to. Children need mothers, especially boys.'

'Blame me, go on.'

'You're not to blame.'

Mary stumbled up the stairs and into her room. She barricaded the door with a chair and like a snake slithered under the bed and found her duffel bag.

She laid the Angel's hands on the bedspread, palms uppermost, the ends of the wrists white and sharp. She touched the left one.

That's my blood.

She dropped Michael's champion marble into the hand; it made a chinking sound. She tried to close the cold fingers around it, but they were too stiff. 'You won it, it's yours.' She spoke into the room.

The bedroom door slammed into the chair but didn't open.

'Open up, girl. What are you playing at?' her dad shouted. 'What's that mess in Michael's room?'

'I don't know.' She stuffed the hands into the bag and kicked it under the bed. She moved the chair. The door flew wide. Her dad was on the landing.

'Did you do this?'

Mary looked into Michael's room. Marbles were strewn like petals all over the rug. 'No.' She was firm. 'Maybe the jar fell.'

'Nobody likes a liar.' His eyes were like marbles. 'Clear it up.'

Mary scooped up the marbles and dropped them into the jar. Since Michael was dead, nothing belonged to him. Nobody had said so.

That night Mary sat up in bed. The woman was in her lighthouse. Mary imagined she was painting the Angel.

She shut her eyes, put her hands together in prayer and in a lullaby voice like her mum, sang herself to sleep.

'Mary had a little lamb,
Little lamb, little lamb…'

Forty-Three

Tuesday, 1 May 2012

The church clock was striking ten as Stella locked up Terry's house and, annoyed by Jack's warning to behave normally, cursorily checked the street. She did keep her keys spiked between her fingers ready for attack.

While trying to shut the gate she dropped the keys. She scrabbled at her feet for them. The faulty lamp-post went out.

'Here you are.'

About to yell for help, Stella gasped. She recognized Marian Williams in the lights from traffic on the Great West Road.

'What are you doing here?' she heard herself snap, and then exclaimed less gruffly: 'What a surprise!'

'Did I scare you?' Marian handed Stella the keys.

'I wasn't expecting you. Or anyone.' Stella leant against Terry's gate.

'I brought you these.' Marian thrust a bundle forward.

Instinctively Stella flinched.

'Flowers.' Marian spoke as if she guessed Stella had expected a weapon. 'A token.'

'Why?' Stella grappled with a generous bouquet. She peered over the top of the paper and recoiled at the heady fragrance of lilies. Funerals.

'For this morning.' It was Marian Williams's turn to appear awkward.

'Anyone would have done it.' Stella disliked cut flowers. They were pointless and lilies in particular made a mess. She remembered Marian had an abusive husband. 'Are you feeling better?'

'Thanks to you. I spent the day on the settee drinking tea.'

Suddenly it occurred to Stella: 'How did you know I was here?'

'I didn't. I was passing and saw lights in Detective Chief Superintendent Darnell's house. Call me zealous, but I like to keep an eye out, especially now he's gone.' She described a circle on the ground with her foot.

'That's good of you, but not at all...'

'We look out for each other in this job. We're family.' Marian Williams gave a tight smile.

'I'm selling the place.' Stella was curt. Had Terry looked out for Marian Williams too? She thought of the condoms in the bathroom.

'It's what he would have wanted...' Her face stiffened and she glanced above Stella's head as if she had seen something.

Stella looked too. The blinds in Terry's bedroom were twisted to open, the slats in position. Had she left them like that? Of course she had.

'It's very late.'

'I'm a bad sleeper. Something I had in common with Terry.' Marian smiled.

'I'd better be going.' Stella jiggled the bouquet.

Marian Williams did not move.

'His house is fine. I was just there,' she said gratuitously.

'I was grateful you were there this morning. DCS Cashman is kind, but no match for... Terry.' She whispered his name as if it was illegal to use it. 'I'm glad I caught you.'

Just what Martin Cashman had said. No one was a match for Terry. If he had found Marian Williams on a dark street he would have made her come in for a cup of tea, whatever the time. After he retired, Marian was a connection to the police station. She worked on traffic: maybe she had alerted him to the pattern in the blue folder. 'Would you like to come in for a cup of tea?' Stella heard herself say.

'That would be lovely.'

Holding the bouquet away from herself, Stella fumbled with the key and opened the door. She was taken aback when Marian reached past her into the hall and turned on the light. She knew where to find the switch.

It would be her luck if a neighbour appeared now and Stella had to introduce Marian. Then it dawned on her. The person at the door earlier was not following Jack; it was Marian. She had been watching the house. She must reassure Jack. It was weird to be checking on the house of a dead colleague at any time of day, but not that weird if you were in love with the colleague.

In her tightly belted mackintosh Marian trotted ahead of Stella down the passage to the kitchen. Stella hung up her anorak and followed. Marian was more at home in Terry's house than she was.

Stella collected up the mugs from her drink with Jack from the draining board, hoping Marian wouldn't notice there were two. If she did it should not matter. She opened the box of tea bags and took out two.

'Terry said that brand had flavour. I used to get it for him.' Marian settled in the chair with the cushion at the head of the table. 'I'll bring you some, if you like.'

Stella shook her head. 'I'm hardly ever here.' If Marian was passing by regularly she'd know that wasn't true. She would have seen the van.

'You must find it hard to bear that he's not with us.' Marian looked around her as if checking this fact.

David had asked her this the night they found the dog. Stella had said that she did. A new thought. Now the question horrified her. She said that life goes on and fled to Terry's living room to find a vase for the lilies. Terry did not have a vase. Marian probably knew this. Stella stopped at the doorway. She dismissed the impression that someone was in the armchair.

In the kitchen, she found an ice bucket branded with Veuve Clicquot – since when did Terry drink champagne? – and filled it from the tap, stuffed the lilies in and put it on to the table. Their heavy scent increased the nagging ache above the bridge of her nose. She opened the fridge and shut it again.

'How long have you been at the station?' She brought the mugs over to the table. 'Sorry, Terry hasn't got any… There isn't any milk.'

Marian flapped her hand at this. 'Since the eighties. Hammersmith Station is a second home.'

She looked about the kitchen again, as if about to add 'after here'. Stella sat down at the table. 'You seem to like your job.' Without milk the drink was scalding and put paid to her plan to down it and leave.

'Your dad used to say, "Marian, love, if we can make the world a little better it's worth it."' She leant forward. 'He was proud of you.' She smiled with kindly eyes at Stella. 'I'm an only child too. You are very like him.'

'I don't think so.' Stella gulped her tea and blinked as it burned her throat.

'You clean up and restore order. Terry wanted bad people off the streets. We have to listen to criminals moaning how their lives are ruined because they're going to jail and demanding victim support when they've wrecked other lives.' She looked about her again. '"You have the patience of a saint, Marian, love," Terry told me.'

'What do you do at the station?' Terry had been Marian's knight in shining armour. Stella glanced out at the garden. If Jack climbed over the back wall, it would be hard to explain it to Marian. This thought was cut short by Marian talking.

'… assign crime numbers for crimes I know didn't happen. I ensure statements are obtained and filed and liaise with victims' families. I used to process road traffic accidents before they moved it centrally. Terry'd say: "We couldn't do without you, Marian." So does Cashman, but it's not the same.'

Stella had to stop herself asking about David Barlow. He had not falsified his claim. She trusted him. Perhaps she could ask about the photographs in the blue file. Marian had helped Terry;

this was sort of the same thing. Marian hardly drew breath. Stella supposed that with the violent husband, she didn't get much opportunity to let off steam.

'… not speaking ill of the dead, but that Mrs Hampson was a time-waster. She didn't spare a thought for the dead child.'

'You must get that a lot.' Stella sat up. Here goes. Marian had been handed to her on a plate. Affecting nonchalance she sipped at the scalding drink.

'I do.' Marian was grim. 'Carelessness kills more than the child. It affects everyone. It affected Terry.'

Stella remarked airily: 'Odd Mrs Hampson saying her husband passing the advanced driving test was fresh evidence. She struck me as sensible.'

'Did she?' Marian Williams rounded on Stella. 'Of course, you knew her.'

'I never actually met her.' Stella was hot with discomfort. Marian hadn't missed Cashman's comment that Mrs Hampson was a client. She did not remark on Stella failing to mention this. Stella was no good at economizing with the truth.

'She relied on your father being a soft touch. I will say this: he could be too nice. "Everyone deserves a second chance," he'd say.' She got to her feet. 'He was a good man, Stella.'

Stella was trying to think where she had heard this phrase before. She took a moment to realize Marian was holding her hand. Her fingers were cold, her grasp strong. 'Yes, he was …' she faltered.

'We're like family in the force,' Marian repeated and set off up the passage. She was going.

Stella's rucksack was by the front door where she had dropped it, the zip undone. One of the photographs, loose from when she and Jack had looked at them, lay face up on the parquet.

Marian Williams picked up the picture. 'This is Tolworth Street. Why have you got this?'

'Oh, I sometimes take photos…' Stella's mind went blank. Her only reason for taking pictures was to capture stains – before and after – for flyers and brochures.

'David Lauren committed suicide here in 1989,' Marian intoned.

'David Lauren?' Stella felt the nettle stings tingle on her knuckles. Her subtle approach was paying off, she told herself.

'Little Billy was killed soon after I started with the police. Terry warned me the first ones stay with you and how right he was.' She opened the front door. 'I was standing here – it could have been yesterday – I told him they all stay with me.'

Elated by the sniff of success, Stella made a snap decision. She would tell Marian about Terry's folder. Marian would know the street. Stella didn't want to talk to the police, but Marian Williams was not strictly the police and, it being Terry's hunch, she would be eager to help. Jack had advised they keep it a secret. He had also suggested she speak to Cashman. Pulling it out from her rucksack, Stella could see no harm in showing Marian. Her phone rang.

'Excuse me.'

'Stella, is that you? It's Jackie. Sorry to call this late.'

Stella shot Marian a look of apology and signalled she should wait. 'You OK?' Something had happened to Jack. She went cold.

Marian Williams was mouthing: 'I'll go.'

'Yes, love, all quiet on the Western whatsit.'

'Can I call you back?' Before Stella could stop her, Marian had trotted down the path and out of the gate.

'I'll speak to you tomorrow, no problem,' Jackie agreed.

'It's OK, go ahead.'

'Do you want the good news or the good news?'

'The good news,' Stella obliged. Jackie shouldn't be working for Clean Slate at this time of night.

'Your nice policeman rang to confirm that Mrs Hampson tripped. She'd had a drink, but not over the odds. Poor love, any of us could do it. You be careful on your dad's path.'

'What nice policeman?' Stella was staring at the path; there was a tile missing. In the rain, she might trip. Jackie had a knack of knowing what Stella was doing. Unlike Marian she would not be checking up on her.

'Earth to Stella! Martin Cashman, your dad's mate? He tried you earlier, but got your voicemail. He wanted you to hear in person so asked me to tell you. What a sweety! Turns out I was at school with his big brother, a cool kid, not like Martin. Will you tell Jack or shall I?'

'I will.' Stella could not remember the name of the man Marian said had died in Tolworth Street.

'Want to hear the other good news?' Jackie did not wait for an answer. 'Amanda Hampson's cousin wants us to clean her house. The police left it in a state and recommended us. They want a deep clean!'

'That's good,' Stella said. At least she had another street name.

'I've settled it with the woman who's handling our contract with them. Mary-Anne Thing.'

'Marian Williams.'

'She brought in the signed forms as I was leaving, bless her. You could have fetched them next time you were there. Funny stick, isn't she? Can't look you in the eye.'

Stella's own experience was that Marian fixed her with a stare. Jackie would have a fit if she told her about Marian bringing flowers; she was protective of Stella's private life. Marian had said she had lain on the sofa all day. Against Cashman's instructions she had worked. Stella would have done the same.

'She looked familiar, but she didn't know me. She has one of those faces. Unremarkable. Anyway, don't you get ideas, I'm giving the job to Jack.'

'It makes up for losing the client,' Stella said. The man was killed in Tolworth Street in 1989; she must keep that in her mind. Since Terry's death her memory was flaky. Surely it was Jackie who said when a parent dies, there's no buffer, you're next.

'Stella, for goodness' sake! Go home and go to bed. You are tired.' Jackie ended the call.

Stella traipsed along to the kitchen. Jackie was not wrong, she did feel tired, but her exhaustion was not from working. A few cleaning shifts, especially deep cleaning at David's, would revive her.

Marian's mug of tea was on the table, untouched. She had brought Terry tea bags. What else had she given him? Company? Love? Stella grabbed the lilies – intending to throw them out. If he were here Jack would stop her. He preferred flowers left to grow wild, but thought once they were cut they should be cherished. She put down the ice bucket. If Marian came back she would see they had gone.

Stella shut her eyes and tried to recapture Marian talking in the hall. To no avail, the name of the driver was lost in a fog.

Marian had said Terry was proud of Stella; she said she too was an only child. Terry must have told her about his daughter. He might have taken her down to the basement and shown her the wall of photographs. Was she jealous? Stella washed the mugs, dried them and put them away. Marian had given her flowers; she wasn't jealous.

Marian had not been following Jack; she could not let go of Terry. Stella folded the drying-up cloth. Marian was not passing; she'd brought the flowers. Jack would say Stella and Marian had something in common: Stella couldn't let go of Terry either.

She texted Jack to meet her outside the police station after her shift the next morning. She would tell him about Amanda and then take him for coffee. That was supporting her staff. Not that Jack was like staff.

Stella nearly said that she had the name of another street and was making friends with the administrator, as he'd suggested, but Jack might ask why she had changed her mind about talking about the case and she didn't know.

Jack had not replied by the time she was back in her flat, had cleaned her teeth and was in bed. Stella stared at the phone, willing it to spring to life. She had no idea where he was. She diverted herself by trying once more to recall the dead driver's name and, unsuccessful, she fell asleep.

Stella awoke some time later and lay trying to make sense of a blue glow on the ceiling. She had received a text.

Will do. Stuff to tell you. Jx.

Jack never put kisses. Stella jolted awake. It was not true that she had no idea where he was. She clicked the location symbol beside the speech bubble and brought up a map in the centre of which a bright blue dot was winking.

Five minutes later, keeping to the speed limit, Stella crossed the borough boundary into Hammersmith.

Forty-Four

> *'Jack be nimble,*
> *Jack be quick,*
> *Jack jump over*
> *The candle stick.'*

In the cold sepulchral hall Jack remained by Reception until he was sure his Host was not in earshot. Stella had assumed the person following him last night was male. He had not corrected her, because the truth had dawned and it was all he could do to hide his agitation. His Host was following him. Stella would not understand; nor did he want her to.

'You're late,' the old man growled.

'Sorry.'

'I like punctuality.' He was querulous.

Jack scooted along the crawl space and popped up beside him in the river.

'That space is cleared for the new build, but I don't have the information. That dealership at the junction is coming down soon.' He stabbed a finger at a low white building on the corner of King Street and St Peter's Square. 'The demolition site will need fencing off when the time comes.'

'Are you sure? That square is listed.'

The man glared at him. Jack snatched up a Stanley knife and poked it into mud at the river's edge.

'The river's crumbling by the Harrods Depository. I could do that.' Jack indicated a threadbare patch near Hammersmith Bridge. On the south bank the towpath went as far as the borough boundary. He knew it well: a night-time route for more than one Host. The willingness of anyone to choose it in the dark told Jack that person had the mind of a murderer.

Jack was pleased the old man had not bowed to convention and painted the river blue. The Thames was never blue. He had coloured it according to differing weather and the currents. At the Bell Steps it was the sheet-metal grey of the thick cloud, with a scrawl of scum drifting downstream. On the north bank, stained cotton signified slime strung from iron mooring hoops – tiny washers daubed burnt umber for rust – exposed at low tide.

'I can start now.'

'Too late.'

Jack heard the key turn. His Host was back.

'You're late.'

'Sorry, I was delayed. It's time for bed.'

The old man dipped beneath the streets and on all fours pushed past Jack along the tunnel. He called out, 'Did you get the new book?'

'No. I had to see someone. I'll get you a nice hot drink.'

From the wheezing and grunting Jack guessed she was helping her father out of the other end. The reek of solvent did not offset the stink of urine. He heard the two move like a slow sack race across the floorboards. Once again the old man had hidden him. The street-mending was their secret. He felt absurdly joyful, it was a long time since he and his dad had built model bridges and tunnels – being engineers together.

'Who were you talking to?' Her tone was bright and by the way.

Jack broke into a sweat. She had been trailing him. She knew he was there.

'Who do you talk to when you're alone?' the man wheezed.

The light in the tunnel was extinguished. Jack heard the door close.

He flashed his torch over deserted streets: a searchlight panning the city. The roads were lit in high relief and he soon found Marquis Way and Britton Drive. The dilapidation was precise: the laundry, the bricks streaked with a mix of putty and typing fluid. Fine wire was sprayed green for weeds; peeling emulsion dried and flaked represented nettles.

The wasteland was lumpy with grit and more green wire for the sycamore saplings. Discarded doll's furniture and scraps of paper lying amid actual soil created seamless reality. Jack was used to passing sprawling acres with ripped sofas, their guts spilling, upturned fridges, splintered planks of wood and rusting oil drums metres from manicured gated communities like Stella's. In these pockets of nondescript land, bounded by razor wire, awaiting regeneration, his Hosts walked unafraid.

One road ran for over a quarter of a metre without interruption and came up hard against the railway tracks at the Chiswick border. Jack moved the torchlight along the long straight tarmac in search of a name.

Spelling Way. Two more streets ran off the edge of the model, one overshadowed by a gasometer and a straggle of rundown warehouses. Taking care not to snap chimneys and aerials he narrowed the beam and found an enamelled square on a wall. From the river hatch he couldn't read it, so he risked discovery and crawled out. If his Host walked in now he would have to introduce himself. Jack was appalled to discover the idea frightened him.

He circled the model and noted another long road. He memorized the name. It had a high wall along much of the length and a disused factory building on the other that looked as if redevelopment had begun and been abandoned. He recognized Mafeking Avenue. It wasn't in any of Terry's photographs. Tolworth Street, not far from where Stella's mother lived, was shorter than the others. Jack had abandoned Stella tonight. He would make up for it with this new information.

He paused outside the kitchen where he could hear the kettle filling. She could come out any moment. He was a high-wire walker without a net, tempting fate. Outside the flat, he made himself take the key down from the lintel, fit it into the lock and silently close the door. He replaced it.

Hush-a-bye, baby, on the tree top,
When the wind blows the cradle will rock...

Singing under his breath, Jack climbed over the wall and affected a stroll up to King Street to stop himself running like a mad thing. The ornate gates to Ravenscourt Park tempted him in, but that was unfair, his Host would never scale them. He must give her a fighting chance. He circled the area, dipping down one street and up another, sauntering like a true flâneur, leading her a merry dance. Jack borrowed the phrase from another Host. Round and round we go.

He was on the Great West Road. The rain was fine, insidious; he hugged into his coat. But, like a veil, the rain soaked the wool and plastered his hair to his head.

When the bough breaks the cradle will fall,
Down will come baby, cradle and all.

Jack strolled down the ramp to the subway beneath the carriageway. He disguised his gait – a precaution against new technical means of recognition – with a slight limp. Without checking the mirror that reflected the passage, he went inside.

A person, hooded and shapeless in the poor light, was waiting halfway along.

Forty-Five

Sunday, 4 September 1966

Her mum had stuck up Michael's map of the world on his bedroom wall, just as in their old house, so he wouldn't miss his old room. But it made Michael think of it and so he missed it more. He could look out of the window and see his new swing; the present for no reason since he'd had his birthday and it was too early for Christmas. Michael was scared of swinging. He didn't like it being outside his window.

There was no map on the wall now. Mary looked for the marks from the tape that had held it up, but couldn't find it amongst all the scuffs and bumps on the wallpaper. Perhaps the map and Michael were made up and had never been there at all.

Her dad was cutting the grass. He had slung the swing over the top bar, making it too high for Michael. Even when it was in its proper place it was too high for him. Her dad was mowing stripes on the lawn. When he faced the house Mary waved, but he did not see her.

Michael's fluffy sheepskin rug had gone. So had his toys and clothes. Mary stood where his bed had been in what was now thin air. The map was a waste because Michael couldn't read.

She was not going to have to change her name when she went to secondary school. She had made her dad cross when she asked. He said to say she was an only child. 'An only child.' She practised the phrase to herself.

She would be going on the bus on her own. Michael didn't know she would do this. He would have been frightened to be on a bus all by himself. She leant on his bedroom windowsill and looked out beyond the swing to her secret mosaic by the bushes. Her dad was pushing the mower too close to it. She prayed he wouldn't find it. She prayed to Michael's Angel.

An only child. There was only her. She did not have to share with Michael or anyone. No one at the new school would know she had once had a brother. No one would like him better than her.

Mary went out of Michael's room and shut the door. In her own bedroom she dragged out the duffel bag from its new hiding place in the bottom of the wardrobe.

The Angel's hands got larger every time she saw them. She laid them out on the carpet, the curving fingers pointing downwards. Slowly she scraped them along the floor. The fingers made a track on the carpet. When she did it the marks were the same. She could have angel hands. Like Michael. She waved one of the hands in the air.

'Whoooh!' She floated it in front of Michael's face, making him fall backwards. 'Scaredy cat!' She laid the hand down on the floor palms up. Her voice caught her by surprise. She tried again.

'Give me your marbles.'

No.

'Now.'

I'll swap some with you.

'You don't have anything to swap.'

You can have my nature collection instead… I have the marbles to swap. What have you got?

Mary scrabbled under her bed and found the sweet jar. She slithered backwards and banged her head on the iron bedstead; it really hurt. 'I have these.'

That's not fair.

Now that he was dead Michael heard everything she said and everything she thought. That was one of the bad things. Mary unscrewed the lid and sniffed inside. The marbles didn't smell of Michael. The glass was hard and cold like the Angel's hands. 'One, two, three, four, five.' That was enough. She grabbed two more and grouped them together. She became a snake to scare Michael. 'Ssssssssss!' She returned the jar to its secret place.

The hands were praying. She had not left them like that. She opened them out again and looked about her. Her satchel was on her table from when she got home. She unbuckled it and tipped out the contents: her pencil case and the book she had borrowed from the school library – *Charlotte's Web*, a story about spiders. Michael didn't like spiders. At last her Trees of Britain collection. She put it in front of the hands.

'I'll swap you these. I collected all of them, which is fifty. You can swap for your marbles.' She gathered up the marbles and tipped them into the hollow of the Angel's right hand, keeping the album in her own hand.

There's only seven marbles.

'You can't count.'

I can, up to twenty. That's seven for fifty cards. Is that fair?

'It's fair,' Mary whispered. Voices in the hall. Her dad must have finished doing the grass. 'Michael, do as you're told,' she added in her mum's voice. It wasn't how her mum talked any more.

The little girl dropped the Brooke Bond tea album and the marbles into the duffel bag and lifted up the cold hands. She dipped her arm into the bag and placed them on top of the album. She tied the drawstring tight and secreted the bag in the wardrobe.

'Come and get your tea,' her dad shouted up the stairs.

Mary, I'm glad you didn't run away after all.

Mary was on the landing. There was no one there. There was only her. Only.

Forty-Six

'Where are you going?' The question resounded in the tiled tunnel.

Above on the Great West Road, traffic rumbled despite it being the first hours of the morning. If Jack shouted for help, no one would hear. There was no one to hear. His tongue like leather, he managed, 'Where are you going?' Stupid to be smart with strangers, he really was losing his touch.

The figure moved into one of the watery pools of light and yanked back the hood.

'I saw you coming out of the school on King Street, near that fountain where I picked you up on Monday night. You promised to stop this, whatever it is.'

Stella. Jack slumped against tiles. Water ran down his face; he rubbed it with a palm. 'It's not what you think,' he protested weakly.

'It's exactly what I think. More to the point it's against the law!' Stella, bulky in her anorak, glared at him. The words tumbled out.

'That person following me is a True Host. I—'

'What exactly is a "True Host"?'

'A murderer. There's another sort: I call them Hosts. They might kill but haven't yet. I have to stop them. You'd do the same.'

This was true. Stella always tried to do what she called the right thing.

'I don't break into houses. That's illegal!'

Water splattered from an overflow pipe. Then came the

rumble of a stream of traffic that had cleared the lights at the Hogarth roundabout. The familiar sounds calmed him. Perhaps Stella too, for in a softer tone she said, 'I'll take you back to my flat to dry off. Hot milk and honey?'

She must think he had gone mad. Perhaps he had.

'I can't.' He was beyond the world where curling up on Stella's sofa with a hot drink could happen.

'There must be lots of killers walking free. It's a horrible thought but it's not up to you to stop them. Nor can you.' Stella was her practical self. 'Jack, it's over. You must let it go. Move on.'

'Like you have with Terry?' The words had slipped out. She was off, heading out of the tunnel on the south side. He felt scared at what he had started but couldn't stop. 'Isn't playing detective just a way of refusing to see the truth?'

'It's clearing up. It's what I do.' Stella quickened her pace.

Jack chased after her. 'You could forget the blue folder. You worry at it like a terrier. You go on about Terry never being off the clock.' He jumped the cracks in the paving without Stella seeing, although she would know. 'Terry's life was refracted through a dark glass of crimes and potential crimes. He saw crime everywhere. But you don't. What if they're just snaps he took for the hell of it?'

'They are not "just snaps", Stella growled. 'And me trying to understand what they are is very different from you stalking people and spying on them in their homes. That's sick!' She stopped suddenly and Jack banged into her.

'It's not stalking. I never follow women. Hosts are men!' He had never lied to Stella before. They were standing on the edge of the kerb to the Great West Road. It might have been an abyss.

Jack should never have told Stella anything about this side of himself. What he dreaded had come true. She didn't like him. Yet he was in too deep. 'My Host has killed. I can't leave it. It's a calling.'

'The only calling you should do is to the police,' Stella quipped. She stepped away from the kerb.

'Stella…' Jack stopped, looked at her.

'What?' She met his gaze.

'This Host is a woman and, yes, I did follow her. It's the first time. I never follow women. My Hosts are usually men. It was my Host at Terry's door.' He felt himself redden. He had brought trouble to Stella, trouble she didn't need.

'I meant to say. It was Marian, the administrator who works for Martin Cashman. She came to bring me flowers.'

'Flowers?' Jack echoed. 'Why would she do that?'

'Why not?' Stella bristled. 'Actually, they were probably really for Terry. She's in love with— Oh, never mind, it's a long story. Main thing is, you weren't being stalked.'

'You have to listen. My Host is dangerous. I was following her, but all the time she's been following me. It's too late to get out.' He mumbled the last words.

'Marian comes to check on the house.'

'You were in danger. So was she. Warn her if she's coming again.'

'She would think I was off my head.' Stella started walking, head down against the insistent rain.

Furnivall Gardens, dark with dense foliage, was on the right. The rain, a clinging mist, blurred the headlights coming off Hammersmith flyover; the passing lights made phantoms of lamp standards and their shadows rotated around the bases like hands of a clock.

Stella was keeping her distance. He was losing her in all senses. Furtively he glanced back. The pavement glistened treacle-black; there was no one there. Stella increased her pace and he had to jog to catch up.

'Where were you going?' She had never questioned him so closely before.

'I identified more streets.' It was true, once he had shaken off his Host it was why he was out, he reminded himself.

'Without asking me to come.' Stella had no side to her. If she was hurt she couldn't help but show it.

'I supposed you'd be in bed.'

284

'I got up.'

'You're out without telling me.' The old trick of turning tables was beneath him but Jack blundered on, 'I've called you several times over the last days, you haven't answered.' There was no satisfaction in hitting home.

'I just texted you,' Stella said.

He had turned his phone off at the school. He took it out of his pocket and switched it on. It throbbed with an incoming text.

Where are you?

'You haven't got the folder. How were you going to tell if the streets were right without me?' Stella put up her hood. He couldn't see her face.

Jack couldn't tell her about the streets in the attic. Hosts were bad enough.

'What have you found?' Her voice was muffled by her hood. She hadn't asked how he had found them. If she did, he would tell her.

'Three more streets. Like our other ones, all in run-down areas. Two are dead ends and the third doesn't lead anywhere useful. Two have CCTV now, but may not have had when whatever happened happened.'

'You went there?' Stella didn't miss a thing. He had the sudden urge to hug her. His secret life lay between them; he couldn't cross the divide.

'It's possible to go on Street View.' He slalomed the truth.

'Three more streets than the ones we know about? Jack, let's not make things more complicated. Stick to the blue folder.'

'I might be wrong,' he conceded. Sure he was not.

'You're probably right.'

Truce. Jack let himself breathe. He could count on Stella to play fair. It was himself he was less sure of.

Ahead the flyover rose higher and higher; when they reached the leafy cul de sac where Stella had parked the van, it cut out the sky. Jack scanned the stanchions for his Host. Surely this time she had been able to overtake? Perhaps it was better that Stella believed the person at the door was her new friend. He had not told her that Hosts never let themselves be seen. The administrator was not the only woman passing Terry's house.

Stella unlocked the van and Jack hopped into the passenger side. Once she was in, he locked the doors.

'Be careful, Jack.' Stella started the motor and the fan blasted out faintly warm air laced with lemon air freshener.

He wiped his eyes with his sleeve and, pushing back his fringe, scrubbed at his hair with the tail of his coat. 'Always,' he said brightly. Stella missed nothing.

'Where first?'

Their altercation had upset him and he couldn't remember the names. He shut his eyes and concentrated on the streets in the attic, his torch searching out the miniature signs on buildings and walls, and from far away came the tune that soothed his four-year-old self. In a lilting voice, to the melody of 'Mary Had a Little Lamb', he crooned:

> *'Mafeking Av-en-ue*
> *Tolworth Street, Spelling Way*
> *Mafeking Av-en-ue,*
> *That's where we're sure to go.'*

'Tell me normally.' Stella reversed the van up and executed a three-point turn.

'Mafeking Avenue, Tolworth Street…' Jack sang.

'David Lauren!'

'Tolworth Street, Spelling Way… Who?'

'The man Marian Williams said crashed his car on Tolworth Street. In 1989.'

'The photographs are private.' It was their secret.

'Keep your coat on, I didn't tell her. Although you suggested that I should. She saw a photograph when she was at Terry's.'

''Spelling Way is closer than Mafeking Avenue or Tolworth Street.'

'What's the reference number?'

'It's not in the file. I suspect Terry's collection wasn't definitive and he knew it wasn't. Spelling Way is long and straight. And Mafeking Avenue is number two.'

'Tolworth Street is number four: there's one photograph. Marian said the man who died there had knocked down a child. A pattern is forming here. Let's go to What's-it Avenue. We should do the ones we have evidence for first.'

Jack typed the name into the van's satnav. 'Twenty-five minutes away.'

At Hammersmith Broadway Stella beat the junction lights and enquired in a 'by the way' tone that did not fool Jack, 'Where are Terry's gloves?'

'They're together.' They were in Colin's wardrobe, but he couldn't tell her this. 'They're safe.' A mistake. Stella didn't believe that objects had feelings. She wasn't worried his hands were cold; she was fretting he had lost her dad's gloves. No present came without strings. He could not mollify her by reassuring her the gloves had each other and were safe from his Host.

'Your hands must be cold,' Stella said. 'Here, take mine.'

''S OK.' She could always surprise him.

'I was with David Barlow.'

'Say again?'

'Last Friday, when you called. I've been out with him twice.'

'The client with the peculiar job?'

'It's deep cleaning, it's not peculiar.'

Jack contemplated his bare hands, palms uppermost as if in supplication. They seemed not to be his own. He stopped himself thinking.

They drove on in silence.

Curving Juliet balconies of blue-painted metal were a clumsy attempt to soften the implacable square building. Stella counted lights in tall windows, many uncurtained, in some the shadows of occupants passing over walls and ceilings. If an accident took place here tonight, there would be no shortage of witnesses. Unlike the other streets, Mafeking Avenue wasn't an ideal place to choose if, like David Lauren had supposedly done, you wanted to kill yourself – help was at hand if you botched the job. More evidence, if they needed it, that the fatal collisions were neither suicides or accidents. On the other side of the road, tingeing the wet pavement orange, was the garish neon of a Sainsbury's Local. Despite what Jack said, Mafeking Avenue was not like the other streets.

'This is hardly derelict,' she said.

Jack nodded assent. 'Maybe the satnav's faulty.'

Stella stretched back into the van and got out the London street map from the door pocket. 'We cut through Melrose Street and went left.' She indicated the page. 'This is the right place.'

The steady rain made the lamplight a fuzzy ball that sent a ghostly glow over the frontage of a graphic design company; giant black and white letters in different fonts appeared to float free of the glass. Through the mizzle sinister shapes resolved against the sky and Stella recognized the twin turrets of Wormwood Scrubs Prison. Terry had grown up near here in Primula Street where one of the dead drivers, Paul Vickery, had lived. This disparate fact might have first sharpened her dad's curiosity. Several men had smashed into trees – counting a telegraph pole as a tree – on lonely streets. Terry had taken his hunch to the grave, but he had left her some vital clues. She would not let him down.

'This place is bristling with CCTV and there's a speed bump.' She clamped the blue folder inside her anorak to protect it from the wet.

Jack didn't reply. It hadn't escaped her that he'd been subdued since she'd mentioned David Barlow. Heedless of the weather or of possible traffic, he strode out to the middle of the road and, muttering, looked about him. She caught the words:

'He's got this wrong, it's still a warehouse. No shop either... won't like it, but I'll have to say...'

'Who are you talking about?' Jack was being deliberately obtuse. Not waiting for an answer Stella went over to the flats. A plaque was set into the wall. She was about to read it when Jack called out.

'Look!' He was pointing up the road.

That was more his old self. Relieved, Stella followed the line of his finger. A tall plane tree stood about twenty yards away.

'This beauty is at least a hundred years old.' Jack circled the base of the trunk. 'Here we are.' He swept his hands over the bark. 'It was some impact. This is at least twenty years old, but the scar is still there – see the faint alteration in the patina?'

A scar made by a vehicle travelling at speed, Terry would say. Stella bent down. Roots pushed up terracotta blocks fanning out from the base. They were new: in Terry's picture chunky cobbles made it look like a Dickensian industrial street. She examined the bricks.

'One is out of line.'

'Imagine this is a chasm leading to the centre of the earth.' Jack poked his finger into a gap between the bricks. 'If you were a beetle.'

'Not now, Jack.' Although Jack being a beetle was better than stalking murderers or saying nothing about David Barlow.

Jack shoved his coat cuffs up. 'Hold one side. When I say, pull as hard as you can.'

Stella clasped the brick, digging her nails into the crumbling mortar between the bricks. Their hands touched.

'One, two, three,' Jack gasped.

Stella felt a grating as it shifted.

'We mustn't let go!' Jack let go. The brick slipped back. 'I can't get a purchase,' he panted. 'I give up.'

'Don't do that. Go again.' Stella gripped the brick, her hands like a vice. Clenching her teeth, she tugged. The stone lifted enough for Jack to shove his fingers into the gap. Together they wrenched the brick out and clear of the hole. Jack placed it against a tree root.

He whistled. 'You are tenacious.'

Stella was gratified by his comment; he was thawing. They were in this together.

She directed her torch into the hole and revealed a boiling mass of woodlice.

'Yes… there we are. Sorry, everyone.' Jack scrabbled amongst them and piecemeal took out what looked like dirty stones. He arranged them on the bricks. One glinted green in the torchlight.

'We must put this back for the woodlice.' Jack picked up the brick. 'No one's disturbed their habitat for decades. Not since the fatal …'

'What do they mean?' Stella felt the same unease as when they were on the other streets, despite there being people nearby. In the time they had been there no cars had passed.

'It's the opposite of taking an artefact from a murder scene for a trophy.'

'He's taunting the police.'

'I don't think the police were meant to know. He was staking a claim. Another for his collection. The glass quantifies his achievement. Like you with your spreadsheets: you collect and file facts towards an objective.'

'Hardly the same,' Stella snapped. She had not thought Jack noticed what she did. 'Dead people. Some collection.' She got to her feet.

'Woodlice have fourteen joints. They curl themselves into a ball as a defence mechanism.' Jack funnelled the stones into a plastic bag 'We've panicked them – if a crustacean can be panicked – but they'll be OK if no one disturbs them again.'

'Shame woodlice can't talk. They could tell us what happened here,' Stella remarked more to herself than Jack. Sheltering under the spreading branches she shone her torch on to the folder and prised apart the damp pages. Water had penetrated the plastic files. She couldn't risk damage. She hurried back to the van and laid the folder on the passenger seat.

As Jack had supposed, the photographs referenced '2' and

'2a' matched Mafeking Avenue. The tree was in the second of two shots. Terry had shot it in the winter when the branches were bare and stark; now it was lush with green leaves. The apartment block was in the picture; despite what Jack had said earlier, Terry had known it was there. She looked again. It was a shell. A defunct warehouse with gaping holes for delivery of goods. These were picture windows done up with fancy balconies. The slogan 'George Davis Is Innocent' was sprayed across the bricks.

'I assumed that Terry compiled this collection over a short period of time.' Jack opened the passenger door. 'But I'd say his suspicions were aroused years ago. No one was living in here when our fatal accident took place.'

Stella got out her grid. Meticulously she wrote in Mafeking Avenue and Terry's photo references. Maybe Jack was right. She did like to collect and quantify.

'They live about two years, although some have made it to four,' Jack got in. 'The woodlice witnesses to the crash were ancestors of these ones. Judging by the age of the scar, it's like the ice age for us.'

'The killer might return to the scene of the crime. He could be here now.' Stella checked her mirrors. Although the street was quiet, he could be out there. She could see a salt bin a few metres away: a good hiding place.

'I doubt it. He takes no chances. He's a collector. He's concerned with increasing his collection, not with playing cat and mouse with the police.'

'He went back to Marquis Way. That was a risk. He wouldn't know the police don't analyse traffic collisions and that someone had not spotted a pattern.'

'Terry did.' Jack scrutinized the stones in the bag. 'Maybe you should talk to your new friend.'

'Meaning?' Stella started the engine. She knew what he meant.

'She'll know her way around their systems. Not much she can't find out. Bet she eats and sleeps her job. You said she instantly recalled the facts about Tolworth Street. She gave you flowers; she might want to help.'

'It's Terry she wanted to help.' Marian would not have bothered with her if she were not Terry Darnell's daughter. 'A moment ago you wanted this to be our secret.'

'Don't say why you're asking.'

'Marian's not stupid.' Marian was law-abiding and hard-working and Stella respected that. She would not ask her to bend the rules. Jack's concept of right and wrong was hazy. Although recently her own morality had been up for grabs. She had not yet found a way to return the green form. She did not say that unwittingly Marian had already helped them. Stella put 'Tolworth Street' into the satnav.

'After three hundred yards turn left.'

'So far we know at least three men died on desolate streets at night and the green glass leads us to be sure they were murdered. The killer marked the sites with seven green chips of glass.' She tilted her head; a car behind them had its headlights on full beam, the light bright in the wing and rear mirrors. 'We don't know why and we don't know how.' Stella accelerated.

'Slow down or we'll have a crash.' Jack was gripping the handle fixed above the door frame.

'There's nothing coming.' A train driver, he must be used to being in control.

'If someone stepped off the kerb, you'd have nowhere to go.'

Stella braked. Jack screamed.

'That's it!' She cut the engine. 'He stepped out and they swerved and smashed into the trunks. No cameras, no pedestrians; no witnesses. He walked away. The events put down as tragic accidents. No one noticed that the dead drivers had all run over children. No one saw the bigger picture.'

Jack grabbed her arm. 'Brilliant, Stella!'

'Although how could he be certain they'd take avoidance action? Some people are slow to react.'

'A potential flaw. I suspect he courts the risk. Like Russian roulette. Later he returns and buries the glass. Job done.'

'Or he buries the pieces before the event. A marker, a promise to himself.'

'Nice one. That's thinking like me!' Jack rattled the glass. 'Although the forensics crawling all over the scene might have found them. A risk too far.'

'Must have been afterwards. No one would draw any significance from the stones. Even though they are at every crash site.' Stella started the van and pulled out. 'No one analyses the data. Besides, as we know, they were not found.'

'He executed the perfect murder over and over again.' Jack put the stones in his coat pocket with the others.

'He's pure evil.' Stella checked her mirror. No cars now. The street was dark.

'No such thing as evil. It's the deed, not the person who is evil.'

'If you commit evil you are evil. Wait a moment.' Stella slowed the van, but didn't brake this time. 'I know what it is.'

'What what is?'

'The glass. It's aggregate, the jade variety. David used it to decorate his wife's grave. It saves weeding.'

'You have reached your destination.'

Forty-Seven

Sunday, 3 July 1966

Her mum and dad were in bed, but she could not be sure they were asleep so was extra specially careful. She had her clothes on over her pyjamas and her anorak over her jumper. This made it hard to walk, but she would be warm.

After tea, when her mum was in bed and her dad was in Michael's room (even though it was empty), Mary had packed provisions for her expedition. Torch, her dad's trowel, some Fruit Salad chews and a ball of string. The last had no direct use, but she had read somewhere that it always came in handy. She was disappointed Michael wasn't there to see, but if he were he would only give her away.

Don't forget the key.

She snatched the key off the hook in the hall.

I'm scared.

Shut up. She cycled down British Grove, head down. The duffel bag was heavier than she had expected. She knew the way without a map. The task was not for scaredy cats, she informed Michael. She had a stitch in her side and despite the biting night air she was hot. She leant her bike against the wall and squeezed through the break in the cemetery railings.

Mary Thornton had not known that in the city it was never dark and found she could see without her torch. The path was a pale line between the graves. She didn't like being so close to dead people; she had made her plan in the sunshine.

The Angel was taller than ever. Mary felt afraid. She would not

294

let Michael see. If he was watching over her like the vicar said, he knew anyway.

She battled through a bush of ground elder, her duffel bag an impediment, and then did a lopsided crawl to a clearing in the middle. She laid down the bag and scrabbled furiously at the earth with her trowel. She dug a hole a foot deep and about eighteen inches in circumference and lowered the bag down.

'*Dust thou art, and unto dust thou shalt return.*'

She clawed at the soil until the bag was covered and then made good the disturbance with a scattering of dried pine needles and leaves. She shoved her way out, splintering and snapping branches, careless of discovery.

The Angel watched the little girl tear up and down maze-like paths until she found the gap in the railings.

Forty-Eight

Wednesday, 2 May 2012

Stella tipped the lever enough to reel the film to fit the screen. She was back in the Hammersmith and Fulham Archives. That morning she had cancelled the rearranged recruitment meeting with Jackie to come to the library. She would do what Terry called good old-fashioned legwork. She had put into the grid the street names Jack had sung to the tune of the nursery rhyme. This had seemed real progress, until the internet failed to throw up an incident for Mafeking Avenue or another one for Marquis Way, apart from Vickery. They could have been wrong about the telegraph pole; it might have been pranged innocently. Then she remembered they had found bits of jade glass there. More frustrating was that she could find nothing for Tolworth Street where Marian said a man called David Lauren had died in 1989. The web wouldn't deliver the Holy Grail.

Last night, when they had gone to Tolworth Street, they had located a scarred beech tree. Jade glass beneath its roots confirmed this was where Lauren had died. Jack was impressed with the tree for surviving the 1987 hurricane and the impact of Lauren's car. He had told it so.

They had a year and a name for number four in Terry's series of seven. There was no tree on Spelling Way, another street in Jack's song. He had been vague about why he had included it. Stella wouldn't put it past him to like how it fitted in the tune. She would discount it for now as they had enough to go on.

She opened her Filofax at her grid and took out papers she had stuffed in there. One caught her eye and she smoothed it out. It was the article about James Markham's death she had printed up the last time she was here. She was about to refold it when a name caught her eye. Christopher Mason. Markham had killed a boy in the January before his own death in November 2002. At the time she had thought little of it. Three dead children was definitely a trend. Green stones at the base of the pole were the only proof something else had happened on Marquis Way apart from Vickery's death. She had the bare details in row six and amended Vickery's accident column to specify the type of tree. Terry would say it was important. They now knew the date of Charles Hampson's death; she filled it in. Although there was a photograph for Mafeking Avenue, again green stones were all they had to indicate an event had happened there. Stella folded her arms and looked at the grid. They had street names for all the photographs except for number one, of the garage mechanic under the car which might not belong in the file.

Pic. No.	Date	Street	Accident	Victim	Child	Date
1	Filed in error	Garage	?	?	?	?
2 (2a)	?	Mafeking Avenue	Hit a plane tree	Found green stones		
3 (3a & 3b)	16th March 1977	Marquis Way	Hit an ash tree	Paul Vickery	James Harrison	17th October 1976
4	1989	Tolworth Street	Hit a beech tree	David Lauren		
5 (5a & 5b)	10th November 2002	Britton Drive	Hit a sweet chestnut tree.	James Markham	Christopher Mason	2nd January 2002
6 (6a)	?	Marquis Way	Hit a telegraph pole	?	?	?

Pic. No.	Date	Street	Accident	Victim	Child	Date
7 (7a & 7b)	15th March 2009	Phoenix Way	Hit an oak tree	Charlie Hampson	Stephen Parsons	8th January 2009
None	?	Spelling Way	No tree	?	?	?

She tried to think what Terry's approach would be and returned a blank. She would use her method of scoping a job. She calculated the square footage, identified specific issues, like stains on a carpet. She broke these down to the kind of stains and length of time they had been there. Step by step. Stain by stain.

The first step was to establish when the warehouse in Mafeking Avenue was converted into apartments. Stella sat up. There had been a plaque on the wall. She tried to picture it, but did not have Jack's photographic memory. He might remember; it was an excuse to call and gauge his mood around David Barlow. No, no point. He had not looked at the plaque.

Stella grabbed her iPhone and brought up Street View. Seconds later she had up Mafeking Avenue on a sunny day. She swivelled the handset to landscape. There was the plane tree. She found she was looking for Jack's woodlice. Concentrate! A few more metres and she was outside the supermarket. She rotated ninety degrees to face the apartment block. The plaque was a fuzzy square behind the railings. Involuntarily she jerked her head to see around them. Zooming in did not help; she couldn't read the inscription. She was about to give up when it sprang into focus.

Th foundation one was lai y

Counc r Vince Har wick

6 ne 01

Two black stripes – the railings – cut out letters but she had enough to go on. Only one month ended with: 'ne'. June. The year had to be 2001. The building wasn't flats when Terry took the picture. It was a lead, a slim one, but a lead none the less.

Stella found the film for 2001 and fed it into the machine. She skimmed at breakneck speed to June. The sixth had been a Wednesday that year. The *Chronicle* was published on Thursdays. She inched along to 7 June and found her grail.

COUNCILLOR FIRES THE STARTING GUN

By Lucille May

Vince Hardwick, Chair of the council, unveiled a plaque for Wilton Retreat, the conversion of the Wilton flour warehouse into luxury apartments yesterday. This kicks off the regeneration plan for Mafeking Avenue. The warehouse, operational for a century, was mothballed in 1963 when flour-production methods changed and bakers didn't need to sift flour. Hardwick used his casting vote to veto a campaign by local residents for a housing association development for low-income families. The apartments, perfect for those with telephone number salaries, include a penthouse and offer spectacular views over West London.

We reminded Mr Hardwick that in 1970 Denis Atkins, who had held his position at the council, died when his MG Midget hit the tree that still stands opposite the warehouse. Appearing flustered he assured us the flats were a fitting monument.

Molly Atkins, 73, who lays flowers by the tree every year, insisted that her husband would not approve of ordinary people being deprived of a home.

If only the clumsy mechanism offered a search facility. With fifty-two weeks of 1970 to trawl though, this truly was legwork. An hour later Stella was rewarded. According to the nightwatchman at the nearby empty flour warehouse, Denis Atkins died on Monday, 7 September, around about eleven-thirty. Lucille May reported his death in four lines in that Thursday's *Chronicle*. Persisting, Stella found another article by May, who had gone to his inquest two weeks later. Despite recent storms, Monday had been dry; there had been no black ice. Atkins had no alcohol in his blood and his Midget was in good repair. The verdict was 'Accidental Death'. She hit 'print' and put the dead councillor in her grid.

She put off searching for clues to the telegraph-pole incident on Marquis Way. David Lauren held more promise. She paced the line of grey metal cabinets. The years were typed in wonky Courier font on browned and crinkled labels. She found the drawer marked '1986 to 1990': 1989 was missing. She checked it hadn't been misfiled. All the years were in order. She slammed shut the drawer and tried the one above and then the one below. It was not there. She balked at combing the entire collection; that was taking legwork too far.

'You're making rather a noise.' The librarian was beside her. 'Can I help?'

'I'm looking for 1989,' Stella barked loudly. She lowered her voice. 'It's been stolen.'

'That can't be.' Stella watched her follow the same process, pausing at the gap in chronology, and was torn between wanting the woman to locate the reel and not wanting to look stupid if it was there all along. It was not there.

'We get few thefts. It's probably being repaired. The films get worn or the boxes collapse, although it's not a popular year. Had it had been 1968 or the Silver Jubilee in 1977...'

While she waited for the librarian to confirm this Stella reread her notes and the size of the task pressed in again. It would be easier with two, but since Amanda Hampson's death Jack had been distracted. The business last night confirmed he was up to something that could land him in trouble or worse. She was disconsolate.

She stared. Something was written on the opposite page to her grid.

'Harvey Gray, aged 53, Marquis Way, Monday, 17 March 2003.'

Stella had jotted down the details of their first search on the newspaper's website in case it was important. This was the other death on Marquis Way. Stella nearly called out to the librarian. She had another street! She retrieved the film for 2003 from the cabinets and, her hands trembling with anticipation, fed it into the microfiche. Soon she was looking at the edition for Thursday, 20 March.

SHOE MAN DIES IN CRASH

By Lucille May

Harvey Gray, owner of Gray Shoes, was killed outright when his luxury Lexus SUV left the road and hit a telegraph pole on Marquis Way W6 late on Monday. Gray was rushed to Charing Cross Hospital where he was pronounced dead.

Ms Carol Jones of Arkwright Buildings, Shepherd's Bush, was on Marquis Way at half past ten and raised the alarm on her mobile phone.

Mr Gray's factory on Britton Drive went into receivership last year. Police are asking an elderly person who passed Ms Jones before she arrived at the scene of the accident to come forward; he or she may possess vital information. Anyone who witnessed the incident or who has information should contact Hammersmith Police Station...

Stella recognised May's name. This was the pushy woman who had written the article about Terry's funeral.

The shots of Marquis Way on Street View were dated June 2009; darts of light bounced off quartz in the paving, shadows were stark in blinding sunshine. Terry went in the winter when

301

the camber glistened with recent rain and a drain was clogged with leaves.

Stella pictured the dilapidated factory outlet in the first street they had visited. Signs and coincidences. Jack's world. The wording was similar to the other articles about accidents also reported by Lucille May. Stella guessed May had got into the habit of trotting out the same phrases for fatalities that over the years must have become routine. Scarcely able to contain her triumph, she slotted Gray into her grid. She noted the figure seen near the crash could have been a man or a woman. A man surely.

Step by step. Stain by stain.

'No luck, I'm afraid. Nineteen eighty-nine has vanished.' The librarian was back. 'Leave me your details and if it turns up I'll call.'

Stella thanked her and studied her grid so far. Marian said that David Lauren had run over a boy called Billy. Charlie Hampson knocked over a child a few months before he died. Paul Vickery killed James Harrison in 1976. Stella looked at her watch. She was standing in for Wendy at a bridal shop in Ealing and didn't have time to check if Harvey Gray killed a child. A hunch told her that he had.

Marian Williams had called David Lauren's victim 'Little Billy' in the sugary manner of Lucille May. Impatient with 'Tiny Tim' sentimentality, Stella had forgotten to put it in her grid. She did so now. 'Little Billy' would have to do until she had his full name.

'Here you are!' The librarian placed a cardboard box in front of her. 'Nineteen eighty-nine! Some of our visitors get numbers wrong or find our cataloguing system tricky. My mentioning 1968 got me thinking and hey presto! This was in the nineties drawer next to 1998.'

David Lauren had died when his car had slammed into a tree on Tolworth Street – the ubiquitous Lucille May didn't give the species of tree – late on Friday, 31 March 1989. The paper splashed a half-page photograph of the flourishing beech deep in floral tributes. The crashed car had been removed. Stella gave Lucille May credit, the journalist had done her homework and linked the crash to the death of William Carter on Boxing Day 1988 in another article with the convoluted headline: 'Christmas Boy-Death Crash Man Dies'.

May described how 'Little Billy' had been riding his Christmas scooter on the pavement outside Kings Court in Hammersmith when Lauren's Vauxhall Carlton had mounted the kerb and 'mown him down'. Stella wrote this next to his full name for good measure. May's tone went as far as she legally dared to portray Lauren as cold-blooded and careless. 'At the inquest, Lauren showed no emotion, apart from a kiss blown to his wife in the gallery. Dressed in a tailored suit…' Maybe this wasn't so routine after all. It was as if the woman took it personally.

Stella found her own emotions stirred. She altered the 'Victim' column to 'Driver'; the children were the real victims. Unable to bear the crossings out, she rewrote the grid on a clean page. She sent the article for printing and, flinging herself back in her chair, reviewed her newly populated grid.

Pic. No.	Date	Street	Accident	Driver	Child (Victim)	Date
1	Filed in error?	Garage	?	?	?	?
2 (2a)	7th September 1970	Mafe-king Avenue	Hit a plane tree	Denis Atkins	?	?
3 (3a & 3b	16th March 1977	Marquis Way	Hit an ash tree	Paul Vickery	James Harrison	17th October 1976
4	31st March 1989	Tolworth Street	Hit a beech tree	David Lauren	William Carter (mown down)	26th December 1988
5 (5a & 5b)	10th November 2002	Britton Drive	Hit a sweet chestnut tree.	James Markham	Christopher Mason	2nd January 2002

Pic. No.	Date	Street	Accident	Driver	Child (Victim)	Date
6 (6a)	17th March 2003	Marquis Way	Hit a tele-graph pole	Harvey Gray		
7 (7a & 7b)	15th March 2009	Phoenix Way	Hit an oak tree	Charlie Hampson	Stephen Parsons	8th January 2009
None		Spelling Way	No tree	?	?	?

Four drivers had each killed a child; she would assume they all had. Her head was pounding. She had twenty-three minutes to get to 'Happiest Day' in Ealing. Gray and Atkins would have to wait. She thanked the librarian, paid for her printing and left.

A keen breeze whipped beneath Hammersmith flyover and blew away Stella's frail sense of victory. Six men had died in five streets. Seven chips were buried at each of the crash sites. A man had stepped out in front of their cars, making them swerve and slam into a tree or a pole. Jack was right, it was a risky modus operandi: if one driver had survived, he could have said what happened. None of them had. The murderer had got away with it.

As she passed the police station on Shepherd's Bush Road, Stella glanced up at Marian's office. In the morning she would return the green form.

Overtaking a number 72 bus, Stella admitted to herself that, at the end of the day, she and Jack were no nearer to knowing who had killed these men and why.

Forty-Nine

Thursday, 3 May 2012

Stella had been at the police station for half an hour when her phone rang. She was guiding her trolley towards Marian's office, the wheels rattling on the parquet, and stopped, appalled. She did not want Marian to hear the phone.

'Your mother's just rung. She couldn't get hold of you.'

Stella guessed, although nothing in Jackie's tone implied it, that this applied to Jackie too.

'This early? And what are you doing at the office?'

'I'm not at the office. Beverly put the phone on divert instead of answer machine again. Lucky really.'

'What did Mum want?' Her mother had left a message last night. Stella had forgotten.

'Jack's number.'

'Did you give it to her?'

'No. I'm afraid that made her cross.'

Stella nodded approval although Jackie couldn't see her. 'I'll call when I've finished here.'

'Have you remembered our recruitment meeting at nine-thirty?'

Stella had forgotten. 'I'll be there by eight-thirty,' she declared. She slipped her phone into her trouser pocket. This was the best part of the day and Suzie had put a dent in it. Her fear about Jack cleaning there had come true; he had displeased her in some way and Stella would have to sort it out.

*

Jackie Makepeace arrived at Clean Slate at seven-thirty. Since Stella's father had died, Stella no longer arrived at six o'clock every morning and worked a twelve-hour day. Recently there were days when she didn't come to the office at all. This had been noticed. Dariusz Adomek, the owner of the mini-mart below, had asked after her, and this morning Sue in the dry cleaner's had wanted to know if Stella was all right. Jackie gave nothing away. Stella would hate to think her movements had been observed, albeit because people cared. Jackie herself had noticed that, since Terry Darnell's death, Stella had changed. Two months ago she had got a speeding ticket for doing three miles per hour over the speed limit on King Street. She had attended a speed awareness course, which had made her evangelistic about speeding and resulted in a section on speeding in the staff manual. Jackie was perturbed. As a policeman's daughter, it was unlike Stella to break the Highway Code. Or any sort of code.

One advantage of the new Stella was that at this time of the morning Jackie had the office to herself, a pleasure she had not had since managing the employment agency.

She made a coffee and began to process the week's employee hours. She tsk-tsked at the three job sheets from Stella; she was doing too much cleaning again. This was not grief; it was Stella doing what she liked best. She had allocated herself two floors of the police station with Donette and Wendy sharing the ground floor. Typical. Jackie saw why. Stella's floors included Terry Darnell's old office and the Braybrook Suite, once the 'Major Incident Room', where Stella's dad had conducted his most famous case. Maybe it was grief after all.

Jackie was certain she would not see Stella today so she did something she had never done before and countermanded Stella's rules. She called Jack Harmon and gave him Suzanne Darnell's number.

Stella left the trolley in the corridor and went into Marian Williams's office.

A dark shape was slumped over the empty desk by the window. 'Please don't worry. I made a promise. It will all be all right; that's what I'm here for.'

Marian Williams was one of those whose home is their workplace. She would believe that Hammersmith Police Station could not function without her. She might be right.

'Don't worry. It will all be all right.'

Stella was surprised by the soothing tone and hoped Marian was not buttering up the violent husband.

Marian Williams was less friendly than she had been at Terry's. She stuffed her phone into her handbag, wheeled herself up to her own desk and fired up her computer. Like Stella, she would not want to be caught on a personal phone call.

Negotiating the doorway, Stella pushed her cleaning cart in and parked it by the window. She turned around and knocked a pot of pens off the unoccupied desk on to the floor. Marian frowned briefly, but her fingers did not stop their canter over the keyboard.

Stella could not equate the taciturn overweight woman squeezed into her chair with the friendly Marian who had thrust a bouquet of flowers into her arms. It was this kind of erratic behaviour that had prompted Stella to write the section in her manual on avoiding being overfriendly with clients. She scrabbled on the floor for the pens, a stapler remover and some paper clips that had scattered across the carpet tiles and poked them back into the pot.

'They have no idea of the damage they cause.' Williams wheeled backwards. 'They think only of themselves.'

Stella gave the briefest of nods. Clients may engage you in conversation and later complain you are slow. Marian would shake her head to Cashman: Not a patch on her dad. She wadded her duster, squirted spray on it and gave the desk a vigorous polish.

'Take this.' Marian indicated her screen to Stella, pecking at the keys with an index finger. 'This chappie cut his hand escaping from the garden of a house he had burgled. He told my colleagues that broken glass on the top of the wall was a "disproportionate response"!'

She hit 'return' and dense columns of words and dates filled the screen. Stella feigning interest, read Marquis Way. 'What's this?' she demanded. Then, to cover up the urgency of her question: 'It looks complicated.'

'He's what I was talking about the other night. He is no longer with us, I am not sad to say. Harvey Gray died on Marquis Way. We put the date there, see?'

Marquis Way was the street with two crashes. The screen swam before her eyes. In 2003, 17 March had been a Monday. Stella forced herself to memorize it in case that was important. 'Did he crash into a tree?' She kept her voice level.

'What makes you say that?' Marian Williams angled the monitor so Stella could no longer see it.

'A joke really. Well, not a joke obviously...' Stella swished her cloth over the desk. She knew it wasn't a tree.

'No. A telegraph pole, which is as good as a tree. Despite the negative tox report, he was drunk. Had to be. Don't shed a tear, Stella. Hanging was too good for him. Robert Smith – his dad called him Rob; I make sure to find out, using a formal name underlines the family's loss – would have been eight two days after he was run over. His parents split up a year later. Mr Smith was drinking and his wife was found dead in bed from an overdose of paracetamol.' Marian clasped her hands either side of her face. 'Not her own bed. She was curled up in Rob's bed clasping his teddy-bear pyjama case.'

Stella suspected that while Marian was genuinely upset, like Suzie she got a certain satisfaction from being the bearer of bad news. 'So he died on Marquis Way,' she said despite herself. So Harvey Grey had killed a child. She wanted to put it in her grid there and then.

'So what?' Marian got up. Stella had to move away from the monitor.

'I know the street,' Stella prattled. 'I had a client there.' She retreated to her cleaning trolley. Marian might be well aware that few lived or worked on Marquis Way, a road so mired in the recession a cleaner was unlikely to be required.

'There's a natural justice in Gray's dying. Poor Rob died outside the Hammersmith and City Underground station. Gray bleated – the man was a teacher, believe it or not – that the little chap dashed into the traffic. No doubt he did, children are impulsive creatures, but we drive to legislate for that, don't we?' She was severe. 'Gray got whiplash. Months later took the coward's way out.' She nodded as if she herself had administered it. 'They say all sin will out.'

Under the pretext of scribbling on her job sheet, Stella jotted down the boy's name, the date of his death and the street.

'We had a "jumper" off Stamford Brook station in January. Family were devastated.' Marian was talking almost to herself. 'I can't say I shed a tear. He didn't think of the tube driver.'

For the first time Stella considered the hazards of Jack's job. He never talked about driving on the District Line. 'Horrible for you too,' she ventured.

Marian shook her head. 'I'm not important.'

'The other night, you mentioned that a David Lauren hit a beech tree on Tolworth Street. He had run over a boy and killed him.' Too late Stella realized that Marian had not told her how David Lauren had died or what type of tree he crashed into. 'Or a bollard or whatever... that's a coincidence, isn't it?'

'Is it?' Marian looked bemused.

'Two men knocking down children and then dying?' There was no way out of so deep a hole.

'Not really. They couldn't live with themselves. If I killed a child I would accept whatever punishment was meted out.' She gave a start as if she had not meant to be so frank. 'So many don't.' She flopped down at her desk again. 'Terry said, "We can't solve the problem, but we can clear up the mess."'

Stella would not tell Marian about the blue folder. She was in love with Terry and wasn't objective. She liaised with bereaved families, filed autopsy reports, collated accident details and supported officers who had attended horrific scenes and seen dead children. While Jack and Stella played detectives, this was her daily life. She would not welcome their interference; she might even resent that Terry had effectively left his unsolved case to his daughter when she was the obvious person. Above all Marian would have no truck with their murder theory. She was convinced that the drivers had ended their own lives. The green glass would not change this. She needed to think they were weak men. It was men like Terry who were strong.

Jack had once said Stella was a bad judge of people, but this time she had it on the nose. Terry had not shared the blue folder with Marian, nor, Stella resolved, would she. 'I'll leave the vacuuming until Friday.' She moved away from the desk.

'Do it now. Joel's parents want to go back to where he died. I'm taking them. I'm popping out to get flowers.' Marian slung her handbag strap over her chest and stood aside to let Stella wheel the vacuum cleaner in from the corridor and then left the room.

Stella plugged the machine into a socket under the window. A patch of condensation on the window blurred the reddish brickwork of Hammersmith Library beyond. Stella rubbed it away. Shepherd's Bush Road was familiar from this angle: Terry's office was along the passage. She left it to last. Cars and lorries were bumper to bumper. Two buses at a stop held up a van, its long wheelbase allowing for a string of writing on the panelling: 'Bridge Cleaning Services ... Medical Hygiene ... Cleaning ... Kitchen Deep Cleaning'.

Competition. The van edged around the buses and squeezed through the corridor between a motorbike and the oncoming traffic. A yellow notice on its rear asked: 'How's My Driving?' Stella's staff must not make slick moves like this to save seconds. She made a mental note to put it in the manual.

It was easy to have an accident. The surprise was that more people had not died. Marian and Terry dealt with evil that was mostly below the line of everyday vision. They had looked after each other.

Jack said people themselves were not evil. For Stella it was simple: she too delved into hidden places, her mission to expunge filth and grime that people had allowed to build. It was always down to people. Stella felt sorry for Marian – Stella would not want to take parents to see where their child had been killed.

She recalled Marian's phone conversation and hoped it had been with someone who cared for her. She hoped it was not the man who had given Marian the ugly bruise on her arm.

The Bridge Cleaning van found a traffic break. Stella should have put 'Deep Cleaning' on her fleet's livery. She would do so on the one van left to paint. This made her think of David Barlow. She brightened; she was due there on Saturday.

Stella unreeled the vacuum cable with great sweeps of her arm and set to work on the carpet, keeping straight lines as if she were mowing a lawn.

Marian was right: children were impulsive. They were less able to judge distance or speed than adults and made sudden decisions or no decision if they blindly chased a pet or a ball. Bewitched by new toys, they raced out in front of buses and cars, stepped on live rails or drowned in a swimming pool too soon after eating a bag of chips. Suzie had peppered Stella's own childhood with dire warnings and pithy commandments. Terry too had lamented what he called 'the failure of the human element'. Evil was a breath away.

She guided the vacuum out and took a last look at the office. Marian Williams was tidy so it took little to keep it spick and span.

An hour later she had finished in record time and texted Jackie to confirm their recruitment meeting. Thinking it would be politic to say goodbye, Stella returned to Marian's office and tapped on the glass. No answer. She popped her head around the door, a bright smile ready. Marian was not there. Her computer glowed in the empty office.

Stella was about to go when she saw that Marian had left the database open her screen. She couldn't have long gone or the screen would have blacked out into sleep mode. Stella stared at it as if at the barrel of a gun. Jack's voice whispered in her ear, urging her on. Stella gripped the door jamb; a strong wind might have been pulling at her, she held it so tight.

Leaving a computer unsecured was a serious oversight. Confidential information was there for anyone to see. Members of the public were not allowed up here without an appointment, but Amanda Hampson had slipped through. Stella should make herself scarce. Marian was upset; when she returned, she would see her mistake and assume Stella had too. First she had left files on her desk and now this.

Stella could close the database and then Marian would never know. Armed with this justification she advanced on the desk. She halted. Was this the pit into which the last cleaner had fallen? Her mouth was dry and every muscle in her body thrilled with the imperative to get away from the computer and its whirring fan.

She heard Jack: Just a peep – dates, streets, victims' names, drivers' names: everything we want and more. Stell, it's all there…

Marian's chair faced her. The velvet cushion, patchworked like some needlework exercise, was moulded into the seat. It might be Marian Williams herself.

There on the screen were the figures and columns Marian had shown her. Stella had the vertiginous sensation of looking down at herself from above. She scanned the ceiling: no cameras. She blundered to the door: no one outside.

Fatal road traffic accidents in Hammersmith between – ooh, say 1980 and 2012?

The shame would be unbearable. Clean Slate would be finished. She would be finished. Stella's hands were ice-cold and clammy. She dashed them on her trouser legs. Marian would be back any minute.

Stella was a policeman's daughter. She had never done anything dishonest or illegal. She was sliding into a drab and dreadful land from which there was no escape.

Her fingers were perfectly steady as she typed in the parameters: 'Road traffic accidents between 1966 and 2011.'

'Enter'. By mistake, she put in the year she was born. The screen went blank. Jack's voice made way for a distant ringtone. Shirley Bassey's 'History Repeating' was cut short when the call was taken.

There were over fifty entries, covering date, location, vehicles involved, time of day, victims, officers. Terry was at her shoulder.

You are no daughter of mine.

Now she was shaking and she clamped her hands under her armpits. The search delivered all road traffic accidents for the period, not only fatal ones. Too many; she did not have time.

You should not be here.

Mafeking Avenue. One of the streets in Jack's song. The entry on the grid where they had no child's name.

Monday, 7 September 1970. Denis Atkins. Collision with tree approx 22.30. Weather conditions dry and cold. Driver thrown out of Ford Consul Capri; found dead at scene. Neck broken, skull fractured in three places. First officer in attendance: Sgnt T. C. Darnell (No.130253) See: Coleman, Colin, deceased 15/3/70.

Atkins was the councillor who had hit the plane tree opposite the converted warehouse flats. Connections hovered just beyond Stella's grasp. She keyed 'print' and thwacked the return key. If Marian came in now she would have to explain what she was printing, that she was printing at all. Time concertinaed. Too slowly the machine spewed out page after page.

At last it went quiet. Stella grabbed the loose leaves, pulled out the plug on the computer and shoved it in again. Marian would think Stella stupid for using it for her vacuum. Stupid was preferable to criminal.

She pulled the duster from her back pocket and wiped the keyboard. An unnecessary precaution: Marian Williams would not do a fingerprint check. Or would she?

Only after she had signed off the sheets for Donette and Wendy and was in her van outside the police stables did Stella breathe properly.

Jack's ramblings about time being fluid usually frustrated her – punctuality was essential – but now Stella wished it were fluid. If only she could go back to the moment when she saw Marian Williams's vacated desk and walk away. She had crossed a line and could never go back.

She turned on the engine and at the same moment, her phone buzzed. It would be Jackie. She had missed their meeting. It was Jack. Stella considered not answering; she knew it was unfair, but she thought he had done enough damage for one morning.

'Yes?' she wheezed.

'I've got it!'

'Don't shout, I can hear you.'

'That's because I'm shouting.'

'What have you got?' It was illegal to use a phone with the engine running and must be more so on police property; she switched it off as if this would redeem her far larger transgression.

'A pattern for the deaths—'

'I've got another name,' Stella interrupted, and then regretted it. She could not mention the computer printout.

'What?' Jack yelled.

'Where are you?' Stella adjusted her mirror and caught sight of her eyes. They were wild, the pupils dilated, her mascara smudged.

'Outside Suzie's flats.'

'Why are you there?' Stella had the sensation of slithering down a steep hillside. She had forgotten to phone her mum.

'She's mislaid something.' Jack's voice was drowned in a series of pops like distant gunfire. Belatedly Stella recognized an Underground train.

'It's not your job to find Mum's things. She loses stuff all the time, mostly her marbles.' Stella was shouting. She shot a brief smile at a young officer carrying a saddle to the stables. 'How do you know anyway?'

'Jackie call— I mean... er, I was passing... oh well, it's no trouble. I won't charge.'

'Yes you will, you're not a charity and more to the point nor is my mum.'

'We have a breakthrough.' Jack's voice was muffled. He would be in the foyer. Stella tried not to picture the glossed Anaglypta wallpaper. She heard the lift gates clang and was hit by the clinging odour of damp mixed with the smell of meals cooked by people long dead as if she were there with Jack.

'Stella?'

Jack must know she had spent the last fifteen minutes committing a crime. 'I'll come over,' she said, but no sound came out.

'I can't hear you,' Jack bellowed.

Stella was hyperventilating; the windscreen was fogging up. She drew a heart, clumsy and misshapen, on the glass. She put the initials 'DB' in the middle and then scrubbed them out, furious with herself. She was not a teenager.

'… I've cracked the code!'

'What code?' Stella addressed the sheaf of database results on the seat beside her. Evidence of involvement in the commission of a criminal offence.

'Your mum's answering the door.'

'She won't answer.' When Stella visited, her mother expected her to use her key as if she lived there.

'Hey, Suz!'

The line went dead.

Fifty

Thursday, 3 May 2012

'Jack!' Stella bellowed. Through the steamy windscreen she saw the stable door open and the same man as earlier, a ghost in the fug, lead out a horse decked in the Metropolitan Police livery; the gigantic animal dwarfed the tall officer. The thought – a bad joke – occurred to Stella that it was too late to shut the stable door.

Jack would be raking through her mother's rubbish searching for an item Suzie had lost years ago or never owned. Stella should rescue him. But despite the acrid whiff of urine-soaked hay drifting into the van, she didn't move.

> *'Mary had a little lamb,*
> *Its fleece was white as snow.'*

A memory of her dad singing her to sleep floated like gossamer across the misty screen. Terry had taken her to see the horses. She had said the raised squares on the stable floor were like chocolate. Something was nagging. She got the blue folder out of her bag and opened it at the first photograph.

Stella was startled by a rap on the window. Marian Williams was outside.

You do not have to say anything. But it may harm your defence if you do not mention when questioned…

About to start the van and drive away, she forced herself to press the window button. Nothing happened. She fiddled with the ignition key and the glass slid down.

'Did I frighten you?' Marian Williams enquired.

'No.' Stella held the folder to her chest to hide how frightened she was.

'I hoped you'd be here.'

'I have forms to complete, calls...' Stella gabbled. Marian had come to lead her back inside.

'I really hope I didn't upset you the other night, talking about fatalities, suicides and all. Terry and me, we used to say we'd learnt to deal with terrible things. With you being his daughter, I forgot that these things upset ordinary people.'

The printout was inches from Marian. Stella snatched it up and crammed it into her rucksack, tearing a page. 'Not at all. I mean, it's upsetting, but...' She bounced the folder on her knee. She didn't relish being called ordinary, but being called a criminal was far worse.

'Do you fancy going over the road for a coffee? I'm owed some time.'

If Marian planned to arrest her for breaking into the police system, she was choosing her moment. Her kindly smile gave nothing away. Hemmed in by guilt, Stella could not refuse. 'Perhaps the office could spare me.' She gathered up her rucksack and stumbled out of the van. They went at Marian's slower pace around to Hammersmith Broadway.

The café was busy with office workers queuing for takeaways or holding huddled meetings at tables strewn with papers and laptops. Marian insisted on buying the coffees so Stella bagged a table near the door while she got them. An umbrella was propped against her chair, but there was no other indication the seats were taken so she sat down.

Stella felt the buzz of a text in her anorak. She had forgotten her meeting with Jackie. If she rang, Jackie would get the truth out of her. Stella looked about her. She recognized the place. She'd come here last year with another client. She should not make it a habit. A woman at the next table was engrossed in a paperback; a middle-aged man and a woman sat over a pile of croissants:

neither was speaking or eating, they were looking out at the Broadway. Never fall in love, Stella resolved. Although being in love was better than falling foul of the law.

'I used to manage the admin on our cases, but since my promotion, it's less hands on, more's the pity.' Marian put down two mugs on the table. 'I don't judge, but faced with the frailty of human nature, it's hard not to have a view. Trick is not to get jaundiced.' The leather armchair squelched when she landed in it. She whacked a sachet of sugar against her mug, ripped off the end and showered granules over the chocolate on her cappuccino.

Stella was alive to threat in her innocuous words. The printout was in her rucksack at her feet. Marian knew. Stella tried to look nonchalant.

'… life has a way of sorting itself … everything balances …' Marian stirred in the chocolate and sugar and licked her teaspoon placidly.

'So you think it's right?' Stella should keep the conversation light and get out as soon as possible. Recklessly she ploughed on. 'Drivers who have killed a child committing suicide.' She could not remember what Marian had actually said. It might be better to confess and get it over with.

'I think people should face their punishments. Killing yourself is the soft way out.' Marian Williams took a sip of her drink and smiled benignly. 'You cleaned my desk.'

Reeling, Stella dimly recalled Jack saying that the best liars tell the truth most of the time. 'I gave it a wipe.'

'You have an eye for detail. Like your father. Do you do a lot of the cleaning? Martin says Clean Slate is very successful.' Marian settled into her seat and contemplated Stella peaceably over the rim of her mug. She had a moustache of foam, but Stella could not tell her.

'Only the important ones.' Stella had not meant to flatter.

'Terry said you take trouble, you miss nothing. Chip off the old block, he reckoned.' At last Marian patted her mouth with a serviette. 'He was proud of what you had accomplished, and impressed. He said he didn't have a head for business; you got that from your mum. '

'Horses for courses,' Stella quipped stupidly and picked up a tube of sugar, remembered she didn't take sugar and put it back. She gulped her coffee. Terry would change his mind now. No amount of deep cleaning would salve her guilt. 'Do you like your work?' she countered. Any minute she would be frog-marched out.

'I take pride in it, which is not the same as liking it.' Marian shrugged. 'I used to love it.' She looked bleak for a moment. Stella guessed she was thinking about the husband.

A young man carrying a laptop case, a newspaper and a card-board tray of coffees struggled along the queue. The bag swung out when he stuck out a leg to keep the door open and glanced against Marian's shoulder, jolting her cup. She shot around. 'Look where you're going!' She reddened and glared out of the window at the departing offender. 'That's what I mean,' she fumed.

'Are you all right?' Stella asked. Marian Williams's chair jutted out into the gangway so it could happen again. They should leave before it did.

'You have taken in everything I told you.' Marian watched the Broadway, two pink blotches on her cheeks.

'Have I?' Stella went cold.

'People like that poor Hampson woman won't accept their loved ones would give up and end their own lives. You saw how that gentleman was too cowardly to offer a simple apology. Imagine what he would do if he killed a child.'

'What you said disturbed me, maybe that's why I remembered.' Lying came too easily. Marian was exaggerating; the laptop-bag man's carelessness was not going to lead to death by dangerous driving.

'They have no remorse.'

'Odd they chose the same way to kill themselves. It's not as if they knew each other.' No mention of the printout so far. 'Hampson and Lauren chose long straight roads like Marquis

319

Way with no cameras or passers-by. There were two deaths in that street. Not an obvious way to commit suicide.' She was a motormouth. Stella drank her coffee to stop herself. She was sailing right into a high wind.

Marian Williams placed her hand on Stella's. Her touch light, but firm. 'Don't think about this, Stella. As your dad said, we try to make the world cleaner and brighter.' She took away her hand and remarked: 'I don't recall saying anything about Marquis Way. Lauren was killed in Tolworth Street.'

Stella banged the tip of the umbrella on the floor. 'In my job, you pick up stray facts.' She lifted her mug to her mouth. It was empty so she pretended to drink. 'I have a meeting in... in fact I'm late.' She leapt up.

'Perhaps Terry told you?' Marian chatted on.

Stella took another sip from the empty mug to avoid another lie. Terry had never discussed his cases with her. She would not implicate him.

'I miss my chats with Terry.' Marian mopped up stray sugar with her napkin. 'This has been nice.'

Marian did not know about the printout. In her relief, Stella was expansive. 'We must meet for a meal.'

Marian had worshipped Detective Chief Superintendent Darnell, and for him she had worked tirelessly. Since he had died the pleasure in her job had died too. She would think it inconceivable that his daughter would enter the database. Stella did not believe it herself. Marian had a violent husband, and had lost her knight in shining armour. She wanted to impress Stella with nuggets of information, but Stella kept undercutting her, demonstrating she knew facts that were Marian's to process, file and store up for a rainy day.

On rare visits to the police station as a child, Stella had occasionally experienced unfriendliness. A receptionist's reluctance to tell her dad she had arrived; some who did not delight in the little girl clutching their boss's hand. They all wanted a bit of Terry. She had never met Marian on those visits. Marian Williams had treated her with respect, even brought her flowers. Stella had abused her authority. The poor woman got enough of that at home. She sat down again and asked, 'Could they have been murdered?'

There was a momentary lull in the shop, a silence with no correlation to external events into which her words landed. She looked about but no one appeared to have heard.

'Why do you say that?' Marian looked pleased to be consulted.

Jack would have seen that the trick was not to be clever. Stella lost her nerve. 'My phone is ringing.' Stella took refuge in her rucksack. In the comparative quiet there was no sound.

'That's an interesting idea. But who would murder them?' Marian persisted.

Stella saw the text from earlier. Jack. He was still at her mother's.

'Sorry?'

'Terry would say: "Who profits by a death?"'

'The family of the child?' Stella had not thought of this before.

'So the families got together and killed these two men? Great idea, didn't Agatha Christie do it? In reality it's more difficult. No one would get away with it.' Marian Williams picked up her bag. 'Do answer your phone.' She stood up.

Stella looked at the silent telephone in her hand.

'It's a text.' She got to her feet.

'Those crashes. Technically they were accidents.' She patted her hair and stepped into the gangway. 'I do what I can, but ultimately I'm powerless.'

Stella guessed Marian was thinking of her marriage. She was tempted to tell Marian about the green glass, but she mustn't do so without talking to Jack. He had asked her not to. She pictured Marian in the toilet, confused and shocked, her arm a mass of purple. She opened the door for her.

Marian took Stella's arm as they walked to the police station. Stella disliked the intimacy, but was glad that Marian wasn't arresting her.

'I would love to have a meal with you,' Marian said.

'How is your arm?' Stella was voluble at the prospect of imminent freedom. She should not have mentioned the toilet incident. It was pointing up Marian's own untruth.

'I am sorry to have caused you bother.' Marian let go of her arm.

'If you need anything, call me.' Marian would not call.

'I will.' Marian trotted up the steps and into the station without looking back.

Stella was getting into her van when she saw she was holding the umbrella from the café. She could return it, but was already late for Jackie. A horrible thought occurred. Marian Williams had seen her steal it. She knew Stella was a thief. If she left the umbrella at the front desk, Marian wouldn't know; the deed was done. Stella tossed it into the back of the van. She was pulling out of the compound when she remembered Jack's text. She stopped and, shielding the phone from the blinding sunshine, opened her Inbox:

Found what your mum lost.

Fifty-One

The draught-excluding curtain was across the door so it would not open. Mary Thornton reached around and coaxed the fabric along the rail. She felt for the light switch. The bulb pinged. She left her bag by the umbrella stand and felt her way along the passage to where light showed under the living-room door.

'Mum?'

The flickering light – her mum watched television in the dark – disorientated her. She waited to get her bearings.

Staring out of the muted set with dull expressionless eyes was the 1960s mug-shot of Myra Hindley. Mary stared back until the iconic image of Hindley was replaced by a prosaic shot of a sprawling building on a dark rainy night, its windows ablaze with light.

An ambulance came out of the entrance towards the camera and then swung out of the frame. A caption on the screen read: 'LIVE: West Suffolk Hospital Statement.' The camera cut to a reporter in a raincoat, collar up. Mary crossed the room and turned up the sound: '... can confirm that Myra Hindley, date of birth the twenty-third of July 1942, died in West Suffolk Hospital at 16.58 today, the fifteenth of November 2002, following respiratory failure. Myra Hindley was convicted of murder at the Chester Assizes Court on the sixth of May 1966 and was serving a whole life tariff. She had been in hospital since the twelfth of November ...'

Mary switched the set off and, leaning over, plugged in the

standard lamp. She had seen the newspaper headline at Stamford Brook station: 'Myra Dead'. The news was no surprise.

Her mother was sitting on the sofa, lolling forward. Mary took in the scene in a series of stills. Pill bottle on the floor. Half-drunk bottle of Gilbey's gin. A tumbler on its side in her lap. Fingers curled as if they still held the glass. One eye open, staring at the damp patch on her lap.

Mary walked out to the hall where her parents' 1960s telephone had sat on the table designed for a phone and directories for over forty years. She dialled three numbers. The dial returned slowly to its rest position after each number.

Nine. Nine. Nine.

'Ambulance. My mother's taken an overdose of tranquillizers. Eighty-one British Grove.' She laid down the receiver.

According to her watch it was five past ten; she wrote this down on her mother's message pad with the stubby pencil attached to a string. That too had been there for four decades. No one left messages. The pad was blank.

Mary Thornton went back to the living room and looked at her mother. Mary did not need medical knowledge to see that this time – the third time to be precise – her mother had succeeded in killing herself.

Jean Thornton, a slight figure, was diminished further in the squashy oatmeal-coloured couch where she had spent most of the past years. She was a slow and steady drinker who never appeared drunk and would have slipped quietly from sobriety to death. Mary did not need to touch her to know her face would be as unyielding as marble. She contemplated putting the glass back in her mother's drinking hand and getting rid of the bottle. It was her job to keep things tidy. But this was a mess that could not be tidied.

She went into the kitchen. The outside light was on. Michael's swing stood in tall grass. The chains had tangled so the seat was at a funny angle and, in the watery moonlight, it appeared to be moving.

As before, there was no note – the wife of an insurance agent, her mother knew better – although she had no life insurance. They would pump her stomach to find the truth. A note would have been helpful. Why today, for example?

The powers that be would conclude that, still stricken by her boy's death, Mrs Thornton could no longer live with the pain. Mary thought it a shame that Jean Thornton had died before Myra Hindley. She would have appreciated knowing about that. Or perhaps she had known.

'That woman deserved to die.'

Her father's brown leather briefcase dangled from one finger. It would only contain the local newspaper. He had been in the library all day. They kept up the fiction that he went to the office.

His raincoat was buttoned to his neck, the collar flat on his shoulders. He had combed his grey hair recently; the tooth grooves were visible. Before going to work he would rinse his metal comb under the kitchen tap and smartly make a straight side parting, flattening it with his palm. He would pass it to Michael. Michael's hair would not obey the comb. Her dad never used Brylcreem; he said his clients would not trust him. She was a girl so she didn't join in.

Mary could not see her father's eyes behind his wire-framed spectacles; the lenses flashed in the kitchen light and it was herself she saw, worn and weary. Time had passed and Michael had been dead longer than he had been alive.

'She didn't mean to do it,' she had said that last time, meaning to comfort.

'Of course she did. She was evil. She never atoned for her crimes, or helped that kiddie's mother. She never put her out of her misery. Now she will die never knowing the truth about her son. Hindley only cared about being released. She didn't atone.'

'Dad—'

'We changed your name because of her. Myra was my mother's name.' He put his briefcase down. 'She destroyed families. She destroyed our family.'

'You never told me why.' There, she had said it. He wasn't listening. She had thought she had done something wrong. Mary. She had hated the name, but now it hardly mattered. Names, like people, came and went. She found she could change her name at the drop of a hat. She picked up the kettle; her mother had filled it. She switched it on.

Next to the saucer for spent tea bags was a scrap of paper. She unfolded it. The writing was her mother's. She could only make out a '10/11', which might be a date. The tenth of November. She knew that date, the pushy woman from the paper was on at her about that. 'Do you know what this is?' she said without thinking.

He snatched it off her and tossed it in the swing bin.

'Dad, I don't think you should…' It was the nearest thing they had to a suicide note.

'It's rubbish.'

She could retrieve it later. She lifted down the Brooke Bond tea caddy from the cupboard. She would rather have a gin and tonic. 'Have you been to the lounge?' To some this would be a needless question. If he had been to the lounge he would have found her mother and his shock would say it all. Not her father – his feelings came out in other ways.

'Dad, come and sit down, I'll get you a cuppa.' She unbuttoned his coat and lifted it from his shoulders. 'There's some people coming. I have bad news.'

'Nothing can be bad with her dead and gone. What's for tea?'

The bell was shrill and insistent. Like the day when the police came to tell Bob and Jean Thornton that their favourite child was dead.

This time it was the woman her parents called Mary who answered the door.

Fifty-Two

Stella slotted the van into the last bay on Margravine Road behind Barons Court Underground station and let herself into the redbrick mansion block. She pressed against the grille and peered up the dust-furred shaft. The lift was out of sight. Most residents – young couples and single professionals – were at work. Again she bit back frustration that Suzanne Darnell would not move to a place where she might meet people, be taken out of herself. Stella took the stairs. The flat door was ajar; she pushed it open.

She was in a brightly lit hall. So preoccupied had she been with the morning's events that she had exited the stairwell at the wrong floor and wandered into the wrong flat.

The layout was identical to her mum's, but instead of the fusty passage that no amount of cleaning could cheer, sunlight splashed through open doors on to a crimson runner. No flecks of paint or blackened varnish. The hallway, with no newspapers, was spacious and made more so by white-painted walls that, though yellowed with age, appeared fresh. Stella traced this impression to beeswax polish and a new non-toxic multi-surface lavender cleaner she was trialling. Whoever cleaned here knew what they were doing. A wild notion of recruiting them was interrupted when she came face to face with the drawing of the dog.

The black Labrador retriever sat beside a bowl half its size and a huge pot with a red flower, petals sticking out in an uneven circle. The background was a strict division of green for grass and blue for sky. The moulded picture frame was too grand for the child's crayon drawing. Stella read the words, written in rounded lower case, 'trixy and tulip. stella aged 6'.

That day the fat waxy crayons had done her bidding and recreated the dog exactly. She had a good feeling in her tummy when her teacher pinned it on the classroom wall. The good feeling went when Stella explained to the children at her table that Trixy was best at sniffing for bodies underwater. She was sent to the headmistress. Her mum had been cross with Terry. Soon after – and so in the seven-year-old's mind linked – her mum and dad divorced. Why was 'trixy and tulip' here?

Stella was in her mother's flat. It was clean last time she visited; this was a transformation. She paused by the open door to her bedroom. The tiger fleece bedspread from her adolescence was draped over the bed; the rabbit knitted by her nana was propped on the pillow. Bunny had gone to charity, how come he was back?

Stella drifted into the room. No dust on the venetian blind. On the shelves above the bed were the boxes of stationery with the original Clean Slate branding and files bulging with Clean Slate's first invoices and receipts. Her mother's electric typewriter was next to them. Gone were the mounds of fabric and the heaps of suppliers' catalogues that Suzie had collected.

'Stella, is that you?' her mum trilled from the living room.

'Yes.' The door swung wide when Stella pushed it and banged against the wall. This was because the carton of clothes Suzie refused to let her chuck had gone.

'You'll dent the plaster!'

House-proud now.

Suzie was perched in her armchair; she too seemed spruce and to have grown in stature. The plaster ceiling rose of carved blooms and cherubs was free of London grime.

Stella did not need to inspect for vacuum marks on the carpet pile, she could see them from where she stood. The scent of carpet shampoo stung her nostrils. The curtains in the two windows were tied back with coloured lengths of material, presumably from the fabric collection. The panes were so spotless they were invisible. Free of its protective plastic cloth, sunlight brought up the finish on her mother's pine dinner table. It was no longer laden with objects. Gone was the box of cleaning samples, along with the 'Bag for Life' bulging with bargains brokered in junk shops, regardless of need. There was no chipped crockery or postcards from forsaken seaside resorts. Surfaces gleamed.

The room was restored to the room of Stella's childhood. The rag mat on which she had played with her dad's Meccano was spread in front of the gas fire.

'I got your message, Mum.'

'We've made you tea.' Jack gestured to the familiar diamond of coconut matting on the coffee table. Stella might be seven; time could be turned back. She took the mug and went into the kitchen. Strategically positioned appliances on the deeply cleaned counter made it a showcase for what is possible in a tiny space.

'What are you doing, love?' Suzie called.

'Sticking it in the microwave. I like it hot.'

'It's hot,' Jack joined in.

'It won't be enough.' She took a sip to prove it and fanned at her mouth. It was hot. She came back and sat on the edge of the sofa, now by the window.

On the Saturdays her mum had her – which was most Saturdays – she let her have a bar of chocolate. Sitting here, Stella ate it too quickly, flicking through the *Beano* and later *Jackie*. She had sat here, washed and dressed, waiting for Terry to collect her. Sometimes he could not come.

'See what a good job your Jack has done?' Suzie tapped on the obligatory cushion; something had not changed. 'Take your jacket off, you're always in a rush.'

Stella shook her head. She was in a rush.

'We have a proposal.' Jack lifted his glass of milk to take in Suzanne Darnell.

Stella sniffed an ambush. Jack was inclined to be sentimental about families. 'Suz, you tell.' He looked at her mother.

'I want a job.' In her effort to get the words out, Suzie Darnell's intonation was aggressive. Her fingers thwacked the cushion. This provided her daughter with the justification she needed to wrest control of the situation.

'You're retired, Mum, you don't need a job. Your finances are healthy and will be even better if you move. The landlords are desperate, they'll give you a lump sum and I'll top it up. We could get a cottage in the country. With a garden. Or sheltered accommodation, maybe by the sea.'

'I'm only sixty-six and I feel thirty-six. I don't want to moulder in a henhouse.'

'Anyone over fifty can live in those places if their partner or husband is older.'

'My husband is dead.'

Stella's tea was exactly the right temperature. Although Jack only drank milk, he made perfect tea and coffee.

'I want a job.' Her mother was appealing to Jack.

Stella jumped up.

'Hang on.' Jack put up a hand. 'What your mum means is she has skills to offer.' Without his coat, in his grey knitted sleeveless jumper frayed at the shoulders, crumpled shirt sleeves rolled halfway up his wrists and glasses perched on his nose, Jack had an old-fashioned authority. He was always looking for a home; it seemed he had found one.

Ghost girl. Stella saw herself cross-legged under the table, beneath a tent of fabrics and blankets, dressed in the Red Indian Chief costume her dad had given her but never saw her wear. After she had constructed the wigwam and donned the costume, she hadn't known what to do next. Nor did she now.

'Stella, did you hear me?' It was Jack.

The wigwam vanished. The girl too.

'What do you think?'

'I told you she wouldn't listen.' Suzie drummed her cushion.

'Yes, yes, she will!'

Stella had never seen Jack angry before. She sat down.

'Your mum wants a job with Clean Slate. I thought this was possible. You are looking for another assistant for Jackie.'

'Doing what?' At the mention of her business Stella bristled.

'You tell me. For a start, typing.' Jack took a long draught of his milk. 'Suzie's speed is ninety-five words per minute with a nil error rate.' He bit his lower lip. 'That is fast.'

'We don't do "typing", as you call it and Mum hasn't had that speed for years.'

'It's like riding a bicycle.' Suzie Darnell addressed the electric fire, her fingers skittering over the fabric. 'The quick brown fox…'

'Your mum types every day.' Jack indicated Suzie's cushion.

Her mother had developed the tic of tapping a cushion when she spoke after Stella had left home. Now she saw what Jack meant. It was a keyboard. Each finger tap was a letter, each beat of her thumb put a space between words. Phantom stenography. Her mum was stressed. If she worked, this would increase.

Stella's mobile was ringing.

'Jackie, hello there!' Timing never better. 'I'm so sorry about our meeting. An emergency with my mother, as you guessed.'

She went through to the kitchen, the phone tucked between her cheek and her shoulder. She dropped a spot of washing-up liquid in her mug, sluiced it under the hot tap and dried her hands on a crisply ironed towel.

'No problem. We need to meet to review the short list though.'

'Yes.' Stella opened the cupboards until she found where the mugs now went. What shortlist did Jackie mean?

Jackie must have guessed her bewilderment. 'Six candidates coming in. Three today and three tomorrow, for the post of my assistant.'

'I'm on my way.' Too late Stella discovered the phone was on hands free. Her mum and Jack had heard the conversation.

'I have to go.' She breezed back. 'I'll give you a lift.' She tipped her head at Jack.

'I've finished here.' Jack reached for her mum's mug.

'Leave that, love.' Suzie Darnell touched his arm and, looking at her daughter, said: 'You don't want to be late for Jackie.' Her fingers remained still. Stella muttered a goodbye.

Jack was quiet in the lift. He took out a tobacco pouch strapped with an elastic band and, opening it, pinched out a twist, shut the packet and returned it to his coat pocket. Stella hesitated over the lift buttons as if there were any way but down.

Downstairs she wrenched open the gate with a clang and followed Jack. He walked head-down, tweaking tobacco into a thin line, the cigarette paper butterfly-like in his palm.

'Your mum said, before she had you she worked for the police, typing reports, cases lists, indexing.' He rolled the paper into a cylinder.

'We're not talking yesterday.' Stella hurried along Margravine Road.

'She typed for Terry – he couldn't read his own handwriting. I didn't know she used to run Clean Slate with you.' Jack cradled his silver cigarette case.

'We're going to see someone.' The words were out before Stella had formed the idea.

'Don't you have interviews?' Jack slotted his seat belt into the socket.

'Jackie can do them.'

'Jackie has a jolly good sense of people,' Jack agreed, the roll-up bobbing between his lips.

In anyone else the pallid complexion and dark stubble would have been a concern, but Stella guessed this was one of Jack's good days. 'Take this.' She lifted down a street atlas from a compartment above the sun visor. 'Look up British Grove.' She executed a six-point turn, crushing a recycling bin against the wall.

'What happened to the satnav? You don't believe in maps.'

'It's broken.'

'British Grove is off King Street, opposite the junction for Goldhawk Road.' He raised the book. 'Is this A to Z yours?'

'Clean Slate's, yes.'

'I've lost mine.'

'Yours is defaced by those letters on each page. Time you got another.' Stella had to be firm with Jack. 'That is not yours.'

'I dropped it and now a stranger has it.' Jack sounded mournful. He believed his possessions were lost without him. Stella scoffed inwardly, but then saw Bunny sitting on her pillow at her mother's. She'd been worried sick about him when he went. However, a street atlas was hardly the same.

Travelling towards the lights on Hammersmith Road, passing the site of the registry office – long gone – where her parents had married in 1966, Stella remembered: 'What was that about cracking the code?'

'Ah yes.' Jack tapped his cigarette case. 'The digits for the dates when the men died all equal seven.'

'Not all. Some have eight numbers.'

'Not the number of numbers, the total of the numbers. Take Paul Vickery, our first death on Marquis Way. He died on the sixteenth of March. That's a one, a six and a three. It equals ten. One and nought is one. Add the year, which was 1977. One plus nine is ten, make that a one again, two sevens are fourteen which is five. Add in our two ones and we have seven. The trick is to think of it like reducing gravy, keep boiling it down.'

Concentrating on keeping to the speed limit, Stella had lost track. 'I've nearly filled in the grid. Get my Filofax.' She indicated her rucksack.

Jack scrutinized the neatly drawn matrix. 'Hey, well done on Denis Atkins. How did you find him?'

'There was a plaque on Mafeking Avenue. I found an article about when it was unveiled, which gave me the year. It mentioned a man called Atkins...' Stella was rather impressed with herself.

'See! The seventh of September 1970. All of that comes to thirty-three. Add that and it comes to six.' Jack's cigarette fell on to his lap. 'And Charlie Hampson's date – the 15th March comes to twenty which boils down to two. What a nuisance.' He found the cigarette and snapped it into his case. 'Something about threes maybe, thirty-three was Jesus's age when —'

'Two of them were killed on a Sunday and mostly in March, including Hampson.' Stella felt excitement building, the answer was just out of reach. They were by Marks and Spencer's. The witness appeal board about Joel Evans's death was still there.

'Very true.' Jack shut the Filofax and popped it back in the rucksack.

'There's a seven in half of the dates, we keep finding seven bits of glass and the boys who died were aged seven. This man has a thing about seven.' Stella was on it now.

'What's in British Grove?'

'Lucille May.'

'Who's she?'

'A reporter on the *Hammersmith and Fulham Chronicle*. She covered most of the accidents. She did that piece about Terry. Don't mention it. I won't say who I am.'

'Sounds like a Hollywood actress. Great name.' Jack whistled. 'Nice one, Stell. Are we telling her about Terry's photos?'

'Absolutely not. She's a journalist.'

'Have to be clever. They have the snouts of porcupines.'

'You'll think of something.' Stella dipped down a road behind the garage where Terry got his car serviced. It had closed down. Hoardings blocked it from view; a sign warned of demolition. Stella saw why older people could resent change. It played havoc with memory. If you didn't recognize a place, how could you remember where, or even who you had been? The garage going put Terry at another remove. The nice man who had given her polo mints while they waited for his tyres to be changed must be dead now. More bloody ghosts.

'They're putting up luxury flats.' Jack dropped her rucksack on the floor. 'Ooops.'

'How do you know?'

'Some man told me.' He pushed everything back into the bag.

The garage gave way to a terrace of redbrick villas. Stella drew up by the first house.

'What's this?' Jack held up the printout from the police database.

Fifty-Three

'Jamie Markham was my schoolfriend.' Jack contemplated his milk.

Stella tapped sharply on the floor with the umbrella, but he ignored her. She should not have left the strategy to Jack; pretending to know the road traffic victim was a bad idea. Lucille May was a journalist. Like a detective, she would be programmed to smell a rat and root it out.

'My dear, you don't look old enough.' Lucille May patted Jack's knee. In a short dress topped with a baggy man's jumper, her stockinged feet tucked under her, she faced him on a leather chesterfield set in a bay window. On a coffee table in front of the sofa lay a London street atlas and the latest copy of the *Chronicle* and a heap of files containing Lucille May's articles. They sipped their drinks.

'I'm older than I look,' Jack demurred.

'My condolences about Jamie.'

Stella thought Lucille May might try to sound as though she meant it. She left her hand on Jack's knee a little too long. Jamie Markham was twenty-nine in 2003 so would now be thirty-eight. This meant it was plausible they could be schoolfriends. Still Jack's ruse was risky; she would have said so if he had told her what he planned to say.

'We lost touch after school.' Jack looked regretful.

At least he was resisting embellishments: unlike her, Jack was a skilled liar. The coffee was lukewarm and sweet. Stella put it down.

336

Lucille May's flirty, rather skittish manner didn't suit either her or her name. She was the woman who had interviewed Stella about her father's death, the article that had prompted David to call. Their conversation had been on the phone, Stella having refused to let her come to the office, so she had not seen her until now. She had mumbled her name at the door, but May's eyes were on Jack. Stella had to hope the journalist didn't recognize her from the photograph used in the article. May had a careworn air that, like Jack, made it hard to guess her age, mid-fifties, Stella decided. She was tall. Stella was always surprised to meet women as tall as herself at six feet. May had invited them in before they could finish explaining why they were there. Stella thought back to the woman's probing questions about Terry and shuddered. 'Lucie, please!' Ushered ahead of her into the kitchen, they waited while she made the drinks so had no chance to confer.

The kitchen had not been decorated for decades. Stella had eyed with distaste chipped blue Formica surfaces, shrunk and faded floral curtains that hung limply. The living room was dingy, the furniture tired and outdated. Despite the rooms having been knocked through and French doors added, foliage around lattice windows let only a dim greenish light filter in.

Jack's 'open sesame' had been his dead friend, Jamie Markham. Fiddling with the cutting on Markham's death, May needed no encouragement to talk.

The room was that of a busy professional. Although worn, it looked unlived-in. A gigantic television divided the room by a green-tiled fireplace. The wall above and the mantelpiece were filled with cheaply framed photographs of May with various low-grade celebrities spanning at least thirty years. They put Stella in mind of Terry's basement wall with pictures of herself. A warped laminate bookcase was packed with garish true crime paperbacks and back copies of the *Chronicle*. Trying to sit properly in a squashy oatmeal settee, Stella saw no sign of a partner or children, although Lucille May wore a ring on her wedding finger, implying there had been someone at some stage.

'The Markhams were newly married and she was pregnant. Well, you'll know that.'

'Not until I read your article. I'd appreciate hearing anything you can tell me about Jamie.' Jack looked sorrowful.

Stella got up and fled to the other end of the room where doors opened on to a garden. So much for teamwork. Since Jack had found the printout, they had not made eye contact.

The garden was a meadow. The grass was too long for a domestic machine; were she doing the job, she would bring in their new rotary field mower. Stella's eye was drawn to a swing. The chains were hanging from a rusting metal frame, the seat green with mildew. Lucille May had at least one child.

Stella got the picture: 'empty nesters' holding on to their kid's stuff for hoped-for grandchildren. No child should use that swing; it belonged in a skip. Lucille May needed Clean Slate's gold garden package. She would get Beverly to pop a leaflet through. She turned back to the room.

'… Markham's son had reared some creature … Let me see.' May was rootling through her files. 'Here we are. A sweet lad. Bit like my brother – how we change!'

Stella returned to the settee. Clearly old, it had recently been professionally cleaned. She could just detect the musky scent of leather cleaner.

'He looks like Jamie.' Jack leaned in and looked at the cutting.

'Nonsense, darling. Kid's fair and Markham had dark hair.'

Stella shot Jack a look, but he was deliberately avoiding her. He read aloud: '"… Damian Markham, aged seven, is now the same age as little Chris Mason was when James Markham's Peugeot RCZ hit him on Shepherd's Bush Road nearly eight years ago to the day in 2002. Markham was cleared of dangerous driving despite a witness reporting he had exceeded the speed limit. Damian, pictured here with a blackbird he reared singlehandedly, never knew his dad. Markham died months after Chris when his car smashed into a tree one night on Britton Drive, North Hammersmith. Why Markham was there late on a Sunday remains a mystery.'"

'Must have put a dampener on Damian's fifteen minutes of fame,' Jack observed drily.

'Chris Mason's death was the bloody dampener. A little boy's life cut short through carelessness.' Lucille May was stern. 'Friend or not, he destroyed the Masons. They didn't have other kids.'

Marian Williams had talked about families being destroyed, Stella thought. Both women were on the sidelines of law and order. Terry tried to make a difference, stop the crime that wrecked ordinary lives. He must have known Lucille May. Stella thought her more his type than Marian; good-looking, a laugh, May would take no prisoners. Something stopped Stella asking her. If Terry had wanted to, he could easily have got May to help. He had not wanted it, she was sure.

'Was it Jamie's fault?' Jack finished his milk.

'There was no film in the security camera. Your man said Chris dashed out without looking. A witness corroborated his story. Technically it was not.'

'Could Markham have committed suicide?' Stella chipped in. Lucille May looked surprised. Perhaps she had forgotten she was there.

'Sophie, his lovely young wife' – her tone was acid – 'said he was upbeat the week before he died, so no, more's the pity. Sorry, sweetie.' She patted Jack's knee again.

'People are often in great spirits before killing themselves. The decision's made, they can be at peace,' Jack said.

'His wife insisted he was full of the future. They were moving to a bigger house, he had put a down payment on a Jeep. Sophie Markham said it was like he'd won the pools. I wheedled that out of her by fussing over her boy and his scraggy bird. She wrote to complain after the piece was out.' She puffed her cheeks. 'Not like the Masons have the luxury of sticking fucking pipettes down blackbirds' gullets!'

Stella noticed that Lucille May spoke without care for Jack's supposed feelings. Like Marian she did not mourn these men. Working on the same cases, if from different perspectives, it was likely the two women had met. She didn't see them getting on. May seemed to view other women as competition. Marian might think May had a hand in the mess she and Terry had tried to clear up.

'My editor wanted something on this house, but I'm saving it for the book. You don't get anywhere in this game by squandering what took hard-won graft.'

'Why did he want you to write about this house?' Jack put down his empty glass.

'You don't want to know.'

Stella leaned forward on the umbrella. They did want to know. A good detective treats everything as important. To her surprise Jack got up.

'Do you mind if I go for a smoke?'

'Be my guest. I could do with some fresh air. I've given up, but once in a while…' Lucille May swiped up a packet of cigarettes and a lighter from the arm of the sofa.

Stella thought there would be more fresh air if she stayed where she was, but grabbing the umbrella she trailed after them.

'Poor you, you've covered a lot of fatalities.' An unlit cigarette between his lips, Jack cleared spiders' webs from the seat of the swing and, sweeping up the skirts of his coat, sat down and gripped the chains. Stella had to admit he drew people out. Particularly women old enough to be his mother.

'I've lost count. Two in Marquis Way – I highlighted that to the police. Paul Vickery and that crook.' Lucille lit a cigarette and, cupping her hand, the cigarette between her lips, proffered the flame to Jack. He shook his head and began to swing to and fro.

'What crook?' Stella asked. May didn't seem bothered that Jack wasn't smoking.

'Harvey bloody Gray. Blew his company's pension fund and then himself. No loss.'

'What did the police say when you pointed out the two deaths?' Jack twisted the swing full circle one way and then the other. The frame creaked ominously.

'They hate you doing their job. The "fatacs" were over twenty years apart so the location wasn't a black spot. Fine, have it your way, said I, gives me free rein.' One eye shut, she drew long on her cigarette. 'One day you'll all come crawling.'

May's gaze fixed on the end of the garden. Stella looked. A bike leaned against the fence, tyres flat. The saddle was the same colour as the seat on the swing. Stella's stomach fizzed. Perhaps May's child would not present her with a grandchild. Her child had died. She tried to get Jack's attention, but kicking with his feet he swung higher. Anyone would think the swing was why they were here.

'It gets to you. The kiddies' deaths, same story over and over, some tosser thrashing his motor. Gives a crap excuse, gets off with a fine or a ban and saunters off into the proverbial whatsit. It's all about speed. Meeting deadlines, beating journey times. Shave off an hour here, seconds there. Keeps the world revolving and the coffers filling and the rest of us as powerless as ants.'

Jack swung between them. 'In fact ants aren't power—'

'Didn't Gray have the outlet factory on Britton Drive?' Stella intervened. It would be woodlice next.

May whipped around. 'Someone's done their homework.' She regarded Stella for a moment and then said, 'Shoes had crap soles.'

Although it was early spring, the air was cold. A wind had got up. Stella should have put on her anorak. Woodlice made her think of Mafeking Avenue where Denis Atkins had died. May had covered that too. She wouldn't be happy about the blue folder: it was treading on her toes. They should leave.

'Don't say you knew Harvey Gray too.' May brushed an invisible speck from Jack's coat. 'Darling, that's ghastly luck.'

'No, I didn't.' Jack's feet momentarily pointed at the sky. 'Both Gray and Jamie died on a street at night. Both were involved in fatal accidents with children.'

Stella wanted to grab the swing. Beneath the flirty persona Lucille May was as sharp as a pin.

'You should be doing my job!' May gave a corncrake laugh.

'Gray killed a boy called Robert Smith. Gray died on the seventeenth of March 2003, my ex-husband's birthday. Bastard.' She narrowed her eyes and drew on her cigarette. 'Gray, that is. Although the husband was a close second. People say you marry your father. My old dad was OK, despite favouring my butter-wouldn't-melt brother.'

'So you don't think the deaths were coincidence?' Stella waved away smoke when Lucille May wasn't looking. Assuming she would be ignored, she was surprised when May replied.

'In my game you get to see that apparent coincidence is exactly that: coincidence. Take my advice and let your friend go and move on. No good comes of raking the coals.' She flashed Stella an on-off smile, put her cigarette in her mouth and, going behind Jack, gave him a push. 'The day Mr Slip-Shod killed Rob Smith was Guy Fawkes. Poor bloody parents were going to have a party. Rob had made the Guy. Just before your lovely Jamie died.' She pushed Jack harder, amidst a plume of cigarette smoke.

Jack flew up and then down like a great black bird.

'Now I'm free to do what I bloody well want,' she said apropos of nothing and gave another clattering laugh.

'There was a witness for Gray's death. Did he ever come forward?' Stella stole a look at Jack, who was swinging back and forth in a world of his own.

'What did you say you did?' May blew smoke towards Stella.

Stella did her best 'Jackie' voice: warm, open. 'I'm a cleaner. I read your articles regularly. They're more interesting than homework.' This was rubbish. They needed to back off fast.

'Stella suggested I talk to you.' Jack landed between them. 'She said it would help me move on, as you say.' Welcome back, Jack! Stella's mind buzzed with how to end this and get out.

'A woman called in the accident, a lady of the night, shall we say. Carol Jones saw a man on Marquis Way before she came upon the crash.'

'Your article said it was an elderly person. It doesn't say it was a man.' Stella couldn't help herself.

'If he existed at all, he was a man.' Smoke clouded out of May's nose and mouth. 'Jones said he was tall, possibly drunk because he wasn't steady on his feet. He was coming from the crash site. Timing-wise he would at least have heard the collision. Suspected suicide. No one will ever know.' She lit another cigarette with the tip of the glowing stub. 'Nine years on and the trail is cold. Jones is dead. Found out when I chased her up. Too slow. My best hunting days are nearly over.'

'This swing is brilliant,' Jack piped up. Feet thrust out, toes to the clouds, he gathered momentum.

'Careful,' Stella cautioned. She brandished the umbrella. She affected a stroll and made for the bike.

'Nice to see it being used.' Lucille May spoke as if Jack was a visiting seven-year-old. 'This place needs life.' She stabbed at the air with her cigarette. 'Oozes misery some days.'

It was a girl's bicycle, its blue paint chipped. On the metal chain guard Stella read 'Trusty Pavemaster'. It was an exact replica of the bike Stella had had when she was a child. Her mum still complained that Terry was prepared to foist stolen property off on his daughter. Stella didn't care who had owned the bike before her. She loved the fat tyres, the vibrant blue frame and the bell on the handlebars. She hadn't been allowed to take it to Barons Court. It was a treat for when she visited her dad on his weekends. The bike wasn't in the house now. Stella had the whirling idea for a second that this was it. She exhaled deeply. Of course it was not. If May had lost a daughter she ought to feel sorry for her.

Beyond the fence she recognized the back of England House: a detached mansion at the end of St Peter's Square that abutted Terry's old garage. She knew most streets here; over the years she had cleaned in houses and flats all over Hammersmith.

Something glinted beneath a holly bush. Stella lifted a branch, avoiding the spikes. A mosaic in the coiling pattern of a snail shell had been pressed into the soil. In the centre was a marble decorated with a twisting of orange snakes.

'Did you make this?' she called.

Lucille May came over with Jack behind her. He stared down as if he had seen a ghost.

'Like I have time for garden design!' Lucille May dropped her cigarette on to the soil by the mosaic and ground it out.

Jack was on his haunches. He traced the shell with a forefinger. 'A child did this, it's too naïve for an adult.' He stood up.

'Hate to hurry you, but I have to get on.' Lucille May waded through the long grass to the house.

'But…' Stella began.

'Leave it.' Jack went after May, giving Stella no choice but to follow.

Stella knew why he had gone pale. What had attracted her attention was not the mosaic, but that it was made with chips of green glass.

Fifty-Four

'She's waving.' Jack tilted his hand at Lucille May on her doorstep.

Stella accelerated down British Grove. 'You might have warned me you planned to seduce her. I was a pumpkin.'

'A gooseberry.' Jack unfurled the printout from his coat. 'By the way, how come you have an umbrella? You don't approve of them – you say they take people's eyes out in crowds.'

'I accidentally took it from a café.'

Jack beamed at her. 'You stole it?'

'No. Well, not exactly.'

Jack settled into his seat. 'That's what happened in *Howards End*. A woman went off with Leonard Bast's umbrella at a concert. It led to his death. Did you accidentally take this too?' He flourished the printout.

'You suggested it,' Stella muttered. 'Did you have to go on the swing?' A cheap retaliation.

'Lucie found it charming and a charmed person chatters like a canary. That stuff about Gray the villainous shoemaker was cool.' He fished out the blue folder from under his seat. 'Incidentally, she'd be a star at Clean Slate; her house hasn't seen a lick of paint for years but it was sterile.'

'She would turn up late or not at all,' Stella huffed. 'She was strange about that mosaic. Did you notice how bitter and twisted she is about the dead drivers? We've been assuming this murderer is a man. Lucille May covered most of those cases about the dead

345

boys. She's got the jade aggregate and she didn't like me knowing about Britton Way. I think she had a child that died, possibly on a bicycle.'

'She's the wrong personality. That mosaic got me, though. Made me feel sad. Did you get that?'

'No.' Jack could be subjective once he liked someone, Stella thought. He had dismissed her theory. 'I think she fits perfectly. The person at the Gray crash was tall. So is May. She was keen to get hold of Carol Jones – why? Lucky for Jones she was dead.' Stella slapped the wheel. Jack's lack of logic was infectious.

'This killer is clever. He, and I think it is a he, has murdered for decades without arousing suspicion. You've met her once and you think it's her. May is an disappointed woman whose prime was way back when and who never made it to Fleet Street.' Jack balanced the folder on his lap. 'This photo is different.' He jabbed at the garage picture. 'We thought it was here by mistake, but Terry didn't make mistakes.' He flattened out the printout.

'That's not true.'

'OK, he missed stuff, but he was methodical. He numbered this "1".'

Stella drew in at the junction of St Peter's Square by the defunct garage. She parked outside England House, a grand imposing building unlike the others in the square. Clean Slate had two clients there. She took the blue folder off him.

'It's a mechanic mending a car.'

'I know that, but why is it familiar?' Jack scratched his chin. Stella noted he needed a shave, although the look suited him.

'It's here! How stupid to miss it. Terry stood where we are parked now. This was his garage. He would have hung around while they mended his car; he had to keep busy so he took pictures.'

The picture was a mid-shot with little background. Now she saw a triangle of the Commodore's wall and on the left a sliver of shop frontage. 'W. R. Pha'. It came back to her. The dental surgery named W. R. Phang had featured on a Pink Floyd album until the dentist made them remove it. Now the surgery had made way for a coffee shop and the garage, once a thriving concern with vehicles every which way on its forecourt, would soon be gone too.

In the picture, the car with the legs sticking out partially obscured an old-style telephone box. The low wall in the photograph was still there, but the phone box had gone.

'Why did he take this?' Jack was leafing through the printout.

He might as well apply water torture to her; Stella felt physical pain as he perused the documents she had effectively stolen.

'Gotcha! Good work for including the 1960s in your search, Detective Darnell.' He snatched a pen from under the dashboard and circled a line of print. 'The sixth of May 1966. A Friday. Listen to this: "Michael Thornton, aged seven, fatally injured. King Street, Hammersmith. Vehicle – poss. grey saloon – failed to stop and left the scene. Victim died on impact. No witnesses. First officer on scene: PC T. C. Darnell. Brackets number 130253 unbrackets."' He described the air with the pen. 'Stella, you are a Wonderhorse! I bet Terry never forgot that day.'

'The date adds up to six.' Stella had broken the law; she did not deserve praise.

'No, and nor was it one or three or a Sunday or in March.' Jack dropped the pen back on the dashboard shelf. 'Trail's cold as ice.'

'I see why it's different to the rest!' Stella snatched up the pen as if it were a baton. 'It was a fatal accident, not a murder.'

'Hang on.' Jack got out of the van and ran alongside the hoarding to the low wall where the telephone box had stood. Suddenly weary, Stella noticed it was past midday. She had missed the recruitment interviews. She checked her phone. Nothing from Jackie. This did not make her feel better. Michael Thornton had been killed just round the corner from Lucille May's house. She tried to corral the fact.

Jack was back in the van. 'Here!' He sprinkled a cluster of green chips of glass on to her palm. 'They were buried by that wall. Your papers say that Michael Thornton was seven when he died.'

'They're not my papers.'

'Other children died, all boys; there are no pictures. This death merited a picture in the blue folder.' Jack held her hand open and stirred the glass in her palm with his finger.

'Terry didn't handle the other deaths, that's the difference.' Stella had resented that Terry would not talk about his work. She saw why. It was too painful. His world was obsessive and ultimately lonely. She shivered. 'Let's go to my dad's and take stock.' She gave the glass back to Jack and started the van.

'The difference is staring us in the face.'

'Hunger is staring at me. I need breakfast, or lunch...' The lights at Chiswick High Road went to amber. 'We'll get sandwiches. I've bought milk.' She took refuge in the banal.

Jack slapped the dashboard with the rolled-up printout. Stella hit the brake. Behind them a horn blared; she steered to the kerb and stopped.

'Michael Thornton was the first boy to die.' Jack's eyes were bright. 'He is the reason for the rest.'

Fifty-Five

Matthew Benson was having a bad week. It had started with the woman in Brentford. She had been as happy as Larry about her shower at the time, even hinting he hop in and give her a demo. Then, at the crack of dawn on Monday, she was on the phone shouting that water was dripping through her lounge ceiling. He knew it would be her hair clogging the trap or a break in the mastic, but when he got there he isolated the problem to the shower valve; he had forgotten to tighten it. Not that he told her; he made out that it was a manufacturing malfunction and got another valve from the van and went through the charade of swapping them. Still, she made it clear she would not want him for her downstairs cloakroom. Back in the day he had avoided her sort like the plague, but now he took any job, however small. Not that Maureen was bothered, since the business of the dead boy she wasn't talking to him. Except to say she didn't know how he lived with himself.

When he had finished with the valve, he found a parking ticket on his windscreen. Madam hadn't offered to pay. Probably let the tosser issue it. She made a wisecrack about the name. 'Perfect Plumbing'. 'Not so perfect, Mr Benson!' Waving the *Chronicle*. She wasn't talking about the valve; she meant Joel Evans.

Today he had parked in the corner bay of the plumbing merchants to eat his bacon sandwich and snatch a kip. At eight in the morning the store was buzzing. Where did these blokes find the work? His diary was on the dash; no jobs today or tomorrow and his credit in the store had run out. The couple wanting new radiators had put him off and he was undercut on a shower and WC in Fulham – even for cash. Or maybe because – the lady turned out to be a copper. Probably knew about the hit and run. His petrol tank was reading empty and so was his bank account. Shit week and it wasn't over yet.

If he went home, Maureen would have a go. Bitch. He should chase up old clients but couldn't face it. He screwed his sandwich wrapper into a ball.

He was startled by a whooping police siren. It was his phone. The ringtone wasn't such a laugh now. 'Perfect Plumbing, hello?' Nor was the fucking name.

'May I speak with Matthew Benson?'

'Who wants him? Callers were creditors or pissed-off customers; he would say he was 'out of the office'.

'It's Porphyrion Insurance regarding the accident that your vehicle was recently involved in.'

Benson shut his eyes. 'It wasn't my fault. The lad was playing chicken – had to be – I had no chance. The police agree.'

'You don't consider yourself to blame?'

'No, I do not. Look, who is this? Are you that reporter?' It sounded like her. She must think he was born yesterday.

'Porphyrion Insurance. I need to establish some facts.'

'I don't have a policy with you. I'm with Principle Star.'

'We are a subsidiary of Principle Star; we handle cases meriting further consideration.' The voice was quiet. 'We may be able to help you.'

'How's that?'

'I have here that you were doing thirty miles per hour; the speed limit on King Street.'

'It's on the camera.'

'You didn't stop to provide an officer with your details. Technically you left the scene.' She inhaled, as if she was smoking. He could do with one himself.

'I was in shock, OK? I went to the police, else the wife would have killed me. Now she's killing me slowly. Or softly!' He'd kept his sense of humour. 'Anyone would have done the same.' Another bloody woman on his case.

'That's not my department or my concern. I'm dealing with your compensation.'

'My what? They said I wasn't eligible. They don't care what it's done to my business.'

'You have a low score on our Culpability Index, Mr Benson.'

'I wasn't drinking, if that's what you mean.'

'On the contrary, it means you are due a sizeable sum in recompense. We take into account disruption to routine, threat to livelihood: loss of earnings and ability to undertake work to the required standard.'

He let his shoulders drop. Someone out there – the husky voice, as if she lived on fags, that went with gorgeous looks – cared. The valve was not his fault; the boy outside Marks and Spencer's wasn't his fault. 'That kid has ruined my life. What sum are we talking?'

'We are talking – as you put it – about seven hundred and fifty thousand pounds, perhaps less, but negligibly so.'

'How much under?' Matthew Benson rubbed his eyes.

'I haven't got the calculation matrix in front of me. There will be minor issues to factor in – your business turnover before the accident, your health. Minor, as I say.'

'Nothing wrong with my business until last week.' He shut his diary.

'Our judgement is reached according to principle. You were not charged with dangerous driving and intrinsic to your punishment was the unfortunate fatality. Your case would not have been referred to me if you were not a clear candidate. It will be a sizeable tax-free sum.'

'Result!' He punched the air and then smoothed a hand down his face. The sun had come out, making the van hot and airless. He opened the driver's door. This would show Maureen!

'For now, this is highly confidential. Payments from this fund do not meet with popular approval so please tell no one, not even Mrs Benson if there is one. Not until monies have been transferred. Any divulgence will jeopardize your claim.'

Benson wanted to shove down Maureen's gullet that now that he was a millionaire – he didn't trouble himself with exact figures – she'd better play her cards right. No debts, no mortgage. No nothing. This changed everything.

'It will be hard not to tell my wife.' As he spoke, Benson saw this wasn't true.

'I am sure you can keep a secret, Mr Benson.'

The woman was a turn-on. 'Can it go into a separate account?'

'We won't detain ourselves with the nitty-gritty. I shall meet you to dot the i's et cetera. All contact with Porphyrion is through me. A single point of contact preserves confidentiality and means we expedite your claim faster. When are you free?'

'I'm busy in the day obviously, or I was until…' He cast about for the right answer.

'I can only do evenings for the next month.'

'Shall I come to your office?'

'No, we're based in Cheltenham and I won't meet at your home for the reasons given. I've pencilled in the sixth of May. I hope you don't mind a Sunday, but the sooner we sort this the better. Do you know Spelling Way?'

Benson was about to say that he did. He'd been apprenticed at a company there thirty years ago and was sacked for persistent lateness. None of it mattered now, except if they were still there, he'd like to rub their faces in it. 'In a pub? I owe you a drink!'

'We all pay our dues. Is nine-thirty all right? I apologize for the late hour.'

'It's fine.' Everything was fine. 'Will you bring the cheque?'

'You will receive a BACS payment into whatever account you choose.'

'Yeah, right. I'm not thinking straight. That kid running out was terrible for me, seems every cloud has a silver lining!'

'Goodbye, Mr Benson. It will all be all right.'

'Bye then… Hey… Hello?'

'Yes?'

'I didn't catch your name.'

'Mrs Hunt.'

Benson had not taken a number. No problem, he could look up the last received call. Number unknown. She had come through a switchboard. He could contact Principle Star if he had to cancel. He would not cancel. It was too good to be true.

Matthew Benson deleted the call entry from his phone. He knew how to keep a secret. He did, however, write the appointment and the street name in his diary. Sunday, 6 May. These days he could not trust his memory or his driving reflexes.

Fifty-Six

Thursday, 3 May 2012

'... last row ... Spelling Way. No tree.' Jack dropped the printout.

Jack and Stella were in Stella's old bedroom, now Terry's office. They had eaten shepherd's pie; the plates were stacked behind the computer monitor. Stella had not put the heating on. Jack was huddled deep in his coat, hands tucked in his cuffs. Stella wore her anorak.

They had transferred the grid of the crashes from her Filofax to a spreadsheet. Stella pressed 'print'. Despite Jack's reliance on her stolen database information, she was enjoying the task. It was like preparing a cleaning rota.

Heads together, they consulted the results.

Pic. No.	Date	Street	Accident	Driver	Child (Victim)	Date
1	Not applicable	King Street	?	? (Poss. grey saloon)	Michael Thornton	6th May 1966
2 (2a)	7th September 1970	Mafeking Avenue	Hit a plane tree	Denis Atkins	Colin Coleman	15th March 1970
3 (3a & 3b)	16th March 1977	Marquis Way	Hit an ash tree	Paul Vickery	James Harrison	17th October 1976

Pic. No.	Date	Street	Accident	Driver	Child (Victim)	Date
4	31st March 1989	Tolworth Street	Hit a beech tree	David Lauren	William Carter	26th December 1988
5 (5a & 5b)	10th November 2002	Britton Drive	Hit a sweet chestnut tree.	James Markham	Christopher Mason	2nd January 2002
6 (6a)	17th March 2003	Marquis Way	Hit a telegraph pole	Harvey Gray	Robert Smith	5th November 2002
7 (7a & 7b)	15th March 2009	Phoenix Way	Hit an oak tree	Charlie Hampson	Stephen Parsons	8th January 2009
No ref.	?	Spelling Way	No tree	?	?	?

'We need the date when the killer of Michael Thornton died.' Stella would not suggest he look in the police printout.

'We won't find it.' Jack clasped his mug of milk.

'Why not?'

'He's not dead.'

'Go on.'

'The killer of these drivers never found out who knocked Michael down. He, or she, never gave themselves up. Your database says the case is still open, remember?'

They had put question marks in the last row. 'Jack.' She sipped at her tea; although it was hot, it didn't warm her.

'What?' Her tone made him turn.

Stella flapped the spreadsheet. 'What is your hunch about Spelling Way? Terry didn't take a photograph.'

Jack stared at her as if she was a stranger. She knew that look. He was hiding something.

'It's like the other roads. You've been there – you know it is.'

'Yes, but why did we go there?' He wouldn't fool her like he tried to fool Lucille May.

'It fits the profile: long, straight, desolate...'

'With no green glass.' Stella looked again at the spreadsheet. 'Why is it here?'

'I could be wrong. Or...' Jack trailed off. 'In the model— er, on the map, it stands out and...'

'Michael Thornton is the reason for the other deaths.' Stella clutched at his arm. She grabbed the spreadsheet. 'This is about revenge. These deaths are rehearsals, stop-gaps, for the one that counts. The driver of the grey saloon. Jack, you're right, this isn't a cold case. The man – or woman – is still out there. He will kill again.'

'Brilliant, Stella! He'll keep on murdering other drivers until he finds Michael Thornton's killer. There's nothing else for him to live for.' Jack pulled in his chair. 'Stella, if I'm ever rude about your spreadsheets again, be rude back.'

'And shut me up if I say anything about your signs.'

Jack consulted the grid. 'Lucie said Carol Jones saw a man leaving the scene of Harvey Gray's crash. She said he was drunk. It's the only sighting of anyone near a crash. Had to be the killer. He slipped up that night. He might be losing his touch.'

'That was years ago – there's been Charlie Hampson since then. The first murder was in 1970. This man must be in his sixties at least. Could he carry out murders like this?' Stella thought of Terry, dead in his sixties. From comments he made, she suspected David was close to sixty, although he behaved like a much younger man. These days sixty wasn't old.

'Did you hear what I said?'

'Yes.'

'What did I say?' Jack was seldom peeved; he went straight to sulking and radio silence.

'That he slipped up.'

'After that...'

'No, then.'

'I said that if he finds out we are investigating these deaths, we are in danger. He may already know.'

The shepherd's pie was a lump in her stomach. 'Jack, I wish you'd listen about Lucille May? She didn't like me obviously knowing stuff and I doubt she bought your grieving-friend act.'

'I just don't think it is her.' Jack shook his head. 'You said you'd trust my signs.'

'That's not quite what … Look, Marian told me the police don't analyse traffic incidents. The only people who might spot a pattern are curious police officers and reporters. Terry was a curious officer and Lucille May is the sort to pick up a scent and follow it to the kill. She's ruthless. She didn't seem to think that Markham and Gray's deaths were suicides even though she didn't know about the green glass. Why would she doubt it? The reason has to be that there's something she didn't say.' Stella remembered the woman's harsh questioning, fired like bullets. 'I don't get the sense you and your dad were close?' Then there was her odd reaction to the mosaic and the proximity of her house to the site of Michael Thornton's death. Not to mention the child's bike and the ancient-looking swing.

'Our killer has to have a powerful motive. Something has kept him going all these decades.' Jack adjusted his reading glasses and scoured the spreadsheet. 'I don't feel it's Lucie.'

'What if she had a child that died?' Stella told him about the bike. She didn't mention she'd had one exactly like it; he would see it as a sign and it wouldn't help her argument.

'Then why the emphasis on Michael Thornton?'

'She didn't mention him.'

'The street where he died is the first photo in Terry's blue folder.' Stella stabbed at the top row of the grid with her finger. 'If this is motivated by revenge, it has to be someone in Michael Thornton's family.'

'Makes sense. So we find out who they are – parents, siblings, cousins – and we've solved it.' Jack stood up and strode over to the windowsill.

'If it were that simple, Dad would have solved it.'

'The deaths are getting more frequent. Three in ten years. Classic serial-killing behaviour. The urge to kill builds so the interval between murders gets shorter.'

'If someone in the Thornton family is doing this, he's not a proper serial killer. He's killing systematically, like cleaning up,' Stella said. 'These men are dying within months of the accidents involving the children.' She turned to the laminated street map of London with which Terry had replaced her poster of John Travolta in *Grease* and, grabbing a pot of multi-coloured drawing pins off the desk, began marking the crash sites on the map in red.

'He's racing against time,' Jack mused. 'It would be clearer on the model than that map,' he added, more to himself.

'He might be dying. He might already be dead. The last death that we know of was Charlie Hampson in 2009.' Stella scrutinized her work. Maybe Terry had solved it?

'Like you say, we should work from the likeliest principle. He left the blue folder out. That was a sign. We'll assume he isn't dead and his next murder site is Spelling Way.' Jack folded his arms.

Stella put a yellow pin on Spelling Way and sat down.

Jack picked up the stolen printout and put on his reading glasses.

'Well I never.' He sprang up and rushed to the door.

'What? Where are you going?'

'Time waits for no man or woman. I'm going to pay another visit to Lucie.'

'Glad you're with me on this. This is the kind of murder that suits a woman: doesn't need strength or knowing how to handle a gun.' Jack always came around in the end. Stella gathered up the plates and mugs. 'We must be careful. I think she's already on to us.'

'She's a pussy cat.' Jack was on the landing. 'I should see her by myself.'

A mug slid across the plate, Stella steadied it.

'Check the address,' Jack shouted from the hall. She heard the front door slam shut.

Infuriated, Stella was gathering up her things to go after him when her phone rang. Jack had changed his mind.

'Have you got a moment?' It was Jackie.

'Yes.' Stella stopped herself saying no. It was past five; working late again, Jackie deserved her attention.

'None of the recruitment interviews was a "yes". You do wonder if these people paid other people to write their applications. Nothing they said matched the quality of the forms.'

Stella rifled through the printout. What address?

'... so my suggestion is we revisit our job description. It's attracting weak candidates. This lot were slow typists, no one could add or subtract and we wouldn't want them cold calling.'

'Good idea.' Stella scanned the lines of data.

'... by the way, did Jack say? I was right about that woman. My friend from school – well, he's not really a friend – said she was in our class. Said she was tough, took no prisoners. That sort. Didn't see it myself—'

In the van Jack had highlighted Michael Thornton's entry, Stella stared at it. 'Jackie, really sorry, I have to go. I'll be there in the morning.'

When he had read the entry out to her, Jack kept to the salient details, so had omitted the dead boy's address.

It was 81 British Grove. The house where Lucille May lived.

Fifty-Seven

'It has a curse on it. Some nights I don't sleep.' Lucille May poured herself a generous measure of vodka chased by a cursory splosh of tonic, cracked an ice tray into a bucket and, with a chef's skill, swiftly reduced a lemon to a pile of thin slices.

Jack was back on the sofa in Lucille May's sitting room, watching her fix herself the 'first drink of the day'. He had refused one himself.

She returned to the sofa and, nestling against his arm as if they were old friends, tilted the glass at him in silent toast and drank. 'A woman topped herself on that settee. Overdosed. Ten years ago this November. Not that settee, obviously.' She slurped her drink. Jack suspected it was not her first.

'Why?' Jack had claimed he wanted advice about getting into journalism, a flimsy excuse that Lucille made no pretence of believing. He draped his arm along the back of the sofa behind her.

'She didn't leave a note. Looked like your typical husband playing away, bored housewife reliant on "Mother's little helper", swigged down with "Mother's ruin". Ha!' She gestured at the ceiling with her glass. 'Same day as Myra Hindley snuffed it. The fifteenth of November 2002. I should have had Hindley, but our fuck of an editor handed it to the new kid on the block. New kid's the boss now.'

'But it wasn't typical?' Jack brought her back.

'Her son was Michael Thornton, a sweet little thing killed in a fatac in the sixties. Hit and run, driver never traced. My editor wanted it revived to spice up her suicide. Boy with the face of an angel who brought joy and laughter eeecetarah! Story had traction: sixties nostalgia, heartbroken mother, empty swing.' She stopped and, uncurling from the sofa, returned to the dresser and sloshed vodka over the melting ice cubes. No tonic this time, Jack noticed. Everything in the woman's behaviour added weight to Stella's theory. Almost everything.

'Did you know that when you moved here?' He risked the question.

'What are you, my psychiatrist? Listen Jackaranda, I'm not superstitious and I'm not easily freaked, but this house is toxic. It's cold even with that fire lit. Look at you all wrapped up in that lovely coat.' She had not answered his question.

Jack pulled his coat tighter. The room was chilly. It was evening now and a dreary grey light penetrated the faux lattice windows.

'She never got over her baby boy dying. No one did.' Lucie stopped still. 'The sanctity of sons! Bet your mother loves you!' She meandered back to the sofa and plonked down beside him, spilling her drink.

'Not sure you ever get over the death of a loved one,' Jack said.

'I wouldn't know, no one sticks around long enough to die on me. I've wanted to kill a few in my time.' She patted her short blonde hair. 'Michael Thornton haunts me day and night.' She glared at Jack as if he too were a ghost.

'When did Michael die?' Jack wanted her to flesh out the facts. 'You said he was a sweet boy. Did you know him?' He held his breath.

'Figuratively speaking. He was before my time! My predecessor covered it in his size-ten hobnailed boots. It was the year the Moors Murderers went down so there was a hue and cry about kiddies. Sixty-six. Clot angled it that the mother was at work when the boy came home from school, a "latchkey" boy fending for himself.' She used Jack's thigh to lever herself up and wove over to the French doors. 'They got sackfuls of irate letters about the mum not being fit to have kids. Blah blah blah. Enough to drive her to top herself. It's a wonder it wasn't sooner.'

'When you went to the police about Marquis Way, who did you speak to?' Jack asked airily.

'Questions! You don't need my help to doorstep anyone! Most of them avoid me even when I help them. It was Terry Darnell, one of the sharper knives in the drawer, always up for a goss at the Ram, that place by the river? A charmer like you is all I shall say, me lud.' She tapped the side of her nose.

She opened the French doors and stepped outside into the garden. Jack went too. Who was charming whom? Terry Darnell had known what he was doing.

'This was Michael's'. She raised her glass at the swing. 'It's bad luck to move it and bad luck to leave it. I'm stuck with the bloody thing. Stuck with this place too. Puts buyers off.'

'Most people wouldn't know the history.' They would feel it. Jack was grateful to be in the sunshine.

'We buy houses with our hearts not our heads. Never mind damp, dry rot or subsidence, we draw a line at the corpse in the lounge and the dead brother on the swing.'

'Brother?'

'Son, husband, brother. The place is tainted.' She gave her raucous laugh. 'Mother never left her home after he died. Not until it was feet first.'

'How did he die?' Jack trod carefully as an idea took shape.

She scowled. 'Sneaked out for sweets.'

Jack looked at the house. The suburban Edwardian villa, apparently benign and homely, leaked profound pain from every brick. Had he come into the garden on one of his night walks he would have known a Host lived here.

'They spent a whack on a fuck-off monument at Hammersmith Cemetery. St Michael, an angel like the boy. It creeps you out.' She stomped over to the fence, close to the mosaic under the holly bush. 'You go to Jamie's grave?'

'I prefer to look after the living.' Keep up. He had forgotten his supposed link with the dead driver.

'You saying a girl made this gave you away.' Lucille May aimed

362

a kick at the mosaic, dislodging a chip of glass. 'Sure you won't join me in a quick drink, darling?'

'I should be going.' Jack longed to restore the glass to the mosaic, but Lucille would interpret it as a criticism. He hadn't said a girl had made it, he had used the word 'child'. 'Gave what away, Lucie?'

'First law of journalism, don't steal from others.' She pouted her lips and ground the glass into the soil. 'I've had it up to here with effing journos.'

'How long did you say you've lived here?' Jack held her gaze.

'I didn't, sweetheart.' She shook her glass, making the remaining ice cubes spin around the bottom. 'You could call it a lifetime.'

'Where is Mr Thornton now? Were there any other children?' No point in holding back now. She had his measure.

'Dead. And he was an only child.' Lucille May eyed her glass. 'Like Robert Smith.'

'I could sort through your material on the accidents? Put it in order? It's the kind of thing I do.'

'And steal my story?' She looked her age, raddled and tired in the cold evening light. Her eyes were watery, as if she might cry.

'I don't have your narrative skills, Lucie. I'm just good at tidying up.' Jack touched her elbow and then let his hand drop.

'What a lovely man.' She stumbled on a tussock and steadied herself on his arm. 'I'm going to trust you. Just pull it together then I'll be off and running.'

Jack closed the French doors. He looked back at the garden. The swing was moving.

Fifty-Eight

Saturday, 5 May 2012

'Your dad was the attending officer.' Jack had Lucille May's file open on his lap. 'Michael Thornton must have been one of his first fatalities. Lucie gave Terry the lead on this case, be it unwittingly.' Jack had told Stella what the journalist had said. He left out the hint that there had been more between them.

'Why is she living there if she hates it?' Stella parked along from a Mini outside the cemetery gates. Saturdays were shopping and chores; she supposed tomorrow would be busier. Jack had done an extra shift on the District line during the day on Friday. She had picked him up by the statue of the Leaning Woman on the Great West Road. Beyond his text assuring her he was fine, they had not discussed the case since Jack's second visit to Lucille May's on Thursday.

'She's a journalist stuck with a story that she can't write and can't abandon. I think it's got to her. She doesn't have the drive to operate a campaign of murder, pardon the pun.' Jack thrust a faded photostat at Stella. She sniffed stale ink on the shiny paper, and read the paragraph of blurred type from Terry's report.

I arrived at the location – Young's Corner, south side of King Street, ten yards from traffic lights, at 15.47 hours. I confirmed that the victim, a male child (dressed in shorts, shirt, one sandal thrown off during incident), was fatally hurt. Checked for vital life signs. I covered him with my jacket. I radioed for an ambulance and police. The vehicle involved in the collision did not stop at the scene. No one present had witnessed the accident. A customer in the hardware shop ten yards east of the location reported a grey car travelling at speed. He could not give the make or the model. Stated was a grey saloon.

'Lucille May knows more than she's let on. Look at all this. Weird that she gave it to you. Did she say anything else about my— about Terry?' Stella looked out of the window at Hammersmith Cemetery. Michael Thornton was buried there. Her dad would have gone to the funeral, probably in the black suit her mum said was past its best when it was new. He would have stood a distance from the graveside ceremony. He'd have made a silent promise to find Michael's killer; he never had.

Someone else had made that promise too.

'Come on.' Stella got out of the van without waiting for Jack to reply.

Hammersmith Cemetery was a half-mile square and bounded by railings partially obscured within bushes. Although sprawling between the traffic-clogged South Circular and the Lower Richmond Road the graves and mausoleums were shrouded within a breath-held quiet. Despite the strong morning sunshine, Stella zipped up her anorak against an insidious chill.

'Opened in 1926 as an overspill for Margravine Cemetery.' Jack paced down the central path reading aloud from his phone. 'The graves are on the lawn principle with a concrete strip at the head of the plot. That means you don't need to wait for the soil to settle before installing the headstone.' He sounded chirpy. Telling her about his visit to Lucille May's he had been oddly upbeat and optimistic. This rather annoyed Stella; he was there to gather facts, not enjoy himself.

'After a coffin's in the hole and the soil replaced, there's ten per cent of the earth left over. Think how much soil that is in a place this size.'

'There are hundreds of graves. We need an index of burials.'
Stella headed for a brick chapel halfway along the path. A chain
was looped through iron handles on the doors barring access
and there was no sign of a warden. She went on a few metres to
where an intersection offered three directions.

'Look out for an angel.' Jack scanned the acres stretching
before them.

'That narrows it nicely,' Stella muttered. 'I can already see
four.'

Jack jogged along the left-hand path to an angel with out-
spread wings. 'First World War casualty.' He darted across the
grass to the next one.

None of the angels marked the grave of Michael Thornton.
Without conferring, they struck off along a track from the
central avenue. The sun had gone behind a stratum of cloud,
casting a flat light that left no shadow.

They were in a secluded section of the cemetery. The silence
intensified. Letters on headstones were missing or worn away.
What dates Stella could decipher were from the nineteenth and
early twentieth century. Coarse grass and creeping foliage disguised plots long untended. The path lost definition and petered
away. Stella forgot to look for an angel. Unable to shake off a
growing unease, she trudged mechanically behind Jack.

'Oh!' He stopped; Stella trod on his heel. He snatched at the
sleeve of her anorak. A figure was framed against the lowering
sky.

Stella was about to pull Jack back the way they had come
when he set off at a run towards the person. He leapt over grave
edgings and tussocks, his coat like black wings. She lost sight of
him behind a clump of bushes.

Stella blundered after Jack, crashing through undergrowth,
blood pulsing in her ears.

Jack was dwarfed by the tallest statue Stella had ever seen. It
was at least fifteen feet high. Upon a tiered plinth, she read:

IN LOVING MEMORY OF

MICHAEL

AGED 7

15TH MARCH 1959 – 6TH MAY 1966

BELOVED CHILD OF

ROBERT AND JEAN THORNTON

'WHO IS LIKE UNTO GOD'

'BONNY AND BLITHE AND GOOD AND GAY'

'Their grief is palpable,' Jack breathed. The statue was enclosed by a marble ledge a foot high, wide enough to fit a car on. The enclosed space was filled with green chips of glass.

'"And the child that is born on the Sabbath day is bonny and blithe and good and gay."' Jack stepped on to the base. He scooped up a handful of glass. 'I have the same birthday as Michael.'

'That would make you older than me.' Stella didn't need Jack and his signs now.

'The date, not the day.' He examined the glass. 'This is the same grade aggregate as ours.'

'How can you know?' But Stella knew it was.

'These markings like rainbows?' He held up a piece between thumb and forefinger. 'Glass grinding against glass. Our man comes here before his next murder and each time he takes seven pieces.'

'Would be more practical to take more and save the journeys.'

'He must return each time.'

Stella didn't like it when Jack talked as if he knew the killer. 'Why?'

'To pay a forfeit to the angel. To atone.' He sprinkled the glass back on to the grave. 'I was born on a Tuesday.'

Stella gave a start. The angel's eyes were admonishing. She

knew about the database printout. Stella could never undo what she had done. 'I thought angels were nice.' She said this more to herself.

'Tuesday's child is full of grace.' Jack settled beside her. 'When were you born?'

'The twelfth of August 1966. What's this to do with Michael Thornton?'

'Which day?'

'No idea. Michael can't have been that good or gay, you said he sneaked out without permission to get sweets.'

'Not a capital offence. Three police officers were shot on the day you were born, you said that was why Terry didn't get to the hospital to see you.' He fiddled with his phone.

Anxious to avoid the angel's penetrating stare, Stella trudged behind the statue. The sense of recrimination did not lessen. 'Surely this thing contravenes the height regulation.' She heard a rustle in the bushes. It was an animal but still it made her skin creep.

'You were born on a Friday.' Jack put away his phone. '"Friday's child is loving and giving."' He nodded at Stella. 'That's you.'

'Ha ha.' Stella shot him a look, but he appeared to be serious. 'Aren't angels supposed to be guardians? This one is like a prison guard. The sculptor was having an off-day.' She stirred the glass with her boot, expecting to expose soil. There was more glass. Whoever was taking it from here would not run out.

'This angel is for a beloved son. No expense spared. That expression of recrimination is not the artist lacking inspiration, it signifies that someone must pay for the death of sweet baby Michael.' Jack put up his coat collar. 'If we stay it will be us.'

Stella was generally immune to Jack's quirky impressions, but not this time. He had used the word 'recrimination', a word she had just applied to herself. The angel would make her pay.

Jack stood in front of the statue. 'Someone's tried to stop her.'

Stella joined him. The angel's arms were slightly raised, exposing thin wrists peeping from the folds of a flowing gown. The wrists ended abruptly. Her hands were missing.

'Vandalism.' In the grey afternoon light the severed ends resembled fractured bone.

'No.' Jack stroked the marble. 'It's a sheer slice. It was pre-meditated. Cold calculation.'

Stella had cleaned up wanton damage after burglaries or parties that had got out of hand. 'Who would do this?'

'The Archangel Michael defeated Satan and kicked him out of heaven. Satan escaped to earth,' Jack said under his breath. 'St Michael is his enemy.'

'The Fallen Angel.' Stella caught echoes of a patchy religious education. 'Michael Thornton committed a sin, you mean?'

'No, Michael's with God. Whoever removed the angel's hands wanted to fracture the power of his guardian angel.'

'That doesn't fit with our theory that the murderer is taking revenge on drivers who have run over children.' Stella squatted down and combed her fingers through the glass.

'The Book of Revelation is stuffed with sevens: John's message for seven churches, seven trumpets, seven seals and the final portent when seven angels each bring a plague.'

'More sevens.' Stella hadn't read the Book of Revelation. 'Sunday is the seventh day of the week,' she offered.

'Sunday!' Stell, you are an angel! Let's see your matrix.'

Stella swung her rucksack off her shoulder and found the spreadsheet tucked in her Filofax. She kept her back to the angel.

'The tenth of November, when my erstwhile friend Jamie Markham was killed, is a Sunday and it equals seven.' Jack sat cross-legged on the glass beside her.

'Charlie Hampson's doesn't, we know this. But—' Stella nudged him. 'Hampson was killed on Michael Thornton's birthday!'

Jack jumped out and went over to the angel. 'Of the seven deaths we know about, four are in mid-March and one at the end of March, the month of Michael's birthday.'

'Lucie said one of the children, Robert Smith, died on the fifth of November, five days before Jamie on the tenth. Mrs Thornton killed herself on the fifteenth, the same day Myra Hindley died.' Jack got out his phone. 'The *Daily Mirror*'s headline was "Gone But Not Forgiven". There has to be a link.'

'Myra Hindley is one person who can't be guilty of these crimes.'

'Lucie made me think. Why did Mrs Thornton wait so long before killing herself?'

'Lucille May also said some things are only coincidence.' Stella swung her rucksack on to her back. 'It was the first time Mrs Thornton succeeded, odds on she had tried before.'

'What if she's our killer? She realized with Jamie Markham's death that nothing had changed, her son was still dead. She saw the futility and ended it all.'

'Good thought!' Stella looked at the spreadsheet. 'Only the shoe man Harvey Gray and Charles Hampson died after she committed suicide.'

Jack had been looking at his phone. 'Michael was killed on the day the Moors murderers were sentenced to life. Lucie told me. That day Mrs Thornton's life effectively ended. Hindley dying brought it all back. She couldn't bear it.'

Suzie had told her that after the Moors murders Terry had vowed never to let his own child out of his sight. Impossible. Finally he left his daughter altogether. Men bottled up feelings for their children. Marian said Joel Evans's father punched a wall and broke his finger when he heard his son was dead. 'We're forgetting something.'

'Likely. My brain's on overload.'

'Joel Evans.' Stella flipped through her diary. 'The boy killed outside Marks and Spencer's on King Street.'

'So we are!' Jack grasped the angel's wrists as if he might heal them.

'Monday the twenty-third of April. The day I found the blue folder.'

'Wasn't it a hit and run?'

'A man gave himself up later. I was there when Marian was told.'

'He will be the next victim! We must warn him. What was his name?'

'Can't remember.'

'If the killer is alive, going by the pattern he won't kill for months after the child died.'

'You said he was speeding up. Something's changed. His health or his circumstances.' She saw again the sandy shape on the tarmac. A child ghost washed away in the rain. 'I'm due at David Barlow's.'

'That's a strange job,' Jack remarked. 'Deep cleaning. A metaphor for cleansing guilt or shame. You should profile deep-cleaning clients. Bet there's a corollary.'

'David's got nothing to be guilty about; he nursed his wife to the end. Not many men would and he was burgled.' Stella hadn't spoken to David since finding the stuff under his bath. Jack would have a field day if she told him. 'I'll drop you at Mrs Hampson's.' She hesitated, struck by the reality of where Jack was going. She would not like to clean there by herself. 'If we delay it, I could come too.' There was more rustling in the bushes, just to add to it all.

'I'm normally there without you.'

'With Mrs Hampson being dead.'

'She's not still there. I should escort you to your deep-cleaning gig.'

'No need.' Stella cast about for the path. The rustling stopped. 'Jack. Come on!' She didn't relish walking across the cemetery by herself.

'What's tomorrow?

'Sunday sixth of May.'

She read the lead lettering on Michael Thornton's monument: '15th March 1959 – 6th May 1966'.

'Ring your friend,' Jack said softly. 'He will kill Joel Evans's driver tomorrow.'

Fifty-Nine

Marian Williams parked her Mini on Staveley Road, a good distance from a van that, despite being plain white, seemed familiar. Everything rang a bell when you worked for the police. She took the bouquet off the passenger seat. When she had seen Stella Darnell outside Terry's, her heart had gone out to her. Stella was keeping her father's house ticking along as if she expected him back. Marian wanted him back too. She had given Stella the flowers on the spur of the moment. She didn't regret it, but it meant that the next day she had come here empty-handed.

Stella wasn't fooled by the bruise. The way she had looked at her, like Terry did, with concern. She had quickly worked it out and no doubt felt sorry for her. Marian didn't want sympathy. Still, with Terry gone, it was nice Stella cared.

A man walked out of the cemetery gates. Marian didn't want to see anyone. She was snatching precious moments out of time. Despite covering her tracks, he always knew what she had done and he made her pay.

Something about the man caught her attention. She lifted the lilies to hide her face and peered through the petals. He was moving with purpose, heels clipping on the pavement. Most bereaved tended to plod along.

She knew him. David Barlow had been burgled. He had lost pictures and valuable silver crucifixes. Dotty to have them on display, she had thought. He brought photographs of the items. Few victims were so prepared. He came the next week to see how the case was progressing. It wasn't. The burglary would have been targeted, buyers lined up, no clues, no fingerprints. She suggested he list visitors to the house – cleaners, plumbers, any workmen. He let slip his wife was terminally ill so there were lots of people coming. Nurses, deliveries of oxygen, drugs, equipment. None of them would steal, he said. Marian didn't like to say you couldn't trust anyone. She saw the underbelly of life; it skewed perception. Poor man was having a hard enough time. Barlow never made an appointment or rang, which would have saved him, and her, time and trouble. Soon she found him a nuisance. Then he began to arouse her suspicions. He didn't seem bothered about the stolen goods; it was the principle, he said. Keep your principles to yourself, she wanted to say. He was taking up valuable time. She had made a note: 'one to watch'. If Barlow was here, Mrs Barlow must have died.

He got into an orange Ford Fiesta. She had not noticed it when she parked. Terry would have seen it. Terry was with her now, spurring her on.

She waited for Barlow to round the corner in the direction of the Hogarth roundabout, then hurried into the cemetery. She knew where the new plots were and found the grave immediately.

JENNIFER BARLOW

LOYAL WIFE OF DAVID

1946 – 2012

A plain, self-referencing epitaph. Nothing about being much missed or deeply mourned. What had tested his wife's loyalty? An affair. That soft-shoe demeanour had to be a sham. She heard voices and ducked behind a mausoleum.

Two people, a man and a woman, walked along the path from the chapel, arm in arm. She had dreamed of bringing Terry here, her arm through his.

She nearly made a noise. The woman was Stella Darnell. The

white van was familiar because Marian had seen it in the station compound. Stella had said nothing about a boyfriend. Terry couldn't have known, he would have said. Marian must get a look at the man; Terry would want to know. She followed them. Terry had taught her his tricks. Keep them in sight, not too close or they will feel you there.

The van pulled away. Marian broke into a clumsy trot. Her lungs were bursting by the time she started her car, an old-style Mini.

Trailing Stella Darnell into Chiswick High Road, she caught a glimpse of the occupants in a shop window. Only Stella. The man had gone. She was hot with shame. He had got out without her seeing. She was very bad. The voice filled the car.

They shall suffer the punishment of eternal destruction and exclusion from the presence of the Lord and from the glory of his might...

Sixty

Marian Williams filed documents, signed forms and slipped them into internal envelopes until her desk was clear. Being off in the week had set her back; at the weekend she could work uninterrupted. She did not like to leave work pending. She began each day with a clean slate. She smiled grimly at the phrase; it made her think of Stella. Stella, it seemed, got everywhere.

She had saved the best task until last. She tapped Barlow's details into the database. She started with vehicle registrations dating from eighteen when he probably passed his driving test.

When computers were introduced to the station in the early 1990s, Marian Williams might have been expected not to get on with them. But she was efficient, and others were mindful to respect her exacting systems. The 'Crime Reporting Information System' was one of many technological challenges. Some staff took early retirement to avoid it altogether, while others, through a mix of carelessness and obduracy, undermined CRIS with minor errors. Marian hunted these down and corrected them. She grew to know it intimately and, awed by its capability, developed a fierce attachment to it. She posed questions. It gave her answers. It never let her down. The answer it gave Marian now was one that she had dreaded one day finding out.

After a time she gathered herself and printed out the result, noting, as she always did, the last time she had printed a response from the database. It made no sense. She never printed in the mornings and never while the cleaners were in the building.

She picked up the receiver and punched in the number of the woman who was supposed to be a friend.

'Is that Stella Darnell?'

The conversation was short. She folded the printout and dropped it in her handbag. She had one more call to make.

The administrator whom everyone knew as Marian Williams put on her coat and slung her bag over her chest like a satchel, a precaution against theft. She trotted out of the station. Before meeting Stella, she would stop at the model shop in Hammersmith Station, orange was an unusual colour, but the man stocked everything, he would not let her down.

Sixty-One

Saturday, 5 May 2012

Stella found a parking space near David's house. While she was hauling the equipment out of the van, a Mini took a vacated slot further down the street. Spaces here were free for less than a minute: a time-and-motion fact Jack would relish. Jack. He should not be in the dead woman's house alone.

'Tea first!'

David relieved her of the Planet vacuum cleaner. His shirt sleeves were pushed up, revealing sturdy workmanlike arms, surprising since he didn't strike her as practical.

He had laid the table with plates decorated with dainty doilies, bone-handled forks and real napkins. A candle burned in the centre of a sponge cake dusted with caster sugar. Another of Jennifer Barlow's creations. Stella was cheered by the cafetière of coffee and a milk jug from which wisps of steam arose. Jack liked cake; if he were here he would see that he had got David wrong.

Stanley was curled up asleep in a bed by the radiator. The dog and the laden table gave the kitchen a homely aspect very different to Terry's. David slid out a chair for her and then slid it back as she sat down.

Mindful of time – she wanted to check on Jack – Stella glanced at David's wall clock and stifled a gasp. Surrounding the clock were the pictures and crucifixes from under the downstairs bath. The jacket she had found hung on a hook cleaned and pressed. Stella had worried that David would not refer to her discoveries. He had put everything on display.

'The cake looks nice.' She was glad Jack wasn't witnessing this. At the same time she wished that he was.

'Last cake.' David sat down. 'I'll have to have a go myself. I've got rather partial.' He patted his stomach, still, Stella noticed, as flat as a board.

The candle flame gave his face a glow, accentuating the start of a tan.

'Make a wish.'

'Now?' she said stupidly.

'I've made mine.' He laughed merrily. 'Keep it secret.'

Stella never made wishes, but this was not the time to say so. I wish we could find the murderer. With too big a blow, she extinguished the light and knocked over the candle. Only then did she think she should have wished something about David.

David flapped open his napkin and spread it over his lap. With efficient chops he divided the cake into exact sixths.

Stella bit off a piece. The sponge was moist and tasted of lemons.

'I bought my Wolseley forty-six years ago.' Barlow nodded at the pictures. Stella clutched the table edge to stop herself trembling and looked to where he was pointing.

She hadn't noticed the car. Unlike the other pictures it wasn't framed but was a print, like the ones Terry did, the colours lurid and dreamlike. David had not mentioned the stolen items.

'Wolseleys are beautiful to drive, even without power-assisted steering.' He detached a morsel of sponge with the side of his fork, gathered it up and popped it into his mouth. 'The smell of the leather, dark red, sumptuous. That shine on the walnut veneer. I was at the start of my career and engaged. At eighteen I was on top of the world!'

'It's hard to manage without a car, even in London.' A lump of cake stuck to the roof of Stella's mouth. She couldn't dislodge it with her tongue, so she gulped her coffee. She would have to say something.

'You've made this place as good as new. And God, in the guise of the good people at Porphyrion, will finish what you started.' He sat back. 'These pictures, those crosses are shackles. Jennifer stitched me up, Stella.' He wiped his hands on his napkin and leant forward. 'She hid them and said we'd been burgled. She was crying, but she never cried. Made me call the police – no, not call, I had to go there. She's adept at dreaming up new modes of torture even from beyond the grave. Divorce would have spoiled her fun.' He appeared to be controlling a rage.

'You had no idea?' Stella could see he was telling the truth. Her skin tingled. Mrs Barlow was dead. She could harm no one. But suddenly Stella felt as if the woman was in the room with them. A malevolent presence. Something nudged at her leg; she leapt back. Stanley was licking her boot.

'Don't feed him. He mustn't beg.' David came over and swept the dog into his arms. He turned to her. 'It's over, Stella.'

Stella reeled. No one had ever ended it with her. Jackie believed Stella split up with men to stop them leaving her. A shame, Jackie said, because men adored Stella and would never leave her.

'No more recrimination.' He was taking the pictures down. He stuffed them into a plastic bin bag, careless, it seemed, of breaking them. 'Tabula rasa. Clean slate!'

Stella was stunned. That word 'recrimination'. David Barlow had asked her to deep clean, his second chance. No amount of scrubbing would rub out her theft. She could not hide the print-out under the bath.

'The police used to drive Wolseleys,' she managed. He didn't want to end it. She was not relieved. If he knew about the print-out, then he would say it was over. Perhaps he did know and was talking about recrimination to encourage her to confess.

'They did.' David threw the bag on the patio. It landed with a metallic crash and the breaking of glass.

Stella's phone rang. Jack. 'I need to take this, it's work.'

In the hall, she tripped over a canister of air neutralizer that had rolled out of the equipment bag. She should not have let Jack go on his own. 'Jack! Are you OK?'

'Is that Stella Darnell?' A girl's voice.

'Ye- es?' Stella didn't know any children. She checked the handset: Caller unknown.

'Could I see you?'

'Who is this?'

'It's Marian.'

'Well, to be honest I'm in the middle of...'

'You said to call if I needed help.'

After the scene in the toilets Stella had encouraged Marian to call and she had meant it. 'I'm with a client,' she heard herself say. Marian had a violent husband. Terry would not refuse. 'I could come afterwards. Are you at the station?'

'I don't work weekends. I can't see you at home.' Marian was wheezing as if she had been crying. 'Do you know Dukes Meadows? By the river at Chiswick, not far from where you are now. It's peaceful. We won't be disturbed.'

Stella would rather they were disturbed. The shoulder-to-cry-on stuff was more Jackie's department. She agreed to meet at six-thirty in the car park by a boathouse, presumably a café. Marian rang off without saying goodbye; she was upset. Bang went the supper with David. Disappointed Stella tossed the air neutralizer back into the bag and returned to the kitchen.

David had brewed fresh coffee.

'Nothing wrong, I hope.' He asked questions without being intrusive. He leant against the fridge, the dog resting on his shoulder.

'A client.' Stella told him she was meeting Marian and how she knew her. Although he would be sympathetic, she didn't mention the marital abuse. She would not break a confidence, even one that hadn't yet been shared. She told him this meant they couldn't have supper.

'If it's any consolation, I can't anyway, something's come up. I'll explain another time.'

'Do you know Dukes Meadows?' She was mildly surprised David hadn't said earlier that they wouldn't be able to meet.

'Lovely spot for a stroll or a picnic. Not tonight, the weather is forecast to deteriorate.' The dog cocked its head as if particularly interested. 'Are you going from here?'

'Yes, apparently it's quite near.'

'Traffic willing, it's twenty minutes. You're younger, but for my generation Dukes Meadows has a darker association. They found a victim of "Jack the Stripper" there in 1959. One of the Hammersmith Murders. I was a lad. Me and my pals went to have a nose. There you go, Fluffkin.' He put Stanley back in his bed and flapped a furry brown bear under its nose. The dog snapped the bear between its jaws and dashed it against the cushion. 'I go back there sometimes. Can't help myself.'

'What happened?' Stella asked out of politeness, thinking about Marian.

'A dawn police patrol found Elizabeth Figg propped against a willow tree. She was a twenty-one-year-old prostitute. It was my first body – not that I saw her; they'd constructed a corrugated iron shelter and shooed us away. One officer said she could have been sunbathing, looking over the Thames to Watneys brewery. Was your dad there?' David was animated.

'He was a boy.' Stella was impressed at his recall of an event of over fifty years ago. But then the Rokesmith murder was still clear in her mind from when she was fifteen. She snapped to: this meant David had to be over sixty.

'Your dad was taken too soon.'

'His first fatality was in 1966 – a boy killed in a hit and run.'

'Where was that?' David snatched away the bear; the poodle whimpered.

'On King Street.' Stella took her mug to the sink.

'I'll give you directions for Dukes Meadows. It's hard to find even with a satnav.'

That a woman had been murdered there made Stella even less willing to go. Amanda Hampson's house was preferable – maybe better the corpse you know. She had no idea how to make Marian feel better. Until David, her relationships were not an example and this wasn't really a relationship.

'We should not forget the Elizabeth Figgs and Michael Thorntons; or we forget ourselves.' David sluiced soap off Stella's mug under the hot-water tap.

'You know about Michael Thornton?' Stella stopped in the doorway. Idle chat was how Terry unearthed clues.

'The car hit him the day Myra Hindley and Ian Brady got life. Sixth of May 1966.' He twisted the drying-up cloth around inside the mug. 'Thornton's sister watched her brother die. I really hope she has forgotten. Her name was Myra, then after the murders her parents changed it to Mary.' He draped the cloth on the oven door handle. 'Myra Hindley was still trying to get released when she died. Jennifer said you can't ever be forgiven for killing a child. A few years earlier, Hindley and Brady would have hanged.'

Myra Hindley was coming up a lot. Mrs Thornton had killed herself on the fifteenth November 2002. Five days after Jamie Markham, who in turn was five days after the boy Robert Smith on Guy Fawkes Night. Lucille May had built a file on the crashes, supposedly for a book she was writing, and she had gone as far as buying the house that the dead boy had lived in. That didn't add up. She needed to talk to Jack.

'Can you?'

'Sorry, can I what?'

'Be forgiven for the death of a child.'

Stella was born a few months after the Moors Murderers were sentenced, but she did remember Terry's frustration when Hindley died, that she had escaped in the end. 'No. Definitely not,' she agreed.

She lugged the equipment up to the spare room, a room that was spare because the Barlows had no children. Unlike her other relationships, she and David agreed about key things. He had risked his life to save a dog. He cared for his wife even when he no longer loved her. He was loyal and steadfast. And certainly there was no way back if you killed someone.

Lost in her thoughts, Stella forgot to phone Jack.

Sixty-Two

Saturday, 5 May 2012

Jack stood in Amanda Hampson's sitting room and listened. Apart from the ticking of the quartz clock on her bureau, the sounds were external. Traffic on the South Circular, an aeroplane's muffled roar and the chugging of a District line train leaving Kew Gardens station right on time.

His phone rang. Clean Slate.

'Hello, love, Jackie here, is it all right to speak?'

'Always to you, Jacqueline!' He laughed happily.

'Stop it! You're at that woman's house, aren't you? I'm checking you're not frightened.'

'Yes and no.'

'Say if it's spooky. I can come out there.'

'It's fine. Stella offered too.' Jack looked about the room. It was horribly empty. Amanda's absence was as large as her presence. He was suddenly less confident. 'What about you?'

'Me? Oh same old... although did I tell you about that woman at the police station? Sent me back, I was a girl again.' She cackled.

Keen now to keep her on the line, he encouraged Jackie to tell him the whole story.

The memory of the night Jack stood in the garden watching Amanda Hampson through the window made him sad. She was not a True Host, but he was wrong to dismiss her. Grubby though she had let her house become after Charlie Hampson died, she had created a home such as Jack had yearned for most of his life.

He regretted that while Amanda was alive he had written off her theory that her husband had been murdered as unresolved grief. He had let her down. The two cases had converged. A man was avenging children killed on roads by careless drivers. One of those drivers was Charlie Hampson. The obvious person was Michael Thornton's father, but Lucie said he was dead. Who else cared that the boy had died?

The answer was obvious. Terry Darnell.

Jack needed air. He plunged outside and slammed the French doors behind him. He blundered on to the lawn. Vaguely he registered the grass was cut, the weeds gone. Stella had sent in her garden crew and made it better than when Amanda was alive. Stella made things better.

Frustrated by the lack of action, had Terry taken the law into his own hands? Gamekeeper turned poacher. Jack rubbed his face. No. It could not be. No.

His tiny bead of doubt was not, could not be, to do with Stella's father. Terry had been a clean copper. Cashman had told Stella the man was his role model. A respected detective, he was not a vigilante. If Terry were the killer he would not have left the folder out for Stella to find. He was too clever for that. Jack let himself breathe.

He looked back into the sitting room. Something was different, even allowing for police and forensics and the urgency of the ambulance crew. The Turkish mat was wrinkled and the dining chairs had been shoved aside to make a gangway for the paramedics to bring Amanda's body through. The curtain ties hung loose. A cushion lay on the carpet and the occasional table that Amanda kept folded was by the sofa. Jack avoided Charlie Hampson's cold sardonic stare.

Papers lay on the open bureau, utility bills and junk mail. Nothing about Charlie Hampson's death or the boy he had fatally injured. Amanda had tidied her file away. The door to the room was slightly open. Any minute she would sail in with coffee, expounding some newly gleaned fact.

'Bring that table over for your drink, there's a love.'

She only put the occasional table out for visitors. Neither he nor Stella had moved it. No one else had need to. The table was folded by the door when he last cleaned.

Amanda had had a visitor. She had not put the table away after her guest had gone because by then she was dead.

Jack put his hands to his face. His eyes were wet and he dashed at them with the cuffs of his coat. He paced the flags where they had found Amanda. The stones were uneven, lifted by tree roots and cracked by frost. His shoe caught the edge of a slab where the path dipped. That night it had rained, making the paving slippery. It would have been easy to fall in the dark. But Amanda wasn't clumsy; she moved like a dancer.

Martin Cashman had told Stella that Amanda's blood alcohol level was 0.29, which he said would have likely caused 'severe motor impairment'. Lucille May dying that way would not surprise him, but he did not see Amanda as much of a drinker.

The meditation temple was unlocked. Jack went in. Amanda had asserted that, being circular, it didn't need cleaning, but dried leaves had gathered on the door mat and scattered on the marble floor. An oval table inlaid with a tableau of a faun peeping out from between spindly tree trunks stood beside a maroon-covered divan grey with dust. White walls, sheer and sweeping, rose to a glass dome in the ceiling, interrupted by a stained-glass porthole, the only window.

Amanda believed her temple was unsullied by earthly cares and, despite her having died on its threshold, Jack did feel a profound calm. In a way Terry had taken the law into his own hands when he had left a file of photographs for his daughter to deal with.

A bloodstain on the divan where the ambulance crew had lain her down had darkened to brown. He could have reassured Amanda it would come out with a good scrub. Gingerly Jack sat down.

Amanda Hampson had been murdered by the man who had killed the car drivers, including her husband. The killer was not infirm or dead. Amanda had not knocked down a child; she had discovered something that made her a threat. From that moment her death warrant was sealed.

'Lucille bloody Ball. I love Lucy, I don't think. Making sheep's eyes at Charlie even when he was dead. She's got me to answer to now!'

Amanda's whisper bounced around the curving walls. 'She's got me to answer to now!'

That last day Amanda had declared she had proof that her husband was murdered. She told the police administrator that Charlie had passed his advanced driving test. A minor fact that had convinced Jack Amanda was kidding herself.

'I have the missing jigsaw piece. The murderer has underestimated me.'

Amanda had got short shrift at the station so she rang Lucille May. This was hitting rock bottom: Amanda disliked the woman, was annoyed she found her husband attractive, even in a painting and so beyond Lucie's charms. Jack, bent on finishing his shift on time, dwelling on Stella's blue folder and preoccupied with the streets in the attic, had paid Amanda scant attention.

Stella believed Lucie May was hiding something. Surely Lucie was not a killer. Amanda could have overcome her with a swipe. If anyone killed anyone it would be the other way around. Jack sat back and surveyed the domed space. He willed the walls to give up their secret and whisper the killer's name to him. The leaves on the floor stirred in an imperceptible breeze.

A hardback book lay on the sill in the porthole window. He expected it to be on mediation or Yoga so was surprised to find a history of motor racing over the last half a century. Not very meditative.

He had seen it before. The book slipped from his grasp and landed on the tiles, pages splaying. It settled on a chapter about the death in Germany of a racing driver called Jim Clark in 1968. The name meant nothing to Jack. He put it back on the sill. The bookmark lay amongst the leaves. It was a ripped section of a letter from the Parkinson's Disease Society requesting a donation. He was about to replace it, guessing the Jim Clark page was the place when he realized with a shock that there was no point. Amanda would not be reading on. Amanda wasn't interested in motor racing. Jack turned the letter over. There was handwriting was on the back.

The door creaked. He jumped and looked out of the porthole. There was no one on the path.

'15th March, 11 p.m., Marquis Way W6. Porphyrion. £££!!'

The day Charlie Hampson was killed. The day that, had he lived, Michael Thornton would have been fifty.

Amanda had this book when she was leaving for the police station. Jack, busy with cream cleanser on the bath, hadn't given it a thought.

'I've won, Jack! Tomorrow we'll celebrate. Now Inspector Whatsit will bloody listen.'

Inspector 'Whatsit' was Terry. Amanda didn't know he was dead. If she had remembered his name, Jack could have told her. If she had shown him this note, scribbled, he guessed, by Charlie taking down a phone message, Jack would have believed her because he had seen Terry's blue folder. He would have assured her that, although retired, Terry Darnell was building a case. He would have told her that he was working with Darnell's daughter on the case. If he had told Amanda this, she might still be alive.

The night he died, Charlie Hampson was meeting someone at 11 p.m. on Marquis Way. The administrator had said the police already knew Charlie had the advanced driving licence. Not knowing about Terry's photographs or the green glass, the administrator had tactfully dismissed her. Amanda had not shown her the Parkinson's Disease letter, she would have wanted to wait to see Martin Cashman.

Jack thought back to his conversation with Jackie. The signs were beginning to make sense. He rang Stella. No signal penetrated the thick walls of the temple.

Sixty-Three

Saturday, 5 May 2012

It was five past six when Stella stowed everything into her van. She looked around to wave. David had gone and his door was closed. She stopped the van around the corner from Aldensley Road, reluctant to arrive at Dukes Meadows early.

She must phone Jack. He had not called her, which probably meant all was well. It could also mean it was not. She was keying in his number when the phone rang.

'Jack! Did you find anything?'

'Sorry to disappoint you, darling. It's not the lovely Jack.' A corncrake laugh. 'It's Lucie-Lou.'

'Hello.' Stella was about to ask how the journalist got her number but, of course, since the interview she had had it. May had worked out who she was, she probably matched the number when Stella had called to fix the appointment at the house. The woman had not lost her investigative touch after all.

'Jack wanted to know about the people who lived here. That boy's a sweety, makes you want to do anything for him, doesn't he?'

On principle Stella was about to disagree, but could not.

'Between you and me, if any post came here for the Thorntons, I'd be a fool to tell you – grist to the mill – but nothing has. They're dead and gone.' Nevertheless she gave Stella the Thorntons' forwarding address.

Stella dashed it down in her diary in the space for today's date. She couldn't put her finger on it, but she didn't trust Lucille

May. She hadn't liked her when the woman rang to interview her and she had been right, the resulting piece had little in common with their conversation. There was something May wasn't telling them.

'If you find the Thorntons, don't be forgetting it's my story.' The journalist rang off.

Stella knew the address. The posh house name was misleading. The building was derelict and awaiting planning permission to become a free school. Since she couldn't see David, she would pop along there after seeing Marian, even though it was a dead end; the Thorntons, it seemed, were lost in the mists of time. If the killer was still alive they were no nearer to finding out his identity.

She read David's directions to Dukes Meadows. His talking about the murder there had made her uneasy. Since Terry's death she had entered a dark world populated with victims and villains and, with the business with the printout, had become one herself. With time to kill. Stella tapped the murdered prostitute's name into Google.

Elizabeth Figg's body was found on 17 June 1959, two months after Michael Thornton's birthday. The young woman was one of several murdered in West London in the fifties and sixties. The case was called the Hammersmith Murders. The killer, dubbed, as David had said, Jack the Stripper because he left the bodies half naked, was never caught. Stella sat up. One of the case files in Terry's basement was labelled 'Hammersmith Murders'. Was he investigating this too? The file was under the sink counter, out of sight. More likely, a collector of unsolved crimes, Terry could not let anything pass. Amazing that David remembered it. His first body, he said. Like Terry he had not forgotten. Thinking of David, she wondered where he would be going on a Saturday night. She stopped the thought.

There was a picture of the murdered woman. Printed on the front page of the *Star* newspaper, thirty-six hours after the body was discovered, it had the caption 'Murdered girl: Yard issue picture. Do you know this Miss X?' Elizabeth Figg gazed impassively into the distance. It took Stella some moments to realise she was looking at a corpse. She closed her phone and dropped it in her rucksack.

When Stella reached the last line of David's directions and parked by the boathouse at Dukes Meadows, she called Jack.

She had no signal.

Sixty-Four

Saturday, 5 May 2012

At the door to the petrol station shop, Jack made way for a young man ripping a Mars wrapper open with his teeth before slipping inside. No customers: perfect. A tall stooping man with rheumy eyes stood behind the till. Lurked was more like it; if a human being could make himself invisible, this man got close.

'Mr Ford?' Jack was warm; Jackie had warned that her friend couldn't say boo to a goose.

'Yes.' Ford blinked rapidly and straightened. He ran a hand over the till as if casting a protective spell.

'I work with Jackie Makepeace, at Clean Slate.' Ford showed no comprehension.

'Yes,' he complied. This was going badly.

'Jackie says you're a wizard when it comes to wood,' Jack prattled as he drew out a Mars bar from the display. He placed it on the counter as if laying down arms. Coin by coin, he counted out change.

'Did you purchase fuel?' The man was expressionless.

'Fuel for me!' Jack grinned and nudged the chocolate. Treating the transaction as life-threatening, Mr Ford took the five-pound note he offered him.

'How is Jacqueline?' Ford quavered.

'Good. She sends her best.' Jack popped the bar into his pocket and rested his hands on the counter, fingers spread. 'You've known her since school, she says. Wish I had a friend I'd known that long.'

'I don't see her often.' Ford stacked Jack's change on the counter by coin size, the five pence on top. 'She was kind.'

'She rates you. A practical kind of guy who can turn to any job. Thing is, I have a flat pack that needs assembling – would that be something you could do?'

'I don't drive, but…'

'I would fetch you and take you home. Jackie said you live across the road from here.'

'I guess, I…'

'Sorted!' Jack clapped his hands. 'She has been kind to me too.' He looked out at the forecourt. There was one car at the pumps. A Ford Fiesta. This man's name was Ford. Had to be a sign. Jack felt positively happy. Yet the car was a nasty orange, surely not a good sign. 'She said when you were little you saw a boy die.'

The man went very still and stopped blinking. Jack faltered. You are dealing with other people's pain. Be kind and merciful. It wasn't in Stella's manual.

'Something happened to me when I was small, that's how it came up.' He frowned out of the window. The man at the pump could have been David Bowie. This was Hammersmith; perhaps it was. He thought about saying so to lighten the mood.

'I wasn't the only one who saw it.' Mr Ford produced a box of Mars bars from under the counter and, reaching over the display, stuffed one into the gap.

'Sorry?'

The man talked quietly; Jack had to move closer. 'Mary wanted to swap. The cards took me ages to collect; my nan gave me ones from her tea, but she died.' He rammed in another Mars bar. 'I wanted Mary's Yew and the Sycamore which was Number Thirteen. She didn't need it.' His face was red, his mouth grim. He spoke as if reading a script. 'She was chasing her brother and, you see, she had my cards so I had to get them back. The boy ran into the road. Mary never saw me.' He shut his eyes. 'My nan said if a thing is wrong, it must be put right.'

'Are you saying he had a sister?' Jack pulled out the new Mars bar and handed Douglas Ford the right money. Lucie had said the family was dead. If Michael was fifty today, this sister must be a similar age. Stella said Lucie was hiding something. She was a journalist; she would know there was a sister.

'I never told tales about the cards.' Douglas Ford slammed the change into the till and screwed up the receipt.

'What was her name? Did she see Michael die? You told the police you weren't there.' Jack had to stop himself yelling at the man.

'I didn't get Mary into trouble. I got there too late to see what actually happened.'

'Mary? Was that her name?'

'I didn't say about Mary, but even so she punished me.' Ford spoke as if in a dream, his voice toneless. 'Nan watches over me, she knows what happened. Mary had me punished.' He said again: 'My Holly for her Yew. Nan said an eye for an eye.'

Behind them the door slid aside. Jack made way for a woman carrying a can of oil. The woman mumbled the number of her petrol pump, added in a bag of crisps, paid and left.'I won't keep you.'

Ford looked startled, probably hoping Jack too had gone.

'Did Michael's death make you angry?' Jack stroked the top of the Mars bars.

'I will have to decline the job.' The man tapped a key on the till and the drawer flew open. He shut it. 'I get tired after work and hate to make errors. Please thank Jacqueline.'

A swooshing sound, Jack turned. 'David Bowie' had entered the shop.

'Yes, sir, can I help you?' Ford looked pleadingly at Jack. He had got to Ford; the man was the colour of wax. Odd, a minute ago Ford had been desperate for him to leave. Jack tipped his hand in farewell and mooched out. Out of sight of the shop he checked his watch and stiffened. A few hours until 6 May.

They should keep a watch on the garage. Jackie had said Douglas Ford was nice. It was the nice ones who caught you unawares.

Sixty-Five

Saturday, 5 May 2012

Jack was practised at entering his Host's home. He removed the window glass, insinuated himself inside, unlocked the back door, went out and replaced the glass.

He half expected she would be there to greet him.

He ran swiftly up the staircase to his dormitory. The bed covers were as he had left them and, poking in the back of the wardrobe, his biscuit tin of trophies was untouched, the contents intact. He did an audit: the lock of hair, his Host collection – photographs held with an elastic band. A wooden clothes peg from a house he had wanted to call home. No time to go down memory lane. Jack shivered and drew his coat around him. Time to find the street atlas and go. For the second time he tried Lucie May's number and got no answer.

In a Host's house he was far away from Stella's clean bright world. Until now he had thought he could move between both worlds, but this school was like an exile from which he feared there was no return.

They had six bags of glass chips; each group of seven represented a life.

He laid the glass from Michael Thornton's grave on the candlewick counterpane. There were seven pieces. He had scooped them up. What were the chances of there being seven? It was a sign. He wrote the location on the bag and fitted them into the tin. A temporary measure, for the glass was not strictly speaking a trophy. He put the tin in the wardrobe and sat on Colin's bed.

He checked his phone. No voicemail from Stella. He called her.

'I am sorry I can't take your call…' He was about to close the line when a thought occurred: 'Hey, Stell. If you see her, ask your friend exactly what Amanda Hampson said when she came to the police station. Tell her why if you have to. We need to meet, there've been developments.'

Diffused light filtered into the room through the grimy panes. He would like to clean them, but without permission it was rude.

The old man would be expecting him. Jack had come to value his evenings working companionably on the streets of Hammersmith. He would tell him about the garage hoarding already being in place on King Street and that Wilson's Warehouse had been converted into flats. The man would not be pleased.

He would be sad to go. He wouldn't say he was going. Cowardly, but he couldn't do goodbyes. Jack wandered across to the next bed.

Steve.

The sky darkened; a gust of wind buffeted the window sashes. He shrugged deeper into his coat. The second bed belonged to Bill, the third to Jimmy. The names were familiar. They were common names; he worked with a Jimmy and a Bill. He had never met a Colin.

Steve. Stevie. Stephen. Jack grabbed the iron bedhead. Stephen Parsons!

The name on the headstone in St Peter's graveyard. The grave his Host had visited. She was a True Host! She had killed the boy. He took deep breaths. Stella would tell him to think logically.

When he had told Stella about the article he had found at Amanda's he'd asked her if the name rang a bell. It had not. Jack could not think why he knew it. Stephen Parsons was the name of the boy killed by Charlie Hampson.

Steve.

He walked to the foot of the bed as if approaching the foot of a grave. The blankets were tucked in nice and tight. Jack did not need Stella's spreadsheet to confirm that seven-year-old James Harrison was hit by Paul Vickery's car on Marquis Way.

Careless of discovery, he went into the other dormitories on his corridor. 'Chris'. And 'Rob' whose mother couldn't live without him.

There was a new label on the 'spare' bed. 'Joel'. Jack got it. These were not the names of boys away for vacation. The term dates on the notice downstairs were wrong, he should have realized. His Host was playing with him. The windows were dirty, the water glasses empty, beds untouched, the blankets stiff and unslept in. The school was closed. These beds belonged to boys killed in road accidents dating from Friday, 6 May 1966, when Michael Thornton died. Jack fumbled for his phone. He punched out Stella's number, his hands were shaking. Voicemail. He left a message.

'Ring the administrator as soon as you get this, tell her to warn that man, Matthew Benson. Ring me when you get this!'

"'O Lord, I love the habitation of thy house, and the place where thy glory dwells. Sweep me not away with the sinners…'" The old man's voice was like the buzzing of a wasp.

"'…nor my life with bloodthirsty men, men in whose hands are evil devices, and whose right hands are full of bribes…'" Jack continued.

The man was pummelling at an apron of concrete with the tip of a long bladed knife. Jack recognized the hard standing outside Harvey Gray's shoe factory.

In a street close to Jack's elbow a grit bin was upended; sand spilled on to the kerb. Jack righted it and saw a chip of green glass, half the size of the bin, wedged against a wall. He was on Phoenix Way. The glass marked the spot where Charlie Hampson had smashed first into the oak tree and then through the wall. The tree was a perfect replica; Jack could vouch for that. The oak leaves must have taken months to cut out and attach to wire branches. These were green and lush because it was May. The man would replace them with russet leaves for autumn and when winter came the branches would be bare.

He heard a noise. A strangled cry. The man was coming towards him with the knife outstretched. The blade flashed. Jack was baffled. He didn't move. When the tip was just feet from him he snapped into action and dived into the crawl space at his feet. Wrong. There was no way out. He kept going. He had no choice. Light leaked in from the room above; he could just see his way and by now he knew the layout. On the turn towards the centre of the model something glinted. A ring handle set into the wood. The eaves. He lifted the ring and tugged it. The door swung open, blocking the space. Beyond was complete darkness. Ignoring the tang of urine, hearing shuffling close by, Jack threw himself inside and pulled the door shut after him.

Blindly he scrabbled away from the door and then stopped. Desperate to get away, he had plunged on regardless of direction. He put out his left hand. Almost immediately he felt cold brick. That must be good. He was heading into the house, not towards the external wall at the side. A dead end in every sense. The bricks to his left were at the front of the house. Jack made himself take stock, as Stella would do. On his right was the partition, meaning he was inches from the attic of streets. He shuffled forward, mindful to make no sound, his progress tortuous. With each move he expected a firewall or a break in the eaves that would make this effort futile. He was attuned to the merest sound, pricking fear weighting his limbs in the suffocating darkness, his blood beating in his ears. His Host was tracking him, keeping pace as he passed by her bedroom, the old man's room, squeezed around the pipes for the kitchen sink. The tunnel went on, his luck thin but holding.

He encountered brick, rough and implacable. Dank and cold. He smacked at the unyielding surface. He had been crawling for a lifetime. Please let this be the wall at the other end of the mansion.

The fusty air was colder here. He must be beyond the boundary of the flat. Jack shut his eyes, the better to picture the house from the outside, framed through the iron gates. It wasn't symmetrical. A wing had been added on the Weltje Road side. A fire escape was attached to the back.

A fire escape required easy access. It made no sense to have a hatch into the tunnel at only one end, there must be other ways in. At any point she could open a door and find him. Jack swept his palms over the partition. He felt an indentation – no, a groove. He stopped. He might have imagined it. He willed it to be so. Again he forced himself to be logical, methodical like Stella. He took his time and listened to what the wood was telling him. There was a groove. He followed it up, a right angle, then along. Down again. He had traced a square. A hatch.

No handle on the inside, Jack flung himself against the aperture. The thump was like a depth charge on the seabed. Surely they had heard it? The wood had given slightly. He launched himself shoulder first and tumbled through.

He was on a rough wooden floor. He clambered to his feet, distantly registering pain in his hip bone from the fall. He was in a long low room, a mirror image of the attic of streets. Although it was completely bare. No streets. Nor were there beds or coffin wardrobes. A thin light drifted through the glazed panels of an external door. Jack wrenched on the handle. It was stuck fast. Push not pull. A typical mistake. He kicked at the bottom of the door and pushed.

The door swung out on shrieking hinges. Jack staggered forward and just prevented himself pitching over a balustrade. The fire escape shook perilously. The rivets had rusted; two had corroded completely away, freeing the ironwork from the wall. Jack gripped the railing as if it would save him. Despite himself, he appreciated the Victorian ironwork stairs spiralling down, each step decorated with a different pattern, diamonds, circles, crosses. Through the ornately fashioned metal he contemplated a breathtaking drop.

He placed a foot on the first step. The frame trembled. The metal was blistered with rusting sores and every so often spindles had sheared off, leaving a gap. As he risked each step, it seemed to Jack that the ground got no nearer.

Far below, the siren of an emergency vehicle whooped and

swooped along King Street towards Hammersmith Broadway. Above the grey brooding clouds came the rumble of a plane descending to Heathrow.

Five steps from the bottom he came upon a barricade of looped barbed wire. Jack gathered up his coat and vaulted over the side railing. Smacking his palms he looked up. The door was open, darkness within. No one had followed him. She didn't need to. She could use the stairs and meet him outside.

Jack tore across the yard, out of the gate, stifling a scream that welled in his chest. He did not stop until he reached Furnivall Gardens. He hung over the river wall close to the slick water rushing below. His reflection was fractured by the current. It might not be his reflection, but writhing black creatures struggling beneath the surface.

A thick pall of mist hung over the river, shrouding Hammersmith Bridge. His watch said a quarter past seven but it felt later. The enclosing fog and dark grey clouds massing at Barnes created a premature dusk.

The old man had attacked him. Why? What had he done wrong? Jack didn't need to ask. The answer was cold and stark. He had been late one too many times, the old man had lost his mind.

He narrowed his eyes at the bushes behind him. Cars passing on the Great West Road lit the branches and ivy tendrils; they pointed and writhed towards the sky. He detected no human movement. He had shaken off his Host. He went along the path a few paces, towards Chiswick Mall. He could never work with the old man again.

Jack checked his phone. Still no message from Stella. He pressed 'redial'. 'I am sorry I can't take your call.' Stella had promised to answer whenever he rang. She had broken this promise when she was out with Barlow. Jack told himself that because of the deep cleaning Stella would treat Barlow as a special client, but he could not kid himself, she liked the man. This was a mistake, but he couldn't say why.

Jackie had told him it was great that the article about Terry's funeral had netted Barlow. Deep cleaning was good for Stella; she had taken Terry's death badly. Jack had reread the piece in Jackie's press cuttings file and found nothing about deep cleaning. Yet, absorbed by the streets in the attic, Jack had let her reassure him; she was the marketing expert.

Stella was cleaning for Barlow now. That did not stop her answering the phone. He felt the stirring dread that he knew to trust. Stella had recognized the green glass because Barlow had used it on his wife's grave. Or so he had told her.

Sixty-Six

Saturday, 5 May 2012

David had been right about the weather. The sky was dark and, as she turned off the engine, a fine rain slicked the windscreen, making it opaque. Stella peered out of the side window. As Marian Williams had anticipated, there was no one at Dukes Meadows and thick scrub on the bank obscured the river. She felt more and more uneasy.

She had parked beneath an oak tree. The branches accentuated the gathering dark. Close by was a building that must be the boathouse. Stella doubted the café was open, but the cleaners might be there. This spurred her on. She liked to meet cleaners and was not due to meet Marian Williams for ten minutes.

When she got out of the van, a gust of wind whipped her hair. She put up the hood of her anorak. It blinkered her view and, nervous, she pulled it down again: better to be soaked than caught unawares. She trudged around the boathouse. Above the wind was a clinking, a sound that chilled. Stella rounded the corner and came upon boats stacked on towing racks. Wind funnelled between the long racing vessels made the hollow bell-like sound. Stella tripped on a metal rigger and grabbed at the boat's bow. St Michael. A sign, Jack would say.

Stella shielded her phone from the rain. She had no signal. If Marian wasn't coming she could not let her know.

She wended her way across the slipway; she would call Marian from the boathouse café. A set of folding doors were tight shut. She cupped her face to the glass. Inside was another boat and piles of gear related to rowing, life jackets, oars. No cleaners. The boathouse was what the name implied. No tea either. And no way to call Marian.

Above her a flag snapped in the wind, wrapping and unwrapping around the pole.

Stella zipped her anorak to her chin and struggled down to the shoreline. She slipped on the ramp and, faltering, became aware of the insidious lap of the tide. Water smacked the pillars of Chiswick Bridge. Feet away, the cover on a sewer outlet creaked as it lifted and dropped, each time expelling a seepage of liquid. The pipe was wide enough to hide in. Stella retreated. She knew how easy it was to be cut off when the river filled. This was an idiotic place to meet. Marian Williams was not thinking straight. Stella hurried along the towpath past the boathouse; looking up the grassy slope she was grateful to see her van, a blurred shape in the misty rain.

It felt as if she were in remote countryside cut off from the city. On another evening Dukes Meadows might be scenic, but tonight the area was fraught with threat. David's story of the dead woman propped against the tree was too real, too possible.

A layer of mist was suspended over the river, tinged with red. Stella caught the looming bulk of the brewery; the red tinge came from the light of the Budweiser logo. David had said that in 1959 a policeman described Elizabeth Figg as apparently sunbathing, gazing over the river towards the Watneys brewery.

The willow tree was on a sloping verge between the road and the towpath. Stella stumbled on thick twisting roots and steadied herself on the trunk. Elizabeth Figg's body was discovered right here. She stared out through long trailing fronds that swept wildly in the wind and saw the glow of the brewery sign – Budweiser now. Then swirls of mist obliterated it. She turned to the tree and heard herself whisper: 'Rest in peace, Elizabeth.' She agreed with David, it was important to remember the dead.

She hurried along the track, now harder to see in the fading light. Wreaths of fog parted and she saw that her van was the only vehicle by the boathouse.

Marian was fifteen minutes late. Stella got back in the van. She was damp and cold and wished herself back in David Barlow's light sunny kitchen. She was startled by a noise on the windscreen; hailstones bounced off the bonnet. She flicked on her wipers, but the chips of ice made them sluggish and the screech-screech of the blades frayed her nerves. She was stuck here. Until she could see properly she could not leave.

After a grindingly long time, the hail reverted to the mizzling rain. Green and brown smudges resolved into the willow tree. Someone was standing under it. Marian had been there all along. Stella depressed the button and the glass slid down. She breathed air heavy with sodden vegetation and river mud. There was no one.

She reversed jerkily on to the road. She would call Marian when she was out of the dead zone.

A figure stepped out of the blackness. Stella slammed on the brake and the van went into a skid; boats zoomed towards her; she heaved on the handbrake. The van turned full circle and came to a stop.

A face was at the window. With relief, Stella recognized David Barlow.

Sixty-Seven

Saturday, 5 May 2012

Fog floated across from the river; it wrapped itself around the boats and made phantoms of trees along the bank; wisps caught like tendrils around the wing mirrors. The wind had dropped and the chinking sound of the boats by the shore had ceased. Stella had left the engine running, the sound lost in the muffled quiet.

'I hope I didn't scare you.' Stanley sat on his lap; head back, chest puffed, he darted swift looks about him. Plain curiosity, she decided. Nothing suggested he sensed the supernatural. Stella's fear finally evaporated.

David's hair hung in dripping strands. His collar up, he warmed his hands at the van's heating vents. That he had turned up in this God-forsaken place was too good to be true. Now she had guessed he was in his sixties, she reflected that he looked much younger. In the dim light his profile, lean and spare, took her breath away.

She gave a sudden laugh. 'I was already scared.'

'I did wonder at your friend suggesting here.' David made a porthole in his steamed-up side window. 'I had to see that you were all right.'

'Thanks.' Stella wanted to say she was pleased but couldn't think how to phrase it.

'The tree where they found her is over there.'

'I'd forgotten about that.' Stella didn't say she had gone out of her way to find the willow tree and had whispered to Elizabeth Figg. He might think her odd. Instead: 'You said you were off out.'

'I wish I could postpone, since your friend's let you down.' He stroked the dog. 'But I can't.' His thigh was centimetres from Stella's knee. 'Call it deep cleaning or tying up loose ends. ' He rested his hand on the dog's shoulder.

Stella braced herself for some personal stuff. It was a bit soon, she told herself. She could tell him about the blue folder. He had remembered Elizabeth Figg; she was sure he would understand.

David must be a little afraid, for, as Jack always did when they were in the streets where the men had been murdered, he pressed the mechanism on the handle and locked the van's doors.

'Next week.' Stella reached out and touched his hand.

Sixty-Eight

Saturday, 5 May 2012

'What is your name?'

'Myra Thornton.'

The paramedics – a man and a lady – were being nice. They lifted Daddy on to a stretcher. It would be touch and go, they warned. She could go with Daddy in the ambulance; Michael was too little. She ordered him to clean his teeth and go to bed.

All the way down the five flights of stairs, she said a prayer to the Angel. 'Please don't let Daddy die.' She clutched his hand and the Angel's jewels dug into her palm. Jade blesses whatever it touches.

Stella Darnell was pretending to be her friend. Mary had been going to invite her for tea. She never asked friends back in case they asked about the empty bedroom. She was proud of her new friend and it was all she could do not to tell Daddy. Not a new friend. She had no old friends. Daddy would forbid it so she didn't. Stella had usurped her trust. Terry Darnell would be proud that Marian had worked out who was in the office when the printer was used. He would disown his daughter. After what she had done, Stella was not a friend.

I'm your friend.

You're my brother. Anyway I don't care about friends, you don't miss what you've never had.

Yes, you do.

The cleaner was not meant to be her friend. She was her salvation. She had led her to David Henry Barlow of Aldensley

Road. If she had not followed her from the cemetery, she would never have found him. Terry said good detection relied on legwork. She could have ignored Stella, laid her lilies at Michael's grave and come to work. God had rewarded her. Stella Darnell had betrayed her. Cleanliness is next to godliness. That was a lie, she would tell Daddy.

I killed the Hampson widow, Daddy. I was sorting it out. Like you do.

You didn't kill her, it was an accident.

I did.

You didn't. She fell. It was an accident.

I didn't call an ambulance. That was on purpose.

She banged her head and became dead. You didn't do that.

Daddy didn't know about David Henry Barlow and how clever she was.

I think you're clever!

'You don't count.' She said it out loud and a nurse passing her chair glanced at her. Myra Thornton smiled to show she was not mad.

Daddy will die and never know.

I know. Have some chocolate, I got it for you.

Stop playing with your food.

All she wanted was to do her job at the police station, come home, make tea and go to bed. She was never late. Every day. Job. Home. Tea. Bed.

Matthew Benson had been nasty when she said she couldn't see him. It had shocked her. David Barlow had been polite. He promised he would be punctual.

I like him.

No you don't, and close your mouth when you're eating, I can see mashed-up food.

David Henry Barlow only agreed when she suggested he donate the money to charity. He had laughed when she called it compensation, as if the word was too big for her. That wasn't nice. Daddy, don't die now.

'Myra Thornton?' The woman who had asked her to wait while they treated Daddy was back.

'Yes, doctor.' She struggled to her feet.

'You can see your father now.'

'How is he?'

'He's suffered a massive heart attack. You being there will comfort him.'

'I have to work.' She could not say that only one thing would bring comfort. He would want to hear that she had done what he asked.

'Come in for a minute or two? Your father is seriously ill.'

The doctor would think her unfeeling. Myra might tell her that she would do anything for her daddy.

At the door to the side ward, she paused. 'Is there a ladies'?' She didn't like saying 'toilets'.

'Up the corridor on the left. Can you find your way back here?'

Mary washed her hands like doctors did and kept washing until she had killed all the germs.

When she came out, the doctor had gone. She hurried to the lift. It was too late for Dukes Meadows. The cleaner had not called to see if she was all right.

Don't cry. I bought you chocolate.

'Brought not bought.' Myra croaked, she blinked back scalding tears.

The streets of Hammersmith were smeared with blood from where she had cut Daddy's hand and saved the man he thought was Michael. Except that couldn't be true because he wouldn't hurt Michael. He liked boys best. The doctor was wrong. It was God punishing her.

Don't stand there. Get the dustpan and brush!

She dropped her satchel and, squatting on the floor, collected up guttering, downpipes, shattered chimney pieces, chunks of brick wall, slabs of pavements, the gables and sign posts, lawns and lamp-posts. 'I'm helping you, Daddy.' She was hot with the effort.

She ducked inside his special trapdoor.

'Who were you talking to?'

Your brother.

'Michael's dead, Daddy.'

It should have been you.

She did not tell the doctor that it was her fault about the man. She had saved her brother from Daddy. She had saved his life. She had. She had.

When she had done what she was told, the Angel would set her free.

Mary heard the big front door open. She had left it on the latch for the ambulance crew and forgotten to lock it. She trotted down the stairs to the landing and looked over the banister. She nearly cried out with joy when she saw her.

She's come about me. Not you. She's being a detective.

Michael was right. It was too late to make a friend. She continued down to the basement and walked out through the basement door, noticing as she went that the putty around the side window was loose and needed mending.

Sixty-Nine

Saturday, 5 May 2012

Jack triggered a clangour of Big Ben chimes. He snatched his finger off the bell. No one came. The house was screened by a hydrangea bush; Jack bent down and peered through the letter-box. At the end of a passage was a table with a teapot.

He stepped away from the door and scoured the upstairs windows. All the curtains were shut. Stella had defended Barlow when Jack suggested he had something to hide. She didn't go as far as saying it was none of his business. Stella was his business.

He had failed Amanda; he would not fail Stella. Her haphazard judgement of character sent her sleepwalking into life-threatening situations. She would trust anyone who presented her with a cleaning challenge. He called Stella and again got her voicemail. He left a message, speaking loudly, as if she was behind the curtains. She must hear. 'Stell? Tell me you're OK.' The curtains did not move. 'Love Jack.' He was practically shouting. He rang off.

He couldn't call the police on the basis of a gut feeling. Stella for one would never forgive him.

A door at the side of the house was ajar. Jack crept down the passage and found himself in one of the neatest gardens he had ever seen. No weeds, and regimented daffodils defined three borders. The lawn could serve as a bowling green.

He felt churning fear. The enforced symmetry and compartmentalized order was the work of a True Host. Jack spent nights searching out such people while Stella attracted them in the

413

course of her work. Naturally she did; Hosts had high standards of hygiene.

He tried a sliding patio door into the kitchen. Locked. He nearly burst into tears. Two washed mugs stood on the draining board. Barlow had made Stella tea. Milky with one sugar. Jack caught his foot on something. A black bin bag spilled its contents on to the grass. He crouched down and stared, baffled. A picture of the Madonna and Child, several crucifixes. Signs. He got no satisfaction in being right.

The window panes above were blank and unheeding. Beyond them Jack visualized deeply cleaned rooms, no dirt, no stains; no proof of life. No proof. His imagination was at full pelt. What better way to dispose of incriminating evidence than get someone to do it for you? Then dispose of the cleaner.

He peered in through the glass of the sliding doors. On a wall beneath a clock was a picture. He cupped his hands around his face to block out reflection. It was a car. He made out a badge on the radiator. A Wolseley. The badge lit up when the engine was running. Stupid facts that Jack enjoying telling Stella. He racked his brains. When they were working on the Rokesmith case, Stella had explained the British vehicle registration system – facts her dad had told her. This car's plate had the suffix 'D': 1966.

Nineteen sixty-six was the year Stella was born. On 6 May that year the Moors Murderers were tried and sentenced. On the same day Michael Thornton was killed in a hit and run at Young's Corner. Forty-six years ago tomorrow.

A buzz in his pocket. At last Stella had texted. Following a lead. Will ring. Stella was not with Barlow. He exhaled deeply. Then he stiffened. Nothing in her text told him this. He didn't need to see Barlow's immaculate garden to know him. The man had a mind like his own; Jack knew him better than he knew himself. These were all signs that Barlow was capable of calmly executing revenge for the death of a small boy.

He rang Stella again. His heart was pounding louder than the rings. Answer!

'Stella Darnell. Please leave a …'

Why didn't she pick up? Surely Barlow wouldn't kill Stella. She didn't fit the victim profile. She hadn't run over a child. But nor had Amanda. Stella was going to tell her police administrator friend to warn Joel Evans's killer. Amanda had got in Barlow's way and paid the price. Barlow would not spare Stella if she got in the way of his lifelong goal.

Jack strode up the street, past a delicatessen; a bicycle chained to a bollard was easy to steal. A sign on a lamp-post gave the number for crime prevention advice. He could ring it.

My friend is with a killer, he is…

Hopelessly he willed the message to yield her whereabouts. Stella had texted an hour ago; he might already be too late. He had no way to warn her about Barlow.

Yes he did.

Beside the text bubble was the symbol of a key. He clicked on it. A map appeared. A blue pulsing dot told him Stella's location, or at least where she had been when she sent the message. Jack was puzzled.

Stella was at Mallingswood School.

'I have the missing jigsaw piece.'

'So do I, Amanda.'

The chawling rattle of a diesel engine coming from the Iffley Road end broke the early evening quiet. An orange light, like a beacon, was coming towards him.

Jack rushed out into the road.

Sixty-Nine

Saturday, 5 May 2012

The headlights flashed in her rear mirror. David took the Hogarth flyover. Stella flicked a short burst with her hazards in response and then joined the Great West Road. Moments later she was in Weltje Road. The digital display rolled to 9.33. David had not told her where he was going. What meeting was he having on a Saturday night? Stella looked up at the dark building. Built of dull grey stone, it was austere and forbidding. No one could live there. Her good mood waned. Whom was David seeing? She berated herself for being distracted; for caring.

Her phone was registering a signal; there were no messages from Jack. It could take a while for data to download. She texted him suggesting they meet at Terry's. She would go there now and have a shepherd's pie. It seemed a very long time since she'd eaten Mrs Barlow's cake.

Meanwhile, Marian was a priority. She had sounded definite about meeting at Dukes Meadows so it was strange that she had not come. Stella did not have her mobile number. She was about to drive off when she remembered Marian had called her. She looked at her phone. Caller unknown. She must have been calling from Hammersmith Police Station.

Stella wanted to call David but that was ridiculous; he had just left her and he was clearly in a hurry. She could still feel his cheeks against hers, smell his aftershave, the silky feel of his hair through her fingers. He was better looking than David Bowie. She brought herself back to Marian Williams. What would

Terry do? He had looked out for her. He would want Stella to check she was all right. Stella dialled Marian's direct line at the police station.

'Cashman speaking.'

'Martin! I was trying for Marian Williams. It's Stella Darnell.'

'This is her extension. I'm chasing up paperwork and doubtless messing up Marian's system.' He laughed. 'As I've got you, can I say what a great job your guys are doing?'

'It's about Marian.' Stella was now seriously worried. 'She asked to meet me after work. I don't normally.' She was flustered. 'This is confidential… about her husband.'

'Her husband?'

'He prevented her coming tonight.' She should have rung as soon as Marian didn't turn up.

'Stella, I think you've got the wrong end of the stick. Marian's not married.'

Marian Williams had never said she was married. It was Stella who had decided the bruise was inflicted by a husband. 'A partner then.'

'No idea if she's seeing anyone. Have to say it's unlikely, Marian's big love is her job. She didn't front up this evening because her father was blue-lighted into A and E a couple of hours ago. She left me a message and I've rung the hospital, but they said she'd had to go to work. On a Saturday! Typical. I'm sending her packing when she appears.' He hesitated. 'As you're her friend, I'll give you her details. She'll appreciate that you care.'

Stella supposed that she did care.

She squeezed the address and telephone number into today's entry in her diary, next to the address where the Thorntons had lived, which Lucille May had given her. The two addresses were the same. Mallingswood House, King Street, London W6.

Stunned, Stella looked at the gaunt mansion looming in the sodium darkness. Mallingswood House. She was outside it now.

Seventy

Saturday, 5 May 2012

The iron gates were unlocked; the chain dangled from the lock. Jack couldn't see a light in the attic window. He pushed through the gates and ran across the turning circle, heedless of the noise his shoes made on the gravel. The front door of the mansion was wide open; inside all was dark. This was terribly wrong.

He tripped on the marble step at the bottom of the staircase and fell on to one knee. He ignored the searing pain and raced up the stairs. The key had gone from the lintel. The flat door was ajar. He blundered in.

'Stella!' His throat tore. At the same time hands grappled with him, holding him. He raised his hand to punch his assailant, fleetingly thinking he had never punched anyone and that he didn't want to.

'Jack!'

The passage light came on.

'Stella! You're OK! I went to Barlow's and when you weren't there…' He took her hands. Then he remembered. 'Where is he?' He looked beyond her down the passage. The door to the streets was open. It was never open.

'How come you are here? Did you speak to Lucille May?' Stella hadn't answered his question.

'Has he hurt you?'

'Who?'

'Barlow.' Jack suddenly felt foolish. He could be wrong about him. No, he couldn't.

'Of course not.' Stella was walking towards the open door. Jack pushed past her, tripped on her umbrella and stumbled. He was blindly aware he must stop her going in. No one behind the door. The house was silent. Too silent. There were too many rooms; he couldn't control them all.

'I agreed to meet Marian Williams at Dukes Meadows. She didn't come. This is where she lives.' Stella chatted on, seemingly unaware of any threat.

'We should get out of here.' He took her arm, alert for the slightest sound.

'… Martin said her father's in hospital. She's not there and she's not here. The most extraordinary coincidence, Jack, could be one of your signs—.' She shook off his arm. 'You went to David's house?'

Brown stains were smeared on the walls and reddish-brown footprints sketched out a mad dance on the floorboards. Jack lifted his foot. It was sticky. Spots of blood made a trail towards the crawl space. He had thought the old man was trying to kill him. Barlow had got to them both. So intent was Jack on escaping, he had not thought the old man and his daughter could be the victims.

'Jack, are you listening?'

He didn't recognize the room. The floorboards were littered with splinters of wood, shards of plaster and torn strips of cardboard. 'He's here somewhere.'

'I know where David is. Will you leave it! Why were you at his house?' Stella was by the model. Along its edges were brown smears of dried blood. 'Marian's father must have cut himself when he fell.' She leant over it. 'There's a horse trough on that corner, isn't that Britton Drive?' She straightened. 'And that's Spelling Way.' She faltered. 'Is this how you knew?'

He saw it in her eyes. He had broken his promise to her and broken into this house. The *A–Z* woman wasn't like other Hosts, but Stella wouldn't see that. A broken promise was a betrayal.

He looked properly at the model. One section was untouched. He went over to it. Aldensley Road was as it had been earlier this evening. There was the hydrangea bush spilling out over a front garden wall and the delicatessen on the bend. There was a taxi turning into the street from Iffley Road. While most of the streets were strewn with rubble, like a city strafed by bombs, Aldensley Road had been spared the damage as if in the eye of the storm. The room tipped, something didn't add up.

'Barlow killed the drivers.' As he said this Jack felt something was not right.

'David hasn't killed anyone,' Stella stormed. 'What were you doing at his house?'

'Looking for you.' He could not say he was worried about her. Stella would tell him she could look after herself. In a way she'd be right. Jack blinked to clear the fog in his head. He had missed something. 'There's a picture of a Wolseley in his kitchen, a grey saloon like the one the police were looking for. Then there's the green glass.' He wasn't listening to the words, his mind racing. David Barlow wasn't seeking revenge. He snatched at the air with a hand as if he might catch the answer.

'It's David's first car.' Stella gripped her umbrella under her arm like a rifle. 'He was eighteen and the green glass is for his wife's grave, I told you.' She fired her umbrella at the model. 'This is Marian's patch. Extraordinary that she made this.'

'Who's Marian?' The mental fog was clearing.

'You know! My friend at the station. She didn't turn up at Dukes Meadows. I was trying to tell you. She lives here. It's the weirdest coincidence. The Thorntons moved to this godforsaken place after British Grove, Lucie May said. That's why I was here. I rang Marian and got Cashman, he gave me the same address.'

'Your friend Marian didn't meet my Host when she brought you flowers that night for the simple reason she was my Host.'

Stella said nothing. He ploughed on.

'She didn't connect me to you or…' He couldn't bring himself to say that Williams would have killed Stella.

Stella folded her arms. 'Or she would have murdered me.'

'Marian and Mary, they are the same person.' Jack felt his way as it fell into place. 'Odd I didn't see the flowers.' He had seen them. The lilies he had squashed near the grave of Stephen Parsons. His Host had misled him. Clever.

'Marian is not a killer.' Stella said in a monotone. Jack noticed she had not mentioned Barlow. It was as if she had not heard what he had said.

'Bear with me. Marian Williams lied to you about what Amanda said when she came to the police station.'

'Marian is law-abiding.' Stella restored a grit bin near the remains of Barons Court Station and repositioned a number 27 bus passing St Paul's Church on the Broadway. 'She doesn't have brothers and sisters. She told me.'

'Strictly speaking, that's true. Her brother is dead.' Jack straightened a lamp standard on Glenthorne Road. 'The need to avenge Michael's death is eating away at her.' The woman who had taken his street atlas was after all a True Host. He had wanted his *A–Z* back. He couldn't explain to Stella that he had intended to keep his promise to her: it sounded silly. Then he had seen the photograph of the family in the bedroom and got the feeling of dread he knew was a sign. Once he'd met the old man in the attic of streets, he hadn't been able to leave.

'Stay there!' He crept into the passage. His Host's – Mary's – bedroom door was shut. He turned the handle. The room was as before. Neatly made bed, coffin wardrobe, bedside table with a full glass of water. No one there. Jack took the photograph.

'There.' He thrust it at Stella. 'The Thorntons, in happier times. Douglas Ford told me that Michael Thornton had a sister and Jackie has just confirmed it, she was at school with the sister. Her name was Mary. You know her as Marian.'

'Not that happy.' Stella tilted the picture to the light. 'Only the boy's smiling.' She paused. 'Michael Thornton was beautiful.' Beautiful was not one of Stella's words; she went for understatement.

Jack looked again at the family. The father blurred, intent on being in the picture before the shutter snapped. His wife looking off camera as if preoccupied, perhaps envisioning what tragedy lay ahead. Like an angel. 'It's as if the sister was blotted out. There's no reference to her in articles about the death and Lucie never mentioned her. Why? And why has this Mary changed her name to Marian?'

'Marian would not do anything illegal,' Stella intoned as if she hadn't heard him.

'She said Amanda Hampson had found out about Charlie passing his advanced driving test. Yet the police already knew. This is what Amanda actually showed her.' He unfolded the torn Parkinson's Disease Society letter he had found in Amanda's temple. 'I made a mistake. I thought Amanda had saved this to show Martin Cashman, but in fact she did show the administrator this and Marian Williams realized it was a vital piece of evidence. It was, as Amanda said, the missing jigsaw piece. Marian knew it too.'

Stella read out loud: '"Change attitudes, find a cure, join us…"'

'Read the back.'

'"The fifteenth of March, eleven p.m., Marquis Way W6. Porphyrion". Then pounds signs and exclamation marks.' Stella flicked the letter with her index finger. 'Charlie Hampson must have been excited. At school we were told to be sparing with exclamation marks. Why didn't Marian tell me this?'

Jack watched Stella. She was flittering about with the model, righting fallen masonry, signs. Clearing up. 'She was worried you'd spot the pattern of deaths. What she didn't know was that you had already spotted it. Or Terry had.'

'Marian worshipped my dad. She would have wanted to help him, not commit crimes herself.' Stella continued her repair work. 'Even revenge for a brother wouldn't make her break the law.'

Jack listened for the front door closing far below. The house creaked and groaned as if someone was moving stealthily closer. 'I think Terry suspected her. He never showed her the blue folder.' He tried to master his nerves.

'If Amanda Hampson hadn't fallen, she would have told you what she really said,' Stella persisted. 'She would have got hold of Cashman eventually and Marian would have been found out. Surely she wouldn't take the risk.'

'Our killer takes risks. We worked that out.' He should tell her about the crawl space: it was a means of escape if they needed it. 'Besides, she covered herself. Amanda didn't fall. Marian visited her that evening and killed her.'

'I know I'm not famed for insight, but this is wrong. Marian wants to make a difference. She loves her job; she is not a cold-blooded murderer.' Stella thudded her umbrella tip on the floorboards in time to her words.

'As Mary she is making a difference. She is murdering reckless and unrepentant drivers who kill boys like her brother.' He paused and looked at Stella. 'I think you're insightful.' Jack felt himself reddening. Stella had seen what he sometimes felt about her. She never failed to surprise him.

Stella was reading the torn letter. 'Porphyrion! I've heard of that.'

'Porphyrion Insurance. Leonard Bast, the man in *Howards End* who lost his umbrella.' He indicated Stella's umbrella. 'Leaving Porphyrion led to Leonard's death. Porphyrion has lured these drivers to their deaths, no doubt with the promise of money. I heard her on the phone.' The murmured voice on the landing, just feet from him. Jack brushed loose plaster off his new tunnel, dimly pleased that it had survived the onslaught. 'Marian Williams – or Mary – relies on her victims not being Forster fans. Greed guarantees they will meet her at a late hour, even on a Sunday, on a secluded road.' He took the paper from Stella. 'Impatient, they speed along the long straight roads. She steps out. They swerve. Bang! Mary Thornton melts into the night.'

'When Martin told her I had found Mrs Hampson's body, she looked odd. I guessed she was jealous it was me and not her.'

'She saw the net closing in.'

As if viewing the landscape from an aeroplane, Jack saw muted patterns like archaeological remains invisible from the ground. Spelling Way, Tolworth Street, Britton Drive. The missing buildings had altered perspectives, creating new views across the city. He caught a glint, like the glowing blue dot that had led him to Stella. It was not a GPS signal. He raked among the debris. A green glass chip. He moved efficiently around the miniature version of Hammersmith and found more. 'She's marked each death on her father's model,' he said quietly.

Stella peered at the remains of Marquis Way. 'There're three chips. That's wrong; there were only two deaths there: Paul Vickery and Harvey the shoe man.'

Jack could feel Stella's detachment. They were not working together. He looked at the model. Glass chips were glued to the pavement beside the wasteland on Marquis Way. They were as big as boulders in the road.

'It's another new murder site.' He breathed. 'We have the deaths for every photograph and an extra one in Spelling Way which we think is where she'll kill Joel Evans's driver.' He shifted a skip blocking the entrance to a defunct industrial unit..

'David is meeting Porphyrion tonight, that's how I've heard of it!' Stella gasped. 'He asked me if a person could be forgiven for killing a child. I thought he meant Myra Hindley and Ian Brady.' She paced the room, seemingly oblivious to the blood. 'He said it was like in the book. I assumed he was referring to the Bible.'

Jack saw it. 'I'm being stupid! David Barlow isn't the killer.'

'I could have told you that.'

'He was the first driver.'

'What are you talking about now?' Stella had gone pale.

'He killed Michael Thornton. Stella, somehow Marian has found out about David Barlow.' Jack couldn't look at her. He could not bear her pain. 'The book was *Howards End*. If Barlow knows Porphyrion isn't real, he might not go.'

'This is his car.' She held up a bright orange Ford Fiesta.'

Jack had not seen the car on the model before, it was new.

But he had seen it before. It was the car that pulled up for petrol when he was in the garage talking to Douglas Ford. The man had gone sheet-white as if he had seen a ghost. He had seen a ghost. Barlow had been standing behind Jack in the shop. His face had haunted Douglas Ford for forty-six years. After Jack's questions, Ford must have believed Barlow had come for him. Jack understood why all the other cars on the model were grey. 'Grey was the colour of the car seen leaving King Street the day Michael was run over.' It was a sign. Mary did have a mind like his own.

'David knew about Michael Thornton's sister. He said she was called Myra. Her parents changed her name after the Moors Murderers were caught so she wouldn't be teased. He was worried that the girl who saw the car hit Michael would never forget it.' Stella spoke like a robot.

'He was worried the girl would not forget him. The police only knew it was a grey saloon. Douglas Ford was the sole witness and he never told anyone that Mary was there. Only the driver could have known that a girl witnessed the accident. Mary Thornton told her parents she was making the tea.'

'None of this makes sense.' Stella's voice was hollow. Jack could see that it was making sense.

'When Marian, or whatever she's called, rang this afternoon she said Dukes Meadows wasn't far from me. I had said I was at a client's house. She knew where I was.' Stella was pale, her eyes unblinking, the pupils dark.

'We led her to David Barlow. I think Marian was there that night on Marquis Way when we hid behind Wilkins Laundry. She wouldn't have recognized the van then, but she's seen it many times since.' The railway lines were exposed where his newly constructed tunnel had split open; everywhere he looked was displaced street furniture. A telephone junction box was ripped from the ground, tiny wires tangling. 'Spotting clues, cross-checking the database, consulting files, it's her job. She learnt from Terry.'

'David was burgled,' Stella said tonelessly. 'His wife made him go to the police station.'

'Then he will be on the database. Unwittingly we helped Mary Thornton find the man she's wanted to kill for most of her life. She left Aldensley Road here because it's where her brother's killer lives. Somehow we led her there. What car does she drive?'

Stella shook her head. 'A Mini, I think.'

'There was a Mini parked near your van outside the cemetery this afternoon. It pulled away when we did. She trailed you to Barlow's and recognized him.'

'Why should she think he ran over her brother?'

'She probably didn't, but if it were me, I'd run a check on him and then I'd discover that he once owned a grey Wolseley and sold it after the accident.' Still something wasn't right. Jack didn't voice the nagging doubt.

'David wasn't burgled. I found the stuff under the bath. He believes his wife was punishing him.'

'Sounds like she set him up. Faked a theft and then made him walk into the police station to report it. A place he'd avoided for decades. She knew he was too cowardly to confess. No wonder he's got you deep cleaning. You're expunging the first Mrs Barlow.' He was hot with sudden anger.

Stella glanced at the door. He turned too. It was open, but the light in the corridor was out; the bulb had blown. The darkness was intense, suspended. They should leave.

'David's not a killer.' Stella was stony-faced.

'No? He killed a boy forty-odd years ago and drove on. The man who killed Joel Evans confessed. So did Charlie Hampson, although probably he had no choice. Barlow never has. He's put the Thornton family through torture. Pure evil.' Overtaken by rage, Jack spat the words.

Stella's eyes flashed. 'You've changed your tune.'

Yes, he had 'changed his tune'. Stella had not refused to take Barlow's calls as she had his.

Stella looked at her watch. 'It's half ten. In an hour and a half it'll be the sixth of May. While we stand here arguing, Marian is going to kill David!'

And he wanted her to stop calling him 'David'. Jack blew dust out of the District line tunnel. It was beyond repair.

'I'm calling the police.' Stella pulled out her phone.

'To say what? One of their valued employees – whose father is critically ill in hospital – is going to commit murder. We have bags of green glass and pictures of long straight roads that prove it? Not forgetting information obtained illegally from their database. Cashman will tell you to stick to the day job. Or worse.'

'We have to warn David before it's too late.'

Jack swept grit off Hammersmith flyover. 'You know, I don't really mind if we are too late.'

He looked up. Stella had gone.

Seventy-One

The house in Aldensley Road was in darkness. No orange car. Jack jumped out before Stella braked. There was no sign of him by the time she got to the front door. She leant on the doorbell. She frowned at the Big Ben chimes.

She ran down the side alley and found Jack tugging at the patio door.

'Can you open this?'

'You're the one who breaks into houses.' She was crisp.

'Don't you have a key? The man's your client.'

'No, David was always here.'

Compared to the afternoon when the kitchen had been richly warm with spring sunshine and the scent of freshly mown grass on the breeze mingling with David Barlow's aftershave, to Stella it now resembled a dark, uninviting cave. She shone her torch through the window. The beam reflected in the polished glass and only a dim glow penetrated. A spark of light caught the electric clock and another bounced off the photograph of the car. Gradually appliances and cupboards, table and chairs took shape.

She shone the torch across the garden and began to tremble. The chairs had been put away; the table was a solitary object beneath the tree. David had put the chairs out for the tea. Three chairs. She shivered.

'What was he wearing?' Jack's voice out of the gloom made her start.

'I can't remember. Trousers, um…'

'Funny that.' Jack's voice was metallic. 'Did he have that on?' He nodded at the glass.

Stella directed the torch at the door again. The jacket she had found under the bath was on the back of a chair. She told Jack about finding it. As she did so, she felt the truth of what he had said. David had killed Michael Thornton. And he had worn the jacket that day. Somehow Jennifer Barlow had known and she had hidden first the jacket upstairs under the bath and later the pictures and the crucifix under the downstairs bath, a punishment that was long and slow. He had unintentionally made a false insurance claim. Stella didn't need to check to know that the insurance company would be the same one that Robert Thornton had worked for. Mrs Barlow had implicated her husband in a lesser crime than driving away from the scene of an accident and forced him to deal with the police. Jack said David had tortured the Thorntons; his wife had tortured him. Drip on drip. Her death didn't release him. David wanted Stella to set him free.

She rang David's phone again. The kitchen lit up with a bluish tinge.

'It's his phone.' Jack moved closer to her.

She watched David's handset judder across the counter, propelled by the vibration, and turn an inexorable circle. At the edge it tipped off and hit the floor, a muffled splintering audible through the double glazing. The ringing in Stella's phone ceased.

There was a scrape on the gravel. Stella swallowed a yelp. A figure emerged from behind the water butt. Marian Williams. Stella's legs went to jelly. She was holding something. A gun. They were in point-blank range.

'Can I help?' It wasn't Marian.

'We were looking for Mr Bar—' Stella began.

Jack cut in. 'David invited us for an aperitif but we're a little late. Or it's the wrong day!' He put on his 'Lucille May' charm.

It was a bicycle pump. Equally lethal in the wrong hands.

'Dave's gone out.' The woman swung the pump down.

'Did he say where?' Jack took Stella's hand, probably intending the neighbour to think them the epitome of a happy couple. He was wearing Terry's gloves, which absurdly heartened her.

'Pub by the river – what's it called? An animal. The Ram, that's it. He said Jennifer would be pleased. Bless her, Jennifer was difficult to please. Dave didn't put a foot wrong, but she still found fault. I never speak ill of the dead, but how he managed all those years with her on at him every turn… That man was a flippin' angel.'

She led the way back to the street. 'Grief plays havoc with the memory. Dave's got to start again. Bound to be hard at first.' She ducked up the path of the adjacent house. 'I'll say you called.' The door slammed.

'That's the pub by the Bell Steps. Come on.' Stella pulled her van keys from her pocket. A paper fell on to the path. She picked it up. To her horror she saw it was the green form she had taken from Paul Vickery's file. She had forgotten to return it. Jack had seen it, he picked it up. 'Terry signed out the file from the General Registry,' she said quickly before he said anything.

'I wonder why.'

'We know why. He had a hunch that turns out to be true.' Stella had a glimmer of pride for her dad.

'Vickery was killed on Marquis Way.' Jack flicked the form. 'Terry already knew, that's why he took the photograph.'

'Marian must have been checking what the police knew about the accidents. Maybe she thought they were on to her.' Stella took back the green form. 'We need to get to the Ram before he leaves. Not like him to forget his phone.' She didn't know what David was like. She didn't know him at all.

'He didn't forget.' Jack shut the gate. 'He won't want it with him. Phones are tracking devices. By leaving it behind, he's killed the scent.

'Now we know where he is, come on!'

'No point.'

'There's every point.' Stella stopped herself yelling.

'He's not there.'

'How do you know?'

'Would Barlow tell the neighbours his business? That woman wasted no time telling us. He was ensuring that no one – you specifically – knows where he is. The bicycle-pump woman was his decoy.'

Stella did not want to think about David. 'Mary Thornton was only fourteen when Colin Coleman died.'

'Kids commit murder and this is an MO for a teenager. No weapons. All she had to do was distract a speeding vehicle. Children do that unintentionally, as we have seen.'

'Lucille May said Carol Jones saw a man leaving the scene of Harvey Gray's crash.'

'She could have been wrong, it was dark.'

'She said a tall figure. Marian is not tall. However, Lucille May is.' She paused. The journalist had gone out of her way to buy the house where the Thorntons had lived. She had kept from them that the dead boy had a sister.

As if he could track her thinking, Jack said, 'It's not Lucie. Why would she give you the Thorntons' address at the school? I heard Marian, or Mary, on the phone. I know she was talking to an intended victim.' Jack had his faraway look. 'Probably Matthew Benson. By leading her to David Barlow, we have saved Benson's life, for what it's worth.'

Stella had heard Marian on the phone too. But for all Jack's crystal ball perception, he had not actually talked to her. Sneaking into her flat was not the same. 'What if she had to take over when the tall man messed up the Gray murder by being spotted and her only victim is Charles Hampson in 2009 on Phoenix Way? She can't use it again: thanks to Amanda's campaigning there's CCTV.' She thought about the laminated map in Terry's study and the different coloured pin she had put on Spelling Way.

'Marian doesn't mark the death on her model afterwards.' She slid into the driver's seat. 'She puts the glass there before. She would have been about to murder Joel Evans' killer, Matthew

Benson, but now she's found the first driver. The third chip in Marquis Way is for David!'

'That's it! Better the street you know. After tomorrow she won't care if the likes of Lucie May – or us – spot a collision pattern, her task will be finished.' Jack scrambled in beside her.

Stella read the clock, two minutes past midnight. 'After today.'

She had swung left on to Ducane Road and they were passing Wormwood Scrubs prison, the turrets gaunt against the night sky, when Jack finally spoke. So quietly she had to ask him to repeat it.

'I think I know who the tall man is.'

Seventy-Two

Sunday, 6 May 2012

'After three hundred yards turn left.'

A flashing light cut a downward trajectory across the Milky Way and a dull roar like distant thunder signalled the descent of an aeroplane to Heathrow Airport.

'Turn left.'

The few lamp standards on Marquis Way cast cones of light on the pavements.

'Slow down.' Jack's voice was disembodied, a shadowy form picked out by the dashboard lights.

Stella let the van crawl. In the rear mirror, she registered that the lights of the Westway had gone. Ahead there were no more lamp-posts.

'Pull in here.' Jack turned off the satnav.

It was where they had parked last week: there was the sign with the fierce dog, warning trespassers from the desolate waste-land. The chain-link fence was upright; Stella vaguely expected to find the model's devastation mirrored in reality.

'This doesn't feel right. Why isn't David here?'

'We're early.'

'Perhaps he won't come? He doesn't care about money.'

'Everyone cares about money. Barlow has been building up to this.' Jack narrowed his eyes.

'What's that supposed to mean?'

'I thought Barlow wanted deep cleaning to purge his guilt. In fact it was to rid the house of his wife. To start again. Drive past

433

Vickery's tree. Keep a steady pace and if you see her, act as if you haven't. Drive to the end of the road and send me a blank text.'

'What? Where will you be?'

'We have to split up. I'll be behind the laundry. Where's your phone?'

'Jack, splitting up is precisely what we shouldn't do.'

'One at each end of the street and we might save Barlow.' Jack did up his coat. 'When you see his car, flash your lights.' He fixed her with a look. 'Don't try to block his path to make him stop. Flash your lights, promise?'

'He'll stop.'

She didn't hear his reply. It sounded like: 'Don't bank on it.'

'Let's stay together,' she urged, now properly scared.

Jack was gone before Stella could protest. She watched him run across to the derelict laundry. Stella glanced over at the dark expanse beyond the fence on her right. When she looked back at the laundry, Jack had gone.

Her finger hovered over the emergency services key on her phone. What emergency would she report? Jack was right; their evidence didn't stand up. She couldn't admit to stealing the printout or the green form. Hours ago she had given Cashman the impression Marian was her friend. If she told him Marian was a killer he wouldn't even humour her. She was a criminal too.

Stella maintained five miles an hour. Her hands were clammy and slipped on the wheel. She stared at the road and her mind played tricks, conjuring flitting figures in the shadows. The ghosts of Paul Vickery and Harvey Gray. Her teeth were chattering. She clenched her jaw as she passed a skip, jammed with rubbish, blocking the entrance to a disused industrial unit. The perfect place for Marian to hide.

A buzz vibrated in her pocket. The central screen lit up with a call. Suzie. Mum! Stella wanted to tell her everything. Her mum would solve it. Mechanically she pressed the cancel button on her steering wheel. Her mum could not help her now.

She passed a warehouse, its corrugated iron roof sagging. 'Gina-Ware Plastics Ltd'. Metal grilles screened the doors and windows; weeds flourished in the parking lot. Gina-Ware had moved on. Stella should do the same. There was the telegraph pole where Gray had died. Despite Jack's instructions she touched the brake. If Marian was out there, she could talk her out of it.

The van juddered. Stella pumped the accelerator. It jerked forward and then lost power. She leant over the wheel as if to coax it on. The engine died. The van freewheeled a few metres but the road had a gentle upward gradient and even as she willed it forward the van trickled to a halt. Stella slapped the wheel. The fuel gauge needle was at 'zero'. She had been so preoccupied with getting to Dukes Meadows that when she left David's she had forgotten to fill up.

A coil of smoke or mist rose from the tarmac, snaking and twisting. Terry had explained the phenomenon; she couldn't recall what he had said. What would he say now? She snatched her keys from the steering column and, slotting them between her fingers, got out of the van. To her left, a ramp sloped to a basement car park. She considered pushing the van there, out of sight, but she couldn't manage it by herself.

The road was quiet. Too quiet. The tree and the laundry were lost in darkness; she had no sense Jack was there. The telegraph pole was closer, surely? Jack said they would be more effective alone. On her own she was no use at all.

She was in full view, exposed. Stella ran down into the car park. Avoiding patches of oil in the bays, she slipped behind one of the stanchions. Closing her mind to the acrid drift of urine, she edged around the pillar, disorientated by shifting shadows and her own cold fear. Stupid to come here: the underground expanse was treacherous. She was electric with panic. Marian was behind one of the columns, black rectangles stretching away into the darkness. Stella's terror was sharpened by the constant spattering of a pipe. She went very cold. In a corner bay, where no light penetrated, was what could be a car. Panic overtook her. She rushed back up the ramp to the street.

She teetered on the kerb. Her job was to stop David, to save him. She whipped around. Behind her was a practice tower for firefighters. Smoky clouds moving fast behind gave the impression the tower was swaying, the pretend windows gaping cavities. There was someone at the top one. Stella squinted up. No, she had imagined it.

Her phone buzzed, she fumbled in her anorak.

Sorry to miss you. At hospital. Fancy coffee tomorrow? Marian.

A flood of relief engulfed her. Marian was not Mary Thornton. She was a civilian administrator at Hammersmith Police Station. She was her friend. Martin Cashman had told Marian Stella was concerned and, as he had predicted, she was touched. They could meet in the café; Marian would see her return the umbrella. Stella would explain about the green form, even the printout.

Stella texted, Meet you at the Broadway – she stopped. The text was a trick. Marian wasn't at the hospital or the school. She was in the car park, or the tower, somewhere close, biding her time.

She broke into a run. She had left the headlamps on in the van. She made for the beams of light. Her legs were leaden and she had to force them to work.

She had not left the lights on. The van was behind her.

The strong lights dazzled her and she tripped on the kerb. David. She shouted and waved. The interior lamp filled his car with a cosy glow. It cut his visibility so he didn't see her. He was driving very fast.

The car sped on, orange dulled to brown. In its headlights she saw white wings, spear-limbs flailing. A creature soared. Then the impression of flight was over and it plummeted, to land with a sickening flump on the tarmac.

Jack!

*

'Ambulance and police!' Stella yelled into her phone. She blundered through a list of landmarks. 'A telegraph pole, tree, car park ...'

A bundle of sacking dumped perfunctorily in the gutter. Stella recoiled. Jack's beautiful face was streaked with war paint like hers as a Red Indian. It wasn't paint, it was blood. The unbearable had happened.

'What is the name of the street, Stella? Are you in danger from traffic? Have you cleared the airways? Two fingers under the chin...'

Jack was stroking Mary Thornton's hair from her face, the same motion over and over. She was speaking, her lips barely moving. He bent close to her, his hair falling forward over his forehead as he listened. His other hand cupped her chin. Blood, bright and viscous, blossomed through her white blouse. Stella drew closer.

Mary Thornton gazed at Jack, her face white as marble. His voice was a lullaby: 'You're safe, Myra. It's over. Sweet dreams, sweet angel.' He repeated the incantation. 'It's over, Myra. Sweet angel.'

'Marquis Way W6. Near the Westway. Halfway down. It's by a tree.' Stella stared at Marian and saw a child. Mary Thornton. Speaking into the phone she said, 'The tree is a sweet chestnut.'

Jack had laid his coat over Mary. Blankly, Stella noted it would need cleaning. His voice was soft and lilting.

'Mary had a little lamb,
Little lamb, little lamb,
Mary had a little lamb,
Its fleece was white as snow.'

Mary stared intently at Jack, her lips working.

'I did it, Daddy. I did it exactly like you told me. Did you see? No hands! One wheel up like a cowboy. Did you see?'

In Mary Thornton's uncurling fingers lay a cluster of green glass chips. 'She's responding.' Stella told the operator.

'I did see. What a clever girl you are, Mary. Daddy's favourite angel.' Jack's voice was warm and lilting. He bent closer to her. 'You have made it all all right.'

A smile flickered over Mary's lips. 'She fell, Daddy. I didn't hurt her. She made me go to the temple. She made me, Daddy.'

'I know, Mary. You're not in trouble.'

'Michael's upstairs, Daddy. I made him fish fingers. He's in his room. I promise that I brought him home and made him his tea. He's upstairs... I made fish...'

'Hush Mary, you did your best.'

'Everywhere that Mary went,
Mary went, Mary went...'

Jack closed his hand over her fingers.

'Everywhere that Mary went,
The lamb was sure to go.'

Mary Thornton's pupils dilated and her fervent gaze resolved to a languorous gaze, sightless. Stella thought of Elizabeth Figg propped against the willow at Dukes Meadows. With the flat of his thumb Jack closed Mary's eyelids.

Stella had never seen someone die before.

'Rest in peace, Mary,' she whispered.

'Barlow didn't stop.' Jack sat back on the kerb, hands around his knees. 'I tried to flag him down. She pushed me out of the way.'

'He may not have seen her.' She lapsed into silence. David had seen.

'Mary knew he wouldn't stop.' In his knitted waistcoat and crumpled shirt sleeves, Jack was a capable stranger.

'Have a wet wipe.' She thrust the fragrant cloth at him.

Jack dabbed ineffectually at the blood on his palms. 'Barlow didn't stop when Michael ran in front of his car. Mary expected that he would not tonight. She knew. She never intended to kill him. She planned that Barlow would kill her. A greater punishment. You were right about Marian. She's no murderer.'

'He might have swerved.'

'He called her bluff.' Jack didn't look at her. 'Perhaps, also, he never wanted to see that little girl's face again.'

Stella's phone rang.

'Stella, love?'

'Yes?' A girl's voice. Marian. Despite the dead woman at her feet, she nearly shouted for joy.

'Remember me, your mother?'

Jack covered Mary's face with his coat.

At the end of Marquis Way blue lights strobed; the road was flooded with light, car doors slamming. Stella spoke over the chatter of radios. 'Mum, I'm sorry, I'm busy.'

'How can you be busy? No one wants cleaning at midnight.'

'I'll be there first thing in the morning.'

'I won't be there.'

'What do you mean?' Stella felt hands on her shoulders: David had given himself up. She turned. Martin Cashman draped a foil blanket around her and guided her out of the path of the stretcher. Dumbly she watched the ambulance doors shut. Ambulances were for the sick and injured. Marian didn't need an ambulance. She shut her eyes against the stinging tears.

'I've had an accident. I'm in Charing Cross Hospital.'

'Daddy, watch'.

Mary heaved the handlebars up and leant back like Clifford Hunt. For a terrifying moment, the sky came down to swallow the ground. She pedalled frantically and lifted it high up. She was a circus clown on one wheel.

'I'm going to go right around the statue with no hands!' she hooted. 'That's harder than a straight line.'

A crack in the path. Unable to save herself, she flew off the bicycle on to the grass. She heard ticking like a clock winding down. The wheel spinning and spinning.

She had gone nearly all the way around the statue.

Daddy!

He was on the bench with Michael. They had not watched even though he had promised. Or he would have promised if he hadn't been pretending Michael was there, when she could have told him Michael was dead. Dead. Dead! She had done it for Daddy.

Mary would not be able to do it again.

Seventy-Three

Sunday, 6 May 2012

Stella was directed to the last bay of a row of six curtained cubicles. She hesitated, nervous of what she would find, then put a hand to the curtain and, as if it were a sticking plaster, whipped it aside. Her mum lay on a bed. The legs that Terry said could win Miss World were bare and crossed at the ankles. Suzie was reading a free newspaper and sipping tea; she might have been on the settee in her flat. When she saw Stella, she laid down the paper.

'What happened?' Stella could not see anything wrong. No bandage, no limb in plaster.

No blood.

She picked up her mother's handbag from a chair beside the bed and sat down. 'I'm here now.' She bounced the handbag on her lap as if it were a recalcitrant baby.

Suzie furrowed her brow. 'I don't remember.' Her eyes glistened. 'You said to ring if I needed you.'

That was true. Stella had not returned her mum's calls or replied to her text.

'They're keeping me in for observation.' Suzie rattled the newspaper.

'Did they say why?' Stella was alert. Perhaps for once her mum wasn't fussing. She had never seen Suzie look nervous before.

'I didn't say the right answers to their quiz.' She gave a quick smile. 'I told the young man that I can read and read him the weather forecast. I said I didn't vote for the Prime Minister and if he did, then he could tell me his name. That put the wind up the lot of them. Serve them right for treating me like a silly old widow.'

Stella noticed that her mum's hands were still. She was about to point out that Suzie was not a widow, but said instead: 'You're not silly or old.' She got up. 'I'll find out what's happening.'

Still clutching the handbag, Stella batted at the curtains and pushed through.

Five minutes later she was back in the little cubicle.

'You haven't fractured your skull, but test results might indicate concussion.'

'Were you doing anything nice?' Suzie's hands stayed clasped on her lap. 'I hope you were having fun. It's Saturday night, half of West London's in here. I had such a lot of fun when I was young, before I met Terry.' She patted at her hair. 'Afterwards too,' she said.

Stella gripped the handbag and flopped on to the chair. 'It wasn't fun, no.' She was tempted again to tell her mum everything.

'You look tired. I told Jack, "My daughter works so hard" – it's good that you do, Stella, I admire you – "but she needs some fun too," I said. Jack heartily agreed. I want him cleaning for me. You doing it will spoil the mother-and-daughter thing.' She addressed a vent in the wall.

'Long day.' Stella was baffled by the idea her mum talked about her when she wasn't there. She fiddled with the handbag clasp. Open close. Open close.

'Mum?'

'Yes, Stella.'

'I was wondering… say no if it's too much… but if you had some time it would help me if you could do a bit for the business. You know, like you used to? Typing, ringing people, chasing up new business.' Stella snapped shut the clasp.

The curtain swept aside and a man in a blue coat twisted a wheelchair through the opening.

'Mrs Darnell?'

'That's me.' Suzie flourished the newspaper.

Stella went cold. Her mum didn't like hospitals and avoided doctors, so would ignore everything: a nagging pain or a blemish on her skin. The doctors were fobbing Stella off; her mum had something worse than mild concussion. She jumped up. 'I'm Mrs Darnell's daughter.'

'Come to take you up to the ward.' The man spun the chair around and clamped the brakes. Stella retreated while the porter transferred Suzie from the bed to the chair. Her mum looked suddenly small and frail, though, at only sixty-six, she was hardly old, Stella reassured herself. Terry hadn't been old either.

'No need for you to come, pet. Go on home to bed. Come and get me tomorrow. Or if you can't...'

'I can.'

The porter wheeled her away. Stella was rooted in the gangway. A few metres away he turned the chair around. Her mum waved. Stella waved back.

'She's asking for her bag,' the man called.

Stella was still holding her mum's handbag. She hurried up the bays and laid it on her mum's lap. Suzie propped it upright on her lap and signalled the man to continue. Stella walked back along the gangway. A pallid young man in jeans and an unbuttoned shirt was being helped onto her mum's bed, his eyes shut.

'Stella.'

The porter was holding open the PVC flap doors; her mum was gesticulating. Stella shrugged, not understanding. She moved towards them.

'That work.' Suzie Darnell was now rootling in her bag. 'I can help you.'

The doors smacked shut behind her.

Seventy-Four

Sunday, 6 May 2012

'Mr Harmon, you needn't do this if you'd rather not.' Martin Cashman was gruff. 'We have officers who are trained. How did you say you were related?'

'It would be better from me.' Jack circumnavigated the question. He would give anything to leave it to Cashman but he owed it to Mary. Cashman would not understand. Stella would. He wished she were here.

'Please make it short.' A female nurse reading a chart on a clipboard barred the way to the intensive care room. 'He's agitated. I'd say wait until he's stronger, but he's not going to make it. If he wasn't asking for his daughter you could leave it.'

When he walked in, it crossed Jack's mind that they were too late. The old man – Robert Thornton – looked dead, his skin grey, his bony features even more cadaverous. He was festooned with tubing beneath a scaffolding of drips. Waste bags draped off the hospital bed. He was so slight he made little impression beneath the sheets. Jack started. Thornton's eyes were fixed on him, bright and discerning.

'Michael.' The voice was strong.

'Actually, Mr Thornton, this is…' Martin Cashman stationed himself at the end of the bed facing the patient. He fiddled with the knot on his tie.

The old man ignored him. 'What can you report?'

Jack sat by the bed, leaning in; he spoke low so that Cashman would not hear. 'Mary did as you asked…'

Thornton's hand began an inexorable crawl over the sheets. He pinched the lapel on Jack's coat. 'You have never let me down, Michael.'

'She found the driver.'

'You are an angel,' Robert Thornton cut in.

'Mary is an angel,' Jack whispered.

'She left you on your own. She lied.' Robert Thornton nodded towards Martin Cashman. 'That policeman brought your sister back. I said, "Keep her, she's not mine, I've done with her." The hand dragged at Jack's coat, twig fingers scraping, groping. 'She tried to killed my boy, but she didn't, did she, son?'

'Myra asked me to give you these.' Jack held out seven green chips. 'It took me too long to work out why Myra wanted my A to Z. She found streets with no CCTV, reported on landmarks for your fantasy land. She told me, she did all she could to make you love her. When you married her mother, you took Myra on too – only you didn't. If she is an angel, then you, Robert Thornton, are the devil.' Jack could smell death on the man and with his words he urged it on.

Thornton gripped the glass. 'That girl wasn't proper police, Mary was a clerk. Where is she now when she should be taking care of you? You need your tea, a growing boy.'

'She always took care of me. She took the trouble to know me. She was the only one who did.' Jack was floating above him on a sea of white. The walls went convex then concave. Someone muted the sound.

Jack was slumped on a chair, his head down between his knees. A steaming beaker appeared. Automatically he took it and, sitting up, held it as if it would anchor him.

'Jack, it's me.' Stella knelt on the floor. 'You fainted. I should have been there.'

'He was going to make her kill Matthew Benson for him.' Jack spoke thickly. 'Mary saw no way out.'

'They only had tea and coffee. I went for tea.' Stella guided the mug to his lips.

'Thornton did the murders, but he got frail. He made her take over.' Jack inhaled the steam from the cup and looked up. Cashman was pacing further along the corridor, talking on the phone. 'According to Lucie's file, Thornton worked for an insurance company until he was made redundant in 2002. On top of losing his job, he was losing his touch. When he murdered Harvey Gray, he was seen by Carol Jones. Without his work, he had no access to accident data. He made Mary get it; her role gave him access to what he needed. She loved her work; she loved your dad. Her own father compromised her. It was unbearable, but she would have done anything to make her father love her. Except murder.' He swirled the liquid in the cup. 'Mary was lost after her brother died. From what you said, her work was her life. Her stepfather ruined it. He's ruined her.'

Stella sat on a chair beside Jack; he shifted closer to her.

'She didn't have to do what he said,' she countered. As she said it, she knew that Mary did. There was so much Stella would have done for Terry.

'She blamed herself for Michael's death. Jackie told me Mary stole Douglas Ford's cards instead of bringing Michael home. Douglas came to see Jackie at the office last night; it's been preying on his mind since a visit I paid him at the garage. She told him he had to go to the police. He said that Mary – we should call her Myra, it was her proper name – chased her brother into the path of Barlow's car. Thornton must have guessed.'

'Could Terry have known it was Marian?'

'We'll never know. Perhaps she wanted him to know so brought him Brooke Bond tea not as a present but as a sign.' Jack rested his head back against the wall. 'I thought the old man was frightened of his daughter. It was the other way around.'

'And I thought Marian had a violent husband,' Stella said. 'Amanda Hampson inflicted the bruises fighting for her life.'

'Amanda would have had the upper hand. Marian's bruises were defensive. Amanda was desperate; her quest gave her purpose. Marian was thwarting her. You thought Marian was jealous because she wasn't at the scene with Martin; she was actually shocked that Amanda was dead. Marian ran out of the house, leaving her by the temple; she had let her die.'

'That old fellow wants locking up.' Martin Cashman was off the phone. 'He told me that Myra, as he calls Marian, should be dead and not his son. Can you credit that? Don't care if he's on his last legs, blokes like him don't deserve children. When I think of what Marian did for him.'

'Martin.' Stella used Jack's knee to stand up. She rummaged in her rucksack. 'You need to see this.' She handed Cashman the blue folder.

Seventy-Five

Monday, 7 May 2012

Pic. No.	Date	Street	Accident	Driver	Child (Victim)	Date
1	6th May 2012	King Street	Failed to stop. Myra Thornton died	David Barlow	Michael Thornton	6th May 1966
2 (2a)	7th September 1970	Mafeking Avenue	Hit a plane tree	Denis Atkins	Colin Coleman	15th March 1970
3 (3a & 3b	16th March 1977	Marquis Way	Hit an ash tree	Paul Vickery	James Harrison	17th October 1976
4	31st March 1989	Tolworth Street	Hit a beech tree	David Lauren	William Carter	26th December 1988
5 (5a & 5b)	10th November 2002	Britton Drive	Hit a sweet chestnut tree.	James Markham	Christopher Mason	2nd January 2002
6 (6a)	17th March 2003	Marquis Way	Hit a telegraph pole	Harvey Gray	Robert Smith	5th November 2002
7 (7a &7 b)	15th March 2009	Phoenix Way	Hit an oak tree	Charlie Hampson	Stephen Parsons	8th January 2009
No Ref.	6th May 2012 (Cancelled for David Barlow)	Spelling Way	No tree	Matthew Benson	Joel Evans	23rd April 2012

Stella completed her spreadsheet of accidents – murders – and, resting her elbows on the table where Terry prepared his prints, allowed her gaze to roam over his wall of photographs. Until these she had seen few pictures of herself. There were the photo-booth snaps for passports and driving licence, but her schools hadn't gone in for annual portraits so her mother hadn't collected the mandatory gallery of gap-toothed grins in blazers that adorned the mantelpieces of many of her clients' homes. The sort of images that accompanied Lucille May's reports of the deaths of the boys.

William Carter, Stephen Parsons, Christopher Mason, Colin Coleman, Robert Smith, Joel Evans, James Harrison. No one would murder Matthew Benson. It was over.

David had said it was important not to forget lives cut short, now she understood the significance of that remark. One name she would remember: Michael Thornton, the boy with the face of an angel.

With the grid in front of her, she wanted to review the case. She regretted not taking a copy of the blue folder before she handed it to Cashman. Stella caught sight of her smiling self over the banana sundae. The blue folder was a police matter now.

Jack had gone to the station to give Martin Cashman a statement about the 'hit and run', as Jack called it. She believed David might give himself up. Jack didn't say it, but she could see he was infuriated by her belief in Barlow.

A police officer was outside David Barlow's house in Aldensley Road. Another was by Jennifer Barlow's grave, in the same cemetery as Michael Thornton. Martin Cashman had reassured them that Barlow would be caught. Jack was giving a detailed account of all they had found out. Giving work as an excuse, Stella had come to Terry's house, but even the sense of Terry had gone and, unable to settle to work emails, she had retreated to his basement.

Stella tracked along the top row of the pictures of her as a little girl. Stella on a bicycle, spooning up the sundae, done up in a painting apron; variously in pigtails, later with shorter hair, sometimes in need of a brush. She looked as if she was having the fun Suzie wanted for her. The adult Stella's different hairstyles reflected the decades and a greater sense of fashion than she gave herself credit for. In one photograph, Stella saw her likeness to Suzie; she hadn't thought she resembled either of her parents. It was out of sequence, in the middle of the third row down, when Stella was around seven. She got up. It was Suzie. Contrary to what her mum maintained, Terry had photographed her. After she left him he put this up on the wall in his favourite room.

She heard something and crept to the foot of the stairs. She recognized the sound – she had heard it before. The flap on the letterbox was lifted. Then it was shut. And again. Marian's ghost.

Ridiculous. Jack knew not to knock and disturb the neighbours. Pleased, Stella took the basement steps two at time and pulled open the front door.

'Hello, Stella.'

David Barlow walked past her into the hall, his dog keeping to heel.

'How did you find me?' Stella fiddled with the kettle. Making a cup of tea was too banal a task.

'I knew you'd come back to your dad's.' He sat at the table. 'I wish I could go back to mine.' He turned to her. Stella switched on the kettle.

'The police are looking for you.' His mackintosh was ripped at the hem and stained with oil. His shoes were scuffed and the back of his hand was grazed. 'Are you all right?' He was not all right.

'Now that I'm here.' He faced her. Stella fixed on the poodle, which in turn was following David's every move, ears pert, chest puffed.

'They're at her grave.' David got up, his hands in his coat pockets. 'Even in death she has set them on me.'

'She's dead,' Stella said.

'That won't stop Jennifer. She knows how to press the right buttons. She's got me. One mistake, Stella. I was a kid myself. We all make them. A fresh start, isn't that your principle?'

'Mary Thornton is dead.' She could smell his aftershave – applied some time ago – combined with his own scent. She thought of what Jack had said and wondered if conversely it was possible to despise a man whose body odour and aftershave were compelling.

'She walked out in front of the car. I had no chance.' Abruptly he took Stella's hands. 'I can handle anything if you're with me. I love you, Stella Darnell. Please don't let Jennifer beat us. She wanted me to pay for my sin for the rest of my life.'

Stella took in the unshaven cheeks, straggling locks of hair and bright eyes. She pulled free of him and sat down. Instantly Stanley sprang on to her lap as if he was putting distance between him and David. She saw David notice it too.

'You hardly know me.' She might have known David all her life. The dog's woolly coat was impregnated with his smell. She moved away and steadied the animal. Its little body was compact and solid.

'I washed the car and got the dent knocked out in a garage in a place called Seaford, a good distance from Hammersmith. When I saw that article about your dad dying there, it – it took me back. I'd never heard of the place since.'

He scrutinized his palm as if expecting to find some answer there. 'Until 15.47p.m. on Friday the sixth of May 1966 I was a good person. Each time you cleaned, you diminished Jennifer's poison. Some people lose their faith when a loved one is taken. When she miscarried, it proved to her that God existed. It was an eye for an eye.

'Jennifer gave me an alibi. I never asked her to. She told the police that I was at home all afternoon building a cot. The officer was sympathetic and crossed me off his list of grey-saloon owners in London and Surrey and that was that. Then, about a year ago, maybe more, your father knocked on the door and asked about my Wolseley. I knew he was on to me. The police didn't know it was a Wolseley, they were looking for a grey saloon. Jennifer was ill by then. I said about the baby coming and needing a larger car.

When I told him about my wife, he went away but I knew he wouldn't give up. When I saw that article I realized he would not return. I wasn't relieved, I promise you, Stella.' He came and sat beside her.

Stella felt the dog lean into her and gave it a stroke. She did not believe him. Surely he was relieved. 'Why did you ring Clean Slate?'

'I told you. I wanted that fresh start you promise in the brochure. Tabula rasa. When you found the jacket I was stunned. Jennifer told me she'd burnt it, just as she told me we had been burgled. I will never forget what happened to that little boy, I visit his grave. That angel haunts my dreams. I did a bad thing, but how long must I pay?'

'What happened to the Wolseley?' Stella stuck to facts.

'I waited a decent interval before selling it, then answered an ad for a Hillman Minx.' He spoke as if in court.

'Why did you put the picture in a frame on the wall? Didn't you think I'd be suspicious?'

'I loved that car, I want to go back to that carefree time. I thought that even if you did guess that you'd understand. And you do, don't you, Stella? He moved closer. The dog gave a low grumble.

'I know we all make mistakes, but—' Stella did not understand.

'I told Mrs Hunt from the Porphyrion Insurance, it was Jennifer who said: Why mess up more lives? I saw sense in that. Mrs Hunt agreed I had been punished enough. After you went to meet the woman at Dukes Meadows I started thinking. That woman didn't believe me about the break-in. She looked at me like she knew me. All those visits, pushed by Jennifer, to check whether they'd caught the thieves. I saw the child by the kerb watching me. I knew she'd never forget my face. It was the face of the woman at the police station. It's the eyes that do it. They don't change.

'My unborn daughter died a week after the accident. If she had

452

lived she would be your age – not that you're like a daughter, you make me feel eighteen again. You said I deserved a second chance.'

The kettle boiled. Holding the dog, mechanically Stella took the two mugs from the draining rack. Moments ago she had been impatient for Jack to return; now she dreaded him finding David Barlow here. She looked in the cupboard for tea bags. There were none.

'There's only instant coffee. I'll go to the shop for tea.' She kept her voice level.

'Instant coffee is fine.' Barlow moved towards her. The dog shrank into her as if it were frightened. Stella clutched it.

'When you turned up, it was love at first sight.'

'I only drink tea.' Two days ago it would have been the word 'love' that scared her. 'I won't be long.' She edged to the door.

'Don't go.' He barred the door, hands outstretched, imploring. 'You drink coffee. I know that, don't I? We are like soul mates, you and me.'

Her thoughts were racing. She wanted Jack to come, but was frightened of what would happen if he did. Jack would not come. He was cross with her about Barlow. Stella tried to regulate her breathing to stop the dog sensing her tension. David must trust she would bring the tea or he would stop her leaving. No, they were not soul mates. That was not it.

He came towards her.

'The wrath of God is being revealed from heaven against all the godlessness…'

The voice, strong and deep, resounded off the walls. Stella's heart tumbled in her chest.

'… and wickedness of men who suppress the truth by their wickedness.'

She had heard the voice before, by the Bell Steps when the river was filling. Then too she had been in trouble.

Barlow was at the back door. 'Where's the key?'

'You'll find it in the fork section of the cutlery drawer.' Jack had come.

453

The dog barked sharply and pushed its hind legs against Stella, scrabbling towards David.

'I will always love you,' he mouthed. She went over and handed him his dog. He folded the poodle into an embrace. Their fingers clutched; his were warm. Stella let go and stepped away.

The kitchen door opened. Then she heard the sirens.

Epilogue

Mallingswood House was separated from the thirty-two acres that once formed part of its estate by King Street and the railway. At Barons Court the District and Piccadilly lines emerged from a tunnel and were carried along a viaduct over streets of Victorian terraces to pass above the remainder of this land which, for over a century, had belonged to the public and was called Ravenscourt Park.

The few in the park at nearly nine o'clock on an unseasonably cold May evening were hurrying to the exits. Tennis players clanged shut the gate to the courts and, rackets under their arms, sauntered into Glenthorne Road. A straggle of teenagers, raucous shouts and laughter clamouring across the lawns, cigarettes glowing in the dusk, spilled out on to King Street. Late commuters scurried along the darkening avenue of cherry trees to Ravenscourt Square or Goldhawk Road. Above them a District line train slid out of the station and, with a rising whine, gathered speed and clattered along the viaduct. Yellow light from its carriages, brighter in the massing twilight, illuminated a figure striding counter to the others between flower beds in which, in the failing light, reds and purples of windblown tulips were particularly vivid.

Stella should not be here. The park was closing. Jack had texted her to meet him under the third railway arch and, quelling misgivings, she had agreed.

Under the viaduct she stopped. His text had mentioned a

slide. Beyond the geometric shapes of a climbing apparatus in the kids' play area she distinguished a paddling pool and a sand pit. No slide. And no Jack. She was alone in a London park at nightfall. She should not have come.

To her left ran a path shaded by the viaduct and bushes. Insipid orange lamps on the railway bridge accentuated wedges of shadow. Reluctantly she went down it. The first arch was boarded up. A grille covered the next arch; through it she made out lawn mowers, a grass roller and other maintenance equipment. The third arch was enclosed with sagging corrugated iron leaving a semi-circular gap at the top. A crude door was padlocked. Stella heard a metallic thrum from within the arch. Frightened now, she clasped the bundle inside her anorak.

'Stella! Is that you?' A sibilant whisper echoed in the vaulted space.

'Jack?' Her heart fluttered. 'Of course it's me.'

'Brilliant! Come on.'

'It's locked.'

'No it's not.'

Stella peered at the padlock. Jack had set the shackle shy of the fastener.

'Come on!'

She dragged open the door. Its jagged edge scuttered along the concrete with a shriek of metal. She found herself in a cavernous chamber.

'I'm here.'

'Where?'

'Here.'

'Oh, for goodness sake, Jack!' Gradually Stella became accustomed to the dark. She gasped and folded her hands over her chest. A tower of criss-crossing metal reached to the apex of the arch. Jack's face was suspended above her.

'How did you get up there?'

'Sssssh!' The sound bounced off the bricks.

It was the highest slide Stella had ever seen. The chute dropped steeply to level out inches from the concrete. Jack was huddled in the doorway of a half-timbered cottage with windows framed by painted roses.

'It's closing time.' But she knew that wouldn't work.

'Have you ever been in a park at night after everyone has gone?'

'No.'

There was a swooshing. Jack whisked down the slide, coat tails billowing, and skidded to a stop beside her, his legs flailing. 'That was fan-tastic! Have a go. I'll give up my turn.'

Stella eyed the structure. 'That thing is not safe.'

'I agree. It's a death slide, a relic of the sixties. Next door there's a massive roundabout which still works, but it's impossible with one person. You'd need to be Batman to push it.' Jack leapt up and scampered into the depths of the arch.

'Superman.' The thrumming was Jack climbing the slide; it shook with each step. 'Why are we here?' She adjusted the zip on her anorak.

His long legs floundered out of the doorway; feet splaying, he positioned himself. 'This is where Mary and Michael Thornton played after school. They should have gone straight home for their tea.'

'How do you know?'

'Jackie told me.'

There were footsteps outside on the path. Jack scooted into the cottage and beckoned furiously to Stella through the little window.

A scrape of shoe leather, closer now. Stella crept around the slide. Her arm across her chest, she put her foot on the first rung of a metal ladder. It shook when she gave it her weight. She could not hurry or she would give them away. Designed for children, the treads were narrow, the handrails low, she could lose her balance and pitch over the side.

Stella clambered up the last two steps and collapsed on to the platform beside Jack. The footsteps were closer.

There was a long-drawn-out mewing sound.

'Ssssh!' Jack put up a hand.

'It wasn't me.' Stella unzipped the top of her anorak. The dog's head shot out and butted her chin. He gave another yawn, quieter this time.

Someone was outside. Jack and Stella stared at the animal. Its ears were pert, its nose twitching; it turned sharply towards the sound, its breathing rapid, working up to a bark.

The footsteps resumed, then receded.

'What is he doing here? Cashman put him in the police pound.' Jack and the dog regarded each other. Stella pulled the zip up to the poodle's chin.

'I've got him for the time being.' Through the gap in the planks she contemplated the drop below.

'How long is time being?' Jack enquired.

'For now. Go on with what you were saying.' Stella had offered to take the dog on a whim. She would take each day as it came.

'Jackie said that Michael got scared and caused a bottleneck. No one could go on the slide and the kids blamed Mary. Jackie said it wasn't her fault, she was kind to her brother and took him with her down the slide.'

Stella appraised the steep silver chute and felt affinity with the little boy who, over forty years ago, had cowered on this precarious perch, scared and paralysed. The ladder was at a precipitous angle, almost vertical. She clung to the housing, unsure how she would get herself and the small dog down.

'You were right,' Jack said.

'Was I?'

'Barlow isn't evil. Just weak and cowardly. I haven't been supportive. Sorry.' Jack had his back to her.

'Cowardly is bad enough.' Stella shuffled towards the opening. 'And you were right, it's more complicated than straight good and evil. David believed he had been punished enough. His wife never stopped reminding him of what she said was a sin. Maybe it was punishment, but David never confessed. He never gave the

Thorntons closure. Robert Thornton sounds like a horrible man, but that didn't make it OK.'

The slide had to be over twenty feet high. Since David Barlow's arrest she had taken every shift going. When possible the dog came with her. Jackie had rung to say that she had received a cheque for David's last deep-cleaning session. What should she do with it? Did they accept money from villains? David had posted it the day he killed Mary Thornton. Stella told her to donate the sum to the local hospice. Jack put in his statement that Barlow had not attempted to stop or take avoidance action. Mary had saved Jack's life, her death would not be described as suicide. He had picked up speed. Barlow was charged with leaving the scene of an accident and reckless driving in two cases decades apart. Martin Cashman reckoned he would get less than five years with good behaviour. Stella told herself she didn't care. Either way she would never see or hear from David Barlow again.

'Robert Thornton had wanted a son – or maybe any child that was his own. He wasn't interested in his stepdaughter. The model was a landscape in which his son was alive. He treated me as his son.'

'He attacked you.'

'He wasn't a well man. Mary saved me. He was bent on one thing – recreating a city where no one died. At least that's my guess.'

Stella followed the progression of a bus along King Street beyond the gates. It passed Mallingswood House where, in the evenings after her work at the police station, Mary had been entrusted with the care of other people's little boys. She had worked there, making their tea and putting them to bed for years until the school ran out of money and closed last December. She hoped the job had given Mary comfort. She had been about to lose another home. She was being forced to take over from her stepfather, now too frail to leave the house. She had only one way to escape.

'I keep wondering why she wanted me to come to Dukes Meadows?'

'Who knows? You taking a printout of the database and working behind her back was a betrayal.' Jack had his back to her at the top of the slide. 'Possibly she would have told you everything. She said she wanted your help.'

Stella let Stanley lick her hand; she had told him her face was forbidden. She had given him a bath but still caught David's aftershave on his woolly coat.

Jack turned around. 'Let it go, Detective Darnell. We solved another case!'

'Terry solved it. We just caught up with him.'

'No. If he had known about Marian – Myra – he would have acted. He trusted you would know his photographs were significant. We finished what he started. Come down the slide with me, it's exciting with two. Or three.'

'I'll use the ladder.' An ear-splitting rumble drowned her response and the sides of the make-believe cottage shook. Then there was stillness.

'The 9.23 Upminster train's on schedule.' Jack knelt at the mouth of the slide.

'Jack, you'll fall!' Stella snatched at his coat.

Jack crawled over to where she was crouching. 'If you sit on the flat bit, I'll hold you. I promise it'll be fun.'

Fun. Was this what her mum had meant?

'If we fall I could squash Stanley.'

Jack blinked. 'Stanley?'

'He's named after... the point is it's too risky.' Stella arranged the dog within the folds of her anorak. Since collecting him from the pound, she had taken him everywhere.

Jack sat astride the flat end of the slide, flung back his coat tails and reached out to Stella. 'Think of a pillion rider leaning into the turn on a motorbike.' He brushed the sleeve of Stella's anorak. 'It's all about trust.'

The dog struggled out of the top of her anorak, button-

460

brown eyes fixed on her intently, his apricot fur defining him in the dim vaulted space. There were flecks of amber in his irises she hadn't noticed before. His nose twitched; he caught a scent. Stella caught it too. Mulch spread around the bushes outside. His eyes flicked about her face as if reading her every thought. He trusted her. Stella scuffled to the door of the cottage and before she could change her mind took Jack's hands and wriggled onto the slide. Jack shuffled along so that he was sitting behind her. Sure that the dog was secure, she gripped the sides of the slide, reassured by the cold metal. She felt Stanley settle heavily against her chest.

'Shove up.' Jack clasped her waist. 'We'll creep forward a bit at a time. Close your eyes if it helps.' He was particularly cheerful. 'We must give ourselves up, don't try to control our speed. Trust it.'

He meant, 'Trust me.' Stella realized that she did trust Jack.

Jack shoved his heels against the lip of the opening and pushed. Bricks zipped past and Stella was flung against Jack. It was over. At the bottom Jack flung out his legs to prevent them tumbling sideways off the chute.

'You were perfect,' he whispered.

Stella got unsteadily to her feet. The dog was calm. It sensed nothing to be frightened of, no threat. No ghosts.

Jack couldn't shut the padlock on the gate; it needed a key. 'The keeper will assume it's kids.'

'He won't be far wrong,' Stella muttered.

She lowered Stanley to the ground and fixed his lead on to his collar. He walked beside her, close to her leg, eyes up to her. She told him he was a good boy.

'He looks rather like you – the way he sniffs the air.' Jack was strolling along as if they were on a Sunday outing. 'Your voice puts a prance in his step.'

He led them all along the avenue of cherry trees, past the tennis courts, the nets like suspended white lines in the dusk. They came to two stone pillars supporting a gate. Stella was relieved to see that the geometric design made it tantamount to a climbing frame. She handed the lead to Jack and shakily inserted her boot above the locking mechanism. She hauled herself up and over.

She had been in a park after closing time. One morning, before dawn, Terry had taken her to collect the first crop of conkers from St Peter's Square.

'Put your jeans on over your pyjamas. Here, wear my jumper. That's it. Do up your shoelaces good and tight. We won't talk until we're clear of the house. Keep close by me.'

Her dad had helped her over the gate. Stella crossed the road and the memory, like the coil of mist on Marquis Way, wisped to nothing.

Ravenscourt Gardens School

Head: Mrs Nelson BA (Hons), Dip. Ed.

The notice, behind a mesh fence, stood in a flower bed of pansies and daffodils.

'Mary Thornton ran away from here in May 1966. Jackie went to this school. Funny that, isn't it?' Jack joined her by the fence.

'I know. I was here for a year before Mum left Terry.' Stella had a recollection of a woman who put her in mind of an animal. Or a bird? She jerked Stanley away from a sandwich wrapper by the school gate.

'Jackie felt guilty she didn't do more for Mary,' she said.

'Mary didn't sound easy. Douglas Ford never forgot her stealing his cards. Jackie was kind to her, he told me.' Jack gripped the fence, hands above his head. 'Could Mrs Thornton have guessed what her husband was doing?'

'We thought it was Hindley's death that precipitated her suicide. Maybe it was, but she could have found out that James Markham had died. She probably guessed. He was going out at night; she must have wondered what he was doing.'

Under the bridge, the roundel sign for Ravenscourt Park station sent a bluish haze over the pavement. The two Thornton children might have been nervous of starting at another school. Stella had wanted to run away from her new school in Barons Court. Leading Stanley, Stella drifted towards the Underground.

She had found notes in Lucille May's file about how the little girl boarded a train here. PC Terence Darnell found her under the flyover at Hammersmith Broadway and brought her home. Days later he went back to the house in British Grove to tell the Thorntons their son was dead. Terry had wanted to make a difference. He treated everything as important; he forgot nothing. Anxious to hold on to the information she had collected, May had kept from them that Michael had a sister, but she knew she would never write the book. She was stuck in the house in British Grove, sharing it with ghosts of her own making. She had given Jack the file; she must have wanted to be helped. Terry might have helped her, but he died.

Stella waited for Jack to catch up. With Stanley on one side and Jack on the other, she walked back to the van in Weltje Road.

'Mary collected cards and marbles.' Jack snapped in his seat belt. 'Collecting objects is a way to quantify life.'

Stella lifted Stanley up and planted him on Jack's lap. 'Like spreadsheets.' She glanced at him. 'I'm getting a seat fitted in the back so I can belt him in. In a collision, even a box of tissues flying off the back shelf could kill you.' She drove out on to King Street.

Jack held Stanley tightly as if he were a source of mortal danger.

Outside Mallingswood House a little girl was jumping on and off the plinth of the drinking fountain. Crazily Stella pictured herself, leaping towards Terry, sure he would catch her.

'We never found out what happened to the angel's hands,' Jack said.

Stella braked at the zebra crossing outside the post office for a woman with a spaniel that refused to walk to heel. She noticed dogs now. Since David's arrest she kept meeting people with dogs, in the street and in the park. Jackie once said that having a dog was like having a child: they brought people together. Stella wasn't keen to be brought together with anyone. Terry struck up conversations with strangers. As you got older you were meant to get more like your parents. Jack was talking.

'... Mary was attached to Michael, but Jackie thought she was jealous of him too. Michael had a father who loved him. She couldn't kill her stepfather, but she could damage the angel he erected for his son.'

'She would have buried them.' Stella was suddenly certain.

'What?'

'The hands. I think she buried them. Stanley buried his bear in the flower bed at Terry's.' Stella glanced across at the dog. Curled up in a ball, in the dark he was a pale blob against Jack's coat. 'The glass wasn't put there by the killer, it was Mary's private mark of respect.' Stella was surprised at herself. She had hardly known the police administrator. 'She couldn't confess to Terry, so the glass was a clue.'

'You could be a detective! We should check the grave.'

'I'm not digging up Michael Thornton's grave.'

'Of course not, but I think we'll find the hands nearby. Stanley might,' he added brightly.

'We must return the glass.' Stella had given the bags to Martin Cashman. She slowed for a bus at Young's Corner. 'I'll ask if we can have them when the case is closed.'

'Six bags for each driver and one for Michael. The glass has done its job and must go back to Michael.' Jack nodded approval. 'Drop me here, I'll walk the rest.'

'You could come back to Terry's house for supper. There's shepherd's pie.' The bus veered away; she pulled into its space. She would not ask where he was going.

'Your house you mean,' Jack corrected her. 'Terry left it to you. It's not his any more.'

The screen in the dashboard lit up. Jackie's name appeared. Stella pressed the 'phone' button. Jack was stroking Stanley. She was gratified that he was making no move to get out.

'Stella, we've had a letter about a parking ticket. We didn't pay in time so owe the full amount.' Jackie's voice came through the speakers.

'It's a mistake.'

'It was issued in the street where Suzie lives. Could be coincidence.' Jackie paused.

'I never get tickets,' Stella said.

Jack leant over. She breathed in the particular smell of the washing powder he used. He was rummaging in the map compartment behind the steering wheel.

'It's the number plate for the van you drive, the one with no logo.'

Jack was holding up a plastic bag. Instead of green glass she saw a parking ticket. The morning she found it on the windscreen was abruptly vivid. The day she had refused to give her mum the job.

'It's OK, Jackie. I'll pay it.'

'Leave it with me.' Jackie could have been there with them, her voice was so close. It seemed a long time since Stella had seen Jackie, longer still since they had chatted over Rich Tea biscuits.

'I'll be in first thing Monday,' Stella confirmed. 'After the police station.'

'If you have things to sort out, we're fine. Your mum's updated the database, designed reports that are easy to understand and yesterday she got us a new client!'

'I'll be there.'

'Then it will be lovely to see you.' Jackie hung up.

'Why are you going to the station?' Jack asked. 'It's not a cleaning day.'

'To return something.' She couldn't say the 'something' was the green form. David had not admitted he had killed Michael. 'I have to give Cashman the green form I stole,' she made herself say. 'I'll let you out here.'

'Aren't we having shepherd's pie?' Jack was playing with Stanley's ears.

'If you like.' Stella slipped the ticket into her anorak pocket.

'We need milk and you've run out of tea bags. I'll pop into that shop. I could get us a nice bottle of wine and maybe chocolates for afters.'

'I have to clean Terry's house tomorrow.'

'OK, your call,' Jack replied cheerily.

Stella watched Jack Harmon jog up to the lights. Although there was no traffic in either direction, he waited for the pedestrian signal. He crossed the road and went into the grocery.

A 27 bus drew up outside what, in the sixties, had been a hardware shop, with a light bulb screwed to the counter for testing batteries. A middle-aged man alighted and went into St Peter's Square. He was too short to be Terry. He walked like him, brisk with head up, missing nothing.

Terry was dead. Stella felt the truth of this. When they arrived at the house where Terry had lived for over forty years, she would not find him there. She would not find her dad in a park early on an autumn morning when the gates were closed. She would not find him anywhere. The house in Rose Gardens North was her house now.

Ahead of her was a beech tree with a spindly trunk, perhaps a couple of years old. In her nearside mirror was a sweet chestnut. She could put her arms around the trunk. It replaced the tree blown down in the 1987 hurricane, another sweet chestnut. Mary Thornton collected trees; she might have noticed it on her walks home with her brother. It was spring then, the leaves as green and new as they were now.

The road where Michael Thornton had died three months before she was born in 1966 had been resurfaced many times. There was no ghostly shape in the sand. No sign of the terrible event that had happened here or of what came after.

She grabbed her phone and pressed a well-worn key. The call was answered without ringing.

'Jack, it's me. Stella. Buy some wine. Choose one you like. They sell chocolates too. And find a treat for Stanley.'

Acknowledgements

I was given much support during the writing of *Ghost Girl*.

Once again I'd like to thank Detective Superintendent Stephen Cassidy, recently retired from the Metropolitan Police. Steve responded in detail to my queries both in person and in writing. Thanks also to Helen Samuel of the Metropolitan Police for her considered advice; and to Frank Pacifico, Operational Trainer for the London Underground: Frank's observations were helpful and illuminating. Any mistakes or errors are mine.

I would like to thank Theresa Meekings for showing me around the building that inspired Mallingswood House and for telling me about its history. Theresa evoked ghosts that morning.

My thanks to Sue Robertson, Course Leader and Senior Lecturer on the MA in Architectural and Urban Studies at the University of Brighton for a reading list and more than one fascinating conversation about cities, buildings and architectural models. And to Professor Jenny Bourne Taylor of the University of Sussex for letting me tap her considerable knowledge on Victorian cities. To Liz Kinning, Facilities Manager at St Peter and St James's Hospice, who gave me hard-core information about deep cleaning and sanitizers that helped me to understand Stella's love of all things sterile. Thanks to Jane Goldberger and Ralph Baber of The Drinking Fountain Association for the spreadsheet detailing cattle troughs in London. I have taken fictional liberties with the data.

I have also taken topographical liberties and redrawn the boundaries of Hammersmith, increasing the jurisdiction of the Hammersmith Division.

The story owes much to my 'first reader' Melanie Lockett,

whose acute perceptions and observations were invaluable. As well as this she helped make the writing possible by doing more than her fair share of the domestics.

Arts Council funding (Grants for the Arts) enabled me to complete a draft of *Ghost Girl*. This invaluable grant for artists was critical to me. I am grateful to John Prebble and Rob Grundy of the Arts Council for their guidance. For their advice and endorsement of my application, thanks are due to creative industries consultant and good friend, Lisa Holloway, Myriad Editions MD, Candida Lacey, and the novelist Martine McDonagh, who generously shared with me her own experience of applying for a grant.

Many played their part in listening to ideas, providing writing space or simply spurring me on. My warm thanks go to: Caro Bailey, Sandra Baker, Melissa Benn, Diana Burski, Juliet Eve, June Goodwin, Marcus Goodwin, Kay and Nigel Heather, Lisa Holloway, Greg Mosse, Domenica de Rosa, Bernice Sorensen, Alysoun Tomkins and Agnes Wheeler.

My agents Capel and Land are right there. My heartfelt gratitude to Philippa Brewster for her staunch support and, as ever, valuable feedback, and to Georgina Capel, Rachel Conway and Romilly Must.

Laura Palmer is a wonderful editor, sensitive and perceptive. Thanks to all at Head of Zeus, in particular Nic Cheetham, Kaz Harrison, Mathilda Imlah, Clemence Jacquinet, Madeleine O'Shea and of course Becci Sharpe. Many thanks also to copy editor Richenda Todd and to proofreader Jane Robertson.

LOTTERY FUNDED | ARTS COUNCIL ENGLAND

Supported using public funding by

Turn the page for a preview of The Detective's Secret,
the third in the Detective's Daughter series.

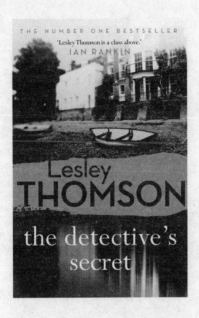

They will learn the city's secrets.
They will learn who plans to kill...

A man has jumped in front of a late night train. Stella Darnell,
a cleaner who solves crimes, suspects it's murder. Now she's
stirring up the past with questions that no one
wants to answer.

Jack Harmon, a driver on the Tube, has a new home at the
top of an old water tower, with a perfect bird's eye view of
London. If he watches through binoculars, he will learn the
city's secrets. He will learn who plans to kill...

Prologue

October 1987

Clouds streamed across the sky. Street lights obliterated the stars; the moon wouldn't rise until midnight, four hours away. A fierce wind rattled reed beds on Chiswick Eyot and tore through the undergrowth. Cross-currents on the river made rib-cage patterns; patches of stillness in the black water resembled corpses.

The Thames was rising, a deadly confluence of tide and turbulence. Miniature waves broke across Chiswick Mall; water welled in gutters, covering kerbstones and lapping at the steps of St Nicholas' church. A storm was gathering force.

At night Chiswick Mall was outside time. Misty yellow light surrounding iron lamp standards might be gas lit, cars were carriages on cobblestones. On the foreshore of the Thames, the clank-clank of a barge's mooring chain against the embankment wall beat the passing of no time at all.

A shape reflected in the river was dashed by a squall; it resolved into a tower. Utilitarian, a cylindrical tank supported by stanchions, the water tower was built in the Second World War to protect riverside wharfs and factories from fires. Long in disuse, the wharfs demolished, the tank was empty, the pipes stripped out. Fifty metres high, it stood taller than the brewery and the church spire and dominated the west London skyline. Against streaming clouds and tossed boughs, the tower, designed to withstand bombs and tensile stresses, seemed as if forever falling.

A cage attached to one supporting column housed five stairways connected by a platform; the last arrived at a narrow metal walkway that gave access to the tower. Violent gusts harassed the grille, testing steel rivets.

A man hurried through the church gates, skirting the water; he ducked into an alley between the brewery buildings and struggled up the staircases into the tower, head bowed against the wind. Minutes later, a woman emerged from the subway by the Hogarth roundabout and went into the alley. Checking about her, she pulled on the cage door and, both hands on the guard rail, began an awkward ascent.

'I hate this place.' Her voice rang in the concrete tank.

He watched as she zipped up her slacks, smacking at dirt although there was none; he kept it clean. Grimacing, she eased on brown leather faux-Victorian boots, doing up the laces with slick-snapping efficiency.

'You wanted secrecy.' The man pulled on underpants, his nakedness absurd as their intimacy of the afternoon ebbed. Her boots had heels. He had advised flat shoes for safety, but was glad she had ignored him. She was his fantasy woman.

He had put himself out to get the key from the engineer. The man had kept it after the developers went bust – as ineffectual revenge for non-payment – but there was no point in telling her of this effort: it would not convince her to leave her husband.

'Come and be with me.'

She had insisted that they leave no spending trail. No hotels, no meals out. No risk of meeting anyone they knew or being remembered by strangers. She had admitted that nylon sleeping bags on the tank floor, drinking wine from the bottle and feeding each other wedges of Brie on bite-size water biscuits spiced up the sex. Strangely there was no handle on the inside: he propped open the thick metal door with a brick and, once she was inside, he locked what he called the 'front door' after her. She'd surprised him by saying that the danger of being locked in made her feel alive.

'You'd feel alive all the time with me.'

She knew that, she had told him.

'*The apartment has a view of the sea.*' He had told her he would take a year's lease. Things had changed, she'd said as soon as she arrived. It had spoiled his performance.

'*Another bloody excuse!*' He shouldn't have said that.

He buttoned his shirt, saw he'd missed a button and started again. She was pouting and air-kissing into her compact mirror. Already she had 'gone', planning the kids' meal, back to her life that was death. The knickers he had bought her lay discarded beside the used condom – just the one this time. Last time she had agreed to leave; today she said her family needed her.

'*I need you.*'

'The flat does sound beautiful.' She appeased him, shrugging into her coat.

'Then leave!' He always tried to be everything her husband was not. Mr Perfect. He'd once let her know the other girls didn't need persuading. She knew there were no other girls.

She smoothed her skirt over her stomach and he was aroused all over again.

'You look lovely.'

'That wind nearly blew me off my feet,' she said again as if she hadn't heard him. 'There's a storm getting up.'

'It's not all that's "getting up"!'

She came over, put a hand on his crotch and whispered, 'Next week.' She didn't usually do this when she was about to go; he dared to hope it meant something good.

'I can't hear any wind,' he said. 'It's nothing.'

'You told me this place is soundproofed!' She looked about her as if she'd just arrived. 'It's like a prison cell.'

'Sea view versus a mauso-bloody-leum!' he snarled. Usually he toned down his accent.

'In my heart I'm yours, you know that.' An off-the-shelf response.

It frightened him that he could hate her. He saw why people killed their lovers. If she were dead, she would stay.

He tensed his jaw. 'Do you have sex with him?'

She was rootling in her handbag. She squirted perfume on her wrists – not for him, but to expunge him.

'You promised to leave.'

'You'd be horrified if I turned up with two kids in tow!'

He tortured himself with a vision of her with a leg over the blubbery husband, letting him pump away inside her. In his dreams there were no kids in tow.

'Bring the girl. Let him have the boy.' Unlike the husband, he played fair.

She laughed and looped her bag over her chest as he advised, for safety.

'I'm leaving on Saturday.' His palms tingled at the decision made there and then.

'You said we had a month.' As he had hoped, she was upset.

'I'll be at the station at three on Saturday. If you're not there, I'm going.'

'It's too soon.' She kicked the brick aside and stepped on to the spiral staircase.

'It's always "too soon".' In her heels he wanted her again.

'I can't just leave.'

Not a 'no'. His venom evaporated. 'Be careful in those boots, that wind is strong.' Too late he recalled he'd underplayed the wind.

'I climb mountains in these.'

Not with me.

He followed her down the staircase and stopped her in the lobby by the front door.

'Promise me you'll give it some thought,' he said, but really he wanted her to give it *no* thought, just to leave. 'I'll be there next Saturday at Stamford Brook. At three. You won't regret it!'

'Darling, don't—'

He cut across her: 'You owe it to yourself. We only have one life – let's make the most of it! When we're settled, we can get the kid. One step at a time. Your life now is like living in a coffin, you said so yourself!'

He went towards her, but she blew a kiss and turned away. The bottom door shrieked when she opened it. He watched until she reached the caged staircase, and then he returned to their room.

Without her the magic had gone; it was a just cold concrete tank. He stuffed everything into the holdall, anxious to follow her, to see her when she wasn't with him. She had left him the Brie, not out of generosity, but because she wouldn't want to explain how come she had it.

Footsteps. She was coming back. He grew excited and regretted packing up the sleeping bags. 'Hon, you came back. I knew you would!'

There was a deafening report.

The tank door had shut, he stared disbelieving at the grey metal. Beware the jokes of those with no sense of humour. The lack of handle wasn't sexy now. She was on the other side of the double cladding, daring him to lose his nerve.

'Good game!' His temples thudded from the alcohol and he needed a pee. This was her revenge for his ultimatum. 'Joke over!'

Wind fluted through vents near the ceiling – she was right about the storm. Daylight no longer drifted in; the street lights didn't reach so high. Bloody stupid to have said leave the boy, he liked him. The walls emanated chill.

'He's a good kid, I'll treat him like my own son.' His voice bounced off the concrete.

There was a distant vibration – the bottom door slamming. There was no keyhole this side; his key was useless.

'Maddie!'

In the dark, the man wondered if, after all, it was not a joke.

One

Forty-three minutes past eleven. Dead on time, Jack brought his train to a stop at Ealing Broadway Underground station. Late-night passengers decanted and straggled up the stairs to the street. As usual he had seven minutes and thirty seconds before his journey to Barking. He would stable the train at the Earl's Court depot and then the night was his.

Ealing Broadway was the end of the line. On autopilot, Jack strolled up the platform to what, with the 'turn around', was the front of the train, glancing into the carriages. There was one woman in the second car. She was leafing through a *Metro* and looked up as he came alongside her. He thought he saw a flicker of fear pass across her face and quickened his pace. At this time of night a woman travelling alone might feel vulnerable; Jack hoped she would see his uniform and know he was a driver and not a passenger who could threaten her.

He opened the front cab door. Being a driver he swapped between different, but identical cabs at each end of the train during the course of a day or night. Travelling up and down the District line, he was never in one place for long: he thrived on the mix of stability and change. As the proprietor of a cleaning company, Stella restored stability in different locations. Pleased by this tenuous link between their working lives, Jack considered texting her. He put his hand in the fleece pocket of his uniform for his phone. But Stella called a spade a spade. His whimsy frustrated her and at this time of night would worry her. When Stella worried about Jack, she allocated him cleaning jobs – he worked part-time for her cleaning company, Clean Slate. Thinking of Stella made him wistful because since her mother had gone on holiday to Australia, she hadn't been herself. The change was fractional: a pause before she replied, an arrangement misremembered, a minute late to meet him because she'd walked the dog. Stella cared about her mum more than she let on.

Her father too. Two years after his death she still cleaned his house, ate supper there and did her emails at his computer with no sign of selling the place. Jack had once asked her if she was maintaining it for her father's ghost. She had retorted that she was waiting for the housing market to pick up. But prices were rising and even next to the Great West Road, the end of terrace in Hammersmith would fetch a small fortune. He dismissed the lurking notion that it was not a ghost Stella was waiting for, but a real live man. When Stella ended a relationship – eventually she always did – the dumped partner ceased to exist. Except her last man, the one who she thought a David Bowie lookalike, had left her with a dog; undeniable proof he had existed for her once.

He felt something in his pocket and fumbling under his phone pulled out a folded slip of paper.

To Let.
Apartment in Water Tower.
A cosy home with detailed views.

If you crave silence and a bird's eye view – Jack squinted at the type in the watery lamplight – *then Palmyra Tower is your home. Guardian wanted for Grade 1 listed Water Tower. You will sign a year-long contract with no breaks and be available to take up residence as soon as your application is accepted.*

It was the flier he had found lying on the doormat when he left the house that morning. He had shoved it in his jacket pocket and, intent on getting to work, had thought no more about it. Reading it now, Jack was intrigued by the imperative *you will*. He touched his face to stop an involuntary twitch and, shivering, zipped up his fleece. The cheap pink paper didn't compete with Clean Slate's glossy brochure.

The style was a marketing ploy that Stella would reject as too obvious an attempt to be different. However the paper did carry an unnerving air of authority, so in that sense it had worked.

Beneath the text was a fuzzy photograph of the tower. It was functional, effectively a tank on stilts; a caged fire escape-like structure attached to one column gave access to it. It stood metres from Chiswick Eyot, an island in the Thames. As a boy, Jack had once tried to climb it, but couldn't open the cage. The steep aluminium staircases and narrow treads were not for the vertiginous.

There was no phone number on the flier. At last he found an email address in tiny lettering: *info@palmyra-tower.co.uk*. Regardless of the amateur appearance, Jack guessed there would be a deluge of responses. For many, the tower would be the dream home. He scrunched up the flier and stuffed it back in his pocket. Leaning back on the cab door, Jack gazed up at the sky.

This section of the District line was above ground. The moon was a waning crescent in the sign of Leo. Stella was a Leo, as his mother had been. Two women with attitude, courageous and strong-willed. Jack's mother had died when he was a boy so what he didn't know about her he made up; this meant she was his particular brand of perfection.

A plane cut below the moon on its descent into Heathrow, the rumble of its engine carrying on the night breeze. Jack thought of the moon as his friend; it accompanied him on his walks. Or it had until he promised Stella to 'stop all that', although he doubted she understood what 'all that' was. The second hand on his watch ticked towards three minutes to twelve.

As soon as he stepped into the cab, Jack had a premonition of what would happen when he turned the key – it had happened here before. The motor whirred, but didn't start. His train was going nowhere.

He reported the train out of service, activated the door at the rear of his cab and went down the aisle of the cars ushering passengers off: seven altogether. Vaguely he noticed that the woman he had seen earlier wasn't among them. Back on the platform Jack felt a pricking at his temples: like last time, this breakdown was a sign. Like all signs, its meaning had yet to reveal itself.

The coffee stand was shut; a metal box covered with stars, it might be a magic trick about to emit a cloud of doves and many wished-for things. The moon had gone behind a cloud and the temperature had dropped. Jack picked up an empty coffee cup from the platform and tossed it into a litter bin two metres away. *Bull's eye*. The tracks hummed. He returned to the top end of the platform and, as the train approached, tipped a hand to the driver. His greeting wasn't returned. When the train was stationary, he peered into the empty cab at the rear.

With no train, he had no set number. Set numbers were the means of identifying a train and allocating it to a driver, but to Jack the set number was a sign. This train's number was 126. The last time this happened, his set number was 236 and led him to Stella.

Jack was tempted to rush from the station to evade whatever fate 126 decreed.

Running away is no escape if you don't know which direction is 'away'.

Jack rubbed his temples to eradicate the voice. Recently it came unbidden, like the voices of a high fever, and uttered dictums like a seer. It didn't feel his own. He looked up and saw the driver walking the length of the train towards him.

'All right?' Jack nodded.

'You're Jack.' The man had acne and looked no more than sixteen. 'They said you'd be here.' He offered no clue as to what he thought about this.

'Yes.' Jack agreed.

'I wanted you as my trainer, but you were fully booked,' the driver continued in a querulous tone.

'Ah.' Jack smiled. 'No matter, we're all the same.' Not true. He knew he was the best trainer, as he knew, although Stella never told him, that he was her best cleaner. Fact. Jack climbed into the cab after the driver. The doors swished shut.

The driver gripped the handle, his every nerve directed to his task. This wasn't the first time Jack had witnessed the terror of a novice driver. For him, responsibility for hundreds of passengers had come naturally when he had settled into the seat for the first time. It had felt right. But Jack wasn't like others.

Hands resting on thighs, Jack gazed out at bunched cables and silver rails converging and parting as the train left the station and increased speed.

On Google Street View, Jack could travel with the roll and click of a mouse. As if operating it now, he zoomed in on Stamford Brook station and focused on the strip of platform a hundred metres away. Yet again he was reminded of the toy station he had bought as a boy. Grey and brown plastic with a detachable ticket office and a couple of sweet-vending machines, added for free because the toyshop man had felt sorry for him.

Jack's train slowed as it entered Stamford Brook station. There was one man on the westbound platform: he would have a wait: the information board was blank. Trains would be diverted to Richmond because of his dead train at Ealing Broadway. He felt a flash of poignancy that he had abandoned it to be shunted without him to the Acton depot. His concern for inanimate things frustrated Stella.

Jack's attention was taken by the headlights of a Heathrow-bound Piccadilly train lighting up the rails ahead. After Hammersmith, it wouldn't stop until Turnham Green.

Nervous of overshooting the platform, his driver was applying the brake too soon. The last time Jack's train had broken down at Ealing Broadway, he had been sitting in the cab of a novice driver. Everything about this man was the same as the other; both moved their lips as if silently talking. The Piccadilly train was nearly on them – its headlights flooded the cab. He braced himself for the slipstream after it passed his train.

Jack glanced again at the platform for Richmond: still no train on the board. No need to hurry, but the man on the platform *was* hurrying. The wheels of the oncoming Piccadilly line train clackety-clacked closer. A tinny announcement came through the platform speakers: 'Stand well away from the edge of platform two. The next train is not scheduled to stop at this station.'

Five metres to go until the end of their platform. Jack's sense of déjà vu was oppressive, as if the last time had been a rehearsal for tonight.

'Take it right up,' he said softly, using the same phrase as last time. 'Get your passengers off. We don't want them pitching on to the line.' The man shoved the handle forward. Jack smelled his fear. 'Keep connection with the lever, coax it. The engine is you and you are the engine.' Something was wrong.

All stories are the same.

Jack banished the unwanted voice and saw the man on the platform lit by the headlamps of the Piccadilly train. The man gave a backward glance and abruptly broke into a run along the platform. Did he think the Piccadilly line train would stop? He was looking at Jack – not a glance, a proper look as if trying to express something. Jack had seen the expression before. Then the man was in mid-air above the tracks, caught in the glare of light as the Piccadilly line train thundered into the station. The man's body hit the windscreen and rolled under the cab. All was over in a second. Carriages jolted along and blocked Jack's view. Both trains halted. Jack looked at his watch. Six minutes past twelve: *126*.

A haunting wail carried across the station. The Piccadilly driver was sounding the whistle for staff to assist trackside. The bleak marking of a life extinguished.

Jack's driver was a waxwork, his hand frozen over the controls. He had berthed their train perfectly, seemingly unaware of what was happening metres to his right.

Later, at the inquest, Jack found that his driver had indeed seen nothing. Only Jack and the Piccadilly line driver, a man called Darryl Clark, had witnessed the incident. The few District line passengers had been asleep or plugged into headphones in a private world and although the other train was packed, it was impossible for anyone to have seen the man go under the front of the cab.

'What's your name?' Jack touched the man's arm, intending to ground him.

'Alfred Peter Butler,' he replied as if reporting for duty.

'You did well, Alfred. We'll stop here, you need a break and I think they might need some help here.' Accompanying Alfred Peter Butler through the carriages, for the second time in an hour, Jack informed passengers that a train was out of service.

Like Stella, Jack was comfortable with emergencies, everyone acting according to their role. While the tannoy announced delays, he and his driver checked seats and gangways for abandoned possessions. In the past he had found wallets, handbags, a tatty London street atlas that he had been allowed to keep, even a Springer spaniel lashed to a pole by its lead.

Alfred Peter Butler escorted their little troop down the stairs and across the station concourse, Jack bringing up the rear. To their right, Piccadilly line passengers were streaming down the westbound staircase, there was the buzz of muted exchange, word had got around.

It was a 'One Under'.

Jack Harmon dubbed himself a *flâneur*; he walked the night-time streets of London, observing others unobserved. Unlike a *flâneur*, he cared about those he watched. Courting mortality, feeling the imminence of death, he hunted out those with darkness in their souls and minds like his own. Jack entered the homes of what he dubbed his 'True Hosts', those who had killed or would kill if he didn't stop them.

Jack was quite aware that he sought a re-enactment of the day his mother had died, a day that for him, as for many, was when his world stopped. As when a film is watched again and again in the vain hope that the next time the victim won't die. He drove in the tunnels of the London Underground to find his way back to *before*.

Affecting nonchalance, Jack strolled across the station, singing softly:

> *'Humpty Dumpty sat on a wall,*
> *Humpty Dumpty had a great fall.'*

His hair blown back from his face by a cold night breeze, Jack guided passengers through the gap in the concertinaed gate to the street. Even though it was after midnight, traffic on Goldhawk Road was nose to tail, slowing for those filing over the zebra crossing. Someone was watching Jack from the top deck of a 237 bus; he supposed it was a man – a baseball cap was pulled low over the eyes. The bus moved towards King Street and the reflection of the blue station fascia wiped the figure out.

In ten years of driving a train, Jack hadn't had a suicide. Some drivers had it twice, while others went their whole working lives without a person jumping in front of their cab. Jack could not shake the conviction that tonight's incident was the culmination of many signs.

The station office reeked of sour sweat. Alfred Peter Butler was huddled in a corner nursing a mug of tea, staring at his feet. The other driver was texting on a BlackBerry, thumbs skimming the tiny keys. Someone on the phone confirmed that the 'customer' was dead. Jack refused tea. He kept to himself that he felt nothing. He told himself that since his mum died, he had nothing left to feel. Jack fastened the grille and ran up the stairs.

There was no one on the platform where the man had been. Lights from the train cast bleak stripes of light across the tarmac. Jack could feel the dead man's presence in the deserted station.

Staff had rigged up lighting gear for the paramedics, due any minute. Confident that the train driver had dropped circuit breakers to cut the electricity, Jack vaulted on to the rails and crunched over the ballast. Sharp stones jabbing him, he peered beneath the train's underbelly.

A splash of red. A hand curled over the live rail. The man wore a wedding ring; the thick gold band spoke of status, hopefully of love.

'*Wake up,*' Jack had said to his mummy.

He leant in and touched the man's ring finger. It was warmer than his own and still pliant.

'*I will save you,*' he had told his mummy.

Blood was soaking the front of the man's shirt. Globules of blood seeped into the ballast. Jack trembled; his teeth began to chatter. The man's eyes – hazel flecked with green, the pupils dilated – fixed Jack with the impassive gaze of the dead.

Eyes are like fingerprints, they don't alter with age.

'I knew that!' Jack found himself retorting out loud. He clambered out from under the train and hauled himself on to the platform. A woman in paramedic green was fumbling with a body bag. He stayed to see the man zipped into the bag and laid on to the stretcher. He accompanied the crew back down to the ambulance.

'Go well.' Jack formed the words silently, touching his cheek to stay a tic that happened at certain times. He watched the ambulance turn on to King Street, heading for Charing Cross Hospital's mortuary. No blue light required.

In his statement about the incident, Jack didn't put that, before he died, the man with the ring had looked at him. It wasn't pertinent.

His shift declared over, he strolled down to King Street and into St Peter's Square as the church clock struck a quarter to one.

The set number was 126. The man died at six minutes past twelve. From the moment he had stopped at Ealing Broadway, his every action and interchange was a sign. For Jack, death was a beginning, it was a sign that something else would happen.

Eyes are like fingerprints, they don't alter with age. The voice got there first. Jack had seen the man before.

With no True Host to watch, tonight Jack went back to his own house. The building was dark; he never left a light on. A wind had got up – forecasters warned of a hurricane-force storm coming – it battered the panes and shook casements swollen from the rain.

His door knocker was a short-eared owl fashioned from brass tarnished with age. Her burnished feathers flickered when she puffed up in greeting. Jack sang:

> *'All the king's horses,*
> *And all the king's men,*
> *Couldn't put Humpty together again.'*

A letter from the publisher

We hope you enjoyed this book. We are an independent
publisher dedicated to discovering brilliant books,
new authors and great storytelling. Please join us at
www.headofzeus.com and become part of our
community of book-lovers.

We will keep you up to date with our latest books, author
blogs, special previews, tempting offers, chances to win
signed editions and much more.

If you have any questions, feedback or just want to say hi,
please drop us a line on hello@headofzeus.com

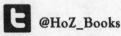 @HoZ_Books

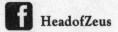 HeadofZeus

www.headofzeus.com

HEAD *of* ZEUS

The story starts here